Crystal Wedding

XU XIAOBIN

Crystal Wedding

Translated from the Chinese
by Nicky Harman

balestierpress

Balestier Press
71-75 Shelton Street, London WC2H 9JQ
www.balestier.com

Crystal Wedding
First published in English by Balestier Press in 2016
Original title: 水晶婚
Copyright © Xu Xiaobin, 2012
English translation copyright © Nicky Harman, 2016
Preface translation copyright © Nicky Harman and Natascha Bruce, 2016

Cover illustration by Xu Xiaobin

Quotes from *The Story of the Stone* (also known as *The Red Chamber Dream*)
are taken from the translation by David Hawkes and John Minford, published
by Penguin Classics, and are reproduced with their kind permission.

A version of excerpts from Chapters 21, 22 and 23 of *Crystal Wedding*
appeared in the magazine *Chutzpah*, Issue 6, February 2012.

This book has been selected to receive financial assistance from English PEN's
PEN Translates programme, supported by Arts Council England.
English PEN exists to promote literature and our understanding of it,
to uphold writers' freedoms around the world, to campaign against
the persecution and imprisonment of writers for stating their views, and to
promote the friendly co-operation of writers and the free exchange of ideas.
www.englishpen.org

 Supported using public funding by
**ARTS COUNCIL
ENGLAND** FREEDOM
TO **WRITE**
FREEDOM
TO **READ**

A CIP catalogue record for this book is available from the British Library

ISBN 978 0 9932154 9 0

To the dark times in life

Preface

This is, at once, both an ordinary and an extraordinary kind of book.

I call it an ordinary book because it is written in an entirely different style to my previous work. It doesn't have the same richness of description; there is none of the mystery or magic of my other writing—the language is simple and unadorned, devoid of symbolism and metaphor. It is the story of an ordinary female intellectual in China, charting the events of the fifteen-year period between her wedding and her divorce. Reflected in her individual fate, we see the changes wrought in the country at large over the course of those fifteen years of Chinese history.

I call it an extraordinary book because this is the first book by a mainland Chinese author to speak so frankly about sex and Chinese women.

At the first mention of sex, people's thoughts usually turn to erotica and pornography. If that's the kind of book you're expecting, however, you will be sorely disappointed. What interests me is another aspect of sex entirely—namely, the fact that for three decades of Chinese history, sex was a completely taboo topic. There was no such thing as sex education for the teenagers of my generation. As a result, when it came to sex, our behaviour tended toward one of two extremes: sexual promiscuity or sexual repression. Naturally, neither of these two extremes is especially healthy, but that's how it was. The protagonist of this novel, Yang Tianyi, is thirty when she gets married, and her attitude towards sex is one of absolute terror. Her husband, Wang Lian, is just as clueless—to the point that, one week after her wedding, Tianyi's hymen is found to be still intact.

While this might seem like a joke to Western readers, I assure you that I did not make it up: this was not an uncommon occurrence among girls of my generation. And those who ended up the butt of this joke were precisely those model students and well-behaved little girls who believed the lies fed to them during that repressive era and, as a result, threw away their youth, the most precious part of any person's life.. They sacrificed their youth for the party and the good of the motherland. That was a popular slogan of the time. Only many years later would they come to realise that, while they were dutifully abiding by all those rules, their great leader was out there living the life of a playboy. Some of them, incensed by this discovery, went on to be wildly promiscuous in their later lives.

In more recent years, sex has become a tool used to bribe senior officials. Dark corners of every city bubble with seedy undercurrents. There are no such things as state-sanctioned brothels, but there are whorehouse signs hanging over the entranceways to every second restaurant. High-schoolers work as escorts, girls from good families have one night stands—and these are no longer things we're ashamed to talk about. People will do whatever it takes to get ahead. Sincerity, on the other hand, will simply get you laughed at. This, surely, is an altogether much more alarming set of values.

The damage to women runs particularly deep. During the Mao era, when they talked about equality of the sexes, about how 'women can hold up half the sky,' what it meant was that men and women were equal when it came to physical work. That girls had to do the same kind of hard labour as men. It was the age of the much-revered 'Iron Girls' and we were girls in the prime of our youth; for us, as for everyone, notions of beauty shifted accordingly. We would think long and hard before wearing an outfit with even a dash of colour. We would curl the ends of our hair—but only ever so slightly—or venture a tiny flash of a pretty collar here and there. If you were fair-skinned, you had to go out and roast yourself darker in the sun, for fear someone would accuse you of being a bourgeois little miss. If you were slim, well, then you had to be even more dedicated, and make sure you worked especially hard, training your calf muscles until they were thick and solid. After this kind of a revolutionary baptism, what hope had any girl of retaining her femininity?

I was sent to Heilongjiang for the wheat harvest. There, male or female, you had to haul 200 *jin* (100 kg) bales of wheat up a gangplank—try to imagine, underdeveloped girls of fifteen or sixteen, carrying weights of 200 *jin* balanced across their shoulders, walking up narrow planks, three metres long and set at 45 degree angles, to off-load wheat into grain storage bins. Isn't it horrifying, to think of it now? Many girls developed ailments that would stay with them for life; many girls, no matter how hard they tried, simply couldn't do it. Me, for example. I was tasked with carrying 100 *jin* of urea on my back—and this was considered benevolent of them—but the strain was still so great that I was practically spitting blood. The slogan during the summer hoeing season was especially absurd: 'Work your hardest while alive, be buried in Heilong when you die.' Human life had no value. During a mobilisation meeting, our leader said, 'Every person, every day, one row of crops. I don't care how many tears you shed in the process.' And you have to understand, 'one row of crops' in Heilongjiang terms, was fourteen *li* (7 km)! I was only sixteen, suffering from severe dysentery, and the old ox cart that dropped off rice at midday only ever made it as far as the places with the most people. This meant that I, always lagging behind, never got anything to eat at lunchtime. So I had to endure the brutal intensity of the work, plus the sickness, without even a bite to eat. To drink, we'd knock over the water vats and worm our way inside like little dogs, just so we could take mouthfuls of the silty water collected along the bottom. Worse than that, when the fields flooded, we were forced to wade through water that came up to our knees and dredge up the wheat plants. This was November, it was bitter winter, and there we were, fishing hemp out of glacial river water; even when we had our periods, there was no respite. Thirty-eight girls slept on two big wooden bunk beds. It was fifty-two degrees below zero and we had no coal to burn. In order to survive, we'd burn bean stalks we dug out from under the snow and drink melted snow we collected in our chamber pots. And every day we had to praise the Great Leader, wishing him a long and prosperous life. I'm still amazed that I made it. Perhaps the only explanation is the natural resilience of youth! That is certainly the only one I can think of.

The 'Iron Girls' era finally passed. Things did not improve, however, because what came next was the era of the 'Little Woman.' What mattered now was not your IQ, but your EQ—your emotional intelligence. And what did it mean to be emotionally intelligent, Chinese-style? It meant that a woman knew how to charm a man; how to charm her boss. There was no question of falling in love, because to fall in love was to lose the game. There was a female student I knew in the 70s, for example, who was not particularly attractive and suffered from a series of physical disabilities. And yet, she would have several men at the same time, all eating out of the palm of her hand. It was about strategy: whenever she needed someone, she'd calculate her moves very carefully, as though carrying out a detailed piece of operations research. She was proud of herself for this; she felt like she'd won. Lots of girls were the same, even the so-called 'elite' ones. They thought they had life all figured out. They knew how to play on a man's emotions in order to win his favour, how to manipulate their way into relationships and wrap these men around their little fingers. They'd figured out how to get rich and they thought this a fantastic achievement. They were the envy of hundreds of thousands of female students, who considered them prime examples of 'high EQ'.

The way I saw it, however, this behaviour showed a serious lack of dignity and self-respect. It was even more degrading than the times of the Iron Girls.

My protagonist, Yang Tianyi, is, without a doubt, a girl of 'low EQ'. In this society where money reigns supreme, she stays true to herself. She has spent her adolescence immersed in romantic novels, from China and abroad. She imagines for herself an ordinary, loving marriage, and a happy family to call her own. But, amid the dramatic social upheaval of the period, her romantic hopes for her future are relegated to the stuff of wistful daydreams. She marries a man who holds a set of values entirely at odds with hers, but she refuses to sit back and accept the hand fate has dealt her. She continues to love another man from afar, unable to give up on her notions of romance. She lives believing she is sexually frigid, before eventually realising that she is simply not the kind of woman who can separate love from sex. She would rather remain celibate than force herself to endure loveless sex. During the Tiananmen crisis, however, she musters her courage and goes to the aid of the man she loves. Her husband soon finds out. The two start to quarrel incessantly, and the tension between them worsens by the day. Finally, after fifteen years, their marriage implodes. Fifteen years makes it their crystal-wedding anniversary. The book, then, is the story of that girl called Yang Tianyi, and her life over the course of those fifteen years between 1984 and 1999.

Yang Tianyi has no interest in politics, just as I have no interest in politics. I was born into a family of intellectuals, descended from a long line of scholars. That's right, China does have intellectuals; we are not all peasants. And the misery endured by China's intellectuals during the Mao era was extreme—indeed, unprecedented.

My father was a very honest, kind-hearted man. He was well-educated and became, at the age of twenty-nine, the youngest Assistant Professor at Jiaotong University. He was loved and trusted by fellow teachers and students alike. His unsparing dedication to his work caused him to contract tuberculosis but, even when he was spitting blood, he continued to take students out on field trips. As a result, he survived unscathed the many political movements that shook China in the latter half of the twentieth century. Even during the terrible Cultural Revolution, the worst that happened was that a few big-character posters accused him of being a 'bourgeois academic authority'. However, his honest and sensitive nature suffered from having no one to open up to, and the pressures that built up led to his untimely death.

I was his favourite child, and the one he worried most about.

I began painting at two or three years old, and a picture of 'The Parrot Girl' that I did at the age of five was spotted by the head of the university's costume doll group and used by her to create a new doll. (These costume dolls were among China's few exports at that time.) At the age of seven, I wrote my first poem in Chinese classical metre, and two years later I read the great novel, *Story of the Stone* (also translated as *The Dream of the Red Chamber*). My outstanding academic results won me all sorts of prizes at primary school and made my father very proud. Interestingly, a fellow student at my primary school was Wang Yi, China's current foreign minister; he was also at secondary school with me, and we did military service together. When I completed primary school, my teacher came to tell my parents that he was putting my name forward for admission to an elite secondary school. At that time, there was a quota from each school of one or, at most, two students, and my school chose Wang Yi and me. Only just then, the Cultural Revolution broke out and everything ground to a halt. To start with, I was intensely curious and rode my bicycle from campus to campus reading the big-character posters. My natural scepticism made me wary of the official newspapers, and I wanted to know the truth. However, I soon lost interest in the slanging matches between the warring factions, and steered well clear of the bloody violence. When I witnessed our elders and betters being paraded through the streets in dunces' caps, the nursery school head being put on a stage in the searing summer heat and spattered all over with paste and ink, the adults around me committing suicide, my father working day and night without a break, my mother being forced to learn the 'loyalty dance', it dawned on me just what the truth was …

Both my parents were engineers and, although they loved to read literature in their spare time, literary studies in those days were not held in high regard. The watchword was 'maths, physics and chemistry will get you anywhere'. Even though the schools were closed during the Cultural Revolution, I often got together with school friends on the university campus and we amused ourselves by conducting physics and chemistry experiments, for instance, boiling water in paper cups over a candle flame, and engraving designs on eggshells. Maths was my chief love, and I dreamed of becoming a scientist when I grew up; reading was just something I liked doing in my spare time. But the Cultural Revolution shattered all our hopes and dreams. Looking back on those days, I realized that my father was intensely anxious about what might happen to me; it was for this reason that, cleverly playing on my love of reading, he brought out the collections of books we had at home (we were fortunate in that they had not been confiscated by the Red Guards) and added to them works translated from western writers, such as *Anna Karenina*, *War and Peace*, *Resurrection*, the complete *Comédie Humaine* by Balzac, and works by Dostoevsky, Turgenev, Mérimée, Zweig, and Stendhal borrowed from the university library. Imagine how bizarre: outside the windows, loudspeakers blared amid a sea of red flags, while behind closed doors, a young girl, bent over those then-prohibited works, was drawn into a whole new world, completely at odds with the spirit of the times. The fantasy world I lived in then is the subject of a novel I wrote years later called *Sunshine on Judgement Day*.

In using books to keep me out of trouble, my father could hardly have imagined that literature would lead me on a secret inner journey; nor did he know that this inner world would prove even more dangerous than the tumultuous world outside. At thirteen years old, a girl is on the threshold of adolescence, getting her periods, beginning to notice subtle changes in her body, feeling the first stirrings of love. An encounter with literature can make her restless for the rest of her life.

Four years later, when I came back from Heilongjiang to see my parents in Beijing, I wrote my first novel, *Young Eagles Spread their Wings*, about two young people from different backgrounds who fall in love. I never finished it but the parts that I had written did the rounds at university, in notebook form. I was always being asked by my friends: 'And what happened next?'

This was the beginning of my literary career. In 1981, I published my first complete novel. From then on, my writing took a completely different path from that of my fellow writers. By 2005, at a time when people's political and moral values had become more sharply divided than ever, I found myself increasingly marginalized. I had to laugh when, a number of years ago, a completely unrealistic story about Heilongjiang appeared. I found out later that the writer had never done a day's labour in the countryside, having been a cadre for his entire life. All these years later, he is still a favourite in literary circles; true, he has made a few comments apparently critical of the system in order to make himself popular with the reading public, but he has also been careful to protect his personal interests. The truth is that in any society, he would be among the elite, because he has a chameleon's ability to assume their colours. He is one among many such chameleon-writers in China: loftily apolitical to the general public, while behind closed doors they scrabble for power and influence, smoothing their career paths with gifts and letters. On Weibo and Weixin, in their blogs and in social media, they pose as honest intellectuals genuinely concerned for their country and their people; then they suddenly turn up in the USA with a green card. As if that is not enough, they claim benefits and tax relief in the USA on grounds of poverty, before reappearing in China to take top official positions on high salaries. These people are clever; they are also the kind of freaks that the system produces. Writers ought to maintain a tension with society, see themselves in confrontation with it, but those who flourish here have done so because they have learnt how to tell lies and make people laugh, how to say what people want to hear, how to win over all and sundry, young and old, men and women, high-ups and humble … They have cleverly persuaded the government to hand over the vast sums of money that it has invested in China's 'soft power push', and they continue to reap the benefits of this ignoble venture. They have become superb actors, indeed superstars, feathering their own nests, while also making themselves nationally popular.

In my novel, *Feathered Serpent*, the hero says: 'The past ten years have allowed the genie out of the bottle; the devil has slipped out and can never be put back in the bottle. The country will rise, economic material will be gained, and we will catch up with advanced countries; but what about the realms of the spiritual and metaphysical? Will they ever be restored? This is a quandary that is more frightening than being poor.'[1] Sadly, all my predictions in *Feathered Serpent* have come true.

As a young woman writing *Feathered Serpent*, I felt acute grief for my beloved country but powerless to change the situation. Along with this pain, I was suffering personal heartache, so every word was written in blood and tears. *Crystal Wedding*, on the other, is a simple record of what happened. When I wrote *Feathered Serpent*, I still had tears to cry, whereas now I am dry-eyed. If anything, hurting and not being able to cry runs even deeper and is even harder to cure.

---

[1] *Feathered Serpent*, Xu Xiaobin, tr. John Howard-Gibbon, Joanne Wang (Atria, 2009:241).

My thanks to Nicky Harman, whose fine translation and hard work in finding a publisher for *Crystal Wedding* has helped make this book available to Western readers; to my publisher, Roh-Suan Tung, without whose perceptiveness and courage this translation might have taken a lot longer to come out; to Eric Abrahamsen, China expert, for his support for this book; and to my agent, Joanne Wang, who brought my previous novels to the outside world, for which I am extremely grateful.

I hope that Western readers will enjoy *Crystal Wedding*.

XU XIAOBIN
(translated by Nicky Harman and Natascha Bruce)

1

A fortune-teller once told Tianyi: 'You'll be single at 30, married at 31.' And that is just what happened.

At 30, she had felt like an old maid, an old old maid—though later, she came to realize that for a woman, at least for her, 30 was really very young, and she need not have been in such a hurry to marry. Every day she had to face questions about whether she had a friend yet—that meant a boyfriend, of course. Aunt Jie from next door, the mother of her best friends, Di and Xian, was particularly persistent. She had already started on finding men for her two daughters, and she knew what she was doing: she could line up several good potential matches for them to meet in the space of a day. She managed to introduce Xian, the more amenable of the two, to quite a few boys. One day, Tianyi looked out of her dimly-lit room to see Xian walking by in a brightly-coloured headscarf, her face vivid with excitement. Tianyi's eyes brimmed with tears, and she felt a stab of—what was it, jealousy? No, not jealousy. Admiration? No, not that either. She was not sure what it was. But she remembered the poem the three of them used to recite, by the emperor poet, Xiao Gang:

> *The sky is frosty, the Milky Way pale, the evening stars are few*
> *A wild goose cries a mournful note—where is it going?*
> *If it had known it would lose its mate on the way*
> *It might have chosen always to fly alone.*

Tianyi felt a looming, terrifying sense of loneliness.

But the boyfriends trickled away one by one, like flour through a sieve. A year went by and Di and Xian were still unmarried. Aunt Jie changed tactics, and began to use her network of friends. She included Tianyi too. It was as if she had realized that her daughters would never get married unless their friend did, as if Tianyi was the root cause of the problem. Only if she was got safely out of the way would her daughters forget all this nonsense and face up to reality. She was probably right.

Aunt Jie made her wares sound highly desirable. In the advertisements she placed for her daughters she gave the girls nice-sounding nicknames then added phrases like: 'very pretty, pleasant nature, university graduate, loves literature, art and music ...' To Tianyi's she added: 'Good cook.'

To Tianyi's utter astonishment, within a month she received almost two thousand letters in reply. And what letters! They came from places as far-flung as Heilongjiang in Manchuria and the Paracel Islands in the South China Sea, from the Pamir plateau in the far west of China to the Ussuri River in the north-east. There were a bewildering array of suitors: from government officials to young farmers, and every other possible occupation, from 50 down to 20 years old. It was really too bad that she moved house several times over the following years, and the letters got thrown away, because on close examination they represented a microcosm of Chinese males in the 1980s. Mrs Wu, who collected the letters for her at her own address, helped her to choose a few of them, all from Beijing and university graduates, and she met one or two, but there was no spark between them ... No doubt the men felt the same. Just the year before, she had published her book *Research into Bisexual Love*, and her feelings about her case studies were still fresh in her mind. Reality did not come close. No wonder she was left feeling unsatisfied.

But the atmosphere at home was so bad that she was forced to think again. After her father died, and her elder sister, Tianyue, moved away, her relationship with her mother and younger brother deteriorated. Home life was stifling and, worse still, she found herself being humiliated at every turn. Yes, humiliated, that wasn't too strong a word for it. There was no one better than her mother at heaping on the insults, and Tianyi was super-sensitive, so there were arguments morning, noon and night.

It had been like this when her father was alive too. When she took the frail old man out for walks, it used to earn her stinging comments from her mother: 'Ai-ya! What a good little daughter! Her father can't move hand or foot until she comes along and then suddenly he can walk!' Tianyi, looking at her father's gaunt, ashen face, could not help herself: 'Mum, what a thing to say!' Her mother's face would darken: 'I'm his wife, I can say what I want!' She might fling out a final insult as she turned to go back into the house: 'Huh! You behave just like his mistress!' That made Tianyi go pale with fury, and her father trembled all over. In her heart of hearts, Tianyi felt that all this was killing her father. It was death by a thousand cuts, a slow torment at the hands of her mother that had gone on for more than 30 years. With the wisdom of bitter experience, Tianyi's father advised her to get away, rather than stay around to die a slow death as well.

Before she did finally leave, she did her best to make it up with her mother and brother, to have some good memories to take with her. But reconciliation was not easy. She started by looking for a job where she did not have to keep office hours, so that she could continue her research, but very soon not keeping office hours came to mean not going to work at all. In the mornings, she went to the University Library, then hurried home to prepare lunch for them. But every time she went out of the door, she was accompanied by a barrage of sarcasm. She put her very best efforts into whatever she was doing but it was no use. She frequently came to the table to eat, having served up the dinner, to find the dishes already half-empty. Her mother and Tianke, her brother, liked their food but she might as well not have been there. Once she had finished the cooking, she was no more than empty air to them. She would sit there, feeling desolate, knowing what it meant to be superfluous. At such moments, she would think: *Just you wait, one day I'm going to leave ...*

As the autumn of 1984 passed, she alternated between hope and despair. The First of October holiday approached and the fortune-teller turned up again. 'On the tenth of the tenth month,' she said, 'you'll meet someone and you can marry him.' Tianyi was startled. She stuffed some money into the woman's hand, and the fortune-teller swiftly disappeared. But her words continued to ring in Tianyi's ears.

Aunt Jie really had fixed up a date for her on the evening of 10th October. The man worked in the Planning Commission and he was called Wang Lian. Aunt Jie was busy at home that day and told them to go out for a walk. Tianyi took him to the small park on the Mingda University campus, where they could sit by the fish pond.

They talked about their respective middle schools. He said he was at the middle school affiliated to Qinghua University and she remembered that her sister, Tianyue, had mentioned someone called Wang Lian in her diary. Her sister had been at the same school. 'That was me,' he immediately responded. 'What a small world!' Tianyi smiled, because Tianyue had not been complimentary. She said that he used to pick his feet during the breaks, and make the whole room stink. When the class monitor told him to stop, he not only took no notice, he made her so

angry that she cried. Lian laughed. 'We were just kids,' he said.
'It's all water under the bridge. Everyone's different now.' Then
he added: 'Best not to tell your sister and the family that we know
each other.'

Foolishly, Tianyi gave her word, and kept it too. She never so
much as mentioned Lian's name to her sister and brother-in-law,
not until the day, sometime later, when she and Lian were off
to the Registry Office to get married. Tianyue looked sick with
worry. 'Lian? He had the worst temper in the whole class. He was
always flying off the handle. Are you really going to spend the
rest of your life with him?' Tianyi smiled: 'Everyone can change.
He's very good-tempered now.' She proved to have absolutely
zero ability as a judge of character. She had forgotten the old
saying that a leopard never changes its spots.

They had liked each other at that first meeting. A couple of
days later, he turned up at her home uninvited. He was wearing
an overcoat in dark blue wool, which looked comically big on
him—the padded shoulders were much too wide. He always
wore ill-fitting clothes but it never occurred to her to look down
on him because of it. She even felt sorry for him. She had met far
too many youths who were rich and handsome. Compared with
them, an ordinary man would make a more reliable husband, she
reckoned, thus committing the cardinal error of believing that a
handsome man was necessarily unfaithful and an ugly one would
never cause any trouble.

The arrival of the uninvited guest that day caused a few ripples
in the stagnant backwater that was Tianyi's home. After he had
gone, Tianke remarked critically that Lian thought too much of
himself. 'Tianyi's always gone out with handsome, well-dressed
men. What makes a squat little man like him, with stained teeth,
think he has any chance at all?' Tianke may normally have been at

loggerheads with his sister, but as soon as an outsider appeared, the family closed ranks, and it never occurred to him that this squat, yellow-toothed man would marry his big sister.

Actually, Lian was not bad-looking, though he did not measure up to Tianyi's former handsome boyfriends. He was of medium height, with regular features, he was very clean and his teeth were not yellow at all, there was just a bit of a gap between the two front ones. After his visit that evening their relationship gathered momentum. He invited her to a pop concert at the Capital Stadium, where the Hong Kong singer, Tsui Siu-Ming, was appearing. Half-way through, they left their seats and sat out the rest of the concert in the lounge of the semi-circular stadium, listening over the speakers to *Any Empty Wine Bottles For Sale*, then a very popular Taiwanese song, and the theme song of the Taiwan film, *Papa, Can You Hear Me Sing*. He bought lots of snacks and they munched them. She felt that he was really nice, dependable and considerate.

Next, they went to the Black Bamboo Garden restaurant for his birthday. The weather was getting cooler, and the duckweed and lotus leaves floating on the surface of the water had died back. With some difficulty, they found a sunny spot near some trees, he spread out a plastic sheet and they laid out all the things she had brought to eat. She had prepared them all herself: smoked fish, salad, roast duck, soy-stewed meat, and pickled cabbage. He tasted everything and pronounced it all delicious. He joked that now that he had tasted her superb cooking, he had better confess that cooking skills were a tie-breaker in a relationship, for him. She had put a lot of effort into this birthday picnic and it made her happy to see him tucking in with relish. They stayed out late, chatting by the lotus pond. He had brought a blanket and, when it got really cold, he draped it around her shoulders. She felt like an ice-cold fish, irresistibly drawn to seeking out a warm current. Love still seemed like an illusion, but marriage … somehow that was very simple, she would marry anyone who was good to her.

A few days later, they were strolling down a path, with him pushing his bicycle, and he put his arm around his shoulder. On and on they walked and never seemed to run out of things to say. As he was seeing her home, he suddenly dropped the bike and kissed her. The clatter of the bike as he let it drop shattered the silence of the deserted street. Whenever she thought back to that night in years to come, the echoes filled her head.

'Let's speed things up a bit,' he said. 'We met on the 10th October, we'll make the announcement on the 11th November and tie the knot on the 12th December. She liked his sense of humour, and laughed. He kept that sense of humour until the second year of their marriage.

The next step, of course, was to pay a visit to his family. He had already told her that the family got on well, that his parents were like a pair of Bodhisattvas, and his maternal grandmother, who lived with them, was very good about the house. But when she met his parents, she just could not make the Bodhisattva image stick. The first thing his mother asked was her age. Then she gave a tight little smile and said: 'You're both old enough to know your own minds, so get it sorted quick, so there's no gossip.' Both parents avoided her gaze, which made her very uncomfortable. His mother was quite ugly, with a pair of piggy little eyes, a very big mouth, and very short legs. Apparently Lian's grandfather had died just ten days after her birth, leaving the young widow to bring her up single-handed. While she was talking to Lian and Tianyi, the father was in the kitchen making dinner. They were all rather reserved at dinner. The father sat stern-faced saying little, except to urge Tianyi to eat, while the mother insisted on putting morsels of food into Tianyi's bowl. Unfortunately, it was all things she didn't like. In fact, having her mother-in-law serve her like this was one of the reasons she came to hate going to eat there. She had been brought up not to waste food and to eat everything on her plate, so eat she must. Finally, she thought she would vomit it all up and had to tip her food into Lian's bowl. When his mother saw her doing that, she grimaced: 'Our Lian's not a slop pail you know.' This was Tianyi's first taste of her mother-in-law's sharp tongue. She was shocked.

The atmosphere that day was chilly. Tianyi tried her best to persuade herself that it was probably because it was her first visit, it was just happenstance, or because she wasn't used to them. Unfortunately, everything that unfolded afterwards proved her first impressions to have been absolutely correct.

On 8th December, they went to get the wedding photos taken, in a photography studio in fashionable Wangfujing Street. You could hire a wedding dress (they had just begun to make a comeback) at the studio. Tianyi had the smallest size; it was a bit grubby but fitted her like a glove. She had a slender eighteen-inch waist back then. The hairdresser cut her hair fashionably short and waved it, and pinned a pink flower on one side of her head. Tianyi sparkled. Soon, Lian came out too: he was dressed in a suit, and white gloves, and his hair looked so shiny you could almost see yourself in it. He was transformed. As the photographer clicked away, he squeezed her hand happily.

Then they went out shopping. She was walking in front, and felt his eyes on her back. 'What a slender waist,' he said quietly, 'it seems to sway as you walk along. Really sexy!' She was wearing a very nice, tight-fitting, steel-blue coat she had bought in a street market. It was only 44 *yuan*, but looked like it had cost a hundred times more. She often bought cheap clothes that looked expensive, for the simple reason that she was poor but she liked looking good.

They did not wait until the 12th of the 12th to tie the knot. Two days before, on 10th December 1984, they were married at the Wang family home. Thinking back to that day, Tianyi felt mortified that the two families had not even gathered for a decent meal together. It was all a far cry from nowadays, with a luxury limo turning up to deliver the bride to her new home. Even by the standards of the 1980s, Tianyi felt hard done by. She remembered pinning a happy smile to her face, consoling herself that she had escaped, finally escaped. No more would she be torn limb from limb at home. Even though she felt bruised, at least she was still in one piece.

Through Lian's job, the Wangs had managed to get an extra room in someone else's house in a nearby street and for a long time after, this was the newlyweds' bolt-hole. There, on their wedding night, Lian smashed his prized plaster statuette of Venus and whispered feverishly in Tianyi's ear: 'Your body is so much beautiful than any Venus!' What woman could not be seduced by words like that? Especially when he sounded so sincere.

There was a lot of fumbling that night but they never managed to do the deed. Tianyi felt exhausted and dispirited, although she was careful to conceal it. She did not want him to feel bad. Deep down, she regarded him as her saviour, because he had taken her from the home where life was not worth living, where she had faced a fate worse than death.

In reality, she had gone from the frying pan into the fire. Her new family was absolutely no different from the old one, just hellish in a different way. At dawn, just as she was dropping off to sleep, there was an urgent rapping at their door—her mother-in-law! Lian was forced to throw on some clothes and open up.

Tianyi was aghast. Should she get out of bed to welcome the older woman or dive under the quilt and hide her face? If last night's dinner-table conversation had merely needled her, her mother-in-law's arrival this morning was like being hit over the head with a truncheon. She later discovered that it was Lian's grandmother who had put her up to it. She had lived so many years as a widow that she bitterly resented the young couple sharing a bed.

A few days later, she went to the hospital for a check-up, where the doctor was astounded to discover that her hymen was still intact. It must sound preposterous to young folks nowadays, but when Tianyi was young, sexual taboos created a phobia of sex in young women, just more extreme in Tianyi's case. In fact, for a long time, she congratulated herself on having found a virgin to marry.

They finally consummated their marriage a week later, on 19th December. They were in bed at her home. They lay under the wedding quilts, one green, one red (the only dowry, along with a gold bracelet, she had received from her mother) and he said softly: 'Sooner or later, it's got to be done. Bite your lip …' She bit down on the pillow cloth as grimly as if she was facing martyrdom, protesting: 'No! What if I get pregnant?' 'You won't,' he said, 'haven't you just had your period? You're safe.' And so, in a daze, she let it happen. However, as she was soon to discover, for her there was no safe time.

She started to feel unwell straightaway. After the Chinese New Year, she began vomiting and the pregnancy test came back positive. The thing she most feared had come to pass: she had fallen pregnant that first night. She had had no time to prepare herself mentally. All she had wanted to do when she married was to escape from home, and now, without pause for breath, she had fallen into a new trap.

Tianyi was afraid to go to the hospital for an abortion so she decided to do it naturally. For the first two months, when it was easiest to miscarry, she swam, played badminton, jumped up and down energetically hundreds of times a day—but absolutely nothing happened. She just vomited worse than before. She brought up every single mouthful of food, and then the bile too. Even the smell of cooking oil made her nauseous. The worst of it was that Lian smelled bad too: he had body odour and terrible breath, and made such a chomping noise when he ate. She tried telling him a few times but it was no use.

Finally she found something she could eat, *wotou* or cornmeal buns. From the beginning to the end of her pregnancy, her belly never rejected *wotou*. Later on, she found she could tolerate the odd tomato and watermelon too. Three months passed, and one morning, the vomiting stopped and she suddenly felt reinvigorated. She looked in the small mirror that hung behind the door, and saw herself cleansed of all foulness and grown beautiful. She peered at herself over and over again: her face looked as if it were lightly powdered, with a peachy bloom showing through the pallor. She had always had fine eyebrows, but now they extended in an elegant arch like those of a classic Chinese beauty, almost as if painted on. Her eyes were like crystalline lake water, so bright they shone almost blue and you could see the shadow of her eyelashes in them. The expectant mothers she met at her antenatal appointment exclaimed: 'Good heavens! You don't look a day over twenty!'

Her complacency was short-lived. They still had no home of their home, and for the time being, lived with her family. Tensions simmered beneath the surface and Tianyi was on tenterhooks, terrified of an impending row. But Lian was determined to get on well with his mother-in-law and brother-in-law, Tianke. Almost every day he brought home a chicken, or a live fish, or some tender pork shoulder for them, and prepared it himself. He was a good cook, neat and clean. His efforts temporarily kept the peace.

But war broke out again anyway. Tianke was going out with Xiaolan, a girl who worked at the same college. Tianyi had met the girl before and reckoned she was a bit of a slut. As a teenager, she plastered on so much makeup, it had left permanent blemishes. Tianke and Xiaolan would never have got together if Tianyi's father had still been alive. It happened like this: after the old man's death, Tianke was given a post in the Accounts Department of his father's university. Xiaolan's father was a cook in the university canteen and her mother guarded the bicycles in the campus bike shed. They had three children, two girls and a boy, and Xiaolan was the youngest. She was helping out in Accounts, having completed lower middle school and then dropped out, and it so happened that Tianke was her line manager. Little by little the attraction between them grew. A girl like Xiaolan was a natural flirt and Tianke, with no previous experience in love, was fair game. It was not long before they were swept up in an affair.

Their relationship caused storms at home. The intensity of their mother's reaction was frightening. For the first time, battle lines were drawn between mother and son. Tianke began to suffer what Tianye had had to put up with in the past, the only difference being that his mother was objecting because she loved him. His mother's hysteria wound him up, the tensions threatened to boil over. Tianke flew off the handle for the most trivial of reasons and, once, even demanded his wedding present to Tianyi back. It was only a cheap diamante necklace, but worse than the fact that he insisted on her giving it back, what really hurt Tianyi was that he passed it straight on to Xiaolan.

Tianyi bottled up her feelings until finally she had had enough.

'Tianke,' she burst out, 'Why can't you behave like a decent human being? If you can't get something like that right, then don't even bother!' Back in those days, she was a feisty young woman. When driven to it, she went for the jugular. Tianke flew into a terrible rage and kicked her violently in the stomach. She was four months' pregnant. That kick was the last straw for Tianyi and Lian. They had to move out.

Many years later, Tianyi recalled that time of her life and thought that her child really must have been some sort of divine gift. Otherwise, how could he have survived the trials and tribulations of her pregnancy and been born such a strong, healthy little boy?

For the time being, Lian's work allowed Tianyi and Lian to have a room in the old Daoist Temple on South Lishi Road. It was shabby and dingy, and they shared the kitchen and the toilet with another couple. The man, a Mr Sheng, did everything in the home. At the start, Tianyi and Lian had no coal stove so they borrowed the Shengs', with Tianyi usually cooking first and then old Mr Sheng. Tianyi was perfectly happy with the arrangement: now heavily-pregnant, she waddled out to do the shopping, then returned to cook. The two families got on well, even emptying each other's rubbish. Lian was moved to comment on how frugal the Shengs were. They hardly had anything to throw away, even a water melon was eaten right down to the rind. Tianyi, aware that old Sheng only ever cooked one dish for dinner, nodded in agreement. Mrs Sheng largely stayed indoors. She had suffered a mental breakdown and had a volatile temper. Just once, Tianyi saw her outside by the stove using the curling tongs. The smell of singeing hair filled the passageway.

One day, Lian's parents came over. It was very hot and Lian's mother wore a short-sleeved blouse and fanned herself vigorously. Tianyi happily showed the old folks her collection of little ornaments displayed in a cupboard, but her mother-in-law ignored them. Instead she asked, eyeing Tianyi's belly: 'Have you had a scan?' When Tianyi shook her head, the older woman looked annoyed. Tianyi cooked four dishes for them and brought the food to the table. Mr Wang took one mouthful and said with a smile: 'Our Lian's a lucky man!' His wife glared at him and asked: 'How come he's not back for lunch?' 'He has his lunch in the canteen most days now,' Tianyi explained. He doesn't want me to tire myself out with the cooking.' 'Aren't you a lucky girl,' was the acid response, 'Dad was never so lovey-dovey when I was pregnant.' Old Mr Wang hurriedly changed the subject: 'Mum's worried none of your clothes are big enough for you. She wanted to buy you something new but wasn't sure what you'd like. Why don't we go down the market after we've eaten, and have a look around?' Tianyi was overcome with gratitude, and said so. She felt as if the new clothes were already in her hands. But when they got to the market, her mother-in-law looked at the goods disdainfully and they left without buying anything.

Tianyi didn't care, though. She had fallen in love with her new life, and with their comfortable little room. She was filled with good will towards all and sundry. At last she had her own home! At last! Every day, as soon as Lian had left, it became her domain. It might be too small to swing a cat, and dreadfully shabby, but it had made her independent. She looked around at the flimsy furniture and cramped space—she had waited thirty years for this!

In the evenings, Tianyi got on her bike, with her big belly sticking out in front, and pedalled to the Film Institute to watch a French film retrospective. There were forty films showing and Tianyi watched one after another, right up until she was due. Of course, the dubbing was not totally perfect, but she was happy.

Although it was the mid-eighties, nude scenes in films were still a big draw. It was odd how people seemed to know in advance about these nuggets of nudity. Every time there was a risqué film on, crowds of people queued up and Tianyi was forever being asked: 'Got any spare tickets?'

Tianyi had loved films since she was a little girl. From the first notes of the film score, she had a strange sense of excitement. She found herself crying and laughing along with characters in the film, even though in real life she hardly ever got emotional. Her friends used to tell her she lived inside art and literature.

Every day, when the film finished, Lian waited for her outside the cinema with his bicycle. Even though her husband was a short man, and ordinary in every way, Tianyi was supremely content with life.

Things had not changed for the Shang sisters, however. When they dropped by to see Tianyi, the conversation was still about boyfriends. Tianyi assumed the air of someone who had been through all that. The maxims tripped off her tongue. 'Don't get so serious about marriage, it's just a threshold. Grit your teeth and step over it!' she advised them. Or, 'If you can't find someone to love, at least find someone who loves you.' Or, 'Whatever you do, don't confuse love and marriage, or you'll never find someone to marry.' Or, 'What a marriage needs isn't love, it's affection' … and so on and so forth. Di and Xian, soaked it all up, nodding as if their heads were pestles pounding garlic in a mortar. They were hardly in a position to quibble, after all.

One evening, Di turned up at Tianyi's apartment. Lian, an enthusiastic host, fried up all five small fresh fish he had brought home for their dinner. Di was a hearty eater and watching her tuck in gave Tianyi an appetite too. Before Lian had had time to dig his chopsticks into the dish, the two women had cleaned the plate between them. Tianyi felt a little unwell after dinner but went out as usual to stretch her legs before getting ready for bed. Then, in the middle of the night, she was woken by stabbing pains in the gallbladder. She endured them for a while until finally she was rolling around the bed in agony. Lian, in a panic, called for a taxi to take them to the nearest hospital, where she was diagnosed with acute cholecystitis. Obviously pain killers were not an option as they might harm the foetus. Tianyi had never been in such agony in her whole life. For the first time it dawned on her that motherhood meant sacrifice. How difficult it was to be a mother, at least a good one, not like her own mother.

Tianyi, although outwardly easy-going, was in truth deeply self-absorbed. Growing up unloved had given her a giant chip on her shoulder and she was always trying to make it up to herself. She joked that she always put herself before anyone else. She had not asked to get pregnant but now she was, and there was nothing to be done except grit her teeth. Her husband, and even the doctor, could only give her moral support, which did not ease the pain at all. Tianyi suddenly thought that you might go to heaven with a companion, but the road to hell you had to tread alone.

2

Tianyi had been determined to go into marriage with her eyes open. That meant accepting that love and marriage were not the same thing at all.

She had, of course, loved, but her love was of a peculiar kind: it was as if, when she was drawn into someone's world, she revelled in the melancholy feeling that her love was unrequited. But as soon as the man began to love her back, it all felt wrong. She was an aesthete, she put beauty above everything, she preferred fantasy to reality. As soon as the man she had idealized departed from the trajectory she had designated for him, she was suddenly appalled. No doubt because she had started reading romances too young, she could not see beyond the ideal. Love for her was an idée fixe, and nothing could change her mind. No surprise, therefore, that she always came to grief.

The first man in her life had come along in the mid-seventies during the Cultural Revolution. After a spell as part of a youth labour team in Yunnan, she was transferred back to Shidu Commune on the south-western outskirts of Beijing. Tianyi was twenty-one years old, in the flower of her youth. Though her looks were no more than average, with a little care and attention she could have appeared beautiful. But she was always drably dressed, in her faded blue jacket and trousers, white-soled black cotton flip-flops, her hair in two long plaits, tied with a rubber band since she did not bother with a hair-clip. No matter how slender one was, a figure-hugging jacket was out of the question, would have been considered indecent, in fact.

Still, she had a good voice and painted well, and her talents did not go unnoticed in the work team. Every commune in those days had a Mao Zedong Thought Propaganda Troupe and Tianyi, with her talents, became a key member and soloist. The first man she ever fell in love with was the accordionist who accompanied her. His name was Sheng.

On the day in question, Qiu, the brigade leader, made a point of telling Tianyi not to go to work in the fields because visitors were coming from the commune HQ. The two blackboards used by the youth labour team of which Tianyi was a member, were set up. Tianyi took a bench over to them, and a bowl of coloured chalks, and began writing and drawing on them. She had not been at it more than couple of hours when snowflakes began drift down from the sky. Tianyi sensed someone standing behind her. After a little bit, she heard a voice: 'How come you're not wearing gloves? Aren't your hands cold?' She looked round—a tall skinny young man was standing there. He smiled: 'You must be one of the new arrivals. Here, take my glove!' And without waiting for her answer, he pulled off his right glove and threw it to her. 'Catch!' She caught it. This, she learned later, was Sheng.

The main reason she liked Sheng was that he was good-looking. He had a prominent nose, long eyelashes, and the merest hint of fuzz around his lips. When he bent over his accordion to play, his eyelashes lowered as if he were asleep. To Tianyi, he was as handsome and noble as a prince. Good looks were important to her, more than to most girls. She was certainly not the only girl in the Propaganda Troupe to have noticed Sheng but the others were attracted to his talent. And girls often display their feelings in strange ways: these ones showed their admiration of Shu Sheng by bullying him.

All the girls in the Propaganda Troupe gossiped constantly

about Sheng in the most malicious terms. Comments like: 'Have you noticed what a lech he is, always eyeing up our chests?!' (from Ping). Or, 'That's nothing! He draws women in the nude!' (from Lili). The girls erupted in embarrassed giggles. Tianyi had had enough. She said: 'Don't talk rubbish like that! You're giving him a bad name!' The others looked at her strangely. Ping spoke: 'Do you know what his nickname is? "Mr Jiffy", because he pretends to be squeaky clean!' Lili pulled out a bit of paper and waved it in front of Tianyi. On it was a rough sketch done with a pencil of a nude woman. It was all out-of-proportion, not at all attractive, Tianyi felt. 'How can you prove he drew that?' she asked. She felt her question was utterly reasonable but the other girls glared murderously at her. After a long while, one of the solo singers, Hong, said: 'You've only just arrived, there are things you don't understand, you'll find out soon enough.' Tianyi was left baffled.

Hong seemed better educated than the others, and was certainly more softly spoken. She was a trained singer—her signature piece was *The Shining Red Star* from the opera *Red Azalea Mountain*— but only had a narrow vocal range. The daughter of a naval family, she had always loved the arts and trained as a dancer too; that meant she walked with her feet splayed out, which made her the laughingstock of Ping, Lili and the others. But the Production Brigade cadres liked Hong, because she was hard-working, conscientious and kind.

The snow kept falling. They could not go to the fields the next day, so Qiu, the brigade leader, said: 'It'll be New Year soon. Why don't the Propaganda Troupe get a show together? That new girl writes well, doesn't she? She can get a programme together for you!' Tianyi was only too happy to oblige. When the programme was ready, the Propaganda Troupe girls gathered in the room, whispering amongst themselves. Sheng arrived and sat down on a chair with his accordion, looking completely focused. The girls fell silent. The Propaganda Troupe leader, Hua, clapped her hands. 'Pay attention! I want to hear *The Tractor Drives into Miao Shan Stockade* first. Wei, you lead off.' Sheng played the introductory notes and Wei and Ping sang:

Rosy clouds over the cliff
Red plum blossom opens to the sun.
The spring breeze brings happy news
The tractor drives to Miao Shan Stockade …

When the melody rose an octave, Hong Wei was unable to hit the high notes, and Ping screeched. It sounded awful. They ran through it once more, and it sounded even worse. Hua clapped her hands for attention: 'Let's have the lead singers leading the chorus through their bit', so the chorus began:

The tractor drives into Miao Shan
a girl in the driving seat
Rice seedlings nod their heads in the breeze
the fruit trees give a wave of welcome …
The tractor drives into Miao Shan
the commune members are so happy
the "iron ox" will plough the commune fields
the air is filled with songs and laughter …
The girl gets down from the driving seat
the old women are so happy
"She's from our village!" they cry
she's driven the tractor back to Miao Shan Stockade …
Springtime has brought happiness to Miao Shan
our sons and daughters have done good

the sunshine bathes the landscape
the hillsides are a blaze of colour
a blaze of colour, as the flowers bloom!

It was not bad. Everyone paused for breath. Then Hua instructed them to do the dance, with Tianyi singing the accompaniment. By the time the rehearsal was over, the snow had stopped falling and the land was wrapped in white velvet. It looked enchanting. With cries of joy, everyone rushed out. They were only young, after all and, in spite of the fact that they were encumbered with thick jackets, there were energetic snowball fights. Tianyi stood there, laughing as Lili stuffed a snowball down Ping's neck. Wild with excitement, the girls began to dance in the snow, and Tianyi sang along:

The flag flutters in the wind
flowers cover the land
each blossom welcoming a friend with a smile …

Suddenly, she heard a quiet voice behind her. It was Sheng: 'Why don't you train as a soloist? You've got the voice, you're a natural!' So Tianyi learned to sing solo, making quite a name for herself in the commune.

Nowadays, Tianyi still loved to sing. Lian asked a Japanese friend to buy a karaoke machine for them and, in the evenings, if he and Tianyi had nothing to do, they would sing together:

I come from deep in the mountains
I bring orchid plants, and plant them in the school garden
I long for them to bloom …

And:

Where have you come from, my friend
like a butterfly, you fly in through my window ...

They had to keep the volume low. Too loud and it might bring old Sheng knocking on their door. The trouble was that Lian sang horribly, stubbornly, out of tune. Tianyi did not have the heart to take him to task over it, but it drove her mad, and eventually she just had to turn off the machine.

Tianyi remembered the two tunes that Sheng loved to play on the commune. One was the Korean song, 'Mangyongdae' and the other was 'The Nightingale'. As he played the accordion, Tianyi would sing:

At Mangyongdae
at the fork in the road
there stands the general
gazing at the open door of his humble home
then hastening towards it.

Finally one day, Sheng had paid her a visit at her parents' home. Tianyi spent an entire morning getting ready for his arrival, even putting out two champagne flutes in her dingy room. Her father's salary as a professor was barely enough to support the family, but Tianyi did not want Sheng to see how poor they were and did her utmost to spruce the place up. However, when Sheng arrived at their home, he seemed oblivious to his surroundings. His attention was wholly focused on Tianyi, so much so that he hardly tasted the glutinous rice balls delicacies she served him. After lunch, the pair of them shut themselves in her room and chatted. Suddenly, Sheng went deathly pale and, clapping his hands to his ears, gave a muffled cry: 'Oh God!' Tianyi leapt to her feet in terror.

Tianyi took him to the campus hospital, where he was diagnosed with acute middle ear infection. It was serious, and agonizingly painful. Tianyi sat at his bedside, silently remorseful. *If only he hadn't come to visit me, he might not have ...* But Sheng displayed an almost superhuman fortitude. He chatted to her about himself: 'I expect you've heard the girls gossiping about me.' Tianyi hesitated, then decided honesty was the best policy. She nodded. Sheng flushed. 'That was when I was much younger,' he said. 'I was very immature.' It occurred to Tianyi that he might be referring to something she had not actually heard before. 'In the fourth year of primary school,' he went on. 'The Cultural Revolution had just begun, and my parents were detained. I got in with a gang of kids, and that's when it happened.'

'When what happened?'

Sheng looked as if he was being dragged to the scaffold. He looked down then, after a long moment, raised his head again. Even his eyes were reddened with shame. There was not a trace of his usual noble, even haughty, expression. He told her how he was led on by the bigger kids and they climbed up to the windows of the women's public baths to watch the women bathing. He finished speaking, and fainted apparently from a terrible stab of pain.

A month later, Sheng wrote Tianyi a letter. The first half page was entirely filled with quotes from Chairman Mao Zedong, including the one about caring for, cherishing and helping each other—it was customary for young people to regurgitate quotes of this sort from Mao when they wanted to write love letters. Then Sheng wrote that he had fallen in love with Tianyi the first time he set eyes on her. He confessed that he had always been attracted to older girls and called Tianyi 'My beloved big sister'.

Tianyi was horror-stricken at the letter. Then her face flamed scarlet. It was outrageously immoral to call a girl 'beloved big sister'. If it had been anyone other than Sheng, Tianyi would have denounced him, and he would have been damned forever.

But this was Sheng. He was nineteen years old, and he was in love with Tianyi, then twenty-one. She was the one who was damned.

3

Tianyi's pregnancy was the happiest time of her life. Every morning, Lian made up a cup of milk for her, from milk powder, or he would fry her an egg. There would be bread or a steamed *mantou* bun. She would have either the milk or an egg. Having both together felt greedy to Tianyi. She remembered vividly something her father had said when he was suffering from TB and spitting blood. He had come home from hospital, Tianyi's grandmother offered him milk and an egg for breakfast, but he had shaken his head: 'Having milk and egg together is greedy.' That was 1959, the first starvation year in China. Tianyi was just six years old, but she never forgot his words.

When she contracted cholecystitis during her pregnancy, Tianyi pedalled herself to the Police Hospital in Dongdan to have acupuncture in her ears, considered the only safe pain-killer for a pregnant woman. But she enjoyed the daily trip. It was an easy ride and did not tire her. She remembered her mother saying: 'You can't afford to fuss when you're poor,' although her mother did. As long as Tianyi lived at home with her, not a day went by without her mother complaining about something. It would start as soon as she got out of bed in the morning: 'Ai-ya! My head hurts! Or 'Ai-ya! I didn't sleep a wink all night!' If it wasn't one thing, it was another. Tianyi was exactly the opposite. Even if she was unwell, she numbed herself to it and refused to admit it. 'You can't afford to fuss when you're poor' made perfect sense to her. She just put up with things.

After her hospital visit, Tianyi hurried home to cook lunch, fish or some sort of meat. She was always in high spirits. She had spent so many years poring over her books, she liked a change of role. *I'll show Lian*, she thought, *that he was so right to choose me, he'll be the envy of everyone.* She was quite certain she would make a good wife and a loving mother. And Lian did feel himself fortunate in those days. He often brought treats home —watermelon, walnuts, chestnuts, once even a live, eight-pound mandarin fish. He really was a conscientious husband, ready to embrace and enjoy their new life. It was a simple life but a good one. He was doing well at work and his bosses liked him. And he felt he had struck gold with Tianyi. He put his feelings of satisfaction into words too, praising his wife to the skies to his friends. Tianyi felt he sometimes exaggerated but she did not mind. She thought it showed how honest Lian was. He clearly meant every word of it.

In those days, they had many friends, and people were always dropping by. Tianyi liked to serve them her speciality, a whole chicken cooked in a small oven that had only cost 60 *yuan*. She would clean the bird and stuff it with a mixture of seasoned, chopped meat and fish, prawn balls and crabmeat. Then she put it in the oven on the highest setting for an hour and a half, constantly turning and basting the bird. Their friends might be in a state of anxiety over the new reforms and liberalization and what the effect would be on their country, but when she brought out the fragrant, juicy chicken, crisp on the outside, tender inside, the discussion gave way to gasps of admiration.

Tianyi's labour began on her due date, thus giving her the distinction of being among the one percent of women who give birth on time. When the contractions started at two o'clock in the afternoon, she went to phone Lian. It was nearly four o'clock by the time he got back, and by then her abdomen was going rigid with each fierce spasms. Lian kept his head and quickly put together the things she needed for the hospital. They got a taxi and the taxi-driver took in the situation at a glance. 'A son to birth, the mother to death, the King of Hell separates them by a hair's breadth,' he recited in a flippant tone. Tianyi was appalled.

A son to birth, the mother to death, the King of Hell separates them by a hair's breadth. Good heavens! What a frightful proverb. In a daze, Tianyi felt the sweat trickle down her back.

By midnight, the contractions were coming fast and furious. Little by little, the mouth of the womb was forced open. With every minuscule dilation, the pain was almost unbearable. Tianyi was woefully ignorant of the facts of life: intercourse, birth and the female reproductive organs. When she was growing up, these were forbidden topics. She had had plenty of boyfriends before marrying but she had stayed a virgin. She had become pregnant from her first experience of sex and, during her pregnancy, they had somehow been afraid to make love again, although Lian had had a wet dream on one occasion.

Tianyi remembered it well. Lian had sat up in bed in the darkness, refusing to speak. Tianyi found his dumb silence unbearable and asked him repeatedly what the matter was. Eventually, he answered in muffled tones: 'What do you think it feels like to have a wet dream with your wife in bed beside you?' Then he buried his head under the quilt and fell fast asleep. Tianyi, however, tossed and turned and did not sleep a wink for the rest of the night.

She felt guilty. Her character was oddly soft and tender under a tough exterior. Just at the moment when she most sternly repulsed other people, a gentle little voice inside her disagreed. Her defiance as a young girl had only been an attempt to get her mother to acknowledge her, to pay attention to her, to love her; she really was a good little girl at heart. Yet few people managed to get under that unyielding carapace. If only Lian had been clever enough to find way in, she would no doubt have been easy tamed. He was not.

Lian sat sleepily on the bench outside the labour ward, along with couple of other men. There was the murmur of conversation but it was almost inaudible because an ear-splitting roaring noise drowned their words. It was a very long time before Lian realized it was the sound of rain pelting down outside. Tianyi's contractions were being accompanied by a torrential rainstorm, the like of which the city had not seen in years. The tumultuous din sounded like the drumrolls of a symphony orchestra, and made the building shudder. Even the stolid Lian, who loved his sleep and could sleep through anything, was shaken awake.

Tonight was his son's birth night, and it was right in the middle of a violent storm … or perhaps he should put it the other way round, thought Lian. Everything seemed confused, although he was vaguely aware that the storm was passing, with even the terrible drumrolls becoming more distant. He heard a cry above the noise but it somehow sounded unconvincing, as if someone was having a bad dream, their mouth yawning desperately in a mute scream. How horrible, as if your head was going to explode.

Tianyi was wide awake all night. She had always found it hard to drift into unconsciousness. As a little girl, she sometimes did not sleep for nights on end. It got worse in adolescence, when the heady fragrance of spring flowers made her feel as if her body was swelling and floating away. Her body … back then she had been delightfully slender and was so flexible she could arch over backwards, her hands on the floor, and lift one leg above her head. Her skin, especially from the neck downwards, was alabaster-pale, and seemed as delicate as almond milk curd, impossibly fragile. When her maternal grandmother was alive, she used to say that in another era, Tianyi would have been an imperial concubine.

Tianyi certainly never became an imperial concubine and she had found it hard to get even an ordinary boyfriend. It was hard to say why. She was not bad-looking. She was intelligent, healthy, competent and well-educated. She had no especial faults in any particular area, it was just that, as they would say nowadays, she just didn't attract the boys. Her friend Di could not understand it. Tianyi's lithe, shapely body, together with her passion for life, should have made her popular and sexy. She was someone who brimmed with sex hormones, even her abundant periods made that clear. Well, that was the impression that Di had, anyway. Tianyi always bled copiously, whereas she, Di, had only scanty periods. When they were girls, Di had lacked self-confidence and Tianyi had been filled with it. Tianyi still seemed full of self-confidence, at least when she was with Di. As far as boyfriends went, Tianyi simply explained to her friend that the boys were too keen; it was she who was not keen. Di looked up to Tianyi so she was more than willing to accept this explanation.

Alone, Tianyi had to face the sobering fact that emotionally she was a failure. She knew quite well why. First, she was too much of an aesthete, constructing a perfect love in her imagination; in reality, she completely lacked either the skills or the courage to fall in love. Secondly, she was too self-regarding—even if she were to meet someone whom she admired, she could not bring herself to make the first move and so she frequently missed her chance. Worst of all, she let her tongue run away with her and often said things that were the opposite of what she really believed. Then, when she was misunderstood, she was too proud to correct the misunderstanding. So Tianyi's excuse that she 'didn't attract the boys' had become a self-fulfilling prophecy and by the mid-1980s she felt she was well and truly on the shelf.

In the agony of her labour, Tianyi could not make out exactly what the terrifying din was. She was quite sure it was not just a rainstorm. It was too loud for that. She was in such a blur of pain that she could not hear or think straight. Every time she had a clear thought in her head, the waves of pain seemed to tear it to shreds. She felt the thunderous noise must be a ringing in her own ears. An even more mysterious thought came to her: was this the noise that accompanied every childbirth? And Sheng, had he heard this noise too, when he got his middle ear infection?

Tianyi had secretly revelled in Sheng's gentle declarations of love, without wanting to examine them too closely. This must be happiness, she felt, and hugged it tight to herself, as if afraid that this pathetically small ray of joy might be scared away.

On the day that the Propaganda Troupe went to the Commune HQ to do their recording, her song was not on the programme. But after the Party Secretary heard all the girls sing *The Tractor Drives into Miao Shan Stockade* in chorus, he was impressed enough to pick out Tianyi and ask her to sing a solo. Tianyi exchanged a secret glance with Sheng. His eyes lit up as he met hers, and he struck up the tune, *When the Communist Party comes, the bitter turns sweet*. This was the Tibetan singer Tseden Dolma's song, and was the Party Secretary's favourite, although Tianyi did not know that at the time.

The commune's recording was broadcast that day and Tianyi's solo was heard all over Beijing. But rumours flew with the song. From that day on, no one looked at Tianyi in quite the same way again. This was the first time it had happened to her, but certainly not the last. She found it a bit frightening, but exciting too. She went looking for Sheng. She liked feeling that the experience had drawn them together and made them forever invincible. She constructed the scenario in her imagination in great detail, convincing herself that it would all come true. Until she saw Sheng. He was crouched over as if he would never straighten up again, and in his crystal clear gaze, there were now flickers of hesitation.

If Tianyi's antennae had been less sensitive; if she had been more easy-going, or perhaps more crafty, or more open and accommodating, the situation could still have been remedied. But Tianyi was the woman she was. She instantly read and understood the hesitation in Sheng's eyes. The spurt of happiness evaporated and she retreated into her customary tragic despair. This was unhappiness Tianyi-style: no matter how the drama opened, the emotional denouement was always the same.

Such was her first love affair. It was a foretaste of what was to follow. A few months later, her youth labour team were allocated factory jobs. Tianyi started work as a machine operator in a cereals-processing factory. One day, Hong came to see her. She was holding a thick envelope in her hand. 'Letters from Sheng,' she told Tianyi. 'You know him pretty well, so tell me what to do, should I go for him or not?'

Tianyi felt her heart leap, then plummet. She was normally good at concealing her feelings but she almost failed this time. Finally, after a long pause, she said in a low voice: 'When did you … did you start seeing him?' 'Oh, ages ago, but there was a time when he seemed to have a change of heart and didn't take much notice of me. Then we started seeing each other again after we all got factory jobs and both ended up in a watch factory. He looked me up again and we had a meal or two, watched a film … that sort of stuff. Lately, he's been pushing me to say how I feel about him …'

Tianyi could not remember the rest of their conversation. Everything sounded distorted, and her heart was hammering so loudly she was afraid Hong would hear. She heard a voice inside her: *You've failed*, it said. Her first failure in love. It dawned on her that the man of her imaginings was a living being and could not wait for her forever, would not stay the same forever. While she spun fantasies in her head, imagining how he would come and find her one day and they would be madly in love just like when they first met, the man of her dreams had gone off in pursuit of something else entirely.

Love had tripped her up for the first time. There would be many occasions in the future when she would trip up just the same way.

4

Tianyi's second boyfriend was the Secretary of the Communist Youth League in the cereals-processing factory where she worked. His name was Yingqi.

Tianyi had been working in the commune for a year when the factory job came up. By rights, she should not have been entitled to the move so soon, but at the crucial moment she wrote a begging letter to the Commune Party Secretary listing all the various difficulties her family faced and why it was imperative that she had a job that would enable her to live at home. Her eloquence proved decisive. The Party Secretary was swayed, not so much by the contents of the letter, but by the letter-writer's undeniable literary skills. He had no idea that he had such a talented writer under his command. At commune HQ, he was surrounded by people who had been recommended as the best of their kind, but none of them came close to this writer. Secretary Sun, a chubby, fair-skinned middle-aged man, sighed as he read it, and thought of his own daughter who had been deprived of education by the ten years of the Cultural Revolution. If this girl, who signed herself Yang Tianyi, was the same age, she must have missed her schooling too, so how did she manage to write so well and with such a range of expression?

Mr Sun made a couple of calls and spoke to the heads of Tianyi's production brigade and Propaganda Troupe about her. The general verdict was equivocal. She was sometimes prone to petty bourgeois sentimentality, for instance, she loved to sing songs like 'Delivering the Grain' and 'Mangyondae', making them

51

sound more schmaltzy than revolutionary. It was true she had plenty of talent, she could arrange performances, she could paint, her calligraphy was good and she had a good voice. In turn, they asked the Party Secretary why he wanted to know. Was there some problem? As soon as Sun put the phone down, he remembered the girl who had sung *When the Communist Party comes, the bitter turns sweet* a year ago. Her voice, with its almost child-like purity had made a big impression on him. The hard-headed Party Secretary suddenly lost his head, and found himself scribbling a note on Tianyi's letter. And so Tianyi's fate was decided.

She became aware of Yingqi the very first day she arrived in the machine operating room of the factory. He was wearing a blue singlet, having just come off the basketball court and immediately struck her as extremely handsome: fair-skinned, deep-set eyes, a prominent nose. There was something foreign in his looks, and she later learned that his nickname was 'the Romanian'. His politics, however, were utterly orthodox—he was secretary of the Communist Youth League—and he employed all the most up-to-date political language at the youth meetings he ran. Later, Tianyi heard about another side of him from Xiao, a young man from the popular science education group and his former classmate, who told Tianyi on the quiet: 'If you'd only known Yingqi at middle school! We used to see him dressed in fancy, long boots, taking his dog for a walk—he was always up to something or other!'

There was an annual national art exhibition, and Tianyi took over organizing the factory's entries as soon as she arrived. She was made directly responsible to the Youth League Secretary. He allocated her a small hut to work in, on condition that they 'get a prize.'

Tianyi was only too happy to move into her little hut. She took up her brush and came up with creative ideas every day. In the three months the factory gave her, she joyfully let her imagination run riot. Every evening, Yingqi would find some excuse to drop by and see her. His visits gradually grew longer, from half an hour, to an hour, then three hours. When he casually asked her to paint his portrait, she could hardly refuse.

The news that the Youth League Secretary was spending most of his evenings hanging out with the girl in the little hut spread through the factory like wildfire. Yet again, Tianyi saw on the face of her fellow-workers, especially the girls, the all-too-familiar, unspeaking look she dreaded. That very year, cruel gossip had driven a girl called Lingyu to kill herself. Personally, Tianyi felt that the girls' silent looks were more than enough to drive someone to suicide! However, Yingqi was calm and unflappable. That, in turn, made Tianyi feel she had someone to depend on and she was grateful to him for calming her. She used to wake up in the middle of the night and wonder: Is this for real? Had she found a real man at last?

When she saw him the day after those long evenings, Tianyi was embarrassed to meet his eyes, although she forced herself to put on a show of nonchalance. She began to make an effort, too, to smarten herself up. In those days where all clothing was drab, she wore brightly coloured under-garments, such as a vest with a decorative edging peeping out at the collar, or she put a hair-clip in her fringe and surreptitiously applied a bit of her mother's old lipstick—then wiped it off again. Yingqi seemed oblivious to her efforts, though. He came every day for his 'sitting', posed, assuming his most 'correct' expression, and chatted as she painted. She did not work quickly, but she was unsure whether she was being deliberately slow.

Suddenly one day, things changed. It was 4th April 1976, right before Tomb-Sweeping Day and in Beijing people flooded into

Tiananmen Square to pay their respects to beloved departed leaders like Zhou Enlai, something the government thought implied criticism of those that were now in power. Tianyi sneaked off to join them. It was drizzling, she remembered, and a young man in glasses stood on a high stone plinth and led them in singing songs. So many people braving the rain, standing on pavements running with water, no one wanting to leave. No one even put up umbrellas. Tianyi wondered if the May Fourth Movement of 1919 had been like this. 'The blood of numberless revolutionary martyrs flowed'—that was what they had been taught as children. It had surely not been shed in vain! Her heart swelled with youthful ardour. She sang at the top of her voice; the only way to feel cleansed was to sing it out. She looked at the people next to her, and their eyes were filled with tears. She was surprised to find that she was crying too, swallowing a mixture of rainwater and salty tears.

Then, a few days later, she saw the banner headline of a newspaper editorial: 'The Tiananmen Incident, "counter-revolutionary"!' Her brother Tianke shoved the newspaper in front of her: 'Look! Look! The government's calling it "a counter-revolutionary incident". And you've been going there every day! Don't tell me you haven't!' She glared at him.

Her father was still alive then, although very frail. He spoke in a quavering voice: 'Tianyi, now you listen to me. I'm your father and I'm worried sick about you, always have been! Ever since you were little, you've got mixed up with the wrong sort of people. You feel the back of your skull, you've got a 'rebel-bone' there, haven't you? You mark my words, my lifetime motto has always been: 'Prudence in all things, just like the old Imperial general Zhu Geliang'. Just remember, be prudent then you'll always be all right!' Tianyi nodded her head obediently. But in her heart she rebelled.

The police began to round up the chief suspects a few days later. In the little hut, Yingqi, looking mysterious, showed her a list: 'Look, these are the people the authorities want.' She looked at the list. She could see he had done her a favour by not putting her name on the list even though he knew quite well that she had been to Tiananmen Square. However, there were many, many people on that list that she knew very well, including his old school friend, Xiao. She looked at him shocked. This was outrageous. By the time they scooped a prize in the national fine art competition, Tianyi and Yingqi were no longer speaking.

Many years later, she heard that Yingqi had progressed up the career ladder, to become official, then deputy head of department. He married but it did not last long and he and his wife separated. He refused to divorce in case it had an adverse effect on his career. That did not stop him collecting around him a bevy of beautiful lovers. That was entirely in character.

5

Tianyi's labour continued all night. She visualized her womb as made of some kind of tough rubber, and did not understand why it was so hard for her cervix to dilate. Other women in the labour room progressed easily to ten centimetres and were wheeled off to the delivery room to give birth. Women came and went, but Tianyi still lay there.

'Doctor, is there a problem with my labour?' she heard someone say. She found it hard to believe it was her own voice. It was so diminished by the pain, it was as thin and reedy as a scrap of paper that the slightest breeze would blow away. 'Too early to talk about problems,' the young male doctor glanced at her. 'It's your first, right?'

'Yes.'

'First labours usually last sixteen hours,' said the doctor. 'Be patient, you're six fingers dilated, things should speed up now.'

Just as the doctor finished speaking, Tianyi felt a surge of sickening pain and warm liquid gushed from between her thighs. She knew it was blood and her legs went limp with terror. She struggled to get up to go to the toilet. 'You're bleeding, hurry up!' the doctor urged her, and she found herself wondering why such a nice young man should be an obstetrician.

It took until eleven o'clock the next morning for her to be fully dilated. It was not good timing: the exhausted doctors had finished their shift and were going off for their meal. Tianyi was left lying there all on her own, almost numb with agony. The numbness and the gradual diminishing of the pains scared her. She instinctively felt that the poor little baby in her womb had no more strength, and was too tired to move.

That was more or less the case. When Doctor Bai, the obstetrician, came to examine her, she noted on her chart the frightening words: 'Foetal distress'. Then, without further ado, Bai asked whether she and Lian wanted a caesarean. It was the dreadful, age-old choice: save the mother or save the baby. Lian's unhesitating response was: 'Save the mother.'

Tianyi never forgot that and was grateful to him, but at that moment, she was incapable to thinking anything. She felt overpowering fear. The taxi-driver's flippant comment: *A son to birth, the mother to death, the King of Hell separates them by a hair's breadth*, seemed to go round and round, banging away inside her head like a drum, making her heart thump in terror.

Tianyi was being wheeled toward the lift when, at the lift doors, Doctor Bai suddenly pulled back the sheet—to reveal the baby's head already crowned. 'Hurry up! Get her back in!' she exclaimed. Then she took the gurney and headed back to the delivery room, leaving the assistants scurrying behind. 'Get a move on!' Doctor Bai shouted frantically as they finally caught up with her. The shouts, the running, all somehow became part of Tianyi's nightmare. There was something else too: the extraordinary moment when the doctor had whipped off the sheet, transforming herself, with that swift movement, into the graceful figure of the goddess of mercy. Doctor Bai had become Guan Yin, Tianyi's very own saviour, at this, the most terrifying moment of her life.

How she had suffered for this baby, Tianyi reflected when she was in the post-natal ward. All the pain caused by this tiny scrap of a creature. I don't even like him. She looked at the rows of tiny heads, lined up in their cots, laid on their sides, pointing left or right, and thought how very ugly they were. But every single one of the other new mothers was overjoyed with her baby. It was as if all that agony had been forgotten in an instant.

In the delivery room, she had heard the big-breasted woman who now lay in bed number two calling her husband all the names under the sun. Never again, she swore, would she go through such torments even if the government changed its single-child policy. Then she saw her baby, the infant girl she absolutely did not want, and fell on her fervently, clutching this tiny creature to her breast. In bed seven, a skinny frail-looking woman was running a fever, but constantly pushed her nipple into her baby's mouth. Quietly, Tianyi watched the other women in the room. Childbirth, it seemed, stripped them of all inhibitions, or rather, de-sexed them, made them invincible. In the stifling August heat, they walked around the room half-naked, as if the doctors were no more than cardboard cut-outs, and those ugly-looking brats in their cots absorbed every ounce of their mental and physical energy. So this is what women, mothers, really were.

Tianyi felt another rush of fear. Why wasn't she behaving like them? She still had her inhibitions, and made sure that every inch of her body was hidden from their gaze. She averted her eyes from this ugly flesh and fixed them instead on a remaining small patch of white wall. As she waited for her baby to be brought to her, she began to count, fully expecting that by the time she got to one hundred, the young nurse would call out: 'Bed one! Look what a handsome little boy you've got!' But something quite different happened. She smelled flowers, and heard the flapping of slippers, then a familiar voice said: 'Tianyi, wake up! I'm here!'

She opened her eyes, to see everyone in the room looking at her. The other women always gawked at any visiting husbands.

Right in front of her was a large bunch of lilies and, behind them, Lian's face, wreathed in anxious smiles. She could still conjure up the scene years later, though the passage of time blurred its clarity somewhat.

It was a long time before Tianyi's son was brought to her. The nurses told her she must be patient. 'He was deprived of oxygen for five minutes, we need to keep him under observation.' Finally, after a day had passed, the matron herself carried a baby into the room. 'Look! Yang Tianyi,' she said, 'there's nothing wrong with your son!' Tianyi took the child from her, and all her imagined worries suddenly evaporated. Her son was perfect, his skin as sleek and smooth as if he were weeks, not hours, old. Tianyi called him Niuniu, little ox, because his birth year, 1985, was the year of the ox.

Niuniu was formally registered as 'Wang Zhe'. This was a commanding, arrogant-sounding name chosen, like his nickname, by Tianyi. Lian just thought it was amusing. He followed her lead in everything and said little, no matter what she did.

Tianyi ran a fever for a week after the birth. One day, she sneaked a look at her medical chart. There were two closely-written pages of notes about foetal occiput posterior position, foetal distress, respiration of the new-born ... and so on and so forth. It was all in medical language that she did not fully understand but still made her feel afraid. There was also a drawing of her vagina, and with two long lines of sutures, clearly marked. Tianyi remembered that the doctor had spent an hour and a half sewing her up after the birth. The cuts had become infected, which was why she had a temperature. They also hurt badly, but Tianyi was surprised to find that, after the baby was born, all the pain seemed numbed, and was quite bearable. Giving birth stripped a woman of her carapace and returned her to a more primitive state. If someone, some day, could invent a civilized way of giving birth, they would be doing immense service to humankind, she thought. Only then could women be truly liberated. Talking about women's liberation and gender equality now was just a nonsense.

6

Tianyi and Lian had nowhere to live. Their old place was gloomy and had no heating, so was too cold for a baby. They had to move into the room Lian's parents had rented for them after their wedding, even though it had a shared kitchen and bathroom. Tianyi was astonished at how glum her mother-in-law seemed, apparently unable to raise a smile. Her father-in-law, however, beamed with pleasure at the arrival of the latest little Wang. On her return from hospital, her in-laws looked after them, her father-in-law doing the cooking and her mother-in-law ferrying it to them, while Lian washed the nappies. Tianyi had slept badly in the hospital for a whole week and longed to catch up on some rest. Lian felt so sorry for her that he bundled the baby up and took him to his mother and grandmother to look after for the night. To Tianyi's surprise, however, no sooner had she shut her eyes than Lian was back with the baby. Tianyi was furious but, when she saw the tears in Lian's eyes, she swallowed back her anger. It was September, there was a cold wind as Lian carried him across the street, and Niuniu set up a loud wail. Tianyi felt wretched.

'They said a baby shouldn't leave its mother.'

'Not even for a night?'

'My grandmother said that a baby should be at the breast the whole time.'

Tianyi felt a yawning chasm open up before her, and smiled bitterly. Lian held both her and the baby in his arms, and tears ran down his face. 'Don't worry, soon it will be just the three of us and no one to tell us what to do.' It was the first time that Tianyi saw Lian cry, and the last.

The next day, her in-laws brought dinner over but Tianyi could not get a mouthful down. By now, she had not slept for ten whole days. Her mother-in-law was grim-faced: 'You two went ahead and had a baby without waiting till you were settled.' She turned to Tianyi and said brusquely. 'You got pregnant rather quickly, didn't you?' Tianyi was struck dumb. Was this the kind of thing a mother-in-law was supposed to say? She wanted to answer back: 'Have you lost all humanity? Aren't you a woman too? Did you never have a child? Aren't you happy to hold your grandson in your arms?' She forced herself to swallow the words back and say nothing. She simply could not be bothered. It was all so boring. How had she got herself into this situation? What was going on? Was this the kind of life she was going to have to live from now on? Heaven knows, it was a million miles from the kind of life she really wanted!

'You got pregnant rather quickly, didn't you?' One woman's criticism of another, the subtle resentment of a young woman by an older one. Tianyi sensed more but could not put a finger on it. She did not discover the real reason for her mother-in-law's coldness until a couple of years later, by which time the cracks had begun to appear in her marriage.

Everything was different now that, seemingly out of the blue, a third person had arrived in the couple's world. Niuniu was ravenous, and was taking three bottles of formula milk a day in addition to breast milk. Tianyi had a lot of milk, white, fragrant and rich. The neighbours all commented in astonishment that a woman of her age should have such good milk. Left alone after their visits, Tianyi revelled in the pleasure of motherhood, picking up Niuniu, marvelling at his soft warmth. 'Look, light,' she pointed out and his face turned upward. He had a funny little face, his little chin round like a button, no neck, and very large eyes between their enfolding lids. As the days wore on and Tianyi was stuck at home, she soon learnt what the 'one-month confinement' meant—pretty much like prison in her view. The only thing that made it better was this little person at her side. She could talk to him, gaze at his sweet little body.

She occupied herself with needlework. She had always done things like that, was better at it than most of her generation. That was thanks to her mother who, when Tianiyi was only six years old, had taught her to knit socks, using those big balls of white cotton yarn. Sometimes, she had used pink, or pale blue. Her mother taught her how to knit a heel and cast off. She was a quick learner, and was soon better at it than her mother. With her unusual aptitude, the socks she knitted looked as if they could have been shop-bought. Then her mother taught her to embroider, to net string-bags, and knit with wool. It took her no time at all to pick up the skills. Her mother had two thick pads of pattern paper, densely covered in embroidered patterns. One of the designs was rather strange: a half-opened flower, at its centre a beautiful girl with very long eyelashes. She practiced the design over and over for a whole evening, using madder pink thread for the petals, light blending to dark and at its deepest at the very centre of the blossom. She made the leaves dark green, and the beauty's cherry-like lips were scarlet. She was pleased with her results, until her grandmother brought out the teacup coasters she had embroidered when she was young. Flowers embroidered in gold thread on sapphire blue satin, and a pattern of lotus blossoms and roots on a pale green satin background. They were exquisite. On the sapphire blue coasters, the flowers were all edged in gold thread, drawn with an extraordinary sureness of line. The effect was like that of Rococo stained glass. On the pale green piece, silver thread predominated, and the lotus flowers were in a jade white. Both pieces had an embroidered edging, executed in a traditional style with particular skill. The embroidery was so fine on the blooms that there was not the slightest gap to be seen, and it looked like a solid piece of satin.

When she first saw the coasters, Tianyi felt truly moved. They seemed to give her a peek into the lives of women generations before. She thought of her mother and her maternal grandmother, their skin lily-white because it had never seen the sun's rays, the figure-hugging *qipao* gowns, with their high necklines, that reposed in their trunks. She suddenly felt a rush of admiration for these old-fashioned women. Perhaps tradition had something going for it after all.

She learned to knit with wool too, and in no time at all was creating all kinds of designs of her own. She progressed to crocheting, tea cosies, and toys crocheted from fibreglass, and then to tailoring. In everything she took up, she was better than any of the girls in their courtyard. Even their neighbour, Aunt Jie, Di and Xian's mother, was moved to comment: 'Your Tianyi is so clever, she can learn anything, and she's so clever with her designs.'

Her needlework certainly came into its own when Niuniu was born. They had no money, so Tianyi bought her own material and made all the baby's clothes. The results fitted well and looked good too. Di gave her some new woollen yarn and she made Niuniu a little jacket and trousers and hat. The garments were so tiny that, years later, Niuniu took a look at them, and refused to believe that he really had been that small.

One bright sunny day, Tianyi was sitting in the sunshine breast-feeding when her mother-in-law came into the courtyard.

'How come he's so pale?' she exclaimed, 'You haven't been putting face powder on him, have you?' So cold towards her grandson, Tianyi felt, but she choked back a retort and said nothing. Her mother-in-law watched the baby from a distance, but did not appear to want to hold him in her arms. She made a few more idle comments, then turned to go. Tianyi could think of nothing to say. Finally, she took the little boy's hand and waved it: 'Say bye-bye to Granny!' These innocent words triggered her first clash with her mother-in-law.

A couple of weeks later, the older woman returned from a holiday in Guilin and made her husband and her son listen as she recounted the incident. She had not enjoyed her holiday, she said, because all she could think of was Tianyi saying: 'Say bye-bye to Granny!' She had understood it to mean that Tianyi did not ever want to see her mother-in-law again, or even that she hoped that she would die down in Guilin and never come home. Her voice was choked with tears and she could hardly get the words out. Lian had to promise to 'have a word with Tianyi.'

That day, Lian clearly had something on his mind when he got home but it took a lot of probing from Tianyi before he finally told her. Tianyi looked scornful: 'Is there something wrong with that mother of yours? Why does she always see things in the worst possible light?' Such an ordinary thing to say, and she had said it so quietly and so naturally, but to her astonishment Lian exploded with rage. Puce in the face, he burst out: 'Can't you stop making trouble for one moment? Can't you both leave me alone? ...' Her husband had become another person, and Tianyi was shocked. He wouldn't listen to reason, he was hysterical, and he shouted so loudly it was as if he was going to bring the house down. Niuniu, asleep in his cradle, awoke screaming in terror. That was the first time Lian lost his temper with her.

Tianyi felt as if her own anger was stuck in her throat and she could neither swallow it nor cough it up. She could not eat a morsel of her dinner. On that occasion, Lian apologized and spent a long time trying to make it up to her. But this became the pattern: he would lose his temper, then suddenly go soft, like a premature ejaculation. It happened again and again. She forgave him in words, but in her heart she was still angry. What could she do? If every little thing she said brought down such anger on her head, what could she say? She longed for her confinement to be over, so that she could go back home. It was as if all her conflicts with her mother and brother had never happened. She just wanted to go home and see her mother.

The one-month party for Niuniu was a big affair with all of Lian's family there. Niuniu, dressed up like a little doll, was passed around to be admired. But Tianyi was completely ignored. No one said: 'This is Niuniu's mother.' Only Lian's grandmother shot her a glance, and said: 'What are you doing sitting there? Niuniu needs a feed!'

Tianyi felt as demeaned as if she were a household slave, as if anyone could tread her underfoot. And this was the 1980s! Her anger threatened to overwhelm her. With great difficulty, she swallowed it back, but it felt like a solid object stuck in her throat.

7

Being back home did not live up to Tianyi's expectations. Her sister Tianyue was at university doing a Masters. Just her mother and brother, Tianke, were there. For the first two days, all the neighbours in the compound came to look at the baby, exclaiming at how bonny he was. They were all old ladies who had known Tianyi since she was a child and greeted her affectionately. Her mother and brother were wreathed in smiles. Lian was anxious to please and went out of his way to be helpful, shopping every day for fresh meat and fish, and preparing all kinds of good food for them. Tianke was busy romancing his girlfriend and in quite a good mood. Everything was peaceful. Then suddenly, one day, nothing was peaceful any more.

It was a gloriously sunny afternoon when Tianyi's friend Di tiptoed in with a mysterious air and whispered in Tianyi's ear. Tianyi instantly said to her mother: 'I'm just popping out, go ahead and have your dinner. Don't wait for me.' 'What are you going to do with the baby?' asked her mother. *What are you going to do with the baby?* It was a question that would vex Tianyi for another fifteen years, and she never knew the answer. But just now she said: 'Give him a little cow's milk.'

What Di had said was: 'Jin's here.' Jin was an old friend of theirs. Tianyi knew that the reason Di was not married was because of her feelings for Jin. He was ten years younger and, in Tianyi's eyes, just a clever kid. Di, however, adored him. He was extremely bright. Four years previously, he had been a student at Fudan University and some friends put him in touch with Di. He came to Beijing to show her a book, *Deep Level Structures of Chinese Culture*, by the Taiwan scholar Sun Longji. It so happened that Tianyi had just published her paper on bisexual love, and she met him with Di. The three of them had a very pleasant discussion. Tianyi gave him an unpublished story of hers, and the next day Jin turned up with a story he said a friend of his had written. Di grabbed it first but, no sooner than she had read the first few lines than she blushed scarlet. She thrust the bundle of paper at Tianyi, exclaiming: 'It's disgusting!'

'Disgusting!' was a word much in vogue with girls back then, and Di and Tianyi were no exception. Tianyi read it too, and also found it 'disgusting', but strangely, the more 'disgusting' she found it, the more she wanted to read on, and in fact read right to the end. It was about a girl who became a stripper to keep her family. The story was completely improbable, had no literary value to speak of, and was mainly one long description of sex. Tianyi suspected that Jin had actually written it himself. Anyway, the two girls gave it short shrift. Jin spluttered in red-faced fury: 'It was my friend who wrote it, it's nothing to do with me … All the same, I think it's very realistic. Not like your story, Tianyi, which is so simple, it's insipid. That's not realistic.'

Jin was on holiday, and after that, came over almost every day. They talked about anything and everything. In those days, Tianyi greatly admired the novel *Rosy Sunrise, Evening Glow*. The author went under the mysterious pseudonym, A-Xiong, and no one had any idea who he was. Quite by chance, it turned out that Jin knew the deputy editor at the publishers of *Rosy Sunrise, Evening Glow*, who told him that the writer was a well-known old Beijing Red Guard leader from Cultural Revolution days. That made Tianyi intensely curious. 'I've just got to meet A-Xiong,' she said.

Jin made sure she did. That very evening, he wrote a review of A-Xiong's work, which he asked the editor to pass on to the author. Tianyi was scornful: Jin was a fool to imagine that the editorial department, always snowed under with submissions, would bother to forward it and, even if they did, who was to say whether the author would ever get around to reading it? He was hot property nowadays, he must get over a hundred letters a day. Did he even bother to open the envelopes? And even if he did, why would he get back to Jin? Tianyi was derisive, but Jin was unabashed. He was quite confident that he would get an answer and, sure enough, seven days later, a letter arrived from 'A-Xiong'.

Tianyi still remembered Jin rushing over that day clutching the letter as if it was a wedding invitation, reading it out in a loud voice: '... Amongst thousands of letter-writers, you are the one who really understands me. Your critique is brilliant ... Please drop by and see me, my anonymous friend, it doesn't matter if you are male or female, young or old ... I do hope we can become friends ...' Tianyi smiled to herself. Such youthful enthusiasm did not seem like the kind of thing a middle-aged man would write, especially one who had been a Red Guard leader.

That summer evening was the first time that Jin got a taste of how inconsistently Tianyi could behave. He eagerly bustled them over to A-Xiong's house, looking over his shoulder to make sure she was following. She was fearful, he could see that, unsure of herself, and he found this funny. She always acted so mature and experienced, but in matters of the heart, she was absolutely hopeless. Like the mythical Lord Ye and his pretended passion for dragons, she would turn tail and flee if one really turned up. But this time, the 'dragon'—his real name was Lu Lixiong—turned out to be so far from Tianyi's ideal, it was no wonder she wanted to run a mile.

Lu Lixiong lived in a military compound designated for senior army officials, and was waiting for them at the gate. Tianyi saw a squat, little man, at least a head shorter than Jin. The moonlight threw dark shadows on his face, and when she looked closer she realized he had hatchet features: protruding forehead and chin, cavernous nostrils and cheekbones. Tianyi took one look and decided this man had to be an imposter. When she was a child, she had seen many Red Guard leaders, and they were all good-looking, 'cool' you would describe them nowadays. Her logic was simple enough. To be a Red Guard you had to be pretty special. However talented you were, if you were ugly, you would not make the grade. Tianyi just could not square A-Xiong's beautiful writing, profound thinking and original opinions with this middle-aged midget. She did not hide her disappointment. When Jin made the introductions, she refused to look A-Xiong in the eye. In fact, she hardly bothered to make an effort to be good-mannered. All she wanted to do was get out of there.

The Lu family's courtyard was sizeable, with a table and benches in the middle. A young woman sat there, combing her long hair in the moonlight. She had obviously just washed it, as she had a big scarf draped over her shoulders. A quiet smile played over her features, and she looked genuinely happy. 'This is my wife, Nan Hong,' said Lu Lixiong.

'You must ... must ... must be the model for the heroine of *Rosy Sunrise, Evening Glow* ...' Jin stuttered. He always had a bit of a stammer when he got excited or met someone new, especially if it was an attractive young woman. 'Yes, you're right!' A-Xiong exclaimed. 'Please, sit down!' Then he looked at Tianyi: 'You must be wondering how on earth I got my hands on such a beautiful girl, right?' He chuckled complacently. He was obviously about to tell them the story of their romance. Luckily, Nan Hong interrupted the flow, to say softly: 'Hey, you haven't offered our guests any tea yet!' It clear to Tianyi that this woman, with her dulcet tones and flirtatious glances, was deliberately playing the siren.

Tianyi suffered through this for a couple of hours, before they were able to leave. Outside, Jin remonstrated: 'This is ridiculous, Tianyi! You insisted on meeting him, and as soon as you get here, you can't wait to go! Was it because of his wife? Why should that matter? It doesn't stop you being friends with him. And he knows so many people, Tianyi, you need to broaden your horizons!' Tianyi did not know what to say. Eventually, she managed: 'Right, I owe you one. I'll make it up to you.'

When Jin next saw Di, he told her how Tianyi had behaved. Di burst out laughing: 'That's what she's like. When she meets a real dragon, she turns tail and flees.'

Four years on from that event, the Jin they met was a very different young man. He still stammered, he still chatted cheerfully about everything under the sun, but he had filled out considerably, and had quite a belly on him. He was a grown man. Something else had changed too: he addressed these two older women as equals, not in the respectful way he used to. Garrulous as always, his main topics of conversation were now politics and agricultural reform. Somehow, he had wormed himself into the confidence of some leading policy makers and thinkers and become their friend.

Just as four years earlier, Di lapped up everything he said, her eyes sparkling with excitement. He found her a most appreciative audience, but what he really wanted was for Tianyi to launch into a fierce debate with him, the way she used to. But Tianyi just could not summon up the enthusiasm. Fortunately, Lian turned up.

Tianyi had said to Di before: 'How come all Chinese men are so into politics? They all act like they're going to be the next

Premier!' Di giggled. 'That must be why they're so frustrated all the time!' Tianyi pulled a face: 'It doesn't seem normal to me.'

Lian, of course, was another amateur politico. His job in the Planning Commission had made him self-important. He began every sentence with: 'In the Commission, we ...' He was delighted to meet Jin, and took to him immediately. He was also deeply impressed at the famous names that Jin dropped—but took good care not to make his excitement too obvious. He commented casually: 'Really! You know Huang Luwei as well? He's quite an interesting man. I read his article, *Meditations on History*, his thinking's pretty much in line with my own.'

'Wow! Re ... really?' Jin responded effusively. Lian was clearly a new soul mate. 'I know him very well, shall I introduce you?' Lian hesitated a fraction. 'There's no hurry,' he said, 'wait until my thesis is published ... But why not take Tianyi to meet him? He's quite a character, and he loves literature.' Tianyi looked at him. She never ceased to be amazed by Lian's self-confidence. She had no idea where it came from, and no inkling that when this self-confidence collapsed, the results would be truly terrifying.

Lian had come to pick her up. Wherever she went these days, he would turn up to take her home. She never said anything, but she liked it all the same. It gave her a simple feeling of happiness that was very precious to her. But her happiness was nothing compared to Lian's. He had it all: job, wife, child, everything was perfect. What more could a man want?

For some time now, Lian could hardly bear to be apart from Tianyi. He loathed business trips for that reason. Whenever he had to go, he bombarded her with letters, at least one a day, sometimes two. It was crazy, especially for someone like him who didn't like writing letters. 'Tianyi, I landed in Guilin airport today and sneezed twice. It must have been my Tianyi thinking of me.

Were you? Tianyi?'

Only a cold-blooded reptile could remain unmoved by letters like this. They seemed to set her alight, as if she had been doused in some flammable substance. Compared to the vague fancies she had had in the past, and her so-called former boyfriends, this was true affection. She had always had trouble sleeping, but since her marriage, she slept like a log, no matter how loudly Lian snored. Lian always said he never got a good night's sleep when he was away on business, because she was not with him. The transition from love to affection felt safe. Tianyi was satisfied with her marriage.

Many years later, however, when she read Milan Kundera's *The Unbearable Lightness of Being* and came across the surgeon Tomas who, in spite of his string of affairs with female nurses, insisted on sharing his bed only with his wife Teresa, she had to smile. It was nonsense for Tomas, or any man, to pretend that he could separate love and sex.

That evening, they were home very late. At the door, she had a premonition that something was wrong. Sure enough, no sooner had she stepped inside than Tianke thundered at her: 'What the hell do you think you're doing getting back this late! You two had this baby, don't dump it on other people to look after! You know Mother's not well! You know my work's crazy! I've been slaving away all day and I have to come home and look after your child! What kind of people are you? What way is this to behave?!'

Tianke's tirades were nothing new but, each time, it carried the same power to wound Tianyi to the core. His eyes seemed about to pop out of his sockets, and his spittle landed on her face. Short of screaming back at him, however, there was nothing for her to do but grin and bear it.

His shouting woke up Niuniu, who began to wail in terror.

'Lian, I'm sorry, our Tianke just can't behave decently,' said Tianyi's mother. She had got up and thrown on some clothes and stood between her son and her daughter, facing her son-in-law. 'He's certainly looked after the baby, carried him back and forth, and thank heavens he had the patience to do that. But now you're back, and he can't help but let off steam. He just can't talk about it, he has to insult the two of you!' Tianke grabbed hold of his mother: 'Don't waste your breath on them! Either I go or they can get the hell out of here! You choose. There's nothing more to be said. I've had enough!' This was too much for Tianyi. 'We're going!' she shrieked. 'How much longer are you going to go ranting on?'

Lian stood looking contrite, saying nothing. Tianke spoke to him: 'Lian, don't worry, I'm not getting at you personally. This family has been arguing for decades, we're used to it! You ask Tianyi, isn't that right?' Then he added:' When you married her, I was worried it wouldn't last, because she's so weird. If she was a good woman, would she have waited until she was such an old maid before she got married?!'

Somehow, Tianyi found the bottle of baby milk flying out of her hand. Tianke ducked, and the bottle smashed into the full-length mirror, making it craze all over into fragments like snowflakes. There was a moment's silence, and their mother burst into floods of tears. 'Oh my God! Now you see what a terrible temper she's got, Lian! That's how she treats us, there's just the two of us, her mother and her little brother, now her Dad's passed on, and I'm a poor old woman, and that's how she treats us!' This was followed by further wails.

Tianyi clutched her baby in arms that would not stop trembling. 'Let's go, Lian, let's go! What are you waiting for?!' Lian picked up Niuniu's bag of things and silently followed Tianyi out of the house. Tianke's furious shouting and swearing followed them all down the road. The Yang family rows made a deep impression on Lian. A dozen years later, when their marriage was truly on the rocks, Lian would stamp in rage and tick off on his fingers all Tianyi's faults. Among them was her family's propensity to loud quarrelling.

Two months after this incident, they finally got an apartment of their own, consisting of two bedrooms and a sitting-room in a modern concrete-built block. It was spacious, forty-six or forty-seven square metres. But for some reason, Tianyi did not take the same delight in this as she had with their first home. They had no money to renovate it properly. Tianyi bought the cheapest furniture she could find in the showroom, and still spent more than 700 *yuan*. It was all made of woodchip, and looked shabby by today's standards, but it was all they could afford. She got a bed, bedside cabinets, a liquor cabinet, a wardrobe and a bookcase. It was obviously not enough, and Lian managed to pick up some wood from a nearby building site and get some migrant workers to knock together a dressing table, a writing desk and a crockery cupboard, and two more bookcases. The workmanship was shoddy and they charged Tianyi over 300 *yuan*, which was a week's food bill. When Tianyi realized just how shoddy, and tried to get them back to fix it, they had vanished without trace.

Tianyi, who held the purse strings in the family, was annoyed. She had been earning her living as a writer for some years now and this money came from her writing, from the sweat of her brow. Money did not grow on trees, and when it was gone it was gone. She asked Lian but he said he did not have a cent in savings, which seemed incredible. But as time went by, she came to believe that Lian really did not have any money. He was a very strange person, one in a hundred, or perhaps one in a million. He was completely scatter-brained in everything he did, acting without planning or forethought. His monthly salary in those days was 300 *yuan*, and he handed over the lot to Tianyi. But he seemed to need double that, sometimes three or four times. He acted like Tianyi was a bottomless purse. Their relationship was like an accounts ledger: Lent: from Tianyi's purse. Borrowed: for Lian's spending. Tianyi came to feel increasingly that Lian was a wild child, grown up in the crack between the rocks, drifting through life completely rudderless. Lian used to say that Tianyi was his rudder. Tianyi was distressed to discover that Lian treated her not only as his wife but also as his mother. It was a terrible thing. The truth was that she herself longed to have a mother who loved her, made a fuss of her. But now Lian had thrust her into a dual role. She had to mother her son and her husband. It was intolerable!

Lian may have had no ready cash but, with an air of mystery, he told her that his family had savings, 50,000 *yuan*. That was a huge sum in the mid-1980s. But the family had only donated 1,200 *yuan* for the wedding of their precious only son. Lian had spent every cent of it, and now there was nothing left.

8

Tianyi really had not made enough preparation for her child's birth, though there was no excuse at her age. In her heart of hearts, she had believed she could reclaim some of her youth by getting married. She did not want a child. She envied the childless yuppies of the west. Let hedonism rule! A late marriage should give her endless pleasure, endless love-making! They would earn big money and buy a car and a house! They would splash out on travel! They would stroll through shopping malls buying fancy clothes! They would have weekends away, go abroad! Emigrate! Whatever form it took, the future promised glittering excitements, but she never even got a taste of the cherry before the child made his grand entrance, and now he was here to stay.

What was even more galling, she loved this child. She felt like she was caught between the devil and the deep blue sea: her baby and the life she wanted to lead. Tianyi had never liked stark, black-and-white choices, but that was what she faced now. Again and again, she had to choose, and it was extremely painful. She had hoped and planned for a different future. Lian never made plans, he just lived from day to day. He never liked thinking very much, and he did not want her to think either.

When it came to looking after her child, Tianyi was intent on avoiding her responsibilities, at least at the start. She felt wounded —by the birth, by her post-natal confinement. She needed a good rest from it all. Whenever she went out, she felt reinvigorated. And she knew that if she was to go out more often, then she needed to do one thing: wean her child off the breast.

Niuniu was two-and-a-half months old. He was such a bonny baby! She used to try and step back, to see him as others did, and her conclusion was always: this little boy was, by any criterion, the bonniest baby she had ever seen. He had beautiful big, limpid eyes, their whites verging on blue, fringed with long eyelashes, enfolded within almond-shaped eyelids; clearly-outlined, cherry lips. His prominent nose and almond eyes were as delicately-crafted as those of a doll. On the day he was one month old, Tianyi took him to the doctor's to be weighed. When he plumped down on the scales, even the doctor's mouth dropped open in disbelief. In the first month of his life, this chubby little baby had put on a whole five pounds!

Tianyi cradled him with the utmost care. His sturdy, supple little body was a translucent, alabaster-white all over, with the exception of a purple birthmark on his bottom, the exact same shape as the mark on that Russian leader Gorbachev's face. Lian joked that their baby had taken the map-like port wine stain off Gorbachev and stuck it on his bum. When he had filled himself with milk, he lay in her arms in the sunshine, and gazed at his mother. One day, his little mouth split open in a smile, such a sweet, glittering smile that Tianyi was almost afraid. It was wholly self-aware, nothing like the instinctive parting of the lips when he had taken his fill. My baby can smile! My baby recognizes me! They said that a baby knows its mother at three months, how come he recognized her at less than two months? He was clearly exceptionally intelligent. Tianyi's secret delight was no different from that of any ordinary housewife. She suddenly felt she had been drawn into the ranks of foolish mothers and, if she did not take care, she would never get out again!

It was no good! She had to pull back from the brink before it was too late. In her research paper on bisexuality, Tianyi had given her opinion that women were their own worst enemies. And the facts proved it. Look at those swollen-breasted women just delivered of daughters, who had scarcely recovered from the pain of childbirth before they started planning for a son. Were women really born masochists?

Tianyi gritted her teeth and dosed herself with Chinese herbal medicine to dry up her milk supply. Weaning proved to be easy, very easy indeed. But for some unexplained reason, Tianyi suddenly lost a lot of weight after she stopped breast-feeding. She became scrawny, and looked unhealthy. Her chin sharpened, dark rings appeared around her eyes, her nose was oddly red, and her face mottled. She had lost all her good looks. Tianyi felt that if her face got any thinner, she would look like a leprechaun. She just could not bring herself to look in the mirror, could not be bothered to. She put away all the mirrors in the house, and wore sunglasses when she went out of doors. Even so, she was recognized by an old acquaintance at the bus stop, the editor of a women's magazine. The woman did not mince her words. 'What on earth have you done to yourself?' she exclaimed. 'Most women look fair and plump after they have a child. How come you've gone so dark and skinny? I hope you're not ill! You need to see a doctor.'

Tianyi laughed it off at the time, but the more she thought about it afterwards, the more afraid she felt. She consulted the deputy-head of the Hospital for Chinese medicine, a very well-known physician. As the old man took her pulse, he looked increasingly grave. 'Have you resumed relations with your husband since the birth?' he asked.

'Once,' said Tianyi.

'You're pregnant again.'

'But I can't be!' I've only just had a period ...!'

'That wasn't a true period, just an indication that you might lose it.'

Tianyi was aghast. Her legs turned to jelly and she could hardly stumble out of the hospital. She found herself looking at a woman at the road-side, guzzling down a pancake wrapped around two fried eggs and dripping yellow oil. She saw the woman's mouth greedily opening and shutting, completely at odds with her scrawny body. Tianyi stood rooted to the spot, watching. How lucky that woman is, she thought, she can eat anything she wants and not get fat. There were, she considered, two kinds of women she most envied in the world, those who could eat all they wanted without getting fat, and the other kind, those who could have as much sex as they wanted without getting pregnant. Unfortunately, she fell into neither category: she put on weight from a sip of cold water, and a man only had to touch her for her to get pregnant. The polar opposite!

A friend fixed Tianyi up with an abortion. She was surprised that, even after having had one baby, the procedure was so painful. The problem was that she was over-sensitive and, even after the anaesthetic had been administered, she could hear every tiny, icy metallic sound. The sounds followed her for years afterwards. If she ever heard anything like that again, she would shake uncontrollably. After the procedure, the doctor showed it to her: 'Look how perfectly formed she is.' That reduced her to tears. A little girl, she thought to herself, that was my daughter, my son's little sister. Poor little girl, to disappear just like that. If she had lived, she would have been one year younger than Niuniu.

'You didn't do a proper confinement the first time,' the woman doctor told her. 'You need a mini-confinement for a miscarriage so take the opportunity to get really well.' Tianyi took the woman's words to heart, and got a nanny to come and look after Niuniu.

XU XIAOBIN

Then she concentrated on looking after herself and regaining her strength. Mrs Zhang, the nanny, was from Anhui province, in her fifties and extremely myopic. Tianyi wanted her to take good care of her baby so she went out of her way to be nice to the woman and Mrs Zhang responded with gratitude. A little while later, when Lian sent Niuniu off to his parents' house to give Tianyi some peace and quiet, the nanny went with him. The day of their departure, Tianyi looked at her baby, a muslin scarf covering his face, fragile as a lily, sleeping contentedly after his feed, and about to be borne away by his grandfather. How he would wail when he woke up! She tried to push the thought out of her mind. She felt her heart was breaking. She finally understood what 'broken-hearted' meant. It was no exaggeration.

In the morning, Lian got up and went to work. Tianyi lay alone in bed, her head teeming with thoughts. Lian was very good to her but she was quite sure that this was not how she wanted to live. When it was nearly midday, she realized that Lian had not taken the pork ribs out to unfreeze. She got up and opened the freezer lid, feeling a sudden chill emanating from the package, penetrating her hand, travelling up her arm. The chill seemed to freeze right inside her and swell. Her palms itched, and she could not bring her fingers together.

Lian arrived back from work to be greeted by a chorus of complaints from Tianyi: 'It was all your fault, you don't look after me, I had to get them out of the freezer myself, I couldn't get a grip on them ...' Lian did not pay much attention. In his view, Tianyi was just acting spoilt. 'Fine, fine, I'll make you a nice dinner. We'll have lamb with scallions, and pork ribs and *mouli* soup, how about that?'

Tianyi had to admit that Lian was a very good cook indeed. He was quick and economical, and everything he produced smelled, looked and tasted great. Tianyi remembered reading once that a good husband should, first, give his wife plenty of spending money and, second, make sure she had nice meals. There was a third criterion but she had forgotten it. In any case, Lian got one of those right, and that was a lot better than men who failed to manage any.

Lian's cooking was always fresh. Now she had eaten his food, she always felt that restaurant food was somehow not very fresh and too oily. His stir-fried vegetables emerged glossy and green. His casseroled meat was appetisingly brown and tender. When they had finished their meal this evening, they put the TV on, and watched right through from the News until shutdown, and the screen filled with snow. Mexican soap operas were broadcast every day in those days. *Bianca* had just concluded and *Libel* was on. The plots were boring but Tianyi and Lian snuggled up together and watched the episodes end to end.

Tainyi felt she was getting stupider by the day. It worried her but she did nothing about it. Her academy was about to host a seminar on issues around women in the Asia-Pacific Region. They wanted her to present a paper, but she could not muster any enthusiasm for it. One evening, Lian suddenly looked at her: 'Tianyi, I know you don't love me anymore.' Tianyi was knitting Niuniu a pair of tiny socks for his sweet, plump, little feet. 'Please, don't start a quarrel,' she said, with an impatient frown. A good quarrel was just what Lian wanted, but he was quelled by Tianyi's expression. Aggrieved and disappointed, he grabbed a book and began to read. It was *The Third Wave*, a hugely popular best-seller in those days. That made Tianyi feel she had been too harsh. For the sake of something to say, she commented: 'That's something new, you reading a book.' Lian's enigmatic reply was: 'Two thousand years ago, the Emperor Qin burned the books and buried Confucian scholars alive but when it came to it, he was overthrown by an illiterate bandit.' It dawned on Tianyi that her husband was not nearly as straightforward as he appeared. For one thing, he had an invincible belief in himself.

Tianyi's judgment was eventually proved correct. Lian was aspirational—or rather ambitious. It was just that his character destroyed his ambitions.

9

Before the 'Women in the Asia-Pacific Region' seminar, Tianyi went to see her baby, who was still staying with Lian's parents with his nanny. To try and conceal her pallor, she put on her fashionable, red velour coat, then sat on the bicycle, as usual riding pillion behind Lian. She was laden with things for her mother-in-law, as well as clothes for the baby. 'It's always good to arrive with presents, it buys you a welcoming smile,' her mother used to say when she was in a good mood.

But every visit to her in-laws filled Tianyi filled with apprehension. She never knew what devilry the old folk would get up to next. At least on this occasion, Lian's grandmother did not scowl when she piled her packages on the table, though she did complain: 'That woman you sent along has eaten us out of house and home, and she expects me to wait on her.' Tianyi knew 'that woman' meant Mrs Zhang the nanny. She looked at Lian. 'Don't go looking at him,' she heard next. 'This was your idea!' The old woman was implacable. In her black woollen top and trousers, she looked just like a crow. 'Mum,' remonstrated her daughter-in-law, 'you wanted them to come, and now they're here, you just …' 'And why not? I've got something to say and I'm going to say it. I'm over eighty years old, and I'm not afraid of anyone!' Tianyi felt incapable of making her usual retort. Lian tried to come to her rescue by making a funny face and having a dig at the old lady, which at least earned him a small smile. She batted him playfully with her fan and said nothing more. Tianyi felt disgusted at the scene, and could hardly raise even a perfunctory smile.

As this discussion was going on, the door opened and Nanny Zhang came in carrying the baby. 'He knew you were coming!' she said. 'As soon as you came down the street, he saw your red coat and cried for you. I'm so blind I couldn't see you but he wouldn't stop struggling and crying. Such a clever child!'

Sure enough, as soon as Niuniu saw Tianyi he launched himself at her. No one else would do. She took him and felt how heavy he was. Like a steelyard weight. She coaxed him back to a good mood by waltzing around the room with him, and the baby began to crow with laughter. He looked so sweet when he laughed that Tianyi forgot everything else. She was just a silly mother! She told herself off, but the little boy's smiles had her completely in thrall. She whirled round and round the room, with her baby in her arms, as if challenging the two older women. She felt their eyes on her, hostile and grim. She found it so strange that these two women seemed unable to exhibit the slightest love and affection for this child, the heir they had longed for. They seemed to have hearts of stone.

That day, she arranged to share Nanny Zhang's bed for her afternoon nap. The nanny prattled away about this and that, then suddenly she raised her fat body and whispered in Tianyi's ear: 'These are two wicked women, you know! They're saying that your mother actually used the Wangs' sewing-machine to make a padded jacket for Niuniu ...!'

That night, a distraught Tianyi finally exploded. 'Your mother and grandmother are like harpies!' she exclaimed to Lian. 'Haven't they ever had children of their own? They've got no idea how to behave!' She ticked off her grievances: 'On our wedding night, they came and knocked on our door. That was out of order! Your mother said the baby had come a bit soon! What did she think she was saying? I'm a decent woman, why shouldn't I have a baby? And why can't that old witch ever get on with me? What have I ever done to get on the wrong side of her? Let me tell you, our family may be poor, too poor to afford a sewing machine, but when my mother wants to make Niuniu a padded jacket, why on earth would she want to use your family's sewing machine? Let me tell you, we never needed you to bring that sewing machine over, but those women kept insisting we should take whatever we needed. And you believed them, you blockhead! How come they only have to say one thing and you fall for it. Whatever they say, goes, it doesn't matter what I say! They're just a couple of peasants! All big talk and tight fists …!'

Even to herself, Tianyi felt she sounded just like any shrew of a wife, but she was unable to stop. Finally, Lian fell on his knees in front of her, boxed his own ears over and over, and she was reduced to silence. She was astounded at Lian's falling on his knees, but even more astonished at herself. She was no better than an ignorant woman like Nanny Zhang, going on and on about things that were utterly trivial, but it was precisely those things that had hurt her, had caused her indescribable pain. How on earth had she ended up living like this? At dead of night, her numbed nerves sometimes sprang back to life, and stabbed her agonizingly. Her reaction was to wrap her armour around herself and drift back to sleep again.

At least she still had her friends. Jin was always dropping by these days. One day, he had an extraordinary request: he wanted to have sex with a girl but they had nowhere to go. Could Tianyi find somewhere for him? Jin's conversation had been turning in this direction for a long time now. He wanted to do some sort of sexual experiment. Tianyi had often hinted that Di had feelings for him. He was quite intelligent enough to understand the hints she dropped, but he pretended to be dumb and so Tianyi let it be.

He was an unusual young man: illegitimate, he had been abandoned at a hospital by his parents when he was a baby, and brought up by a foster-mother. His foster-mother could not have children of her own, and lavished all her energies on his education. When he was very small, she taught him to read stories of the ancient philosopher Meng Zi and the widowed mother who had schooled him. Then his birth mother wanted him back. Perhaps she could not bear to see the boy subjected to such a strict educational regime. He certainly achieved academic success but it was not a normal childhood, and he had been left with a gnawing feeling of unsatisfied curiosity. As time went by and he grew up, his feelings towards his adoptive mother became more complex. He kept trying to please her and had nothing but praise for her kindness in taking him on. But somewhere in his heart, he also resented her for casting a baleful shadow over his life. She was always there, watching from a distance, spying on him, so that he never dared overstep the limits.

His emotions were like a prisoner desperate to break out of jail. His sexual urges grew stronger and at dead of night he masturbated constantly. It sapped his energy and made him depressed. Only a girl could save him from himself. That girl could have been Di, but he liked his women curvaceous and wild. Di was too flat-chested to interest him. If truth be told, Tianyi was the one he really fancied. She was a lovely young woman, married but with the quiet simplicity of a girl and, best of all, she had curves. However, she also had an air of dignity that awed him and put her far out of his reach.

Now a girl had finally appeared to rescue him. She was in her final year studying piano at the Conservatoire and had heard him gabbling away at a meeting. Somehow that touched her sympathies. On their first date, in the park, they got down to some serious petting. He gave Tianyi a blow-by-blow account, making her blush with his frankness: 'She undid her bra so I could feel her breasts,' he stammered. 'Then she pushed my hand down there ...'

'Is she pretty?'

'No, but she's curvy, and she's really hot.'

'So she fits the bill?' Tianyi asked with a touch of sarcasm.

'Yes, yes she does,' Jin went pink. 'So I need your help, I've been wanting to do an experiment, to watch a girl's reaction to having sex ...'

'That's not fair, if she really loves you ...'

'But I might fall in love with her during the experiment. So there's nothing unfair about it ...'

'It's crazy.'

As with everything else, Tianyi told Lian all about it. To her astonishment, Lian not only did not condemn Jin, he evinced great enthusiasm for the plan and, of his own accord, went looking for a room. This gave Tianyi a whole new level of respect for him.

The one he found was next-door to their own apartment, and belonged to a friend of Lian's on the Planning Commission. He had gone abroad for six months and left Lian with a set of keys so he could keep an eye on the place.

Jin was hugely grateful, but Tianyi had a few more chores now, as she had to take them a thermos of boiling water, and sometimes breakfast too. Naturally enough she got to meet the luckless girl who was to become the object of the sexual experiment. It was true she was not pretty, but she was very fair-skinned and her full, high breasts strained against her T-shirt. To Tianyi, the older woman, she was shy and deferential. With Jin, according to him, she was sexually voracious. She liked it dozen times a day and Jin began to flag.

'She twists her head on the pillow when we're having sex. What does that mean, is it from pleasure ...?' Tianyi was amused and entertained at the things he told her, until she realized he was staring at her own breasts, which she did not like at all.

'Anything else? Off you go then!' she would interrupt him brusquely.

'We ... we need more condoms ... the last lot got used up ...' he stammered.

Tianyi felt as if she was trapped in a world of make-believe, forced to play the clowning assistant.

One day, Jin brought a big stack of photographs to show her, all nude pictures of the girl, in all kinds of poses, some of them very revealing. 'These are a bit over the top,' Tianyi remonstrated. 'Did you force her into this?' 'No ... it was her, she wanted to do it. Are all girls a bit masochistic?'

His question struck home and Tianyi shivered. Was she masochistic? It seemed like it. Her sex life had never given her any pleasure. Was it because Lian was just too nice to her? Too gentle? Did she need someone a bit rougher? Not too rough, she wasn't looking for violence, just a masculine sexuality, a masculine strength. If the man wasn't strong then the woman wouldn't be gentle. A man had to be a man before a woman could be a woman. Some men could penetrate, caress, embrace a woman just by looking at her. Did such men still exist?

In time, Tianyi really did meet a man like this. It was two years later. Jin had gone to America, and the girl had graduated and been allocated a job back in her native Liaoning province. Tianyi was invited by a social science journal to a symposium in Zhangjiajie, Hunan. Zhangjiajie, an area of mountains and forests, had only just opened to tourism and its gorgeous scenery was still pristine. The journal had invited a group of top scholars to attend. Tianyi was the only woman present, and so enjoyed privileged treatment. And there she met Xiao'ou, spotted him straightaway. A guide took the whole group out for an evening stroll along Golden Creek. Tianyi hummed as she walked, infected with an almost irrepressible excitement, her footsteps dancing in time to the song in her head. She was still young, after all.

It was this renewed vitality that restored her to health, not the mini-confinement after the miscarriage, which had only added to her ailments. For instance, her fingers swelled up and she could not grip properly, and her periods became irregular and very heavy. The practitioner of Chinese medicine she consulted just said she 'had deficiencies in her blood and her *qi*' and prescribed endless herbal tonics. None of them did any good at all and she decided she might as well stop them. Her complexion was dull and sallow and there were dark rings around her eyes, although they were still bright.

Xiao'ou was a research student, with a job as a newspaper reporter and a talent for writing. He was tall and very handsome, with a husky, deep voice, and was a wonderful conversationalist. It was hard to find fault with him, in fact. It was an eight-hour bus ride from Changsha, the capital of Hunan, to Zhangjiajie and they sat next to each other and chatted all the way. There seemed to be so much to say. She did most of the talking and he listened attentively. She liked listeners who paid attention. She felt small and delicate next to a man of his stature, and she liked that feeling too.

As they got nearer to Zhangjiajie, the temperature began to drop. She was cold and huddled up in the seat. He noticed immediately and took off his down jacket and draped it around her shoulders. The jacket carried the smell of his body, and made her feel cosy and warm. In the course of eight hours, they became intimate, almost like lovers. Their fellow passengers even began to make jokes: 'Hey, has the TV soap finished yet?'

He recommended *Last Tango in Paris* to her, and she did manage to get hold of it when she returned to Beijing. She watched it, flushing, her heart pounding. She did not understand why he would like a film like that. Of course, Marlon Brando was brilliant, but she did not like him in his old age, nor did she like this nightmarish sex.

After she got back to Beijing, they carried on meeting. He told her he wanted to go abroad, to set up some kind of 'cultural enterprise'. She helped him by finding the right people and pulling strings. She brimmed with enthusiasm, unstinting in her efforts, especially happy to help someone that she liked.

Xiao'ou was always unhurried and unflustered. He often phoned her at unexpected moments and, when she heard his deep tones, it would give her a frisson of excitement. Once he said: 'Why don't you come over? I'm in the Erligou Hotel, room 203, we're going to do a TV drama. The screenwriter and the actors are all here, come and meet them, talk through some ideas, they're really keen to hear your ideas.' 'You're so funny,' she said. 'How come you're always doing something different, even TV dramas?' He laughed: 'Right, do you find that a bit of a let-down? This is the second TV play I've directed, the first was two years ago but it's never been broadcast.'

So she went. There was a noisy scrum of people in the room. The screenwriter was the author of a best-selling book, *The Complaint*, a man called Dong. He wore his hair long and clearly thought he was the boss of the show. There was a lame man who walked with a stick, an attractive figure who had played a Christian priest in a previous role but this time was the male lead. The female lead was a stunner. She was dressed in a black leather coat and long, black boots that made her look like a Nazi Stormtrooper. Xiao'ou introduced her as Wenshu. Tianyi found her spirits dampened by how casual and relaxed Wenshu and Xiao'ou were together. She made an effort to act cheerful and laugh and joke but secretly wanted to make her excuses to leave at the first opportunity.

They watched the rough-cuts and she made some general comments, then stood up. To her surprise, the others were all on their feet too: 'We'd better be off.' Xiao'ou raised no objections and they left. All of a sudden, quiet descended on the room. She looked at Xiao'ou and found he was looking at her too, with an expression of tenderness. The warmth of his gaze startled her and she averted her gaze. But her heart dissolved, like a cloud that at the slightest touch would seep moisture.

'Come on, let's go and eat, there are some good places around here,' he muttered, looking at the floor. She followed him out of the hotel and, as a sudden breeze caught her in the face, she felt filled with warmth. They walked along, side by side, getting closer until she felt an arm drape itself gently around her neck. They huddled close together against the evening wind. She felt that the journey to the restaurant was all too short.

He ordered masses of food but did not touch it. She, on the other hand, tucked in while he sat and chatted idly. He talked of his family and childhood, telling her that he had been a wild child, and did not get any schooling. 'But you'd never guess,' she put in. He carried on as if he had not heard, telling her how much he had missed a mother's love, how all neglected children were troubled adults. 'What did your mother do?' she asked, feeling she could ask that now that they were growing closer. He said his parents had been in the Ministry of Defence. He mentioned their names, and she nearly jumped out of her skin.

'But don't get the wrong idea,' he said. 'I've made my own

way in life. Have you had enough to eat?' He only picked up his chopsticks once she had set down hers. How strange, she thought, but that was how it was every time they ate together. He simply refused to start until she had finished her meal. It was very puzzling. 'Let's eat together,' she urged him. 'It's delicious.' But he would not budge. 'My parents are workaholics. My mother hasn't given up work even now she's got cancer, she ...' 'Your mother's got cancer?' she exclaimed. 'Yes, breast cancer, she's been admitted to Hospital Number 304 for treatment.' '304? Isn't that the one near here? Then why don't we go and see her?' 'Fine, we'll go when we've had dinner.' His expression never varied, she thought, and wondered if he would be as impassive if the house caught fire.

She bought bags full of delicacies in the evening food market. He made an effort to stop her but she would not be stopped. She was driven by an odd kind of urge, the urge to be good to his mother. When she actually met his mother, she was taken aback. He was so handsome, she had expected his mother to be equally good-looking. But the old woman was hideous. It was not down to the hospital treatment, she was naturally ill-looking. The oddest thing was that he had told her: 'I take after my mother.' Were all Chinese men so tied to their mothers' apron strings? They did seem to love mothers much more than their wives. As far as heterosexual love went, they seemed to be stuck at the stage of oral fixation and then to go straight from that to premature ageing, so that they were always little old men who never grew up. Poor Chinese women! She thought.

The old woman had endured a double mastectomy and Xiao'ou seemed very distressed. 'The breasts are so important to a woman,' he told Tianyi. Something came floating back into Tianyi's memory, something from far back in the past. Instinctively, she touched her own right breast. It was the slightest of movements, that even the most observant person would not have picked up. Still, she still shot Xiao'ou a wary glance in case he had seen, but he was immersed in his own tragedy and had shut the rest of the world out.

Afterwards, quite suddenly, an impulse came over her. An impulse to unbutton her clothes, take off her top, and show herself to him, show him her splendid breasts, her crowning glory. There were few, if any, Chinese women with breasts like hers, she would say bluntly. Since she was fourteen years old, she only had to walk into the public baths to draw the stares of every woman in there. Her breasts were so dazzlingly white, they might have been crafted from silver, surmounted by nipples like pale pink jewels. They made people wonder about her ethnic origin, because Oriental women certainly did not have breasts like that. White women had breasts that colour but not of such a fine shape, nor did black women or Native Americans. The shape of Tianyi's breasts was most like those of a woman from South-West Asia or North Africa, small, jutting cones, but the skin colour was different, pink and white. Only a girl who was God's best beloved could have these most glorious of God's creations, the most bountiful of God's gifts.

But she should have remembered that the world abhorred perfection. Those whom God loved could just as easily be abandoned. The instant God had abandoned her, she had been knifed in the breast, and now she bore a scar that would never fade. She wanted to show him her scar.

It happened when she was university and had just split up with her third love, a fellow student called Jianyu. She was looking even more haggard than usual, her eyes dark-ringed, her skin sallow. Her periods, when they came, never seemed to stop, and then one day she found a lump under her armpit. It was hard, and rapidly getting bigger. She was scared and went for a checkup. She saw the head of surgery, a nice old man who kept trying to relax her by making facetious comments. But it only made her more tense, and she kept asking: 'What's wrong with me, doctor?'

The doctor said he was admitting her to hospital so that they could examine the lump. The evening she arrived, the door to the ward silently opened, and a tall young doctor came in. 'Dr Lin,' the nurse introduced him. 'You'll be under his care.' He was wearing a facemask but she could see a pair of beautiful eyes. She had never seen a man with eyes like that. They were a very unusual colour, blue-grey, distant like moonlight on a mountain crater.

She tensed up immediately. 'Open your gown,' he said. His voice had a professional detachment. She quietly untied the tapes and the loose, shapeless gown fell away from her body. He looked dazed.

He bent over and began to examine her. He still had a professional gravity but she could see the flush that rose up his face under the mask. She tried to clear her head and focus on the *chakra* beneath her navel but it was no use. A surge of heat travelled up her body and she felt her face flame red. Good heavens, she was a grown woman, wasn't she? How could she be so easily reduced to such embarrassment? The truth was that, although she was twenty-six years old and had had three boyfriends, she was still a virgin, had never been touched by a man! This was the first time it had happened to her. It felt peculiar, yet entirely natural.

The young doctor's name was Lin Fan. He descended on Tianyi like the Angel Gabriel, giving her a new reason to fantasize, a very good reason. Many years later, she still remembered that instant of crippling embarrassment. She was acutely aware of his experienced fingertips, his quiet muttering. There was the pressure of his fingers on her breast, probing, caressing gently, the strange medical words that he murmured, his way of fending off his own discomfiture. She felt mortified at this man's hands sliding over her smooth skin, his palms broad and warm, blessedly unsweaty. On the surface they were doctor and patient, interacting in a normal, formal manner. In reality (and there was absolutely no way they could deceive themselves), they were not doctor and patient but a young man and a young woman. Doctor Lin's first examination exposed something real between them, something they recognized from the word go, and were inescapably drawn into.

The girl in the bed opposite watched them goggle-eyed. She was a sixteen-year-old who had grown up in a Beijing back street, and he was a good-looking man, a fine surgeon too. He was obviously from a good family, and had everything a young man like that should have. That was another attraction. An uneducated young girl was just as skilled as any university graduate at picking a likely prospect. And this girl had really taken a fancy to Doctor Lin.

On the operating table under local anaesthetic, Tianyi was upset and in pain. She cried and cried. Eventually, Doctor Lin himself grew distraught and the attending nurse had to intervene. Tianyi was roundly told off: 'What on earth is all this fuss about? This is just a minor procedure, what are you crying for? An educated woman like you! Pull yourself together! Doctor Lin is a very kind man. Any other doctor would refuse to operate at all!' At that point, Doctor Lin stemmed the outburst.

She was wheeled into a single room. Late in the evening, it must have been eight or nine o'clock, she was still crying, or rather the tears were falling silently. Night was falling and a corner of the curtain lifted and fell in the breeze. She was thoroughly chilled from all the crying, and clutched the thin hospital blanket around her, shivering uncontrollably. At that moment, the door opened. Doctor Lin came in, wearing his ordinary clothes. It was his habit to check up on all the patients he had operated on that day, before he went off shift. He saw her reddened eyes, and the bowl of rice porridge sitting untouched on the table and asked: 'Has no one come to sit with you?' She shook her head. She felt a great longing for him, though she could not say why, all she could do was cry. His expression, it seemed to her, grew much softer and his eyes filled with pity.

'Why haven't you eaten?'

'I don't want anything to eat.'

'So you just want to cry?'

She was a little embarrassed and bit her lip.

'It was only a minor operation. Is it very painful?'

She hesitated. Then she said in a low voice: 'It's not because of the pain …'

'Then why?'

She said nothing. The tears stubbornly welled up again. He saw patients cry almost every day but for some reason, could not bear her tears. 'I'll go and buy you something to eat.'

'No! …' She slid out of bed, clutched the hem of his jacket, frantic, swayed and almost overbalanced. The stitches pulled painfully and she cried out in pain. He turned quickly and put his arm around her to steady her. Her whole weight lay against him. He had never felt such a soft body. He, who had always thought of himself as self-possessed, felt consumed by a surge of heat. She was as tense as he was, and for a long, long moment they stood stiffly, silently motionless.

Finally, he helped her to lie down and laid the quilt over her with great gentleness. The tenderness and restraint of this young man flooded her heart and the tears came again, but now she was completely soft, as if he had dissolved all her stiffness. At that moment, if he had laid his finger anywhere on her, her skin would have seeped like ripe fruit, but he did not touch her. His expression told her that he liked her, liked her very much, but it would be wrong.

The characteristic that all good Chinese men share is that they do not want to hurt a woman. The trouble is that they do not understand what really hurts a woman. It was a good man like that that she had met—and fallen madly in love with.

After she was discharged, she made frequent visits back to the hospital, even though it meant a long journey and changing buses three times, just so she could see him. The first story she ever wrote, for which she won a prize, had Lin as its main protagonist. On New Year's Eve that year, she suddenly received a phone call that made her heart skip a beat: 'Is that Yang Tianyi? ... This is Lin, I'm on duty tonight in Emergency ... If you have nothing on, would you like to come and keep me company?' Her heart pounding with excitement, she dressed up and put on some make-up, then finally scrubbed her face clean and wore something very simple. She wanted her face to be completely naked.

Flickers of emotion softened his stern expression. His first words were: 'Your story. I read it.' Her face flamed.

Twenty years later, when she met him again, the years had given her complete self-possession. Or so she thought. After all, it had been twenty years, she had surely changed out of all recognition, would he even know her? In fact he recognised her immediately, and he flushed, just as he had twenty years before. The sign on his door read: 'Professor Lin, Outpatient Services', but nothing else had changed. There was the same unresolved tension between them, as if twenty years ago was just yesterday. He finished writing a prescription for the patient he was seeing, making, then correcting, four spelling mistakes. Then he saw the patient out and shut the door without calling the next one in. Just like twenty years ago, his consulting room was theirs.

Of course, he had aged, but not much. His face looked the same, though his hair was thinner and there were a few sombre frown lines on his forehead. However, once again, she had missed her chance. She asked a wise friend for advice. The response was: 'Of course, because you are both too noble. Who needs nobility nowadays?' Was that really true?

The same thing happened when she stayed up late into the night with Xiao'ou. Precisely nothing. Three months later, when Xiao'ou's TV drama was about to go on air, he called her. She focussed all her attention on his tone of voice rather than the words, and discovered that that tone had changed. It was not that she was being over-sensitive, he really had changed. She put down the phone with a sigh. She realized that yet again love had passed her by.

She had not understood that the male of the species was an utterly pragmatic animal. There was not a man in this world patient enough to have a platonic relationship with her. Worse, none of them had the courage to bring this goddess down from her pedestal and turn her into a real woman. Only that rude boy Lian. He boldly took his chance, and actually succeeded.

10

One day Lian came home from the office and said to Tianyi: 'They've let Mrs Zhang go, and they've got my cousin's daughter Jiaojiao in to help with Niuniu. First, she's family so she can be trusted and, second, she's young so if there's stuff she doesn't do, the old folks can make her do it, it's not like with a nanny, you have to tiptoe around them.' Tianyi gave a faint mutter of assent, and carried on with her writing. Lian was always most respectful when he saw her scribbling away. He was in almost superstitious awe of the written word. He had had an article published in some newspaper once, had kept a copy, and had it still. Far from being scornful, Tianyi actually felt sorry for his foolishness.

Jiaojiao's arrival had entirely unforeseen consequences. It triggered a crisis in their marriage that rocked it to the foundations.

That afternoon, Tianyi and Jiaojiao lay on the bed in the extra room Tianyi and Lian rented opposite her in-law's home, as Niuniu slept soundly between them. It was just the two of them, chatting quietly because Lian was away on business, and Tianyi had come on her own to see her baby. Jiaojiao was a skinny girl, with a long face and protruding teeth. She was not pretty but she was young and had good skin, so was not unattractive. Tianyi had given her some clothes and a few knickknacks, the sort of things that girls liked, and that broke the ice. On that pleasantly warm afternoon, Jiaojiao began to whisper an alarming story in Tianyi's ear.

'Uncle Wang keeps everything to himself,' Jiaojiao said. 'I bet he hasn't told you that your mother-in-law's his step-mother.

'Uncle Wang's real mother is a peasant,' she went on. 'His father left her behind and got a new wife when he moved to the city, that's Uncle Wang's step-mother. She's my auntie.

'When she couldn't have children, Uncle Wang's father wanted to bring him from the countryside, but his real mother wouldn't let him go, so his father got two relatives to kidnap him. Uncle Wang's real mother was out of her mind with fury. She was so mad she started to pull the *kang* to pieces with her bare hands ... you know, the mudbrick beds we use in the countryside, with a fire underneath to heat them ...'

Tianyi was struck dumb. The whole story was almost too fantastic to be true! She felt devastated, totally unprepared for a revelation like this. Her first reaction was: *How could he have kept such a big thing from me? If he could keep that from me, what else might he be hiding?* Her second reaction was: *If it's true, then the whole family's completely immoral!* Her third was: *How traumatic it must have been for him.* Jiaojiao said it had happened when he was seven or eight years old. In that case, he must remember his birth mother. So why had he never mentioned her, or acknowledged her? What a dreadful business!

No, she could not believe that Lian knew about it. She could not! Jiaojiao must have mis-remembered his age, he must have been too small to remember. Lian's honest, earnest face floated before her eyes. It was impossible that such a guileless man could have pulled the wool over her eyes. He could not possibly know. She must tell him, immediately, it was too tragic for him not to know who his birth mother was! She did not sleep a wink that night.

And that was the cause of Lian and Tianyi's first proper fight. As soon as Lian came back from his business trip, Tianyi burst out with her appalling revelation. To her amazement, he said nothing, nothing at all. Instinct told her that he had known, had known all about it. He looked completely unmoved, just as if it was all quite normal, and the more worked up she got, the more he withdrew into silence. She frequently said things that were unwise when she was in a state. And he seemed to be deliberately winding her up, leading her to say things which would have been better left unsaid.

'Why don't you say anything? Did you know about it, or not?'

'I want to know how you feel about it! That's really important to me!'

'Tell me something! Are you going to go looking for your birth mother? She may be a peasant, old and poor, but she's still your mother! You knew when I had Niuniu how much a mother bleeds and suffers when she gives birth! How can you forget your beginnings like that?!'

She probably said a lot more too, she didn't remember. What she did remember was Lian's sudden, silent explosion of rage. It left her absolutely terrified. First came a crash so loud that she was quite sure the whole building must have heard it and been shocked into silence. Then she saw her beloved tape-recorder. It was in tiny pieces.

She had acquired it in the third year of university. She had asked a classmate who was good with electrical stuff to come and choose it with her. She was a girl who lived frugally, and when she bought something, she chose with great care. She and her friend went through every item on the shelves, until they finally settled on a Taiwan-made machine, of decent quality. That was 1981, and she had one of the best tape-recorders in her year group. Now, after looking after it so carefully over the years, it had come to a sorry end.

When the echoes had died away and quiet descended once more, she said nothing more. She put on her coat and scarf, flung out of the door and into the teeth of a snowstorm. She peddled madly through the storm on her bike. It did not bother her—she was still young and energetic, still physically fit from her time in the commune. But very soon she realized there was someone chasing her, going as fast as she was. She trod furiously on the pedals but he caught her up at the junction of Weigongcun Road.

'Get lost!' she screamed into the whistling gale. The dark figure on the pursuing bicycle braked. She heard: 'You're so fierce, no wonder Lian doesn't stand up to you!' Up close, she saw the black figure was very slender. It was Di.

The snowstorm that evening seemed to swallow up all the houses. It was too late for Di to go home, so she stayed with Tianyi, and Lian slept on the sofa. Di had little sympathy for Tianyi's rage. She just said, over and over again: 'Lian has his reasons. Don't go making wild guesses, and stop forcing yourself on him.' The two talked far into the night. The next day Lian apologized but Tianyi felt instinctively that he did not really think he had been in the wrong.

When they separated many years later, Tianyi spent a long time searching her memories. She came to the conclusion that that night, when he broke her tape-recorder, was the beginning of the rift in their relationship, a rift that never healed. It showed how different their values were. Tianyi even believed that if Lian had told her about his mother at the start, she might well not have married him. Of course, that was just conjecture.

11

Niuniu had been such a lively, chubby baby, but when he came back from Lian's parents he was listless, and thinner too. His legs looked scrawny and short, as if he was under-nourished.

Lian went on a frantic search for remedies, buying up all the bone-strengthening infusions, zinc and iron supplements he could lay his hands on but nothing made any difference and, when Niuniu started at nursery, he was the smallest in his class. Tianyi just said: 'What on earth were your parents doing with him?' Lian pressed his lips together in a furious silence. This made Tianyi even angrier. The more she thought about it, the more she felt it was her in-laws' fault. Every day when she picked him up, she rushed to the school canteen and peeped in through the crack in the door. She spotted his large head immediately. He was not eating, she could see that. He just played with his food, poking at it with his chopsticks. She found it distressing to watch. This was her son, the beloved baby she had nurtured for nine months in her womb, and given birth to in such agony that the first time she set eyes on him, she glared at him, convinced the nurses were giving her the wrong baby. Of course, the second time, she was in no doubt. He was hers, this small person with his smooth head and flawless complexion. She would never forget his sweet smile when he was two months old. It was more beautiful than anything she had ever seen. He had his father's mouth, small but very mobile and widening into a startling smile. He had been such a sweet child, sucking down his mother's milk with resounding, greedy gulps that astonished all the other mothers in the ward. Yet this baby, so bonny at birth, had turned into a skinny little runt, his bright, intelligent eyes now dull and listless. It was common in children who did not get enough love. She felt ashamed. She hid her shame deep inside her, but it was exquisitely tender to the touch.

Good mothers needed to love selflessly. She was not a good mother. Firstly, she did not sleep with her baby, the way most mothers did, because his slightest fidget woke her up. Actually, she could not share her bed with anyone. So when, all those years later, she read Milan Kundera's *Unbearable Lightness of Being*, she felt a shock of recognition. The surgeon Tomas was an inveterate womaniser yet was unable to share his bed with anyone. Except Tereza, the girl who drifted into his life like a little basket bobbing on water; with her, he had been able to sleep, hand in hand. No doubt many Chinese readers found that sentimental, but personally Tianyi understood it only too well. She felt she was just like Thomas. People like them, whether they were God's chosen or God's rejects, or one way or another had been singled out by God's patronage, had an unequivocal need for their 'other half'. If they failed to find their other half, then they were reduced to flotsam, destined to drift alone and lonely in the world for the rest of their lives. God had not endowed this child she had thought so wonderful with any natural gifts at all.

There were more and more rows with Lian, too. 'You have no sense of responsibility to your family … You weren't made for marriage,' were just some of Lian's accusations, no matter how hard she tried. Maybe it was true. She felt torn between her undoubted love for her child (and she really did adore him), and a dreadful feeling that having a child was a life-sentence. She loved nothing more than to let her creative imagination take wing, but she could only do that at night. On paper. She wrote one story after another, finish it, read it, then bin it, showing it to no one. It was like having sex, she got it all out of her system, and then her body was at peace. Until one day Lian happened on the novel she had just completed and read it.

It was called *The Tree of Knowledge*, and it had a simple dedication: 'To H Z.' Who was H Z? An old flame? Lian was not bothered by her past loves, they were all child's play in his view, so they did not count. But he sensed she had really lived this experience as he read this story. She made her hero sound very attractive: 'This young man's features were almost perfect. He had a bright, clear forehead, a prominent nose, the pupils of his eyes were not black but the translucent colour of lake water, brimming with light. He had a noble air, but it was the nobility of a fallen prince ...' she had written. Lian discovered, apparently for the first time, that Tianyi's prose was beautiful. It was certainly wasted on her academic writing!

Back then, a new generation of young film directors were quietly emerging. *Yellow Earth* and *One and Eight* had just come out, among other films. They made a big impression on Lian. He felt instinctively that Tianyi's novel should be made into a film and, without telling her, he wrote to a director called Ji, recommending it and signing himself 'A Reader'. He mailed the letter and forgot about it. Two weeks later, out of the blue, he received a reply from a production company overseas. It was signed with a flourish by none other than the celebrated Mr Ji himself. Lian was thrilled.

Another two weeks passed and Tianyi and Ji met in person. He was pretty much as she had imagined him, fashionably bearded, large, expressive eyes. They had a very enjoyable discussion: Ji said he liked her story, though of course he had a few criticisms, it would have to be worked on, and so on and so forth. He said he wanted to use this film to get one up on Zhang Yimou. Tianyi was taken aback. He was talking about using the film to get one up on another director, before he and she had come to an agreement? But she was soon swayed by Ji's obvious ability. After all, jadeite was still jade, wasn't it? You couldn't afford to be too picky with your friends in this business. Or so Tianyi told herself. She had to admit that Ji treated her with much more respect than most directors accorded their screenwriters. 'Your writing is very good,' he told her, 'I'd like to bring you in during shooting, to write a few extra scenes.' The assistant director, who was in on the meeting, told Tianyi: 'The director's never praised any screenwriter for writing well before. Why don't you do an article about working with Ji when you have time? After all, people were always publishing stuff about working with Zhang Yimou, so why not Ji? Tianyi looked at him, then gently suggested that they should stick to what they were good at and not try and compete. Ji looked at his assistant too: 'Mrs Yang is right. We should get on with our own project, and let Zhang get on with his, and let's see who does a better job!' Tianyi couldn't help smiling to herself. What children these film people were! What she said was: 'Please don't call me Mrs Yang! Tianyi is fine.' The three of them talked some more, then Ji got to his feet. 'Time for lunch! Let's find somewhere good.'

The fashion for sumptuous banquets had yet to sweep through China; people's taste in food was not terribly sophisticated in those post-Maoist days. However, the restaurant they went to near Weigongcun Street was one of a few really fine ones, and had a grand name to go with it: the Luxury Seafood Centre. They ordered cod with shrimps and egg yolks, ham with broad beans, steamed shark, soy-stewed goose wings, crispy fried pigeon, stir-fried bean shoots, and ham and wax gourd soup. The dishes had no sooner arrived than a young woman breezed in, as if she had deliberately picked her moment to make an entrance. Tianyi, who had met few actors in person, was startled at her appearance: a dark ruby-coloured skirt accentuated the whiteness of her skin and her scarlet lipstick. At first glance, the girl looked fresh and unsophisticated, but when Tianyi looked more carefully, she realized she was being distinctly flirtatious. Her arrival certainly seemed to make Ji perk up. He looked like a different man.

Ji made flattering introductions: 'This is Tianyi, the celebrated writer. And this is Kexing, the celebrated actress.'

Kexing beamed smiles and extended a small delicate hand, shaking Tianyi's, as lengthily as if they were old friends. 'How nice to meet you, Tianyi' she said, in a hoarse voice at odds with her fragile beauty. 'Ji has said so much about you, he says you're a terrific writer.' Tianyi never knew what to say to comments like that. She made a dismissive gesture: '... Oh, no, really!' A long time later she realized that everyone dropped comments like that, it was the done thing. There was nothing personal about it at all, and her embarrassment simply came across as asking for more compliments.

Tianyi's admiration of beauty predisposed her towards Kexing, at least at the beginning. On the surface, she seemed a charming young woman, utterly likeable, the sort who would be popular in any day and age. She knew exactly what to say to butter people up, knew how to smile and talk her way into everyone's affections. Her flattery was so sophisticated it sometimes verged on the insulting, before veering off at the last moment to compliment the subject. There was hardly anyone to match her in the art.

But Kexing was not just a superlative flatterer. Gradually Tianyi learned about the other killer weapon the young woman had up her sleeve: sex. The 1980s were a time of social as well as economic liberalization and Kexing was up right there in the vanguard. She made a clear distinction between lust and love and was willing to have sex with any man, with one purpose in mind: to get whatever it was that man could give her.

Tianyi had a good time at the banquet that day. But not long afterwards, Ji phoned to ask her to recommend a woman for the female lead: 'Anyone who comes to mind who you think would be right for the role? Have a think … someone you've met, with the temperament that fits the role, anyone you can recommend …' Finally, Ji threw in anxiously: 'It could be someone you've only just met!'

But Ji was out of luck. Tianyi was ultra-sensitive, but her sensitivities did not lie in that direction. No matter that Ji talked round and around the subject, Tianyi just did not get what he was hinting at. The trouble was that Tianyi was too straightforward. She did not understand subtexts. As Ji spoke, she was racking her brains as who might play the lead role. Who would be right for it? Suddenly she remembered having watched a film called *Youth* two years before, where the female lead was a young woman with a hazy look in her eyes, impoverished, a devout Buddhist. She was called something like …

'Lina Duan!' she cried. Ji, at the other end of the phone call, said nothing. Tianyi was nonplussed. Why wasn't he saying anything? 'That girl's eyes are remarkable, don't you think? Even though she was dressed in rags, her character shone through, like a princess fallen on hard times, don't you think …?' She babbled on until she ran out of things to say. It dawned on her that there was still silence at the other end of the phone.

It was an afternoon in the middle of summer, and Tianyi had gone to the neighbourhood residents' committee office to take Ji's call, as they did not have a phone at home. It was quite a business to apply for a phone to be installed in those days, and it took a long time, so Tianyi always gave people the residents' committee number and got the woman to come and fetch her. The phone booth window was open, and outside some old ladies were fanning themselves in the shade. It began to drizzle, and a great dark cloud settled overhead. The old ladies picked up their stools and, holding their fans over their heads, scuttled for cover, all except for the one in charge of the phone who came into the booth. Then something happened that Tianyi was never able to explain: there was a clap of thunder and a streak of white light shot from the telephone. Instinctively, Tianyi flung the receiver from her but just at that moment, it was as if something stabbed her in the ear. I'm finished, she thought. But it only lasted an instant, no more. Then it was gone, leaving nothing behind. And Tianyi could not recall what the pain had felt like, except that it was like a solid object thrusting into her ear canal. Days later, when the pain had completely gone, Tianyi suddenly realized that she was feeling a wonderful emotional release.

While Tianyi was still in this elated mood, filming began for *The Tree of Knowledge*. The female lead was Kexing and finally Tianyi understood the director's laborious hints. But then she put her foot in it once again.

'You can't have Kexing!' she burst out without thinking. 'She's the very opposite of how I imagined the female lead would be. How can she play her?' She was talking to the assistant director. Then she added: 'She can't play the heroine. But she could play Shanshan, she's got the right kind of shrewdness.'

At the next production team, Kexing dropped all pretences at affection and went stony cold on Tianyi. Ji was as polite and respectful as he had always been. 'Mrs Yang,' he said, 'when the film is finished, I hope you'll help us with promoting it.' In those days, Tianyi had no idea what doing business meant.

She did not sleep well that night. Insomnia was a chronic problem, and she never found a long-term cure for it. It had got better for a short time after she got married, and she was actually able to sleep through Lian's stentorian snoring. But after her baby was born, it got worse again, because she was not sharing a bed with Lian. He had the baby in his bed, she had to sleep alone.

She was nine years old when the problem began. (Heavens! Was she really that young?) The culprit was the novel, *The Story of the Stone*. The complete set of volumes had just come out in an illustrated edition, and her father bought them for Tianyue, who had just started middle school. However, there was no way he was going to let Tianyi and Tianke read it.

Each of the three children had their place in the family, and Tianyi was her father's pet. He never stopped treating her as his little girl, even when she was grown up, but he never knew what really went on deep in his darling daughter's heart, nor the extent of her curiosity. The very evening that he issued his edict about *The Story of the Stone*, Tianyi scrambled to the top shelf of the book case at dead of night. She took down the book, still fragrant with the smell of printing ink.

As she leafed through the book, looked for the first time at the fine-line illustrations, and read the names of the star-struck lovers, Baoyu and Daiyu, she was gripped. She had read about love before, mostly in the huge assortment of children's picture books (more than 400 of them), most of which had been collected by her big sister. Tianyue was neat and tidy and kept all four hundred-odd books arranged in four drawers, to keep them clean, and had listed every one so that if any of the neighbours' children came to borrow them, she could note down the date they were borrowed and the date they were returned, and it was all nice and clear.

As a small girl, Tianyi loved copying pictures of pretty ladies from these children's books, in fact she filled a whole notebook with her drawings. She copied the 'Parrot Girl' from a calendar they had too, a girl dressed in ancient costume, smiling and holding a fan with a parrot perch on a circular stand behind her. Mrs Feng, who ran the local library saw Tianyi's efforts, and liked them so much she offered to teach Tianyi to paint. Mrs Feng made traditional costume dolls and was somewhat reclusive, so when she offered to take on Tianyi as her pupil, the news swiftly spread through their compound. Tianyi instantly became known as their 'little artist'.

These picture books, with their cast of female characters, passionate, tender or staunchly heroic, imperceptibly stole into Tianyi's young heart, so when she opened the first volume of *The Story of the Stone*, she immediately recognized the hero and heroine, Baoyu and Daiyu, picking them out from among dozens of other characters. She chose the bits in the book that were about their love story, reading obsessively through the dark hours of the night, until finally she read herself into a state of complete mental exhaustion. Night after night, she went without sleep, going to school the next morning feeling unwell, her eyes and face puffy. Back then, Di used to drop by so that they could go to school together, and one day she found the book lying by her bedside. She read the first line: 'The author had a dream and spake ...' 'Oh!' Di cried, 'So the author of *The Story of the Stone*'s called "Spake"'. Scornfully, Tianyi said: 'Whatever do you mean, "Spake"? "Spake is the past of to speak! How could you get to third grade without knowing that the author of *The Story of the Stone* was Cao Xueqin?' Di, an unsophisticated girl, had always looked up to Tianyi, and now admiration turned into hero-worship. She put Tianyi on a pedestal, deferring to her in everything. There was no one to beat her friend, in her view, for knowledge, bravery, intelligence and good looks.

But too much living in fantasyland can take its toll on a little girl's mental health, and Tianyi actually became delusional. She was put to bed, but even then, when no adult was watching her, she would sneak her copy of *The Story of the Stone* from under her pillow, and carry on reading. She got to Chapter 97, where Lin Daiyu burns her poems to signal the end of her heart's folly and Xue Baochai leaves home to take part in a solemn rite.' In her mind's eye, she saw Daiyu, the hapless heroine, ashen pale, vomiting a stream of blood. Tears poured down Tianyi's face like a tap that someone had forgotten to shut off, drenching the pillow cover, as she read Daiyu's deathbed exhortations to her maid Nightingale. Increasingly self-pitying and troubled, she became convinced she was the dying girl. She was sleeping no more than a couple of hours a night, and her father became desperate to find medical treatment for her. Nothing worked however, and his darling daughter was becoming thinner before his very eyes. But the grim Reaper was not ready for her yet. One day, her paternal grandfather turned up.

Her grandfather still lived in the old family home in Shayang county, Hubei province. He was no ordinary granddad, having joined the Northern warlords and risen to a high rank in his youth. He had three sons and a daughter, but had passed down his love of military matters only to his eldest son, Tianyi's Uncle Huairen, and not at all to her father or the youngest son.

Tianyi's military uncle was a source of pride for the whole family, especially the children. Ever since she was a tiny child, Tianyi had known that she had an uncle in the People's Liberation Army. All the kids wanted to visit him. He had a big house and a car, and a fancy cooker that good things were cooked on. Anything they asked for, they were given. Tianyi had been a greedy child

—her maternal grandmother always said she was reincarnated from someone who had died of starvation. Whenever she got to her uncle's house and smelled the cooking smells, her stomach would rumble. During the Starvation Years, between 1958 and 1961, Tianyi was especially keen to go and see him. The family and their neighbours in the large compound seemed to live in another world. They had no need to go digging up bitter greens or collect fungi to fill their baskets, or gather elm seed pods, or locust tree flowers, to steam with rice, or carefully eke out the wheat flour with corn husks, and cook them up together. 'Gold-wrapped silver', that was called, but no amount of fancy names could disguise the fact that they were truly scraping the bottom of the barrel. When Tianyi went to her uncle's, she tasted preserved eggs, roast duck, steamed shad, all for the first time. Before their little brother Tianke was born, Tianyue and Tianyi used to be dressed in their nicest clothes and taken to see Uncle Huairen and his family often. They were pretty girls back then. His wife, Aunt Hui, was a pretty woman too. Tianyi admired her outfits and hair-do. She was always nicely turned out and, since she had never had children, had a beautiful figure too. She had a Shenyang accent, but a pleasant voice and was very talkative. Given the chance, she would go on for hours criticizing her husband's army aides. None of those stayed long. Tianyi's beautiful, clever aunt reckoned they were coarse and inferior, and did not measure up to her exacting standards.

It was obvious that Aunt Hui even looked down on her relatives, especially the female ones, and that included Tianyi's mother. Actually, Aunt Hui was much younger than her sister-in-law. Only nineteen when she married Tianyi's uncle, she had been a nurse in a field hospital, her family were comfortably-off market gardeners, and she had completed several years of schooling.

Like Tianyi's mother, she then stopped work and devoted herself to looking after her husband. Years later Tianyi found out how hard it was to be a housewife. Being cooped up at home all day destroyed many women, especially if they had no children to look after.

In Tianyi's childhood memories, her aunt was always there together with the delicious food smells. Tianyi liked to stand next to her as she cooked, and learned from her how to slice onions on the slant, chop silk gourd into chunks, and how to scrub the chopping board till it was clean of all food stains. She admired her aunt's pale green flowered, gauzy terylene housecoat, her apron embroidered with doves, her feet, very white in their silver-grey slippers. She loved the décor in her uncle and aunt's house, where there was not a speck of dust anywhere, and even the tablecloth in the kitchen was fashionably foreign. She knew that her uncle had been to the Soviet Union, India and Morocco. In fact, the kitchen tablecloth with its fine check pattern had probably come from India. As a child, she had adored these things, yet strangely, as the years passed by, she became increasingly puritanical, rejecting all the blandishments that the material world could offer, acting as if she were a monk doing a self-imposed penance. But in her youth, when she was more uncomplicated and before the urge to put on an act took over, she craved everything that came from abroad, collecting whatever she could get her hands on. She knew her mother's father had once travelled to Germany and Belgium, and her grandmother had a trunk in which she kept a complete German silver service, and toilette boxes, cups and perfume bottles from Belgium. Her grandmother had been dead for many years, but her mother still kept the trunk locked and would not take things out to show anyone.

Once, when her grandmother was in a good mood, she gave

Tianyi one of the wooden Belgian toilette boxes, its lid carved in complicated, baroque patterns. Her grandmother had used it for her delicate perfume bottles, covered in engraved silver patterns, and face mirrors with Louis XV ladies painted on the back. The box held a lingering fragrance, even though it was fifty or sixty years old, and the scent should have gone long ago.

In Uncle Huairen's house, Levitan landscape paintings hung on the walls, and on the table were sturdy boxes, imported from China's 'big brother' ally, the Soviet Union. Tianyi knew they held fruit candies. She also knew, young though she was, that the better-off of her father's students had those boxes at home. In the 1950s, they were a sign that a family were going up in the world. Their neighbours, Di and Xian's family, were like that. Their father Mr Shang had been to the Soviet Union too and the Shang sisters had a prized Soviet-made doll, which they swopped for a painting of a courtly lady Tianyi had painted.

Uncle Huairen was often in the USSR. Each time he came back, it was like a dream come true. The first time, he brought back two pure lamb's wool scarves, hand-knitted in beautiful bright colours. Most recently, he brought dresses for Tianyi and Tianyue. Tianyue's was fashionably foreign-looking, of ivory cotton with collar and cuffs with a wide blue and white border, like a girl in a fairy story. Tianyi's was even prettier, in white seersucker, with a bodice of *broderie anglaise* flowers, through which was laced a bright red ribbon. Tianyi looked like a doll in it. At New Year in 1961, the sisters put on their new dresses and paraded down the street. They certainly attracted attention, and not just from passers-by; even the local policeman stopped to look.

That evening, Tianyi ran up and down the cobbled pathways on the estate where her Uncle Huairen and Aunt Hui lived, happy in the knowledge that she was going to be called in to dinner at any minute. On the table would be what she and her sister called 'glass' eggs. The dark green yolks of the preserved eggs made her feel sick, and once she nearly *was* sick, when her aunt fed her a spoonful.

There would be steamed shad too, her favourite. It was from her aunt that she learnt that shad should be steamed with the scales on, so that the steaming process dissolved them into fragrant fish oil, even tastier than the delicate flesh itself. Those were happy times for her, before Tianke was born. Everyone petted her, she was everyone's princess, the family revolved around her. She had good food to eat, pretty clothes to wear and was the prettiest and brightest of children! Everyone loved her. Jealous Tianyue nicknamed her Fat Gesang, after the villain in the play *The Fox and the Grapes*, by Guilherme Figueiredo, who, like Tianyi, was very plump. Tianyi did not care. Having seen a play called *Iris*, she nicknamed her sister Old Cat in return, Old Cat of course being the villain of that piece. And so it went on: with each film or book or drama they saw, they nicknamed each other after the baddies.

After dinner, Aunt Hui usually got into an argument. Her opponent depended on who was on hand that day. At one point, the woman she was most irritated with was Aunt Yuman, a young woman who had just married Hui's brother-in-law Uncle Huaiji. Uncle Huaiji had grown up in his older brother's house, and was the baby of the family. His sister-in-law browbeat him constantly, so that he lacked self-confidence and allowed himself to be pushed around. It was only when he went to university that he finally acquired a girlfriend, a young woman from a wealthy Shanghai capitalist family, called Sufan. She was very good-looking, with plaits so long they came down to her calves. Not surprisingly, she came in for a heavy dose of my aunt's criticism too. However, for first time, Uncle Huaiji dared to go behind Aunt Hui's back and began to conduct their love affair in secret. Needless to say, it did not last long, and in actual fact, Uncle Huaiji only had himself to blame. Apart from the games he liked to play with his two nieces, he had absolutely no experience of women. He soon fell out of favour with Sufan. The final row that finished them off came from an argument about *jiaozi* dumplings. Uncle had said he liked *jiaozi*, so Sufan and her one-time capitalist mother made some for him with their own hands. They made more than ninety, and steamed them, and Uncle Huaiji polished almost all of them off without waiting for his girlfriend to come to the table! He left only four, and that was because he had stuffed himself full.

Uncle Huaiji never did understand why, after steadily working his way through all those delicious *jiaozi*, he was politely shown the door, and then abandoned by his girlfriend.

For a long time after that, Uncle Huaiji went around in a daze, until one day his colleague at work, Yuman, told him bluntly that she had fallen in love with him. Yuman had a pretty name, but an extremely masculine appearance. When she was taken to meet the family, Aunt Hui cold-shouldered her. But regardless of her opposition, the couple eventually married. Worse was to follow: they immediately had a baby, and another, and another, until there were four children! Yuman became the butt of Aunt Hui's jokes for ever after.

That made Aunt Hui a comrade-in-arms of Tianyi's mother, Siqin, who only had to see Hui imitating Yuman flapping her fan around and fidgeting on her feet or in her chair, to burst out laughing. Tianyi heard her mother's ringing laugh and her words: 'You've got her to a tee! I can't take her off half as well!' But, child though she was, Tianyi also sensed that if her mother was not there, her aunt's sarcasm might well find a new target for her jokes instead, and it might just be Siqin. Aunt Hui mimicked her mother's affected complaints: 'Oh dear me, how my stomach aches, how my liver hurts ...'

But when Tianyi's grandfather arrived, the butt of her aunt's sarcasm changed again. It was now an old man, her father-in-law. 'Such a feudal old stick,' she said. 'He comes rushing over here because now he's got a grandson.' She threw Tianyi a wry glance: 'It doesn't matter how clever you are, or how hard you study, you're just a girl! Your grandfather's such a feudal old stick. He's certainly not come to see you!'

She was right, too. But the trip to Beijing to see his grandson was a disappointment to the old man. Tianke, was stubborn as a mule. Apart from stuffing his face and going out to play around in the streets, and mastering the most basic maths with the greatest difficulty, he never learned anything more. Not that many of his schoolmates bothered to study. As soon as classes were over, the kids ran off to their games. Especially at the height of summer when people came out of their houses to enjoy the cool evening air, it was common to see crowds of boys gathering in the lamplight, arms folded across their chests, laughing and telling jokes. Tianke was a past master at telling tall stories. And of all the kids in their courtyard, there was no one who could beat him at killing birds with a sling-shot! Years later, when Tianke had been fired for the nth time from his job, the only thing he could boast about were those long-unused childhood skills. He would stand there, paunchy, middle-aged, with grizzled hair, and tell his stories: 'There was one time when my Dad used to be able to shoot a dozen birds in a day! And all you can do nowadays is play on your Gameboys! Once I saw a really fine bird...!' Every time he got to that point, his wife, Xiaolan, would pull a face. She already had a lover and was demanding a divorce, but Tianke would rather be cuckolded than divorced. How on earth would he look after himself if he divorced Xiaolan, let alone his son and his elderly mother?

Tianyi's grandfather racked his brains for a way to win the boy's affections and decided to take him to a film. The weekly showing was *Tunnel Warfare*, and Tianke had been desperate to go and see it. But as soon as he heard his grandfather wanted to go, he changed his mind. He had so much homework, had to stay at home to do it, and so on and so forth. Tears trickled down his grandfather's face and he set about buying a bus ticket home. Tianyi's father was upset at his distress, but he could not control his son. The only thing he could do was sigh heavily and twist his good-hearted eldest daughter Tianyue's arm. At his instigation, she offered to take her grandfather out for a stroll but the old man shook his head so vigorously, his snowy white hair and beard shook too. To Tianyi, he looked more like a hoary old wizard from a fairy story than a real person. In any case, he sat there in a wobbly old rattan chair, stubbornly refusing to go out with his eldest granddaughter. In those days, they had no TV, only a dilapidated old radio. Her grandfather told Tianyi to turn it on. It was a *Story Time* programme, Tianyi's favourite.

The old man soon looked bored and got out some maths problems he had brought from the school in his home town, for Tianyi to do. It was a bit of a stop-start process at first, but once they had done a few sums, the old man's eyes began to shine. When Tianyi's father came into the room, his face was wreathed in smiles: 'Ai-ya! What a little treasure you've got here! She got the right answer to sums that even our senior middle school students can't do! It's amazing, really amazing! You were never that bright when you were a child!' Tianyi's father was a considerate son and when he saw his father's joy, a great weight fell from his shoulders. Even better, the child being praised was his favourite daughter.

He beamed along with his father, a white-teethed smile of rare genuine happiness.

Siqin immediately jumped in. 'What are you smiling about? Come on then, tell us so we can share the joke!' When Tianyi's father told her, she looked disdainful. Ignoring her father-in-law, she said pointedly to her husband: 'So he's heaping praise on that daughter you always make such a fuss of, is he? Well, "like father, like son", why should I expect any different? The old man's just saying what you've always felt!' And she stalked off. In fury, Tianyi's father shouted after her: 'Isn't she your daughter too?' His wife turned around and retorted: 'And Tianke's not your son? Why do you give him such a hard time? If Tianke ever manages to please his granddad, you make a point of turning the old man against him! He's not the brightest kid, he takes after me in that, but that's no reason to dislike him so much!' Under normal circumstances, her father would have backed down but today his own father was with him and he could not allow her to browbeat him. He parried, and the arguments went back and forth until finally Tianyi's grandfather intervened with his daughter-in-law:

'Now listen, Siqin, you're in the wrong here. Your son and your daughters, they're all yours and you should treat them fairly. While I've been staying with you, I've been watching you. My son goes to work and when he gets back, he has to rush around cooking dinner. That's not good at all. You should take a leaf out of your sister-in-law's book.'

Tianyi's mother never forgot the old man's words, and never let anyone else forget them either. 'Take a leaf out of my sister-in-law's book? That's a joke! The old fool has no idea the kind of things Hui says about him behind his back! My trouble is I'm just too kind-hearted. I should have told him straight up. He would have been furious! It was time he knew who should take a leaf out of whose book!'

Tianyi's mother was a very odd person. She gave the impression of being timid and naïve, but when she got fired up, she was anyone's match. She was a wily strategist and tactician, playing weak, but adept at stealthily muddying the waters and turning the proposition on its head. Tianyi's father was an intelligent man but, when her parents quarrelled, he never failed to fall into her traps and ended up bamboozled and defeated.

Back in 1962, the third of the famine years, when she was nine years old, Tianyi spoke out in favour of her grandfather. Her mother always favoured Tianke, she said. She, Tianyi, had become a sort of Cinderella, she said. Were there really such old-fashioned folks in the countryside who paid no attention to a mere girl? She asked.

Tianyi's grandfather's arrival put a stop to her obsession with *The Story of the Stone*, and made her feel suddenly that she was not only clever but should not hide her gifts. When he left, taking with him Tianyi's 'Parrot Girl' painting, it was very clear that although he had come to claim his grandson, it was his granddaughter that had brought him comfort.

However, the insomnia triggered by *The Story of the Stone* persisted, and had disastrous and enduring consequences. Many years later, Tianyi reflected on her own marriage and realized that it was sleeping in different beds that put paid to a marriage. After that, there was no going back. It was one thing to share a bed but have different dreams, quite another to dream in different beds. That was the true end of a marriage.

She could never forget the morning after their wedding day, the frantic hammering on the door, the loud yell, startling the couple awake. It took a while for Tianyi to work out that her mother-in-law was shouting her son's name, 'Lian! Lian!' as if he was being kidnapped or murdered. She was not just startled, she was very annoyed. What peasants! But surely, even countryfolk did not act like this? People always said you should steer clear of old women widowed too young. They were so embittered by not having had a normal marriage that they would do anything to stop the rest of the world being happy!

As time went by, she was proved only too right. Lian's grandmother did nothing but issue orders through her daughter, Tianyi's mother-in-law. The child must absolutely not have its own cot, it absolutely must sleep either with father or mother, it must be breastfed round the clock ... in short, the two women did everything in their power to prevent husband and wife sharing the same bed. Tianyi privately considered it amusing. What on earth good did it do them?

Thinking back on it, Tianyi realized how naïve she had been. If she had her time again, she would have paid no attention to the pair, she would have talked and smiled with them but completely ignored their injunctions. She would have treated them like so much hot air. Her failure, she felt, lay in being too honest. If she looked at the people around her, no one remembered the honest ones, they were here today, gone tomorrow. People did what they wanted nowadays, only a fool would put any value on honesty in this fast-moving, materialistic age.

The old women's strategy must have been effective. Tianyi fell pregnant on the night her marriage was consummated and, as soon as she found out, did not dare share a bed with Lian, thus quenching his ardour. Once the baby was born, they only had sex once more, and she fell pregnant again. After that they kept to separate beds, right up until they separated. Of course, when Niuniu was still a baby, Lian would burrow into Tianyi's bed for some cuddles while the baby was asleep, but the occasions on which they had full sex grew fewer and fewer. On the odd occasion it happened, Tianyi realized her husband was increasingly unenthusiastic. She, however, was just the opposite. It seemed that childbirth had lit a flame in her that could only be quenched by sex. Tianyi began to feel as if she was on fire. Very soon the flames would consume her until only ashes were left.

It was not that she had not thought of finding a lover. For instance, if Xiao'ou had taken the initiative, she would not have turned him down. The trouble was, a man like Xiao'ou was not in the habit of taking the initiative and, even if he did, it would have taken someone cleverer and more sexually experienced than her to take him up on it.

Tianyi was in torment. The best way of sublimating her desires was to scribble stories. Sublimation was not a new idea by any means: Freud had talked of sublimation too. So Tianyi wrote as if she was giving birth to another baby. During this period, she wrote so many articles that, years later when she looked back at them, she was astonished. In this era of family planning, when men were not like men nor women like women, a woman like her, brimming with vitality but deprived both of sex and of giving birth, could only throw herself into writing reams of articles, covering sheet after sheet of paper. They were beautiful pieces. If she had been able to transform them into children, they would have been beautiful children, but what good was beauty? Tianyi had always put too much value on other people's tastes, and readers' tastes ran in the direction of crude writing and vulgar content, not her sort of work, never mind that every word contained pearls of wisdom.

No matter. Tianyi could put up with the slights, because she was in love, wholly and completely in love—with the mysterious H Z.

12

The Tree of Knowledge won a major prize at the Karlovy Vary International Film Festival. Karlovy Vary was a town in the south of the Czech Republic. Ten years later, Tianyi was lucky enough to visit it, and it took her breath away. It was as pretty as a child's picture book. It was autumn and the entire city was gilded by autumnal foliage that blazed and shimmered in the breeze. A building in the distance looked like it had been built from a child's wooden bricks. Near that building, she found and bought a set of gilded crystal wine glasses.

At the time of the festival, however, she knew nothing of Karlovy Vary. Though she had heard its name, she did not have a clue as to where it was and even had a vague idea it was in Africa.

The Tree of Knowledge was only shown in China after it had won the prize. On the opening night, the deputy director had a number of complimentary tickets, and the first person she thought to invite was her H Z.

There was no real mystery about who H Z was, it was just her abbreviation for Hua Zheng. In Tianyi's eyes Zheng was a beautiful and dangerous man, especially beautiful precisely because he was dangerous. She first met him at the beginning of the 1980s, in the house of a friend. He was a formidable figure back then, with eyes that blazed so bright you could not see the pupils. Her friend Peng introduced them, saying with a laugh: 'Tianyi, we all know you writers are fascinated by Che Guevara. Well, here he is in a modern guise. Have a good talk.' Peng was given to hyperbole, but this time he was not exaggerating. Zheng and Tianyi hit it off straightaway and talked non-stop for seven hours. Peng had to bustle around and do the dinner without any help from them, but he did not grumble. He provided a good spread too: scrambled eggs, stir-fried cabbage, a dish of potato, aubergine and green pepper, stir-fried shredded pork, beancurd and mushroom casserole, and a sour and hot soup. But even eating could not stop the chatterers' mouths, as Zheng and Tianyi talked on and on. Tianyi discovered that this lovable, boyish man liked nothing better than a good argument. He could not seem to help it: if you said east, he said west, and if you agreed west, he immediately changed his mind to south. Tianyi felt he was being argumentative for the sake of it, but Zheng defended himself: 'A lot of the time, I try and start an argument because, when people argue, it livens up their thought processes.'

Tianyi heard it from Zheng first: 'Mao Zedong is not a Marxist, he's a peasant revolutionary imbued with a feudal king's thinking.' At the beginning of the 1980s, this was a risky thing to say, but to Tianyi's surprise, she realized that these words clarified her innermost feelings.

'I think that China's biggest problems are, one, that there's no religious faith and, two, our links to the finest things in our national culture have been severed. We've lost our traditions, so even though our economy may flourish, at a spiritual level I can see us becoming impoverished and degraded,' Tianyi said despondently.

'Most of the world's rulers impose their rule by means of religious faith,' Zheng replied. 'But China is a country whose religions, Confucianism, Buddhism, Daoism, have all been smashed. Even Maoism has been smashed!...There are no standards, no bottom line, so value judgments are confused.

Glass gets treated as diamond, vermicelli as shark's fin. It's really terrible!

'When the Qing dynasty was overthrown,' he went on, 'old-style scholars spent a lot of the time debating which was the best for China: a monarchy, a constitutional monarchy or a republic. Actually, during the Republican years, a number of educated reformers did emerge but it's true to say that for the last one hundred years, we have not only not gone forward, we've gone backwards. For instance, did you know that there was actually a legislative assembly at the beginning of the Republic? So I feel that after these latest economic reforms, we need corresponding political reforms, otherwise the consequences will be unthinkable.'

'I like the Song dynasty,' Tianyi suddenly said.

'Why?' Zheng, brought up short in the middle of his tirade, looked hard at Tianyi. Before him was a woman who might have stepped out of an ancient painting; she had a dignified, cultured air and, he was coming to realize, a rare purity of heart. He was captivated. Making an effort to cover his emotion, he asked: 'Is that because intellectuals enjoyed a high status under the Song? I agree. I especially like the injunction of the Song philosopher, Zhang Zai, to intellectuals, "To establish the spirit of Heaven and Earth, and a good life for ordinary people" ...'

'... "To protect and perpetuate bygone wisdom, and maintain the whole world in peace forever",' Tianyi finished off for him. They fell silent and stared at each other. There was an instantaneous vivid flash of delighted surprise, of mutual recognition. Then each of them hurriedly looked away.

Tianyi decided she liked Zheng very much indeed. Oddly enough, her liking was entirely platonic. She felt no physical desire for him, still less any desire to use him. She felt about him the way she might feel about a heavenly emissary, or a sage. From their very first meeting, she did not treat Zheng as an ordinary man. And that was the root of the problem, because Zheng fell in love with her at their first meeting, even though she was four years older than him. Not that that put him off. He said to Peng: 'Jenny von Westphalen was four years older than Marx.' Peng did not repeat this remark to Tianyi straightaway, for one simple reason: he was in love with her himself.

One day, Tianyi suddenly said: 'Zheng, I don't think you're cut out for politics.'

'Why not?' he asked, startled.

'It's simple, you're not a politician. You're an idealist. Born in the wrong age.' Then she added (and Zheng would remember her words for the rest of his life): 'You're the ultimate idealist.'

Because of her feelings for Zheng, Tianyi was constantly dreaming up pretexts to spend time at Peng's. It was the same with Zheng. So they regularly bumped into each other there, and chatted, cooked a meal, worked. Peng's dad was the boss of some big company and had quite a bit of money put by. The family owned a two-courtyard home, and Peng's father gave it to his son, thus making Peng one of the very few young people who owned their house at the beginning of the 1980s. It was a wonderful place for his friends to gather.

Over time, increasing numbers dropped by, and they dreamed up more exciting things to do. Often, they went to the Miyun Reservoir outside Beijing. They were so young then, Tianyi reflected. Nowadays, it was a long journey, two hours or more. Back then, it was much simpler, they just got on their rickety old bikes and pedalled there, talking and laughing.

They usually got to the Miyun Reservoir towards evening. They would start with a swim, then gather under some nearby trees and have their picnic. There were always plenty of provisions, though of course 'plenty' in those days only meant soy-stewed beef, coarse-grained bread and snacks, and a variety of pickles: sweet-soy 'eight treasure' vegetables, Korean chillis, home-made pickles, mouli in soy-paste, and so on. And salads and fruit, of course. Tianyi usually decided on what salads to bring, and she and Zheng made them up together. They made the mayonnaise for the salad in the most basic way. There was a bowl of peanut oil, heated up then left to cool; the oil was slowly added to the egg yolks—it had to be added a drop at a time, just a little bit too much and it curdled. That was the key to making mayonnaise, the adding of the oil at the beginning. At this crucial moment, the person in charge often added the oil too fast, curdled the mixture and had to be rescued by Tianyi. She always added the first few drops personally. When the mixture had begun to thicken, and the salt, sugar and vinegar had been added, then Zheng took over. He beat the mayonnaise with vigour, and a single-minded concentration that was comical and still raised a smile with Tianyi all these years later.

Zheng was ham-fisted when it came to practical things, but he was terribly earnest, especially when Tianyi asked him to do something. He had big fleshy hands, with fat fingers that looked like pickled mouli. He had big feet too, and stomped heavily along. But his handsome face, his bright eyes and his eloquence far outweighed any impression of clumsiness.

On this particular day, the mayonnaise was especially well-received and was soon finished. Dusk had fallen and one by one, they put on their costumes and went for a swim. Tianyi always enjoyed wearing her costume. It was very striking and looked good on her dainty figure, unlike the clumsy, baggy garments most women wore for swimming. Tianyi had found hers in a shop on fashionable Wangfujing Street. It was obviously a smuggled import, and caught her eye instantly. The fabric was light and thin, the bust was well-cut and it was a pretty colour, bright red scattered with big and small white spots. Tianyi fell in love with it straightaway. It was more than 70 *yuan*, shockingly expensive back then, but Tianyi bought it without a moment's hesitation.

Tianyi's shopping fell into two categories: things she absolutely had to have as soon as she laid eyes on them, and bargain buys that she wore a couple of times, then discarded. The swimsuit fell into the first category, of course. And so, come dusk, Tianyi, her beautiful figure clad in her equally beautiful costume, was frequently to be seen swimming at the Miyun Reservoir.

To Tianyi's surprise, Zheng made no attempts to conceal his admiration. His feelings were as transparent as a child's. As soon as she went to swim, he got in too. When she went in one last time, he had been lying sprawled, exhausted, on the embankment, chatting to friends. But as soon as he spotted her in the water, he jumped in regardless.

They were very conspicuous, since there was no one but the two of them in the reservoir. Everyone else was on the bank, watching them as if this was some kind of performance. It was getting quite dark and there was an evening breeze. Tianyi found it delightful. Slowly she slid through the water, heading for a little boat that bobbed up and down. It was a ramshackle craft, probably belonging to a local peasant who kept there for catching fish or clams.

As Tianyi remembered it, a girl on the bank was making fun of Zheng's swimming style: 'He looks like he's banging a drum with his arms!' she laughed. Tianyi glanced back and, in that instant, the old man in the sky got angry. There was a loud clap of thunder, followed by streak after terrifying streak of lightning. A fierce wind gusted and churned the water around them.

The girl's teasing comments were still ringing in Tianyi's ears but around her everything was different. The heavens had darkened like the bottom of a cooking pot, and dense clouds boiled like pitch. Tianyi felt as if her body had been dyed black by the pitch. She reached a pale arm above the waves, reached as high as she could, out of the pot, but her head was still submerged. She swallowed some water, water that boiled like pitch, and was scalded by a gut-wrenching fear.

She was fully aware of what was going on, however. Before long her hand bumped against the boat but it bobbed up and down and she could not keep hold. Finally, her fluttering fingers touched a solid object, and her flutters of anxiety eased. Next, the sturdy arm she had felt gripped her, and anchored her firmly to the boat.

It was the first time in her life that she had embraced a man while almost naked, though it meant little to her in her state of terror. Even so, she saw his body. Down his back ran a long knife scar. She fingered the scar ever so lightly and he instinctively shrank away, as if he did not want her to know about it, so she withdrew her hand. After a long moment, she became aware that she was in his arms. He seemed quite bashful and held her with great diffidence.

'You were trembling,' he said. She pushed away from him, and he from her, and let go of her hand.

'Was I? I didn't realize ...'

With an effort, after a long pause, he managed to get out: 'Did you see the scar on my back? From an operation I had when I was young.'

'What operation?'

'When I was little, my elder brother got some scalding rice porridge spilt on him. He needed a skin graft.'

'And they used your skin?'

'Yes. That was OK, but the problem was that afterwards, a large area of skin got infected, and they had to cut out a lump of flesh and sew it up again.'

'Good heavens!' Tianyi exclaimed. 'it sounds like you were carved up by a butcher!' And they both laughed.

Her favourite reads at that time were Ethel Lilian Voynich's *The Gadfly* and Turgenev's *On the Eve*. She was entranced by their cool super-heroes, who could suffer any amount of pain without a murmur of complaint. As regards the infatuated Arthur in *The Gadfly* and Insarov (in *On the Eve*) and their heroines, she did not particularly take to Arthur's Gemma but adored Insarov's Elena. She even made a series of paintings of Insarov and Elena, portraying the Bulgarian revolutionary in bold outline, forceful, with a lean, rather pale, face of magnetic attractiveness. The Gadfly she imagined in the same way. These revolutionaries, in Tianyi's fantasies, became her ideal men. Thus, when she met Zheng for the first time, she was magnetized by his casual willingness to suffer anything without a murmur of complaint.

Sadly, Zheng was not lean and lanky, he was healthy and sunny-natured, with a pair of beautiful crystalline eyes, so translucent that it seemed unimaginable they would ever cloud over.

Tianyi put her fingers gently on the scar again. This was an extraordinarily bold gesture for her to make, quite out of character. She expected something earth-shaking to happen. But now it was Zheng was missed his chance. So like a man. He had put the girl he loved on a pedestal. He could only do as he pleased with a girl he did not love, or even despised. He was also embarrassed to admit that he was still a virgin, and had no experience with girls.

His feelings towards Tianyi were conflicted. He loved her but he respected her at the same time. She was a woman he could only admire from a distance and could not be intimate with, even though he wanted her, badly. In a word, he wanted her to make the first move, even if it was just to give him a clear hint. After all, she was a highly accomplished writer—she must be able to express her feelings for him in words, spoken or written. If she kept him at a distance, it must mean she did not love him. Having misinterpreted her attitude and convinced himself that she did not love him, he resigned himself to having her as his very best and closest friend. So on this stormy evening, the most important of Tianyi's life, when she was sure something would happen, Zheng fatally misjudged Tianyi's bold move.

Just now, in the boat, Zheng was in turmoil. If the sky had been a bit lighter, Tianyi would have seen his face flush as scarlet as a drunken prawn. This was the moment when Zheng should have striven for victory, but he failed to seize the opportunity. He said: 'Do you think the people on the bank can see us?' The words, so trivial, were like a bucket of cold water to Tianyu. She instinctively looked towards the shore, but their friends had all ducked inside the tents for cover, and were just black shapes.

No doubt Zheng lived to regret his mistake. But the person who really got it wrong was Tianyi. Her great failing was that she took everything too much to heart. Even the smallest slight, and she wanted to get her own back on the perpetrator. Tianyi felt wounded at Zheng's failure to respond to her hint, very seriously wounded.

The worst of it was that she buried her feelings very deep. No way was she going to let on that she had been hurt. She covered it up, and so well that no one would have known that she was not happy. She put on a mask, beneath which she supressed her unhappiness. Let no one say that she was petty-minded. We have already said that Tianyi was an aesthete who put beauty above everything. It was not only other people's image that mattered to her, her own image did too, very much so.

At dead of night, when all the others were asleep in the tent, Zheng sat quite still outside. Tianyi went out and quietly urged him: 'Go to bed, or you'll get bitten by mosquitoes.'

A few days later, when a friend fixed her up with a date, she was happy to go along. He was a salesman with a company set up by a famous politician and entrepreneur, one of the first to make a lot of money in the eighties. He had certainly taken a lot of care with his appearance, he was wearing a white jacket and trousers, with his hair combed into neat waves. He exchanged just a few words with their mutual friend and then Tianyi found herself swept away with him. His idea of a date was comical. He had bought a twenty-one-inch colour TV (beyond the wildest dreams of ordinary Chinese families in those days) but it so happened that the lifts in his apartment block were out of action. So he got Tianyi to help him carry it up to his thirteenth floor flat. They heaved the huge TV up floor by floor and Tianyi gasped for breath. By the thirteenth floor, she was exhausted and sweating profusely —but still immensely curious about Yuan. She always had been incorrigibly curious, and had never been able to resist pursuing the object of her curiosity until it was thoroughly satisfied, even at the price of sweat and exhaustion. When they finally arrived at his flat, Yuan poured her a glass of water and offered her a chair. As he fiddled with the TV, he said: 'I hear you write novels. What are they about?'

'People. Life.'

'That's a big topic! Life …' He muttered, with a faint smile. She felt the subtext was: *And what would a chick like you know about life?*

'Why do you write novels?' he asked next.

'Because I've got things to say.'

'Excellent. That's a good way to say things.' He smiled slightly again. 'But has it ever occurred to you that the China of the future won't be a world of literati, or of politicos, it will be a world of business people.' She was startled. What a strange man. She had never come across anyone like him before.

'Do you know why I've never married?' he asked.

'You're a Marcusian?'

'No, no, no, I'm actually quite traditional in these things. It just so happened that, when I was at university, the girls in our class were so young, they could have been my daughters, so any daughters we had would have been my granddaughters...' He laughed. 'You see, I may look very lively and outgoing, but really I'm an old stick-in-the-mud.'

'You remind me of the story about the man who buried a stash of silver and left a note saying there was no silver buried there. His neighbour A-Er dug it up and left a note explaining that he couldn't possibly be the culprit!'

'Shhh,' he put his finger to his lips. 'Don't talk so loud. It's not A-Er who's my neighbour, it's the head of the Romance Section of the Marriage and Home Research Institute.'

She burst out laughing. What an interesting man, she thought, he could be a friend. With this thought in mind, she took him to Peng's. She was obviously getting her own back on Zheng. In the past, when she invited Zheng to a meal, he usually brought along another girl, a dazzling array of them, in fact. Zheng actually had no ulterior motives, except perhaps a desire to show off a little.

She had forgotten that the day of her date was her birthday. Zheng had not, however. He got to Peng's early and was busy making dumplings, which were cooking when they arrived. Everyone was astonished that she had brought a man along. Zheng exchanged a few brief courtesies with him and soon made his excuses and left. A week later, Tianyi found out he had gone to Changsha, apparently to start up a new company. He did not say goodbye. Tianyi knew that something had changed forever in their feelings for each other. Still, she thought: *Why was it OK for him but not for me? What double standards!*

Of course, she split up with the man before long. He never did understand it. How had he offended this odd woman?

In reality, Tianyi never stopped loving Zheng, even while she was getting her own back on him. So when *The Tree of Knowledge* had its first showing in China, he was the first person she thought of. She had dedicated the story on which the film was based, to him. The assistant director gave her a dozen tickets, and she got a friend to give them to him. As a result, half of his institute turned up for the showing. Before the showing, the cast and production team met the audience. Zheng saw Tianyi, petite and beautiful, standing on the platform, and felt a rush of emotion. He had been away from Beijing for not quite three years, and in that time, Tianyi had become a mother. This was the first time he had seen her since then, and his heart ached. Tianyi, for her part, was shocked at how much he had changed. Those sparkling eyes had dimmed, and she wondered what on earth had happened to him.

The opening sequence of *The Tree of Knowledge* was very interesting. Brilliant red berries gleamed in dense woodland, like the Garden of Eden, from which a young woman serenely emerged. The titles rolled: first came Yang Tianyi, writer of the original work and the screenplay. The theme music was mysterious and evocative, just like Tianyi's unfathomable inner world. Unfortunately, Zheng did not tumble to the fact that the lead male role was actually him. He had no idea that that was how Tianyi felt about him. He even found the man irritating, unappealingly pretentious.

It was Peng who got the clues. He said to Zheng: 'The lead character is very like you.' Zheng was scornful: 'You're pulling my leg! I'm not as argumentative as that.' Tianyi overheard this exchange and was suddenly furious. Tears filled her eyes and it was only with a huge effort that she forced them back. She was a good actress, and her smile took everyone in.

Later that evening, however, Tianyi's acting skills were to desert her. Lian had made them a huge dinner, including his specialities, winter melon balls, plain-fried beans, red-cooked chicken wings and so on. Tianyi tucked in happily, did the dishes and was sitting in the sitting-room, one leg crossed over the other, reading the paper, when Lian suddenly came out with: 'So H Z is Zheng then?'

His words hit home. Tianyi looked at him, and seemed to be seeing a stranger. Her head was whirling with questions. Lian calmly carried on reading the paper. She could read nothing from his face. Finally she took a deep breath and came out with: 'You seem to have been thinking about for quite a while.' 'No, it was just a gut reaction.' Lian looked up, still impassive. 'It's obvious you were in love with him, and you still are. No,' he put his finger to his lips, 'don't deny it. I understand. If I were a woman, I'd fall in love with a man like that. He's very attractive. Do you believe me? I like him.'

Tianyi could think of nothing to say. It occurred to her that either Lian was the most forgiving of men, or the most terrible. She had underestimated him. But she was not to be outdone. 'Fine,' she said, 'if you like him so much, why not invite him over?' Lian's smile was genuine: 'No sooner said than done! I'll cook, you invite him, and that's settled!'

It was a lively dinner party. It so happened that their friend Jin was home from the States to visit his family, Di was about to leave for the States, and her sister Xian had just got married, so it was a send-off, a welcome-back and a celebration all rolled into one. Lian bustled in and out the kitchen and in due course, more than a dozen dishes appeared on the table.

Di, who was used to plainer fare in the postgrad canteen, gazed hungrily at the food and exclaimed: 'Tianyi, you've got a house-husband and he's worth his weight in gold!' Xian's marriage must have been making her happy, she seemed to have grown prettier. She laughed and told her sister, that 'house-husband' was not a proper word. Di protested: 'But "house-husband" is exactly what I meant! You know what Tianyi's like. She's just the kind of woman to get herself one!' Everyone laughed, with the exception of Zheng, who was deep in conversation with Jin about the economic reforms. Tianyi had the feeling, however, that he was trying to conceal how despondent he felt.

Tianyi began to observe Xian's new husband, Du. He was a whole nine years younger than Xian, only just above the legal minimum age for marriage. He was a handsome young man, nearly one metre ninety tall. According to Aunt Jie, Di and Xian's mother, he was a friend of Xian's from college, where he was doing management studies. He was so obsessed with going to America that he had suffered depression and ended up at Student Counselling Services. He was from the North-East, from a very poor family, so getting to university was a big deal for him. But he needed to pass his English test or he would not get to America, and would have to go back home. That put him under immense pressure so he was in and out of Counselling and, in so doing, got to know Xian.

Xian was a girl with no obvious faults, but little to distinguish her either. As a child, she had idolized Tianyi, just like her elder sister Di or perhaps even more so. But now she was grown-up and was a bit disappointed in her former idol. She found it hard to say why, except that she had felt Tianyi was destined for greater things. Some things were not worth bothering about, of course, but she realized that Tianyi was not only not too bothered, she really could not give a damn. Tianyi was just like any ordinary woman: she was an over-fussy housewife, preoccupied with the usual domestic trivialities and fell out with her mother-in-law. Xian liked Tianyi just as much as before, but she was no longer the Tianyi she had put on a pedestal in their youth.

A poor young man like Du needed someone just like Xian, to give him her complete attention. Xian was very good at listening. That was the role she used to play with Tianyi when they were growing up together so she fell into the role easily the next time it was demanded of her. By that time, Aunt Jie was at her wit's end in her attempts to marry her girls off. Xian was a dutiful daughter, so when finally a suitor turned up whose only drawback was that he was a few years younger than her, she accepted his marriage proposal with alacrity. Aunt Jie was over the moon, and went around saying to anyone who would listen: 'Our youngest girl just couldn't find anyone, and now look what a handsome boy she's found!' Of course, doubts still nagged at her. She had a quiet word with Tianyi's mother: 'He's so much younger than her, if you look at them together, does it make our girl look too old?' Tianyi's mother could be very nice when she wanted to be, at least to people's faces. She was quick to reassure her: 'Of course not. Your Xian has such a young-looking face, she looks three or four years younger than girls of her age.' Aunt Jie was not comforted: 'But the lad's nine years younger than her!' 'So what? He's old-looking, four or five older than his contemporaries, that makes them exactly even, doesn't it?' Aunt Jie beamed with delight: 'You certainly have a good way of putting things.'

But it was a different story when Aunt Jie had gone. Tianyi's mother grimaced and said to Tianke: 'The thing is, if a family has pretty daughters, the suitors will come to them. But she's turned it upside-down, and gone running after the boys' families. She's so keen to get those two girls married off, she's lost all her self-respect. It's a good thing you and your big sister got married before them. Otherwise, you'd all have been tarred with the same brush.' The fact was that Tianyi's mother normally never paid much attention to her. But as soon as there was an outsider in the picture, she became protective, as did Tianke. Tianyi was their flesh and blood, after all.

As far as Du was concerned, the significance of his marriage to Xian went far beyond the union itself. First, it meant he could stay in Beijing, and take his time over the TOEFL test. If he had had to leave Beijing, he would never pass it.

However, although Aunt Jie believed that she had thought of everything, there was one important thing she had not taken into account: the feelings of her eldest daughter, Di. She had no idea that Di had had her eye on Du from the moment they first met.

At that point, Di was pining for Jin as well. He had conducted his 'sexual experiments', (Tianyi had told her a bit about that) and then he had rushed off to America, where he wasted no time in falling fall in love with his tutor's daughter. However dumb Di was, once she found this out, she knew that there was no future in her feelings—they were just wishful thinking.

One evening, Tianyi found the three of them together. Both sisters lavished attention on Du, Di helping him to the choicest bits of the food they were eating, and Xian carrying on a running commentary on his inelegant table manners while fanning him gently. Tianyi smiled: 'You'll spoil the boy, the pair of you!' She saw Di's fierce blush and thought, *I shouldn't have said that.*

On the night of their dinner with Zheng, Lian turned the

conversation to *The Tree of Knowledge* and the prize it had won. By now, he had drunk enough to become effusive: 'I've only ever met two really intelligent people in my life—the man was Jin, the woman was Tianyi. I don't know how I managed it, but I married her!' There was a burst of laughter and much clinking of glasses. 'I think Tianyi's novel is sensational,' said Di. 'It's so truthful emotionally, and it's so beautifully written. I don't think the film's as good as the book.' 'I absolutely agree, it's not nearly as good as the book,' Lian said. 'But film and TV is so much more influential, and there's nothing we can do about that.' His voice sounded distorted, as if he was talking through a microphone.

'I've just seen the rough cut, and I didn't know what to think,' said Tianyi, slowly sipping her tea. 'But then I figured that the film is like the child of the novel, once you've made up your mind to sell it, it doesn't matter to you whether it ends up dressed in velvet or in rags.'

'You're quite right,' said Di, her face flushed cherry red. 'Why are you not saying anything, Zheng? Are you angry because Lian didn't say you were one of the two most intelligent people he knew? Honestly, you can't be very intelligent because Tianyi's novel's about you and you still haven't said what you think about it!'

Zheng had been keeping his head down and drinking, but now he went scarlet. Before he had time to speak, Lian hurriedly butted in: 'It's true I didn't say Zheng was the most intelligent man but I'm quite sure he's the most attractive. I told Tianyi, if I were a woman I'd be very attracted to him.' Everybody laughed. Zheng joined in too, but it sounded forced.

Zheng left early. Tianyi suddenly took pity on him and was about to see him down to the ground floor, but a subtle change in Lian's expression made her change her mind. 'Bye bye,' she said, as casually as she could manage, and carried on talking and laughing with the others.

Tianyi's casualness stung Zheng. A month later, he started dating a girl and, in another month, they announced they were getting married.

Then, before she left for America, Di startled Tianyi by saying that she and Du loved each other. She made a point of saying not 'fallen in love', but 'loved each other'.

Tianyi's first thought was to wonder if she should tell Xian. Di must have guessed, because her next words were: 'You absolutely mustn't tell my little sister!'

'What's going to happen with Xian, then?' said Tianyi.

Di was apparently so engrossed in her new-found happiness that she had no answer to this question, except to say: 'Let's wait and see.' Yet she had been unable to keep the thrilling news to herself. She had to share it and it had to be with Tianyi, no one else.

It had all started with the English test and some American dollars. Xian had some because she wanted to go to Italy on an academic exchange. Du asked for $50 to register for his TOEFL exam. But Xian dug her heels in and said no. 'Why right now?' she protested. 'You're married to me and settled in Beijing. Register next year, or wait until I'm back and register. That won't be too late.' But Du dug his heels in too, and there was a massive row. At the crucial moment, Di stepped in. She had $300 saved and offered Du a hundred. Du had never seen that much money in his life and, the day after his wife left for Italy, he took his sister-in-law out in a rowing boat on Beihai Lake. They were out until late in the evening, whispering sweet nothings to each other like a newly-married couple. Du certainly knew how to please a girl like Di: he bought her an intricately braided string of coloured garlic.

It was a most original necklace and Di accepted it and put it on.

When Du discovered that Di was still a virgin, he was amazed. He never imagined in his wildest dreams that two virgins would fall into his lap, just like that.

She bled copiously the first time, Di told Tianyi. Du had been a very considerate lover. She blushed scarlet, then pulled the string of garlic from round her neck and showed it to Tianyi.

'What are you going to do now?' Tianyi asked. Di told her that they had decided to go to America together. Di would get herself a research place there and go, and as soon as Du had passed his English test, he would join her.

'But what about Xian?' Tianyi said again. Di looked pensive, then raised her head and said with determination: 'Time heals all wounds.'

Tianyi was chilled by her words. My god, she thought, and these are sisters! If even sisters can betray each other like this, then morals have really changed!

Tianyi did not know what to say to her old friend. After a while, she ladled out some chicken soup and gave her a bowl. Di took a mouthful and said how good it was. Then she said sadly: 'It's going to be a long time before I taste your cooking again.'

Before he left China, Du divorced Xian.

When Tianyi next met Di, ten years later in a restaurant in Hong Kong's Wanchai harbourside, they were both in their forties. Di had aged greatly. *I've been blessed*, thought Tianyi, *I was once so desperate to leave China but I couldn't get away. Now look at all my friends who did leave. None of them have got along well.*

Di was single again. She lived with Du for a year after they went to America, then they split up. Du had lied to her—he had a girlfriend on the side. Having got hold of Di's money, he spent all his time having torrid sex with the other girl. Tianyi was not surprised. Du was just up to his old tricks, she said. A man who could betray the woman he had only just married was capable of anything!

But something even more terrible had happened. When Di finally caught Du out, the shame made him fly into a terrible rage. 'What the hell do I owe your family anyway? You were just a couple of old birds fighting over who was going to push their fannies in my face first?! Don't you ever look in the mirror? Have you any idea how old you look? Why would I want to fuck you?'

Di fell seriously ill, and found it particularly distressing because she was away from home. Finally, she pulled through. An American researcher who had worked at her institute in Beijing came to visit her. His name was Brian Brown and he had always liked her a lot, only he never got a look in because Di had been involved with other men at the time. First it was Jin, then it was Du. They were both ten or more years younger than her—she obviously went for younger men, because Brian was also four or five years younger than her. Di, on the rebound, quickly took up with him.

Her letters to Tianyi tailed off, so when Tianyi had a spare moment, she dropped in on Aunt Jie to ask for news. Di's mother said proudly: 'Our Di's going out with an American. They're getting on really well. Didn't she tell you?' Aunt Jie sounded comically enthusiastic. 'Yes she did,' Tianyi reassured her with a smile. 'It's just that I'm still a bit worried.'

Aunt Jie laughed heartily. 'You're so old-fashioned! Even I'm more open-minded than you! Loads of girls marry Americans nowadays! You marry, you get your Green Card, then two years afterwards, you can get American nationality!'

Tianyi did not know whether to laugh or cry. Was Aunt Jie really so keen to get an American son-in-law? She wondered.

Then she heard Aunt Jie say: 'My two girls are always out of step. Di's thinking of getting married just as Xian's got divorced!' 'Xian, divorced?' Tianyi pretended this was the first she'd heard of it. 'Yes, that wretched man Du, he was only using her to stay in Beijing. Then as soon as he left for the US, he divorced her! Xian was so generous to him that even when she knew she was going to be dumped, she went to see his family and bought them a colour TV?'

Aunt Jie's words that day came back to Tianyi in a rush of sadness when she met up with Di, now divorced herself, ten years later. At the time, she had paid little attention to Di's American marriage. She was absorbed, body and soul, with another event, the catastrophe that was 1989 in China.

13

Just after New Year in 1989, Tianyi fell ill and was admitted to hospital suffering acute abdominal pain. It was the Year of the Snake, her birth year. Dire things always happened to her in the Year of the Snake, as it did this year to the entire country.

The doctor diagnosed acute appendicitis; they would have to operate. This would be Tianyi's third operation in ten years. She lay on the operating table feeling very unwell and weak. Then the anaesthetist came in to inject the local anaesthetic, and the surgeon took a thin-bladed knife and sliced into her abdomen. She felt some pain and made a big fuss: 'It hurts! It hurts!' Other women in the ward had told her that that was the way to get more anaesthetic and make the operation more bearable. But she had forgotten that everything came with a price.

The anaesthetist made her curl up and inserted a needle into her spinal column. When the surgeon next asked if she felt pain, she had no feeling at all. Her body seemed to be fluttering downwards, almost weightless. Then the operating lamp was extinguished, plunging the theatre into pitch darkness. The surgeon and nurses around her turned into demonic shadows, and she wanted to scream but no sound came out. She felt someone bend close to her ear and, in a remaining flicker of awareness, she sensed that he was listening to what she was saying. Then a mask was put over her face, and for a few seconds, she had time to think: *So this is dying, this is what dying is like. The colour of death really is black.*

But she would not give up, her voice had not been extinguished, she would put up a fight. A voice inside her said: I won't die, I won't die, I'm not going to die! She saw her lips form the words as she formed the thoughts. She suddenly realised how important willpower was. If you refused to give in, even death had to back off. The dead were people who had been ready to abandon hope, and had abandoned it. If she did not give up, then no one could force her to.

When she was recovering from the operation, she asked an intern at the Beijing Hospital, who had been present: 'What happened?' The young man stammered in embarrassment: 'If you promise you won't tell them, absolutely promise ...' 'I promise.' 'It was like this ... they put the anaesthetic in the wrong place, it caused an anaesthetic accident.' 'And what does that mean?' 'Well, it can be fatal.' 'Exactly.' 'What do you mean "exactly"?' 'I was very near to dying.' 'Don't joke.' 'Really. I've found out what dying means.' She said nothing more. She did not want to say that she could tell just by looking at him that he had not an ounce of spirituality. Even if she did say it, he would not understand.

She had vomited all that night after the operation. It may have been a reaction to the anaesthetic, it may have been something else. The violent retching was agony and she felt as if the incision was going to burst apart. The woman sharing her room thought so too, but Tianyi looked and there was no blood seeping through the gauze.

The wound was painful but she was not bent double like the other patients, so the next day, she got up and, holding herself very straight, she walked up and down. Lian stayed with her for the first night but was impatient with her, quite unlike when Niuniu was born. That gave Tianyi a choking feeling in her chest, and her wound felt even more painful than before.

What eventually relieved her pain were the posters that

appeared in the Triangle at Peking University in April. Lian always said that Tianyi was someone who thrived on chaos. As soon as the unrest started, she made a rapid recovery. Was it because she had something new to focus her energies on, she wondered? At any rate, for a while, she felt elated and spent every day at the Triangle. She was astounded at the intelligence of the posters. She felt that no one in the world understood politics like the Chinese. Every political movement threw up extraordinarily perceptive insights. For example, during the Cultural Revolution the posters that appeared on every campus had been very perceptive at the start though, sadly, the movement had quickly degenerated into bloody infighting and the students' antics eventually dragged the whole nation down with them.

But in mid-April 1989, two decades later, politics on the university campus found far gentler and more cultured expression. One of the posters, written in the form of a traditional couplet, was a commentary on Deng Xiaoping's attack on his former colleague, reformer and supporter of the students, Hu Yaobang. The couplet used the language of mah-jong moves and involved an intricate play on words, but there was nothing veiled about the references to the political situation and to the author's feelings about it. There were many other similar posters, and the campus became a forum where the brightest brains of the university displayed their political and literary talents.

Riding her cranky old bicycle around the campus that day, Tianyi recalled the outbreak of the Cultural Revolution in 1966. She had only been thirteen, in the sixth grade of primary school, and none of her fellow pupils shared her enthusiasm for politics. She cycled from one school to another to see what was going on, until in December of that year, she fell ill. There was no clear diagnosis but she was in bed for three months, running a high fever. By the time she recovered, everything had changed: spring had arrived, she had suddenly grown beautiful, and she had written her first poem, entitled *Enlightenment*. Before the end of the year, she also got her first period.

In those days, there were no sanitary towels. Her mother looked out an old 'sanitary pocket' for her. It was a rectangular piece of checked cloth, with a strip of towelling sown on top of it. When no one was around, Tianyi slipped into her room with a washbowl, shut the door and washed herself. Then she tore some ordinary toilet paper into strips and stuffed the pocket with them. She was scared. She had seen the way women walked up and down the street and did not want to end up looking that way. She was grateful that after three or four days, the bleeding stopped and she felt like a girl, playing the usual boisterous games with Di and Xian. The dread returned, however, with another period the next month and accompanied her as she grew up and began to walk like those other women she saw in the street.

On one of those brilliantly sunny spring days in 1989, she received a phone call from Zheng. Once more, his voice dispelled her angst and turned the day bright again. 'Tianyi, we're in the Square! Come and join us!' His voice also seemed to turn the clock back, to turn them back into the young man and woman they had been all those years ago, unmarried, without children, when they had lived their individual lives, belonging only to themselves.

That day, Tianyi put the phone down and got on her bike. Zheng's voice had succeeding in soothing the pain from her wound, and she pedalled speedily along, leaving the other cyclists far behind. Ever since she was a girl, she liked to ride fast. It had frightened her mother and father.

That day, the students who had marched into Tiananmen

Square were from Zheng's university. Everyone knew him and many stepped out of the march to greet him. Before Tianyi's very eyes, he was transformed back into that brilliant, handsome youth she had once known and loved.

Tianyi was very late home that day. Lian and Niuniu were both asleep, but Lian threw on some clothes and came out to say: 'Your mother called. Your aunt and uncle have arrived from Taiwan, can you go over tomorrow?' Then he got back under the covers and was asleep. He had scarcely opened his eyes to talk to her. He liked his sleep, for sure, but this was different. He was secretly very angry, Tianyi knew, and did not want to look at her. His resentment had built up over a long period, and was seeking an outlet. The outburst would not come right now—the middle of the night was when he was at his least belligerent—but come it surely would, when he had bolstered his strength.

Tianyi lay in the single bed in her little study, overwhelmed with excitement, unable to sleep. All she wanted to do was to share today's excitements with someone, but she knew it would not be with Lian.

Next day, Tianyi's eyes welled with tears when she saw her Taiwan uncle and aunt for the first time. The pair looked so frail and old. But what moved her most was the way her uncle was so clearly devoted to his wife and attentive to her needs. Her mother told her how, when her sister had married him, their parents had feared that he would turn out to be a philanderer. Her uncle had been an up-and-coming airforce officer in the Kuomintang, romantically handsome, while her aunt was the least good-looking of the sisters and girl cousins in their family, in fact she was frankly ugly. But the parents had no cause to worry.

Her uncle held himself erect, like the soldier he had once been. He hurried back and forth, bringing water and a towel, and wiped his wife's face. Her aunt had had a stroke two years before, and her mouth was still lopsided. The two of them were fond of children, and immediately took to Niuniu, whom Tianyi had taken with her. Niuniu saw the piles of toys they had brought him and was wild with excitement. He was a solitary child who had few other children to play with, being the only child in the family as yet, so he was thrilled when all the assembled adults vied to pet and spoil him.

The size of Xiaolan's belly was alarming; her face was puffy too and her heavily-pencilled eyebrows crawled across it like a couple of black snakes. Pregnancy had given her a voracious appetite for deli-style food like soy-stewed pigs' trotters and kebabs. Tianke went out every day, determined to find her what she liked. Tianyi, watching her eat her way through mountains of meat, felt her gorge rise.

Lian went out of his way to please the old folks, producing his party piece, stir-fried shredded eel in sizzling oil. Tianyi's uncle and aunt were greatly touched by his efforts. The trouble was that Xiaolan demolished half the dish, so Tianyi, embarrassed for her, hurried off to make an extra soup.

Tianyi's mother was talking about their youth when their family had fled the turmoil of war, arrived in Hankou and had had to rely on her sister's husband's family for hand-outs. Tianyi had always found it hard to understand how the older generation were related. This story shed some light on it: her aunt was her mother's older cousin, not her birth sister. Tianyi's maternal grandmother was the wife of her aunt's father's younger brother. Her mother also had a brother, now dead, who was her aunt's younger cousin. To tell the truth, before Tianyi met her uncle and aunt, she had heard nothing but negative things about that side of the family. Her mother used to say that when she and her family fled to Hankou, her own mother had given her brother-in-law a lot of silver dollars, while the rest of the family got only a little food. Tianyi's mother's brother did not even get enough to eat. The old woman had stored valuables at the brother-in-law's house, and that branch of the family never gave them back. And so on and so forth. Tianyi's mother had a poor opinion of Tianyi's uncle as well—but then she had an extremely sharp tongue. Anyone she approved of must be a saint. As she listened to the stories of the old folks' lives, what most moved Tianyi was the story of her mother's brother and the Taiwan uncle: the brother had been separated from the others, and went down with cholera as they fled the battle zone. It was the Taiwan uncle, at that time the youngest officer in the Kuomintang airforce, who had come to the rescue, carrying the sick man on his own back to the best hospital he could find. When mother and daughter talked of these things afterwards, both were always reduced to tears, and the child Tianyi along with them.

Now they were reunited, and all the bad feeling had vanished. Her mother was beaming with a happiness rare for her, and looked genuinely appreciative of their visit. How sad that her father had died, otherwise he and her uncle could have become good friends, Tianyi thought.

Her aunt and uncle had planned to visit the Old Summer Palace the next day, then the Lama Temple the following day, then on the fourth day, go to the Great Wall or the Forbidden City, they had not decided yet which.

But in the event, there was no fourth day for the old couple. On the night of the third day, their longed-for trip back to the mainland was cut short, and was never resumed. By the time, some years later, Tianyi went with a tour group to Taiwan, her aunt had died, and her uncle had dementia and was in an old people's home. When Tianyi visited him, he was beyond recognizing her. Tianyi's foolhardy behaviour that afternoon amazed the residents of the entire university campus. After the cataclysmic events of the night before, Beijing had an air of desolation. Tianyi got out her old bicycle and, pedalling furiously, headed through the city streets to her mother's house. At first, she did not notice anything odd. Her mother's home was in the northern outskirts, and as yet no one there had heard the news. It was only as she rode down Weigongcun Street past the universities that she suddenly felt a wave of panic.

Niuniu, then four years old, sat in a bamboo seat secured over the rear wheel of her bike. Relegated to this position behind her, Niuniu was always leaning to one side so he could see ahead. Just as she reached People's University—Tianyi would never forget this—he suddenly pointed off to the side: 'Mum! What that?' All those 'What that?' (never 'What's that?'), along with the endless repetitions of 'Why?', were usually just irritating, but this time his question made Tianyi's heart pound with fear. He was pointing to a blood-soaked shirt, hanging conspicuously from the main entrance gate to the university, next to an upturned car that belched black smoke. Something terrible's happened! The blood rushed to Tianyi's head. Her first thought was: *Zheng!* Where was Zheng? Was he in danger!

Tianyi knew Zheng better than anyone. They had talked on the phone the day before. He had been acutely aware then of the looming danger. 'Where are you?' she had asked. 'I'll join you.' But he said: 'No, don't.' 'Why?' There was a long silence at the other end, then he answered: 'I don't want you to get dragged into this.' As the years went by, the import of those words 'I don't want you to get dragged into this' gradually became clear. Then Tianyi knew that Zheng had loved her, loved her more than he loved himself.

One month earlier, towards the end of May, Zheng and Peng had turned up at her house one day. Zheng's first words were: 'Tianyi, have any of the detainees been given the death sentence?' Tianyi felt as if she had been stabbed in the heart. Ignoring Lian, she spoke directly to Zheng: 'You'd better go to Shenzhen. It's near Hong Kong. I've got a good friend there who can fix things for you.' Zheng looked intensely at her, and she felt as if there was no one else in the room but the two of them. His eyes gradually brightened and she saw in them the resurgence of something she had thought gone forever. His gaze was tender, piercing and beautiful.

'What a stupid idea,' Lian snapped. 'The situation in Shenzhen's even hotter than here.' This, it transpired, was a lie, although at the time he sounded genuinely concerned. Lian was much smarter than she imagined.

Just now, Tianyi's arrival at the Mingda University campus with her son behind her, caused quite a stir. The crowd of people who gathered around her she had known since childhood, had grown up with, and, looking at their appalled expressions, it dawned on her how serious the situation was. Xian, a shopping basket over her arm, pushed in and confronted Tianyi. 'How could you be so stupid as to come here with Niuniu?' she said severely. 'Go home, right now! This afternoon, there's a curfew in Haidian. If you don't go now, you won't be able to!'

Xian sounded completely different from her normal placid self, but Tianyi was calm. *So it's happened,* she thought, *there's no going back. What will be, will be.* She thanked them all for their concern, but stubbornly got back on her bicycle, pushed through the crowd and headed back to the shabby old apartment where she had been born. When Lian was in a good mood, he used to compliment her for the way she kept her head in a crisis. And it was true. The bigger the crisis, the more decisive she was. For instance, during the catastrophic Tangshan earthquake of 1976, she had roused everyone in the street where they were then living. Then she had guided each member of her family to safety, one after another, before going to help the neighbours.

Today, everyone in the house—her aunt and uncle, her mother, Tianke and Xiaolan—looked traumatized. Tianyi went and boiled water for tea, feeling they were making too much of a fuss. All the same, she could not help feeling sorry that the disturbances had coincided with her aunt and uncle's long-awaited visit home. 'Life's not really like this,' she wanted to say, 'It's sheer bad luck that it's happened now, we're normally fine.' Then Niuniu announced loudly: 'We saw a luddy shirt at the school gates.' Luckily the old folks did not understand him, and Tianyi was able to steer the conversation into other channels.

What was really worrying her was her aunt and uncle's return to Taiwan. They did not want to stay a moment longer. They had lived through wartime and they understood far better than the younger generation how serious this was. Lian came around in the evening, and they all put their heads together to figure out how to get the old couple out of Beijing. The problem was not their plane tickets but the fact that, overnight, all the taxis seemed to have disappeared. It was at least 50 kilometres from the university to the airport and they could hardly be expected to walk.

It was the night of 5th June 1989. They talked until half past ten at night, when Xiaolan went to bed. The rest of them went on talking until, at eleven o'clock, they suddenly discovered that Tianyi was no longer with them. In these extraordinary times, they were in no doubt that she had sneaked off for a reason, and there was panic in the room.

It was close to midnight by the time Tianyi pushed her bike into the army compound. Security had been tightened and there were two extra gates now. As she went through the first gate, she heard the sentry pull back the bolt of his rifle with a clatter, but Tianyi ignored him. If Tianyi had looked up at the guard, no doubt she would have been scared witless by his watchful stare. In fact, she never even gave the sentry a glance. He shouted a loud question, she gave an indifferent, unhurried answer: she was going to the night school to see a friend. This was a prestigious night school and everyone knew they rented rooms at the army academy, at a cost of 700,000 *yuan* a year.

She followed his directions to Reception to fill in a visitor's form. She really did have a friend at the night school and some of the teachers really did have accommodation here. What mattered now however, was that her relaxed, unhurried manner made the keen-eyed sentry relax his guard.

By the time she had passed through the three security gates, Tianyi's collar was soaked in cold sweat. Next, she had to cross the garden with its bamboo fencing. Tianyi had on a red silk T-shirt top, a deep yellow fishtail skirt and matching shoes, and wore her hair bobbed. She dressed with style and had a nice figure to go with it. When her top snagged on the bamboo as she went into the garden, she fingered the pulled thread with a pang of regret, but there was no time to dwell on it. She knocked on the door of apartment A10, and waited. There was no sound from inside.

Zheng's mother, Ke Zhilan, told Tianyi later that she had been too frightened to open the door in case it was had news. When she finally opened up, she saw a good-looking girl whom she took to be in her late 20s. (Actually Tianyi was 30-something by that time.) As she let her in, Tianyi's first words were: 'Excuse me, Mrs. Ke, do you have any news of Zheng?'

Mrs Ke was immediately taken with Tianyi. She made her sit down beside her and peeled a pomelo for her. This was the kind of special treatment that her daughter-in-law Yiyi, Zheng's wife, had never been accorded. Yiyi, of course, was a thoroughly bad lot. This family was living proof of the old adage that mothers- and daughters-in-law were natural enemies. In Mrs. Ke's view, Yiyi was a calculating young vixen, whose main aims had been to seduce her precious boy, and stir up trouble in the family. Zheng was her second son and her outright favorite. The eldest, Lin, and the younger boy, Jun, were both more streetwise than he was. He was the brainy, kind one who always got a raw deal. What made her heart ache was that he never complained about it. Like when he went to Changsha to set up the company; that must have been really hard because he was very ill after he got back. For a long time, he hardly spoke, and even those bright eyes of his looked dull. She kept asking but he had refused to say a word. He just buttoned his lips. That slut had spotted her opportunity and got her claws into him! The pair of them weren't even married and she was cheerily calling them 'Dad' and 'Mum'. She was shameless! thought Mrs. Ke. But now that Zheng was in trouble, she simply vanished without trace. Not like this girl she had never met before who, though she was not exactly beautiful, seemed quite out of the ordinary. She was a well-grounded young woman, you could tell that at a glance. So Mrs. Ke roused her husband Hua Liankai and the old couple bustled around treating her as if she was family.

Mr Hua had helped run this military academy until his retirement two years ago. Never strong, he became depressed after falling out with his headstrong, disobedient sons, and his illness worsened. However, their midnight visitor made his eyes brighten. He thought he had rarely come across a girl of such shining purity, so thoughtful and idealistic, but still lively. She was someone special, he could tell that. He smiled as he listened to his wife probing questions.

'How old are you, young lady?' Mrs. Ke asked, her eyes fixed on Tianyi. 'About 25 or 26?'

'Heavens, no, I'm over thirty!'

'And you're still not married?'

Tianyi laughed: 'Oh yes, I've been married for a while. I've got a son of four years old.'

'Ah, our boy's out of luck then! Have you known him long?'

'Oh, a long time ... eight or nine years ...'

Mrs. Ke looked astonished. "You've known him that long, girl, and you never thought to come and pay us a visit?"

Tianyi was lost for words. It was true, she had never thought of that. When Zheng took her in his arms the night of the storm at the Miyun Reservoir, he had seemed like a child who had squeezed out of a crack in the rock, a solitary loner. When she thought more about it, it was true that she had never sought out the families of any of her previous boyfriends. Unless she absolutely had to, the thought that she might 'go and see the parents' never occurred to her. She had been married five years, but she would have been hard put to say, if asked, what Lian's parents were up to. And Zheng was pretty much the same, she thought. There was one occasion when he had taken her home because it was raining and had met her parents, but that was all. They both preferred to be free to enjoy themselves as they wished, beyond the reach of parental supervision. On this point, they were very similar, while Lian was just the opposite.

Fortunately, Mr Hua changed the subject and said to his wife: 'The girl's here to ask about Zheng, what are you going on at her like this for?' Tears started to run down Mrs Ke's face. 'He hasn't been home for more than three months!' she said. 'The last time, he just dropped in to pick up some medicine, then left. He was running a temperature then, and I don't know if he's better now!'

'Have you any idea where he might have gone?' asked Tianyi, very worried.

'Probably Changsha. That's where he had the company,' Hua Liankai said. 'But don't you go looking for him, girl, whatever you do, it's really dangerous out there.'

Tianyi was very late home that night. For the first time ever, Lian had waited up for her. He did not ask her any questions, just said: 'Get yourself washed and go to bed.' She could not sleep. Some time later, around two o'clock, they suddenly heard trucks thundering by. Lian crept out of bed and tiptoed to the window. She followed him and they peered through a crack in the curtains. Down below, they saw a convoy of military trucks full of soldiers driving past, the dim street lights shining eerily down on them. Then the silence was broken by the sound of a gunshot. Shocked, Tianyi pulled the curtains open and looked to see where the gunfire was coming from. Lian, just as swiftly, pulled the curtains together again and glared at her. 'What do you think you're doing? Do you want to get us killed?' Tianyi returned his stare: 'Will it come to that?' 'Of course it will,' he said, through gritted teeth. 'You lot don't understand a thing!' The solitary gunshot had caused a commotion in the street and Tianyi threw on some clothes so that she could go out and look. But Lian grabbed hold of her angrily. 'Cool it, OK? We've got to get your uncle and aunt to the airport tomorrow. There are no taxis, I'll have to take them on a tricycle. Dammit, just let me get some sleep, will you?'

Lately, Lian had been prone to flying into a temper, swearing, bellowing and smashing anything within reach. She did not understand what was up with him. It was the middle of the night so she just had to put up with it, but she was not a patient person by nature and felt increasingly resentful. She tossed and turned, unable to sleep. As soon as it was light, she'd leave, she thought, and go to her mother's house. She would see her uncle and aunt off and then go to Changsha to look for Zheng.

Plans dreamed at night rarely survive the cold light of day, however. When she woke, she was too giddy to get out of bed. Lian was already up. 'Hurry up,' he urged her. 'The later we leave it, the more difficult it will be to get there.' He seemed in a much better mood, however. She was aware that his mood swings were worsening: he either lavished endearments on his wife and son or acted as if he wanted to kill them. Once Niuniu had confided to her: 'Dad's crazy.' Another time, she overheard him say to Momo from next door: 'I'd like to mash my dad up into a meat patty and take a chunk of him.' She laughed at first, then thought about it and decided actually it was not good at all. It was the first sign of hostility the boy had shown towards his father. The effects on Niuniu of his father's mood swings were all too obvious: the little boy's bottom was black and blue with bruises. Lian was either cuddling him adoringly, or he would pick him up with one hand and begin to thrash him with his trouser belt. The worst was when he made him kneel on the washboard. Tianyi naturally found this unendurable and shouted furiously at him.

The rows had become more frequent. Tianyi was thoroughly fed-up with marriage and home. But as soon as this thought came to her, Lian seemed to sense it and behaved better. Now he said: 'Get yourself ready and I'll go down and buy some breakfast.' Tianyi hurriedly got Niuniu up, washed and dressed him. Niuniu always liked snuggling up in bed. Tianyi's way of dealing with this was to pounce and snatch him from the bed, singing: 'Arise you heroes from your slumbers!' And his face widened into a big smile, making his right cheek dimple. Today she dressed him in the outfit her uncle and aunt had brought him, a striped, short-sleeved shirt and dungarees. He looked very smart. By the time they were both ready, Lian was back with soymilk and *shaobing* sesame cakes. He rushed in shouting: 'Tianyi, guess what! That gunshot last night came from a police motorbike patrol. They were turning the corner, right by the grocery store downstairs. Some people were playing chess under the streetlights and when the police drove by, they shouted abuse, and the police fired. There are still a bunch of people standing around down there now, looking at a bloody shoe that's been pinned to the wall. They're saying the person got shot in the foot, and was taken to hospital but wasn't badly injured.' Tianyi was busy tying Niuniu's shoelaces. 'Shooting someone so casually ...' she muttered to herself. 'This is a major disturbance! Of course, they're going to shoot,' said Lian, taking a big bite of sesame cake. 'Those people were asking for it.' Tianyi said nothing. She did not want to get upset this early in the morning. But Lian had not finished. 'I'm telling you, you've got to be careful what you say and do, wherever you are, at work or anywhere else. You shouldn't go to work if you can help it ... You think I don't know where you went last night? I bet you went to Zheng's.' Tianyi quivered, but said stubbornly: 'So what if I did? I just went to find out what was going on. I can't just back off when a friend's in danger ...' She almost choked on the last words, shocked into silence as Lian struck the table with his fist and roared in a voice so thunderous it made the building shake: 'Now you listen to me, Yang Tianyi! You're not on your own any more, you're a mother! You've got a responsibility for Niuniu. Those sort of people are under surveillance 24/7 just now, so don't go playing heroics! You really don't understand a thing, do you?'

Tianyi was astonished at her dumpy little husband's outburst and accompanying leap into the air. In any other circumstances, it would have been funny. But Niuniu was too small to find it funny and burst into terrified tears, which further ratcheted up the tension. Lian, apparently feeling guilty at having made his son cry, smothered his bad conscience with more shouting. Normally, Tianyi would have shouted back but she was so upset today that she did not have the energy to raise her voice.

She could not remember how long these appalling thunderclaps of rage had been going on. They were terrible, but on every occasion she tried to contain herself. She wished she did not have to, but having the whole building hear their rows was too shameful. She could not bear it, she was too thin-skinned. She never wanted to go out afterwards because the neighbours gave her peculiar looks. As if guessing how she felt, Lian had become more and more intemperate. His shouts grew louder and were punctuated with the sound of smashing crockery. Tianyi usually forbore to answer back but she was not a forbearing kind of person and, inwardly, she seethed with anger. Her health began to suffer: her chest felt tight, and her periods went haywire. Eventually, when she could not take his temper anymore, she forgot about keeping up appearances and would shout back at him. When the fight was over, she felt drained. She forced herself not to think, not to remember, because after each fight, Lian would go out of his way to make it up with her. He would become human again, as gentle and considerate as he had been when they were in love. He would make such an effort to coax her out of her mood that she felt there must be some hope left for them. And, over time, she grew used to this vicious circle.

That day, Tianke, Lian and Tianyue's husband, Wei, put her aunt and uncle and their baggage on a goods tricycle and took it in turns to pedal them to the airport. They did not see a single taxi on the way.

At the end of June, it was as if peace suddenly descended on the country. This unearthly calm sometimes made Tianyi feel as if she could not breathe. At the Academy of Letters where she worked, the ferreting out of 'dangerous elements' was more or less finished, although a few matters remained to be 'clarified'. Luckily, she was not a Party member, still less a government cadre and so, for her, matters were allowed to rest.

The worst of it was that it was time for Niuniu to go back to kindergarten. She was left not knowing what to do with herself, what she wanted to do, or could do. She simply could not write new stuff. She was reduced to digging out some old wool she had put by and knitting jumpers. In Lian's view, knitting woollens in such hot weather was crazy, to say nothing of the fact that she was no longer a good knitter. What she knitted, she unpicked, what she had unpicked, she knitted again. Lian guessed aloud that she was missing Zheng.

She was not only missing Zheng. There was Di, and Jin too, friends she had been so close to that they could and did talk about anything. She felt they had all abandoned her. Niuniu was still a little boy, and she felt a depth of loneliness it was hard to put into words. The monotonous clacking of knitting needles helped to calm her fears and, as she knitted, then unpicked, unpicked and re-knitted, she was grateful to whoever had invented this simple, repetitive work.

At the beginning of July, a letter arrived that shattered her fragile calm; it was sent to her mother's house. On the phone, her mother brought her up to date on what had been happening at home. Xiaolan had had her baby. It was a boy, and they were calling him Long. His birth was a ray of sunshine amid all the turmoil. Xiaolan, as the youngest and the pet of her family, knew all about pampering herself. So she put herself down for a hospital near where Tianyi lived, so that, as she put it, she could 'eat Tianyi's good food'. So Tianyi would have to cook for her every day and deliver meals to the hospital. She grumbled to herself that no one had treated her like that when Niuniu was born. Even if she had gone back home, her mother was never going to wait on her for her confinement month. It would just have triggered more rowing.

That was not all: her mother had something to get off her chest, and she, Tianyi, was going to be her confidante. Tianyi sensed that things had shifted. The family rows were no longer between herself and her mother, but mainly between her mother and Xiaolan and, secondarily, between her mother and Tianke. Tianyi was in the happy position now of being her mother's ally, for the first time in over thirty years.

Her mother said a letter had arrived for her. She could come and pick it up. Tianyi knew her mother missed her, and wanted to talk to her, to re-hash the usual old stuff, and the letter was just an excuse but she went. Her reaction, when she opened the envelope, left her mother dumbfounded. She had never seen her daughter let her guard down and bawl her eyes out like that.

A sheet of paper had fallen from the letter, a photocopy of seven mugshots. The letter was from Peng, and the seven were all wanted by the police. Top of the list was Zheng.

It was Zheng's familiar smile in the mugshot that set off the tears. He was such a good man, with a belief in heroism that belonged to another era. He wanted to be a hero, and so he imposed heroic demands on himself, always putting others above himself in a way that was rarely seen in this day and age. It was ridiculous, but he stuck to his guns, and if nothing else, it made him hugely popular. But what use was personal popularity? It was a fragile thing. Peng wrote in his letter that Zheng had been betrayed by his political friends, and more than once. It was as if he was committed to being betrayed, Tianyi thought, angry and distressed. Without Judas, where would Jesus have been?

Peng wrote that he had reliable information that Zheng had been detained at Changsha Bus Station, and was now being held incommunicado in Qincheng Prison. Coincidentally, Peng was the son of the famous entrepreneur for whom the boyfriend with the TV had worked. Peng was devoted to his studies but had inherited none of his father's genius. He was the kind of person who turned his studies into a kind of mania, making them his whole life. Unfortunately, his results were no better than those of bright students who never put any effort in, the ones who coasted along, spending their time sunning themselves, playing tennis or chewing gum and just absorbing knowledge into their bloodstreams. The bright students had knowledge in their genes, and just learning one small thing allowed them to extrapolate the bigger picture. Zheng was a classic example. While poor Peng was a classic example of the other type.

But Peng never gave up. He was convinced that he could become a second Zheng. These troubled times would give him a chance him to display his prowess. He adored Tianyi, and had done for a very long time. His letter was like an elegy to revolutionary idealism. It contained a long poem, telling her of his staunch faith in the future and his undying love for her. He finished by telling her that he was hiding out in Shaoxing, had changed his name to Wang Lin, and was working for a small business. Could Tianyi send him some books? There was a list of books, including Marx and Hegel. Tianyi had the feeling that the list may have been as much for her to see as for him actually to read. The awkward-sounding foreign names made Tianyi's head swim. Peng really was off his head. It was bad enough shutting himself away in a place like that. Why on earth didn't he choose some light reading to cheer himself up? The romantic image of the revolutionary (male) hero who pored over Marxist-Leninist tracts with knitted brow was so old-fashioned. The nineteenth-century Italian 'charcoal-burner' societies were much more interesting (or at least less hypocritical) in this respèct. The type of revolutionary Tianyi most loathed were the ones who were keenly aware of women as 'other', but who nevertheless pretended to genderless. She secretly suspected that Peng was one of these. But these were exceptional times and Peng was Zheng's best friend, and she was bound to stick by him.

She was home very late that day and Lian looked extremely grumpy. Niuniu, however, welcomed her with open arms and sang her a song he had just learned in kindergarten: 'Mummy, mummy, please sit down and have a cup of tea. Let me kiss you, my good mummy.' His out-of-tune singing reduced Tianyi almost to tears and she gave him a big hug. He was no longer as pink-cheeked as he had been, nor as sturdy. That was because he was not eating well in the kindergarten. Tianyi thought, kissing his little face. *Sweetheart, you've been really unlucky to end up with such a restless mother. I'm a bad mother. When you call me a good one, I feel so ashamed.*

Lian interrupted their cuddling with a scowl: 'That's enough. Stop babying him and do something practical, why don't you? We'll eat and you can give him a bath!' Lian had started being very brusque to her, his past endearments gone for good. Their honeymoon was well and truly over, she thought.

14

Niuniu was not in the slightest bit musical. When she was four months pregnant, Tianyi did something she had read about in a book on pregnancy and childbirth: she got out an old-fashioned transistor radio, placed it five centimetres from her belly and put on some music. The pieces she played most often was Sibelius, *D Major Violin Concerto*, and Saint-Saëns, *Le Cignes*. It was beautiful music but it did not appear to have penetrated the walls of that mysterious thing, the womb.

Niuniu's first song startled her: apart from the voice, it could have been Lian singing. Genes really were astonishing. Such a tiny sperm, invisible to the naked eye, could invest the embryo with a host of innate characteristics. Many years later, when Niuniu was a young man, she was forced to face the fact that he was a clone of his father. Apart from the face and the voice, he was like him in every way. Was there something wrong with her eggs?

With the first royalties from *The Tree of Knowledge* she had bought Niuniu a piano, and they scraped enough money together from their meagre salaries to hire a piano teacher. But, three years down the line, the teacher gave up on his pupil. When, the following Christmas, they asked him to play Silent Night on the piano he made a complete hash of it. Under his stubby little fingers, the beautiful tune sounded like the huffing of a bellows. It was as if the piano keys had turned into a computer keyboard; Niuniu could strike the notes but was quite incapable of drawing out any feeling or spirit or beauty. His parents listened, applauded encouragingly, then fell silent.

But when Niuniu opened his little mouth and sang his song, 'Mummy, mummy, please sit down and have a cup of tea', Tianyi felt quite differently. It didn't matter that he sang completely out of tune. The only thing that counted was the feeling he put into the words. The little boy may have murdered the song but he sang right into her innermost being and told her that he was part of her flesh and blood, and the only thing that really mattered in her life was to have that flesh and blood person close to her.

Niuniu may have been a very ordinary little boy in most respects, but he was exceptional in one way: he had an unerring eye for beautiful things. She first became aware of this when he was three and she brought home a French fashion magazine. She turned each page for him to look at and was astonished at his appreciation of the elegant colours, the kind of colours that she loved too. None of their subtle gradations escaped him: silver-blue, golden-brown, olive-green, sunset red … the beautiful hairstyles and the jewellery, all uniquely beautiful. Much later when he grew into a man, Niuniu was, predictably, a snappy dresser, and extremely fussy about the labels and style of her clothes too. In her son, Tianyi had her strictest judge, and every time she had to attend a special occasion, she consulted him for his opinion on her outfit. Without his approval, she would not go out of the door.

During his childhood, she was a real playmate to Niuniu. In those days, computer games had only just arrived in Mainland China, and they were extremely basic. You had to plug one end of the cable into the console, and the other end into the TV. Then mother and son sat down to play together, mostly a game called *The Jungle*. They became warriors, not only doing battle but crossing mountains, plunging into seas, chasing away fiery dragons, leaping off precipices. In the course of all this, a firm friendship was cemented which went beyond their relationship as mother and son, or friends. They were comrades, and the bond this created drew them together in their confrontations with Lian.

There was one game, however, that Tianyi never got the hang of, though Niuniu was adept at it: *A Fistful Of Dollars*. An armed guard kills a man and robs him of his money—and revels in it all. Tianyi found playing the game extremely disturbing. When she played the guard, killing and robbing at will, it made her feel that doing evil was immensely pleasurable, stimulating and seductive. But she was never as decisive or as quick off the mark as her son. And if you hesitated for a fraction of a second, the money would be gone. If you did not kill your man, he would kill you. She suddenly thought fearfully that these were the rules by which people played in real life, that moral maxims were no more than a thin veneer, masking the harsh reality beneath—that you had to kill or be killed. Only by understanding this could one become free. And those who had never had any morality or ideals or faith were freest of all. She watched, shocked, as Niuniu well and truly trounced her in *A Fistful Of Dollars*, as he robbed and killed, robbed and killed. He was not weighed down by any sense of responsibility. He loved money, he was cold-blooded, and that was that.

The whole thing filled her with terror. She sensed that today's youth were a brand new generation. When they were grown up, she would be truly old.

15

Zheng's trial was delayed until August. It was Tianyi who got him a lawyer, a man called Xia Shi. Having consulted a friend at the College of Law, she was told that without any doubt Mr Xia was the best in North China. Tianyi was a simple soul in some ways, and simple souls have a way making the complex utterly simple. She did not even bother asking for his phone number, just got his address and went straight there, not forgetting to take with her a gift, some genuine ginseng from the Changbai Mountains.

Mr Xia's residence was not the intimidating place she had imagined. The furnishings were informal, the atmosphere casual. The celebrated Mr Xia was something of an eccentric, but prepared to be indulgent to a young woman like Tianyi. He seemed unsurprised when she turned up without an appointment and did not enquire too closely into her relationship with Zheng, as Tianyi had worried that he would. He simply listened calmly to what Tianyi had to say, and gave a simple answer: 'Yes, I can take on being his defence lawyer. But I need to get my assistant in on this. He's in Henan province at the moment.' And he accepted Tianyi's gift of Changbai ginseng.

Years later, Tianyi realized just how much it had meant to her to find a lawyer like Xia. He was extraordinarily perceptive; his calm questioning told him everything he needed to know, and he could see right into the deepest recesses of her being. After the trial was over, the old man (he was nearly seventy) was left in possession of some potentially explosive documents, the thirty-six folders pertaining to Zheng's case. He did not give them to Zheng's wife, or any of his friends, or even to his parents. He handed them all over to her, to Yang Tianyi, a woman who had no blood or other formal ties to the accused. And he did that because he had seen through her. He believed that she was the right person to keep these folders and that eventually they would pupate like butterflies, and take wing in the form of her stories.

Tianyi was not allowed to be at the trial itself. Yiyi was, as his wife and so were the others who had been active with Zheng. Peng had come back especially to testify in Zheng's defence. Other friends came too.

Zheng's parents were not present, however. His mother, Mrs Ke, phoned Tianyi and asked if she would go over and see them. Of course, Tianyi went straightaway, taking a bag of prawns with her. Prawns were a luxury back then. Tianyi realized, as soon as she arrived, that the old couple had asked her over because they were frantic with worry. Although his father had been a high-ranking military officer, and well able to look after himself, now he was elderly and fragile and sometimes he let his defences drop. Mrs Ke for her part found it most strange that Zheng had had numerous friends, especially from the last few years, who were forever knocking on their door and knew his house as well as their own—and yet the only one who dropped by now was a young woman whom they found rather mystifying. Tianyi was no longer young and, at first glance, was nothing special to look at, but she had a physical presence, something that made you want to trust her and tell your innermost feelings. Mrs Ke felt that Tianyi was worth a second look, and the more she looked, the more she found beauty. Not prettiness, which in any case was confined to the face, but a kind of beauty that emanated from the inside, a kind that blurred someone's age. Mrs Ke felt that it pervaded the room, in a way she had never experienced before. Very early on, she formed an idea (albeit prematurely) about this young woman, *How good it would be if this girl became my daughter-in-law!*

Tianyi sensed the old couple's expectations and did not like them one bit. But she felt she had to play her role, and play it brilliantly, because these were exceptional times. She got dinner ready for them, something she was adept at, washing and chopping the vegetables, shelling and de-veining the prawns, all in complete silence. She did not even clatter the bowls and plates. And all the while, Mrs Ke stood in the doorway of the kitchen, as if she was watching her own daughter-in-law. Tianyi might look too delicate to do the cooking but she actually knew just what she was doing. Mrs Ke watched as Tianyi unhurriedly lit a match, poured oil into the clean wok and stir-fried some chopped onion, lifting and turning the pieces in the smoking pan with the shovel-ladle. As the fragrance rose into the air, Mrs Ke thought what a good girl she was. Why had her son given her up? She wouldn't have meddled ordinarily, but these weren't ordinary times. Why shouldn't she try and make things right for her son? She was an uneducated old woman, with little schooling, but very determined. Once she made up her mind, she went right ahead and did whatever she had decided on. In point of fact, she was stubborn to the point of pig-headedness.

They got news of the case in the afternoon. Peng and a few other friends who had testified came by, and Peng, his eyes red-rimmed, told them what had happened. With three video cameras trained on him, Zheng delivered an impassioned statement. Thus far, this was what Tianyi expected. Zheng was nothing if not eloquent. Several years of practice in university elections had taught him that. What she had not expected was the news that Zheng had contracted hepatitis and it had flared up. Only a gigantic effort of willpower had kept him going in the court. More surprising still, after the judgment was given, Yiyi had flung herself at her husband and made a heart-rending scene. Peng looked disdainful as he recounted the hullabaloo she had kicked up. No one said anything.

Zheng was sentenced to thirteen years. Thirteen years. Longer than the anti-Japanese War and the War of Liberation added together. Tianyi made a rapid calculation: she would be well into her forties by the time he got out, nearing fifty. And Zheng would have given the prime of his life to prison and by the time he was out, he would be finished.

Looking at the tears streaming down Mrs Ke's cheeks, Tianyi knew she must hold her own back, and she did—until the evening when she was alone. Then she cried a small river. Luckily, Lian was away on business. Her cherub Niuniu was sound asleep, so soundly that not even a military band could have woken him. Then, at dead of night when all was quiet, there came a light knock on the door. Tianyi was startled. Had someone betrayed her? Was this the police come to get her? She imagined the arrest warrant, the handcuffs glinting as they were fastened on and she was taken away. It was a nightmare she had had countless times. As she opened the door, however, she felt no fear. What would be, would be. There was no avoiding it.

The man came in bringing a gust of warm air with him. Without waiting for a response from her, he embraced her. She did not have to see his face to know it was Peng. He must have been drinking—his face was flushed and his eyes suffused with red, too. He opened his mouth and tears rolled down his cheeks as he said: 'Tianyi, I can't bear it! I can't bear it!'

What happened next seemed entirely logical. Peng carried Tianyi to the bed and she did not resist. She felt as if she had been drugged. She had a vague feeling that they had suffered so much, these 'fighters for democracy', that she had no good reason, or the strength, to refuse to console him. In her heart of hearts, there was also an opposing voice, but she did not hear it clearly and she did not have time to sort out what she was thinking. It was all happening too fast, everything rational was being stripped away along with her clothes. She just had time to wonder how he had become so adept at taking off women's clothes.

Once she was naked, he knelt in front of her. 'You're so beautiful,' he said. 'You've always been my goddess, but always unattainable. When I was in that damned place in the South, you were the only one I wrote to and you actually sent me books. I flipped through them but I couldn't read them, all I could see was you, and when I thought of you, I ... I used to jerk off ... I never imagined that I would see you again in this life. I can't let you go now. I can't let you go ever again ...'

She could not refuse him. She shut her eyes and tried to imagine that this man caressing her was Zheng. His hands lingered on her breasts, caressing them, sucking them, and they gradually distended and her nipples hardened, and her body, starved of caresses for so long, came back to life. Like all the men who had seen her body, he admired her breasts. Then his muscular hand slid down to that secret place and she suddenly began to tremble.

'What is it?' He sounded anxious.

'Nothing, nothing. Don't talk.' She turned off the bedside light and focused on turning this man into her beloved Zheng. Her Zheng, her tormented, persecuted Zheng. Zheng, who had never once touched her intimately. At the thought of him, her eyes filled with tears.

At the crucial moment, he stopped. 'What is it?' She turned the light back on. 'I don't know, I've gone ... soft,' he mumbled.

Wretchedly, he pulled himself off her and sat up, naked, his face covered in sweat. His penis was so pitifully shrivelled, it looked as if it would never grow erect ever again. She looked away. She did not know why, but the male genitals were still an impenetrable mystery to her, something ugly that she did not want to look at. She still had such horrible memories of her wedding night. She used to dream about penises and, each time, been filled with terror. She was genuinely frightened of them, they had only ever brought her pain and distress.

Peng went to the bathroom and masturbated for a long time, then came back and tried again, but it was hopeless. 'Maybe I got too excited,' he stammered. 'Let's talk instead. Maybe it'll be better if I'm more relaxed.' She forced down her scorn and impatience, and turned over. 'You're just too tired,' she said distantly, 'Let's get some rest.' But Peng was not about to give up. 'No, I'm not tired at all … let's try again, one more time.' 'No,' she sat up and put her pyjamas back on. She did not look at him. It was as if he had vanished into thin air. 'Why don't you get washed and get some sleep? You may not be tired but I am … And anyway, how did you know Lian was away on business?' she flung at him. Then she turned out the light, and went to sleep in her study. She knew that her last comment would keep him awake for a good while.

In the early hours of the morning, she finally heard a light snoring coming from the next-door bedroom. She tossed and turned, her eyes fighting to close, her mind ever more wakeful. Her re-awakened body was still in a state of excitement. She was startled at how easily the flesh could betray the spirit. She reached between her legs and discovered she was dripping wet. An old maid could not write, she thought, or only stuff that was dry as dust. Creativity depended wholly on this mysterious juice, this fruit of the Garden of Eden. The west's concept of passionate love, the east's symbiosis of yin and yang, attested to that ancient truth. Denying it meant denying oneself. And yet here they were, in a society that had 'evolved' to utter barrenness!

The tears welling, she caressed herself fiercely. Her breasts, swollen and hard, her cunt moist and smooth like jade ... her orgasm came quickly. Her pelvis jerked and she came to an urgent, hot-flowing climax. She felt an involuntary quivering in her fingers and toes. Then she gradually relaxed and her body cooled down. She suddenly felt utterly desolate.

What a tragedy to be a woman in this barren society, in this barren epoch. A woman had only herself to depend on, for even this small thing bequeathed to her from ancient times. She buried her head in the bedclothes and wept.

Back in the office, she found a letter lying on the desk. It was from America, from Wright State University, Ohio. An invitation. She read and re-read it, her mind in a whirl. She knew all the English words but could not make sense of them. In the end, she had to take it home for Lian to read it to her.

When he came back from his business trips, he always needed to sleep a whole day. He also swept the bedroom with suspicious eyes. Tianyi accepted it, acting calm, although she secretly found it amusing. It was like when she was a child, hiding some mischief from adults, she even got a malicious enjoyment from it. *I've really gone out on a limb this time, Lian,* she thought. *Now you just see if you can spot it with your beady eye!*

Lian looked at Tianyi's invitation letter and threw it back at her: 'Wright State University in Ohio have invited you to go to America, it's too bad they're not offering to pay.'

'What do you mean?'

'Isn't it clear? An invite where they don't pay is crap!'

'Where are you getting all this bad language from, all of a

sudden?'

'Lian suddenly yelled: 'I'm telling you the truth! The truth is ugly! If you want pretty language, go and find it from someone else!'

He was obviously about to explode with rage, and Tianyi turned away. She went to her study and slammed the door. She could still hear Lian outside. He was yelling: 'I'm telling you Tianyi, we've got this flat through my job. If you crack the walls banging that door, you'll pay for it!'

Tianyi made a hurried phone call, to Tianyue, who had completed her Masters and was home from America. She had changed, grown much prettier, with bright, expressive eyes. It must be love, thought Tianyi. Her sister must be in love.

She was right. Tianyue was involved with someone. Some years ago, she had told Tianyi what was going on in her life, though for a reserved girl like her, that must have been extraordinarily difficult. She said she and Wei had only done in it fifteen times in as many years. Incredible. There was something wrong with Wei, said Tianyue, but he would not admit it. (Actually, Wei once told Tianyi that it was her sister who had the problem.) Tianyi stepped in and made the pair of them go the hospital for a check-up. The results were inconclusive: there was nothing physically wrong with either of them. That just left incompatibility as the cause.

So Tianyue and Wei sat down and negotiated a very private agreement. They never told anyone the details, but the agreement they drew up basically said that they would keep up the appearances of being married but were each free to go their own way. It became clear that this benefited Tianyue because, from then on, she never looked back. Her current lover was called Yang and was thirteen years younger than her.

When Tianyi set eyes on Yang, she did not like him. He was

fair-skinned, on the chubby side, with a small eyes and a turned-down mouth. He was from Hunan and was in Beijing to make money. He did a bit of business and quickly discovered that, to make big bucks in the capital, you needed a foreign language. He enrolled on a very expensive language course, and who should be his teacher but Tianyue.

Yang's boldness and enthusiasm were genuine, though he was a bit like a bull in a china shop. He also lacked perseverance. He was a young man from a small mountain village in Western Hunan, and the moment he set eyes on Tianyue, he saw her as his saviour. Tianyue, for her part, was bowled over by his initial enthusiasm. She and her husband had got so stale, it seemed hard to believe that there was someone as fired up as Yang. Yang did not even trouble to avoid Wei. He spent all his money on expensive food, which he would bring over to their house and set to and prepare for Tianyue. Tianyue and Wei were barely scraping by in those days, and their idea of a treat was going to a café to have a bit of Sichuan spicy food. So eating well felt special. Wei even said quietly to Tianyue that he actually really liked Yang coming to their house because 'he brings pork shoulder steaks with him'. Tianyi had mixed feelings: she was happy for them, but also amused and shocked. She understood why her sister despised Wei; he was happy to accept handouts, even if it meant pimping his own wife. Tianyi thought with relief that Lian may have had a bad temper but at least he had some self-respect.

Gradually, Yang began to push the boundaries of good behaviour. He would lie on their double bed even when Wei was in the house. Wei was angry but did not dare object. If he wanted to continue accepting Yang's largesse, he was hardly in a position to speak his mind. His resentment grew, however and, with no one else to talk to, he finally came to Tianyi to get it off his chest.

He had been tidying the house one day, he told her, and he found a big bag in the cupboard full of condoms. He also said that when Yang was around, even Tianyue had no respect for him. Sooner or later, he and Tianyue would split up for sure, he said.

But Yang was extremely deferential to Tianyi. He certainly knew how to turn on the charm and Tianyi let herself be charmed, and was affable in return. Why on earth should she offend Yang just for Wei's sake? She thought.

On the phone to Tianyue, Tianyi said she was going over there this evening and would take the three of them out to dinner. Tianyue was delighted. It did not matter how much she ate, she was naturally skinny and never put on weight. She easily ate double what Tianyi ate, even though she looked as if she was deprived.

Tianyue was someone who was ruled by her emotions. Towards Tianyi, she was both jealous and admiring at the same time. This little sister of hers seemed like a different generation because of their differing experiences during the Cultural Revolution, even though she was actually only a few years younger. Added to which, Tianyi had always been a strange little sprite of a girl, so terribly intelligent that, in many ways, she made her elder sister feel inferior and she knew it. But her Masters degree and her love affairs had changed her. Tianyi seemed just so-so now; she, Tianyue, had worked hard and was the better woman, certainly more glamorous. Tianyi no longer paid much attention to her appearance, probably because of the child, and had lost her youthful prettiness. It all made Tianyue secretly glad that she was childless. It kept her looking much younger than her years.

They ate dinner at a Uighur restaurant near Tianyue's house. Tianyi discovered to her surprise, as plate after plate of roast meat appeared before them and was devoured, that her sister was uninterested in the Wright State University invitation. It was the two men who were enthusiastic and discussed it in detail. Yang pronounced magisterially: 'First, you should get the agreement of your workplace, then figure out a way of getting a financial guarantor, otherwise you'll have to be your own guarantor.'

'What does that mean?' Tianyi asked.

'Being your own guarantor means photocopying a statement of your savings when you apply for a passport with the police. They just need a statement in dollars, the amount that's written in the invitation letter. You've been invited for six months, right? How much do you need? $8,000, that's it. So long as your statement says $8,000, you should be OK.'

'Good heavens! Where on earth am I going to get $8,000?'

'There's nothing to worry about,' said Yang, sounded like God Almighty. 'Everyone contributes, that's how all my fellow students did it. How much have you got right now?'

'I …' Tianyi was embarrassed to mention it. 'I've only got $2,000.'

'No problem. We'll get together $10,000 within three days. You get ready to deposit what you've got in the bank, and when you're ready, call me and your sister and we'll transfer the rest at the same time.

Yang spoke just as if he were her brother-in-law. But at that instant, to Tianyi, he was more than that—he was her saviour. As soon as she got out of the country, she thought, she could appeal to the world to protect Zheng. Zheng's present predicament was truly terrible.

Three days later, Yang fulfilled his promise. The next step was for her work place to confirm that they would release her. Tianyi put on a show of optimism but was secretly worried. She could not be sure that they would let her go.

Meanwhile, the post-Tiananmen political situation was getting steadily worse. Her colleagues at the academy proposed a march in support of the students. Of course, Tianyi threw herself into it and personally made an 'emergency appeal'. She sounded just like a proper announcer, everyone said. Tianyi was pleased and repeated it to Lian, who replied coldly: 'When are you going to stop being so childish and act like a grown up?' Perhaps not surprisingly, someone took it upon themselves to tape her speech and broadcast it throughout the march. The entire staff of the academy were thus able to hear Tianyi's impassioned plea, delivered in the classic tones of Mao's speech, 'The divergence between Comrade Togliatti and Ourselves'! Back then, all broadcasters sounded like revolutionaries forged in the flames of battle, not like today's mild-mannered anchor men and women.

But it was not the time or the place for revolutionary enthusiasm. One day, Peng insisted on pedalling after her to Fuxingmen Bridge. He leapt off his bicycle and whispered in her ear: 'Don't go on the demonstration. I've just heard the authorities are condemning the protest movement as a "counter-revolutionary riot".' That scared Tianyi, but she had been brought up on revolutionary films, she knew just what traitors looked like and she knew she would never leave the revolutionary ranks to become one. What they were doing might be dangerous but they had to carry on, or how would they face themselves in future? She sent Peng packing and carried on. But those around her must have heard Peng's words, because gradually they melted away. She was utterly scornful of them at the time. Looking back though, she felt that they had been wiser than her, and that Peng had behaved like a real friend that day.

The authorities had turned a blind eye to her part in the appeal, but now she was applying to go abroad and the subject was raised again. Tianyi had never been subject to such scrutiny by the Party Committee and the Personnel Department. Again and again they summoned and interrogated her. The Party Committee members, whom she had always regarded as wimps, questioned her relentlessly. It all boiled down to just two points: 'Who wrote the appeal? Who got you to read it out?'

Of course she could not tell the truth. She had not forgotten the old saying: 'Tell the truth for a lighter sentence, and you'll be in jail for your whole life; refuse to confess, and you'll be out in time for New Year.' She kept her answers simple and consistent: she had seen the appeal lying on the table and recorded it for fun, certainly not especially for the march. No one made her read it and she had no idea who wrote it. They repeated the same questions again and again, and she repeated the same answers. Until eventually she figured that, at worst, they might not let her go to America but what did that matter anyway? Going abroad was not a big deal. Being disloyal was.

She had only ever heard tell of, or read herself, old stories about, the attitude of Chinese people towards political movements, but this was the first time she had seen it with her own eyes, experienced it. She had thought that that era, when people spied on and betrayed each other had passed, never to return. But when the authorities at the academy had gathered together in all their dignity, she saw how their attitude had undergone a 180 degree turn. As each one pontificated in turn, she stared at them, and thought that in just a few days, these people had become unrecognizable. Just a few days before, they had wholeheartedly supported their students, because they did not want to be seen as behind the times. While now, with tears in their eyes and grief in their voices, they searched their souls and expressed the deepest remorse. Good heavens, would this cycle ever be broken?

This was not the right place for her, she thought. She was simply too healthy in body and mind to be this shameless, let alone this slavish. She wanted to leave, she must leave, to live the kind of life she wanted to live. But just as she was thinking this, either because someone from above took pity on her, or because her answers were unshakeable, finally Personnel certified that she had not been involved in any violence. Clutching this piece of paper, she went to the police to arrange her passport.

At that time, the passport office was still housed in a nondescript office in a narrow street near the Forbidden City, Dongjiaomin Xiang. Two police officers, a man and a woman, sat at small tables, behind each of which stretched a long queue. The officers wore severe expressions and their brusque questioning terrified her. As she queued for long hours, time seemed to freeze her into immobility, and every movement required a huge effort. At midday, the officers went off for lunch but the applicants did not dare move, as if budging an inch might shatter even that tiny remnant of hope they clung to. No one talked. Everyone held their forms close to their chest, as if afraid someone might see what they written on it. If they happened to meet someone else's gaze, they immediately looked away.

So off she went to the passport office, filled with enthusiasm. She chose the male officer, figuring it was easier to do business with someone of the opposite sex. Then she discovered that although she could be quick-witted when the situation demanded it, her physical reactions were awkward. Just seeing the police officers made her feel guilty, as if she had something to hide. She didn't know where to put herself. It took six visits before she finally got her passport. On that occasion, she brought a copy of *The Tree of Knowledge* with her, and presented it to the male officer. He looked up at her: 'Hey, if you write stories, why didn't you bring two copies?' Alarmed, she shot a glance at the woman officer, who had taken the book and was flipping through it with keen interest. In her discomfiture, she stammered: 'Next time ... next time, I'll bring you a copy.' She always stammered when she was at her most uncertain.

But there was no next time. A short-term passport was there for her to collect. It gleamed before her eyes and suddenly she was blind to everything else. She certainly never imagined that it would be America, not China, that would bar her way.

The two weeks before she went for her visa interview at the US Embassy she spent preparing her answers until she knew them off by heart and back to front. She carefully read up on the kind of thing the visa officers liked and disliked, and how to deal with them. The day before the interview, she could not sleep, and got up to take three sleeping pills, which finally reduced her to a fuzzy-headed doze. First thing the next morning, she got up and put on a new woollen skirt, with a grey stripe on a dull red background, which Peng had bought her down south. She wore an unusual necklace, made of black threads, interwoven with tiny shells. Thinking back on it, she felt she had got her outfit wrong. She should have worn something more ordinary. But it was impossible to foresee everything, things happened so randomly. In the event, on her first visit to the American visa office, she blundered irretrievably. All the same, some things could only be blamed on fate. Previously, in the Chinese passport office, Tianyi had been able to make her choice between a male and a female officer, but in the American visa office, there was no way she could choose her officer. So when she was called to Window 3, she had a gut feeling that she was finished.

Many friends had warned her to avoid the old woman at Window 3 like the plague. She would refuse your visa application for sure, especially if you were a woman. Yang had made a point of telling her that if she was called to Window 3, she would be better off playing deaf, and missing her turn. She almost did that, but was overcome with a sudden urge to take her chances. Maybe she would be lucky.

She approached the window to which she had been summoned, with all the poise she could muster, in the manner of a gallant Communist Party martyr in a film epic. She saw the legendary 'old woman'. She was not old, forty-six or forty-seven at the most, but she was scrawny and old-maidish. Tianyi registered the frown lines on her forehead with trepidation. She would never be able to stand up to a woman with frown lines like that.

The 'old woman' questioned her closely, first in Chinese, then in English. She tried to answer in English, and the woman appeared to be listening earnestly, nodding away. Tianyi felt better and better, until she finally got out the entire spiel she had prepared, in fluent English. Finally, the old woman stopped asking questions and picked up the sheaf of papers as if she was going to sign on the spot. Then suddenly she put another question, one which Tianyi did not hear properly. She said: 'So, apart from your child, you wouldn't need to come back to China at all, would you?' The question would have sounded convoluted enough in Chinese, let alone in English, let alone after such gentle questioning. Tianyi fell right into her trap and, nodded dumbly even though she had not understood, thus, in a single instinctive response, undoing all her previous efforts. The woman's face grew serious. Tianyi realized she had committed a fatal error.

Her short-term passport was stamped with a visa refusal. At that instant, she suddenly thought that the hatchet-faced visa officer was just like the soft-faced woman in the academy's Personnel Department. It did not matter whether you lived in the east or the west, it was all essentially the same, people counted for nothing when it came to national interests. Both the policewoman and this woman were the padlock on the shackles, the guardians of authority. She had schemed and fought so hard for freedom—but ultimately she was to be disappointed.

Lian, however, got a visa with no problem at all. Three months after Tianyi was turned down, he went to America as part of an investigative team from the Planning Commission.

His first letter from America was a long one. He gave her a blow-by-blow account of everything that had happened. He had travelled on his own and had no sooner got off the plane than he discovered he had lost the address where he was staying. A kind-hearted elderly American couple took him under their wing and to a hotel. He was so grateful that he gave them one of the small gifts he had taken with him, a satin pincushion in the shape of a pumpkin dolly. He could not say enough good things about the Americans he met—and enough bad things about the overseas Chinese. He finished by adding portentously that although America was wonderful, it belonged to the Americans, just the same as China belonged only to the Chinese.

Tianyi had to admit to herself that Lian was quite clever. A lot of what he said and many of the conclusions he came to were pretty much right. She even thought that Lian would be best-suited to a job with a think-tank—he was excellent at dreaming up wonderful ideas for other people, no good for anything else.

After he went, leaving Tianyi and Niuniu at home, she felt a sense of release. Like many people, she had an instinct for avoiding freedom and another instinct that longed for freedom. Now, she found being stuck at home for too long unbearable.

Tianyi took up the activity she had been good at as a child, painting. She had not lifted a brush for many years, and soon found herself engrossed in it. Apart from a couple of visits each week to the academy and caring for Niuniu, she spent the rest of the time painting. She felt inspired: she used abstract lines to express her life and loves, in a way that only she could understand. She found the fineness of this technique intoxicating, and was completely and utterly absorbed in her own little world. If there is real happiness in this world, then that summer of 1990, Tianyi found it.

When, a month later, friends came to visit Tianyi, they were flabbergasted at the paintings that filled the apartment. After a long pause, there was a chorus of exclamations: 'You must have an exhibition! It would be such a pity not to show these paintings!' So, that autumn the Yang Tianyi exhibition was shown at the Central Gallery of Art. Almost all Tianyi's friends in Beijing attended the launch, including one that Tianyi had never imagined in a million years would come. Her name was Qing, and she was twenty-three years old. Peng brought her, and introduced her as Zheng's girlfriend when he was in the South.

Tianyi had mixed feelings. On the one hand, it was quite normal that Zheng should have had a girlfriend—after all, he was a hot-blooded young man full of life and energy. On the other hand, it niggled her that Zheng had never mentioned the girl to her. For 'Zheng's girlfriend' suddenly to spring out of nowhere was hard to swallow. But Qing was a very likeable young woman. She immediately treated Tianyi with a warmth that the latter, who hid a soft heart under her sharp tongue, found hard to resist.

Qing's rather flat face, large eyes and mouth that tilted up at the corners as she spoke made her look like a doll. She said she knew all about Tianyi—on her first trip to Beijing, she and Zheng had cycled with a group of friends to Haidian and on the way, Zheng had suddenly braked, pointed to a grey tower block and said: 'That's where Tianyi lives.' 'Take us to meet her,' said Qing, but Zheng said firmly; 'No, I can't do that.' Peng had said with a wicked laugh: 'You don't know but this woman's Zheng's secret goddess. He'd never agree to take you ordinary mortals to see her!' Zheng had flushed and then lapsed into silence, said Qing. She had been very struck by that.

'That was when I knew who he really loved,' she concluded. Tianyi felt her heart swell. Then the tears came.

Qing's candour made Tianyi take the girl under her wing. From the autumn of 1990 to the spring of 1991, when Lian returned from America, she stayed at their house. The two women got along well enough. Qing was good-hearted, although she had a young girl's failings—was sometimes scatter-brained, loud-mouthed, unable to look after herself, and so on. But on the whole she was a good girl. What most touched Tianyi was that while the exhibition was on, Qing spent two whole evenings mounting the paintings one by one. Even Tianyi got fed up with the mounting, but Qing kept on working away. So as soon as the exhibition closed, Tianyi agreed to Qing's request: she would take the girl to meet Zheng's parents.

The exhibition made Tianyi one of the hottest artists in town. After the turmoil of 1989 through 1990, the autumn of that year should have brought peace and quiet, but the special exhibition at the Central Gallery of Art had everyone at a fever-pitch of excitement. In the Visitors Book, someone had written in large letters: New! Wild! Amazing! Early one morning, the Chinese art world's leading critic, Wu Mengshi, paid a visit. The old man was taken around in his wheelchair and, when he saw the paintings, his eyes lit up. He nodded, and muttered to himself: 'Only someone without formal art training would dare to paint like this.' Tianyi shot a quick look at him and felt that this was high praise.

Then two art dealers asked to buy the three largest paintings in *The Tree of Knowledge* series, offering to pay $3,000 for each. Tianyi was suitably impressed but, having thought long and hard, decided that she could not bear to part with them. Each was a one-off, there would never be another one like it. Each line, she thought, was drawn from her flesh and blood. She could not let the paintings go. Of course the money was good, but she felt money had little to do with her.

But one man's arrival proved to be a turning point for Tianyi. His name was Feng Dayuan, and he was the father of Kexing, whose lead role in the film of *The Tree of Knowledge* had made her a household name. In 1990, Dayuan had just taken over as deputy director of a film production company. He had already taken note of Tianyi and *The Tree of Knowledge* in his previous post, heading up its literary department. This was no thanks to his daughter, who was highly ambitious and never recommended any works to him, especially when it was by someone of the same sex. Kexing by dint of toadying to all and sundry, did make it abroad and became the first actress from the Chinese mainland to make it in Hollywood. Of course, in a dozen years there, she only managed to play walk-on parts and, even though she appeared scantily-clad, her body was too scrawny to attract attention.

Dayuan had not come to see the pictures, but to meet the author of *The Tree of Knowledge*. At their first meeting, he was disappointed. Dayuan liked three kinds of women: the young and pretty ones; those who were older but were sexy and flirtatious enough to pique his interest; and those who were not pretty but were young and unsophisticated, had a personality and were articulate, even a bit mouthy. Sadly for him, Yang Tianyi fell into none of these categories. She was young and female but physically, she looked matronly. Her writing was beautiful and highly individual, but as a person, she was neither pretty nor did she have much personality. Older women, even at thirty-six or thirty-seven, could pass as quite young if they looked after their appearance. But Yang Tianyi's outfit was dowdy, she had a sallow complexion and dark circles under her eyes, and seemed exhausted. Whatever was wrong with the woman?

Tianyi was a woman ruled by her emotions: when she was happy, she was combative and brimmed with energy; and when she was depressed, she looked haggard and dragged herself around as if she could hardly stand upright. Dayuan must have caught Tianyi at her lowest moment. Fortunately, the success of the exhibition lifted her spirits just a little, and banished some of the shadows from her face, allowing a ray of light through. Dayuan walked around the exhibition illuminated by that light. When he came back to see her again, he had made up his mind what he was going to say to her. His producer's eye had unexpectedly been caught by one picture. He wanted someone who could paint like that, it did not matter if she was a rubbish-collector. So for the moment, he suspended his judgment of her as a woman.

Dayuan was not particularly knowledgeable, or enthusiastic, about art. Put simply, he liked that picture because it was the spitting image of his daughter, the actress Kexing. In the picture, she was holding a bass guitar in her arms, her face curtained in sleek black hair, below which her white neck was visible. The tones of the picture were cool, the background a violet-blue colour, the kind of colour the Russian painter Vrubel so loved. Dayuan did not really understand the finer points of the painting, but he knew that was the colour his daughter most loved. How he wished he could fly her back from the other side of the world to look at the picture!

So, for the sake of a painting, this middle-aged 1990s director approached this woman who otherwise fell far short of his standards, and spoke: 'Yang Tianyi, would you like to join my production company?'

Tianyi felt this was her lucky break. Leaving her sinecure at the Academy of Letters, and making a new start, all proved very easy. Once she had sorted out the paperwork, she prepared to take Qing to see Zheng's parents. That morning, Tianyi helped the girl with her makeup. She knew how to apply make-up but only seemed able to use her skills on other people.

Qing was a typical provincial girl from a modest family, unsophisticated and without much taste. She had nothing suitable to wear, so Tianyi opened her wardrobe and picked out a suit in silvery blue with phoenix tail flowers embroidered on it in silver thread. Then she took out the necklace of black thread interwoven with shells, and got Qing to put it on. She put her hair up for her and put the finishing touches to her makeup. Qing smiled at herself in the mirror: 'It's true what they say, Tianyi, people need clothes the way a horse needs a saddle! I'm ready to audition for the Central Academy of Drama now!'

Tianyi put on a pearly-gray pencil skirt with an embroidered linen top, and they set off in good spirits. On the way, they bought some gifts of food. Tianyi thought that if Zheng's parents were going to visit him in prison this month, they could take him some. But nothing worked out as she had expected.

When Zheng's parents saw Qing, they looked anything but happy. Tianyi did her best to break the ice, but they were extremely reserved towards her. Tianyi racked her brains but could not imagine what the problem was. Qing seemed oblivious, as she smiled and chatted to Tianyi's mother. Mrs Ke peeled a juicy Sichuan orange for her, but it seemed to Tianyi that she was only going through the motions. In between mouthfuls of orange, Qing talked on and on about Zheng. Then she said: 'Tianyi, you go home, I'm going to spend a couple of days with Zheng's Mum and Dad.' Tianyi saw the beseeching look Mrs Ke gave her, then the older woman said: 'Tianyi, maybe next time ... The thing is the house is in a terrible mess, I haven't cleared up.'

Qing butted in before Tianyi could speak: 'Mrs Ke, don't worry, I'll do it for you. It's no problem, I'm really good at cleaning and tidying.' She smiled sweetly at Tianyi. 'You go on home, Tianyi. You've been cooking my meals for a couple of months, you deserve a rest.'

Tianyi walked out into the courtyard feeling utterly helpless. Qing seemed to have cast herself in the role of the Hua family's future daughter-in-law. Of course, there were a few problems with this but Tianyi could not bring herself to break the truth to her. For a start she had no idea how Zheng felt. Qing's version of events was that Zheng really did love her, and when his parents told him that Qing was with them when they visited him in prison, then it would be a huge boost for his morale. Also, if Tianyi absolutely had to be the one to puncture her illusions, Qing would never forgive her. The girl would be convinced that she, Tianyi, was putting obstacles in her way out of jealousy. Tianyi felt the only thing she could do was to back off.

As it was a Saturday, Tianyi went to pick up Niuniu, who was now at a different nursery where he boarded, coming home only on Wednesdays and Saturdays. She took him straight to a restaurant where they often ate because, even though it was a bit small, it was spotlessly clean, and offered good home-cooking. Niuniu loved it, and normally ate well. But today he picked at his food, and the reason was simple: Auntie Tianyue and her boyfriend Uncle Yang were eating with them.

Tianyue knew the restaurant well, because every time she visited, if they had nothing good to eat at home, Tianyi and Lian brought her here. The trouble was that Niuniu did not like his aunt, and liked Yang even less. As soon as he saw them, his little face clouded over. Tianyi, who had always thought that her son had a tendency to be grumpy, had the greatest difficulty in making him to say hello to his aunt and uncle. Some people just took an instinctive dislike to one another for some reason, and that was how it was for Niuniu and Tianyue. But compared to how he was with Yang, he was politeness itself to his auntie. Yang he treated as his natural-born enemy.

Tianyue was radiant that evening. She said to her sister: 'Yang and I have both taken the English test, Tianyi. Do a reading for us and tell us if we've passed?'

Amongst her circle of friends, Tianyi was famous for doing readings from the I Ching. But that night, before she had had time to do one for her sister, Tianyi had a strange dream. A glittering golden tiger was standing at the entrance to a tunnel, looking back with a great yearning in its eyes. Then it waved its tail and it was as if a pure gold fan splayed open, and folded together again. Then it walked into the darkness and slowly disappeared. She dreamed it at four o'clock in the morning. Dreams she had at that hour were generally very accurate. Her sister was born in the Year of the Tiger and the dream clearly meant that her sister could go, and that going would bring her good fortune.

When Tianyi did the reading, next day, the results confirmed this even more clearly. The trigrams told her: *In autumn the tiger's coat is gorgeous and it is a favourable time to wade the great river.* Exactly what her dream had said. So Tianyi called Tianyue and told her: 'You can go. This autumn.'

By the middle of August, Tianyue had still not received her

acceptance from the college. This was unusual and Tianyue had almost given up hope, but Tianyi encouraged her: 'You will go, just be patient.' 'Of course I will, but not this time, right?' said Tianyue. 'No, it will be this time,' Tianyi insisted.

One day at the end of August, Tianyue finally received her letter. The envelope contained a brief apology too, saying that they had written the address wrong and the letter had been returned undelivered, and they had had to re-send it, and so on and so forth. The first thing Tianyue did was to phone Tianyi. 'You got it absolutely right, Sis!' she exclaimed.

16

Qing left Beijing at about the same time as Tianyue. She did not seem happy to be going. 'Tianyi, I'll never forget how good you were to me,' she said. 'But I just don't know why Zheng's Mum took against me. I never asked for anything except just a word from Zheng and I would have waited for him, I would have waited thirteen years, but I didn't get a single word. I reckon that his parents never said anything to him about me. What do you think, Tianyi?'

Tianyi slowly shook her head. To be honest, she did not know why Zheng's parents had been so cold to Qing, either. Was it that they just didn't like her? Even if they didn't, they must see that Qing had travelled all the way from South China to Beijing for him, and deserved a little courtesy and warmth. As these thoughts passed through her head, Tianyi tried to comfort her: 'Don't think like that, there's probably a lot more going on than you imagine. You know he's still married to Yiyi, even if they don't have feelings for each other. His parents have fallen out with her, but she is still legally his wife. Even his Mum and Dad can't do anything about that. And they're old, they might even be worried that a divorce would be messy. After all, they're getting on in years, and things upset them. If Yiyi made a fuss, it would be terrible for them, wouldn't it?'

Qing was silent for a long time. Then she said: 'I don't agree with you, Tianyi. You see, his mother...she just doesn't like me. It's true. She doesn't like anything I do. If I touch something in their house, she looks like thunder. She won't even let me wash the bowls, it's as if I'll bring the family bad luck by touching them.'

Tianyi could not help bursting into giggles. Oh my god, she thought, mothers- and daughters-in-law ...!'

'What are you laughing at, Tianyi?

'Just at the way you described it. That's enough, girl, you go off and live a good life and if I ever see him one day, I'll speak up for you.'

Tears streamed down Qing's face as she said goodbye. She would miss her friend and mentor so much. She had been like an older sister to her. When would she ever find someone like her again?

But Tianyi was no saint. True, she had done something most women would not have done, made a huge effort and taken her former boyfriend's girlfriend under her wing, but deep down she was not happy about it. Perhaps that was when her feelings of closeness to Zheng began gradually to fade. A man as attractive as Zheng was always going to have countless girls openly in love with him, or pining in secret. But Tianyi was a proud woman and she had no intention of being yet another of his admirers. She would rather be a true friend in his hour of need. She remembered when she was a young girl reading Balzac's *La Cousine Bette*. One bit had made a particular impression on her: Lisbeth quotes the Old Testament story where the rich man has whole flocks but 'the poor relation has one ewe-lamb which is all her joy.' She preferred to be that one ewe-lamb.

Tianyi dreamed of being loved deeply by one man, a man that she loved and that she was not competing with anyone else over. But this seemed impossible in a society where every individual, particularly someone who stood out for some reason, was surrounded by crowds of others. Unless they were on a desert island, of course, or in prison, as was the case right now. She thought that when Zheng came out of prison would be the time to break with him. She could imagine the number of young women who would descend on him when he came out. But she would turn and leave without allowing herself to look back, like the mermaid who saved the prince. Unless ... unless her prince cast off everyone else and came in pursuit of her, and asked her to marry him.

Qing had no sooner left than Lian returned. Someone called from his work to tell her that he would be back that night, around two o'clock in the morning Beijing time. The office bus would arrive at half past ten. Tianyi got Niuniu ready, took thick jackets for them both and set off. On the bus, Lian's colleagues kept asking: 'Niuniu, have you been missing your daddy?' But Niuniu refused to open his mouth.

Tianyi knew what her son was thinking: Why has he come back so quickly? Her cherubic little boy, plump as a doll, had been jealous of his father from when he was tiny. It was not just that he used start crying if he touched his father's moustache in bed at night. It went much further. 'Wait till I'm grown up and I'll mince Dad up into meat pancakes and take a chunk out of him.' That was the kind of thing that came out of this sweet kid's mouth.

Tianyi found it funny. She really had no idea when this animosity between father and son had started. Lian was strict with Niuniu, that was true, but he adored his son. Tianyi tried to redress the balance by telling the boy: 'Daddy loves you. Daddy's put much more time and effort into looking after you ...' But Niuniu turned a deaf ear.

It was the early hours, past three o'clock, before Lian walked through the Nothing to Declare channel and Niuniu had been sound asleep for some time. Tianyi, leaning on the barrier, stared as he emerged clad in denim jacket and jeans. The outfit really did not suit him, he just looked awkward. As he wove his way through the crowd towards her, she saw that the sun had burned his round face much darker than usual. *Is this really my husband?* She wondered. *So much picking and choosing and this is who I ended up with.*

Yet he still felt like family, even though he was ugly, awkward, dull, wrong in all sorts of ways, compared to all the handsome guys she used to go out with. For years to come, she would have conflicting feelings about Lian: she felt close to him but uncomfortable with him at the same time. It was an odd feeling. If they were apart, she quickly forgot even what he looked like. Then she saw him again, and there was no one but him.

He really was her family. Jetlag had not yet caught up with him, and when they arrived home they sat up talking until daybreak. He had brought her a complete set of Italian gold jewellery, had spent several hundred dollars on his purchase. He told her about his colleagues' astonished reaction. She could believe it. This was the early 1990s, and very few people like them, educated but not wealthy, could afford stuff like this. Suddenly her spirits lifted a little. No matter what, I still come first for Lian, she thought. Even his beloved son is only getting a Gameboy. But a few days later, something happened that astonished her.

Peng brought a guest over, and not just any old guest either. Tianyi recognized him instantly; he was one of Zheng's closest friends, Tong. A short man with a broad forehead, he bore a striking resemblance to Bukharin in the film, *Lenin in 1918*. She had nicknamed him Bukharin and he had laughed and acknowledged it. He seemed a good-tempered sort—only a very few friends knew he was prone to terrifying explosions of rage. He had been convicted of assaulting his ex-wife and scarring her face for life, but he did not serve a sentence because his wife refused to press charges. The wife told her parents from her hospital bed: 'Don't cause trouble for him. He's a good man.'

Tong was as spontaneous by nature as Zheng. He had met his wife when he was sent to a commune in Inner Mongolia in the Cultural Revolution. He fell madly in love and they courted on horseback. It was most romantic. But the problems started in Beijing.

When they came back to the city, his wife, Ying, suddenly discovered that Tong was shorter than she was, by a good head. Other discoveries followed: the attractions of city life for instance, and the fact that her husband was not god's gift to women, after all. She could not find a job and that bothered her too. She started arguing with Tong, until the latter, who still loved her deeply, began to feel that there must be another man coming between them. The anxiety caused by his suspicions had the effect of making him impotent. In despair, he began to tail her. Finally, his patience snapped. One freezing winter night after he had been following her for a whole day, he caught up with her and slashed her face with a knife. 'You want to be another Carmen? Let me help you be her!' he shouted. (*Carmen* featured a lot in popular culture back then.)

However, what added to the drama was that the wife with the slashed face refused to bring charges against him. It was as if her husband had proved his love with this action. Men would never understand the twists and turns of women's logic.

Like Peng, Tong had fled south, returning to testify for Zheng at his trial. However in Tianyi's house, he did not get the kind of welcome Peng received. When Tong began spouting to Tianyi the kind of fiery rhetoric popular in the protests of a few months previously, Lian launched into an attack on him. Lian had had enough and, face to face with yet another 'revolutionary' whom he did not know particularly well, his antipathy boiled over. Only Tianyi knew Lian's rages. Peng and Tong had never seen anything like it. Subdued by his violent outburst, they made an ignominious exit.

But Tong was nothing if not devious. A few days later, he came to Tianyi's house again and put a photocopied document on the table. 'Have a look at that,' he said. Tianyi took one look and realized what it was: Lian's 'personal report', written for his bosses on his return from America. He wrote that when he left China he realized how great his homeland and its Communist Party were. 'This has spread like wildfire,' said Tong with a sneer. 'For the authorities, he's become their knight in shining armour. They've distributed the document to every departmental Party Committee.'

Tianyi flushed scarlet with humiliation. For a whole day, she did not eat a bite of food or say a single word and, that evening, she put the Italian jewellery back in Lian's drawer. She lay awake all night, staring at the ceiling. A feeling of utter desolation took hold of her.

17

Less than a month after Tianyi transferred to work at the film production company, the head of the literature department stepped down. A new man was sent to take over, one was said to have studied overseas and had a doctorate in popular communications. He was clearly not interested in being a new broom, contenting himself with calling a meeting of all the staff. He was younger than she imagined, just a year older than her. His name was Wei Qiang, and he was very tall, at nearly six foot, slim but solidly-built, with broad, level shoulders. His hair was neatly combed, he wore a baggy shirt in unbleached cotton, and he was fine-featured but with a determined look ... he was just the kind of man Tianyi found most attractive.

Six months went by and Qiang, now settled in the job, set Tianyi a task: 'Yang Tianyi, you can write a screenplay for us. Didn't you write *The Tree of Knowledge* in the mid-eighties? Write a love story even better than *The Tree of Knowledge*, right?' Tianyi looked at him. 'OK,' she said.

When Tianyi agreed to something, she threw herself into the task. From then on, she worked long hours on the project. It was exhausting, but she thought, *I'm doing this for Qiang.* She surprised even herself: she would never have been so passionate about it if she was doing it for herself, but because it was for someone else, even an imaginary person, she would put herself under immense pressure, working until she was physically and mentally exhausted. But she avoided close contact with Qiang, keeping her distance in just the same way as she had nurtured a silent crush on boyfriends in her youth. *He's an intelligent man,* she thought, *he doesn't need things explaining to him.*

Throughout her life, Tianyi had misunderstood men. She had always tried to conquer them through the beauty of her mind. She overlooked the fact that what almost all men wanted was a physical relationship.

Work threw Qiang and Tianyi together a great deal, and she could see that he was interested in her. He no doubt saw the adoring looks she could not conceal, but he pretended not to. He was married, after all, and he was her boss. All the same, he found plenty of opportunities to spend time with her. For instance, they had a friend in common, a man called Ren Dong, writer of the novel, *Blame.*

The first time she met Dong was at Xiao'ou's house, but he had made little impression on her. They met again, on subsequent occasions, and she discovered that he was by no means the long-haired, extrovert yuppie he posed as—in fact he was rather shy and retiring. But he was also very amusing, always delivering high-sounding maxims and apparently convinced (this was funniest of all) that he was such a celebrity that even the country's decision-makers were interested in him. Once he said with the utmost earnestness: 'So-and-so says that Dong must be handled calmly and a solution must be found. You see? If so-and-so says that, then what have I got to worry about?' Tianyi and Qiang looked at each other, then Tianyi burst out laughing, and a chuckle even escaped the normally serious Qiang. All the same, Dong reacted with the utmost gravity: 'What are you laughing at? It's true! You can go and check at his office, the director told me in person!' Helpless with laughter, Tianyi said: 'Oh, Dong, you must be the most self-deluding person on the planet!'

One of the effects of Dong's buffoonery was to draw Tianyi

and Qiang closer. Whenever he commissioned scripts, Qiang took Tianyi with him, ostensibly because 'Tianyi knows a lot of writers.' The real reason was that the two of them understood and were comfortable with each other.

One evening in springtime, Dong invited them out to dinner. The three of them went to a restaurant serving Demoli Fish Stew, near Beijing Zoo. A pleasant feature of this smart restaurant, with its brand-new resin-carved white chairs and tables, was that the food was served outdoors. They were well into springtime now and the breeze was soft. Tianyi felt as if her long-frozen heart had come back to life again. A few sips of red wine and she felt an uprush of heat through her body. Then she mocked herself, *Spring may be the time for love, but I'm all of 37 years old!* She sneaked a glance at Qiang, sitting opposite her. He was staring at her with those dark eyes, normally sardonic, but just now full of warmth.

A few days later, he called her into his office. It was a plainly furnished room, no doubt intentionally so. 'Have you heard of the novel *Old City*? It's had a lot of media hype. Can you ask around and find out who's publishing it and try and get us a copy. You know everyone in the literary world. Get straight onto it.'

Of course she had heard of it. *Old City's* author was the famous Yu Wusheng. There had been huge media hype even before it hit the bookshelves. For the publishers to hype up a book like this, pre-publication, was a relatively new phenomenon, and Tianyi found the whole thing strange. She never imagined that 'media hype' would become such a durable phenomenon in the book world, one which refused to die.

Old City had been widely headlined in the newspapers as, *'Ten years in the making ... the modern-day Red Chamber Dream,'* and so on. Actually, in spite of the novelty of this media hype, it made little impact. Most ordinary folk just ignored it. On the other hand, the author's name was very well-known, it almost advertised itself. His novel *The Snare of Love* had been adapted into a hugely popular TV series which had the entire population glued to their TV screens, handkerchiefs at the ready. All of this spurred Qiang to take a punt on *Old City*—he badly needed to make his mark in the company.

Tianyi had the failing common to so many women, that she would do anything for the man she loved. And she had another failing too, one few women did, and that was pride. There was no way she wanted the man to know just how much she was doing for him, as if he would respect her less if he knew. That was why she had particularly liked the story *Letter from an Unknown Woman* by Stefan Zweig. The heroine was a girl in her early teens whose unrequited love for a certain man lasted her whole life—the man did not even know who she was. Finally, on her deathbed, she wrote the man a letter, pouring out her feelings. And what a love it was! It put traditional love stories like *The Red Chamber Dream*, firmly in the shade! For a very long time, Tianyi was fixated on one-sided love, secretly convinced that it was the only true and beautiful form of love, the acme of love in fact. So much beauty and suffering emerged from loving and not receiving love in return; unrequited love gave the lover so much, forcing her to strip away the mask and expose the lies that lurked in her subconscious. That kind of beauty and suffering was absolutely authentic. As a writer, Tianyi was convinced of that. Over the years, she had revelled in the pain of platonic love, unquestioning love that asked for nothing in return. For Tianyi, the love that lived and died in her heart alone, had grown into an enormous tree, nourishing her soul, nurturing her creative urges. The trouble was that worldly relationships gave her nothing, and never would.

She did not know if she was in love again. Some vague thing swelled in her heart, swelled erratically and inexplicably until it completely took her over. Around then she received her first screenplay fee and she invited Qiang to a meal in a restaurant in Muxidi, just west of the centre of town, old-fashioned but clean. As he got off the metro, he saw her waiting for him, clearly anxious, waving a frantic greeting, anything but graceful and relaxed. She was wearing an ill-fitting crepe georgette, pale pink short-sleeved blouse, over a black skirt she was fond of. Her new glasses seemed constantly in danger of sliding down her nose and every time she spoke, she had to keep pushing them back again, a gesture that he found almost comical. Then he stopped finding her comical and began to compare her to all the glamorous actresses he was normally surrounded with. This middle-aged woman in front of him seemed to give off a wholly different aura, one that was intriguingly unfamiliar. Qiang, who knew a thing or two about seductive women, felt Tianyi lacked all seductiveness because she was incapable of dissembling, and yet was peculiarly seductive for that very reason.

She had brought some gifts for him. And what gifts! Eight weighty cans of eight-treasure rice, a Playboy T-shirt, a Reebok neck tie, an imported cigarette lighter. As she laid them all before him, he wondered if it was simply to show how grateful she was for the work he had put her way, or was there something more? The canned eight-treasure rice had just come on the market and was a luxury. She had brought such a lot no doubt envisaging how pleasurable it would be for a man living on his own, as he was, to go home and relax on his sofa, and eat a piping hot bowl of it.

Qiang could not help being touched. His wife and child were living abroad and when he was not at work, time hung heavy on his hands. He was a highly intelligent man, but he had the kind of intelligence that would never become wisdom. Wisdom required something a little bit more than intelligence, something of a different quality. A moral quality. Be that as it may, Qiang was very acute, indeed ruthless, when it came to other people's characters. He had seen through Tianyi instantly. She might write good love stories but her knowledge of love was purely theoretical, her practical experience in these matters very superficial. She had not had many deep-going relationships, and was especially inexperienced where sex was concerned. She was so innocent, still like a girl, even though she was a mother. He had once joked that she acted as if she was suffering the pangs of first love. She was so startled that she nearly dropped her glasses on the floor. It was as if he had found that chink in her armour.

Qiang began to be interested in this woman who wrote about love yet clearly did not understand it, who had reached middle age yet had the mentality of a girl. He pursued her with phone calls, on any pretext that came to mind. They were very relaxed in these conversations, forever cracking risqué jokes, although at work they kept up a dignified appearance as if, face to face, they were two completely different people. Sometimes they were on the phone for a couple of hours, or more. It has to be said that Lian was remarkably tolerant of this, no doubt because he had absolute trust in his wife. After all, he had never had any cause to complain.

There was also another reason: he was quietly preparing to quit his government job and start work for a commercial company. To his surprise, the 'personal report' he had worked so hard on after his return from America had not received the rapturous reception he had anticipated, even after it was cascaded to the other departmental Party Committees. He had the impression that his superiors were not going to get around to promoting him for a while. So he decided to move to B.O. Holdings, a company that was making a lot of money. Post-America, Lian had made up his mind to become rich and powerful, like so many of his contemporaries. He was so fixated on the idea that he hardly noticed his wife spending hours chatting on the phone. So Lian started work as Deputy CEO in charge of Finance in the kind of big company where so many people dreamed of getting a job in the mid-nineties. The company CEO, Qiankuan, was a good friend of his. In the 1980s, he had often dropped by with his wife, lured there by Tianyi's fragrant roast chicken.

Qiankuan was originally from Hunan province, and was an only child like Lian. There, the similarities ended: Qiankuan was tall and slender, and carried himself with an easy grace. His wife, Yufan, had a figure like a model, and was ultra-fashionable. Tianyi was fond of Yufan and always liked trying out some new delicacy on them. When Yufen was pregnant, Tianyi felt that she should make a special effort to be kind to them as neither sets of grandparents were in Beijing. Very soon, the couple were treating Tianyi's house as their second home, dropping in whenever they felt like it. The two men would go outside to talk politics and economics, while the women stayed inside chatting. So when Qiankuan was head-hunted by the B.O. Chairman of the Board, the first person he thought of was his old mate, Lian.

Everybody wanted to be rich nowadays and Tianyi was no exception. She and Lian had been married ten years and Niuniu was now nine. She felt it was time to draw a line under their hand-to-mouth existence. This has got to stop, she thought, looking around her cramped, shabby study. She had had enough of visitors staring and exclaiming: 'So this is where you do your writing?!'

Lian's new job brought a succession of changes—first, he started bringing home presents from clients, followed by gift vouchers, then one brilliantly sunny day, a shiny blue Chevrolet drew up in the courtyard below their apartment. Niuniu had always had an eye for cars. Even as a small child, he could tell one make from another, however far away they were. Standing at the window, he shouted in excitement: 'Mum! Come quick! Dad's got a car!'

Tianyi and her son stood close together at the window and watched as Lian leapt out. He stood there and took out of his pocket a rectangular thing with an antenna. 'Hello?' they heard him say into it, and then the house phone rang. That was how Tianyi discovered that the rectangular thing was a mobile phone, then called a Dageda, or Big Bro Phone. When Tianyi and Niuniu got into the car, they learned that it had a phone too, a car phone. And then … the young driver looked around with a smile, and Lian said to Niuniu: 'Say hello to Uncle Xiaoming. Tianyi, this is Xiaoming.' Tianyi nearly jumped out of her skin: he was the spitting image of Zheng as a young man, perhaps even more handsome. There was something very noble in the way he held himself. Where on earth did that come from?

Bursting with pride, Lian took his wife and child to the Dragon's Vein Hot Springs in Xiaotangshan, on the outskirts of the city. Tianyi and Niuniu were thrilled at the sight of the pools filled with jade-green water. In the changing room, Tianyi looked at herself in the mirror. She had put on a lot of weight, she discovered, and not just in her chunky arms and legs, but in her already generous bosom too. Red with embarrassment, she draped herself in a swimming towel before venturing out. She instinctively felt that she did not want the driver, Xiaoming, to see her half-naked.

The water was delicious. It spurted from the fountains with enough force to knock you over if you stood too near. Lian and Niuniu splashed each other energetically, and Tianyi found another spot where she could swim. She did a few circuits then found the hot pool to soak in. Comfortably relaxed, she stretched her arms wide and floated lazily on her back, quite unaware of how seductive this made her look. After a little while, she felt a pair of eyes on her. She sneaked an uneasy glance in that direction and met Xiaoming the driver's bright gaze. He seemed even more embarrassed than she did, flushed scarlet, and looked mutely away. Tianyi decided it was time to get out—although that exposed even more of her body to view.

In the interval between swims that day, they had lunch at the hot springs restaurant, an open-air eating-area set with chairs and tables between the pools. It was simple home-style food too, but today it tasted especially delicious, perhaps because swimming had given them an appetite. Lian ordered stewed beancurd, stir-fried wild greens, Mao-style red-cooked pork, asparagus and 'vegetarian roast goose', actually made of sheets of beancurd. This they demolished in no time at all, and Lian had to order two more dishes, catfish with aubergine, and shredded pork vermicelli. When this, in turn, had been consumed, the girl brought them tea, and they sat back, feeling pleasantly full, and chatted. Somehow it made Tianyi think of Mister Ma the Second in the Qing dynasty novel *The Scholars* who, on a visit to Hangzhou's West Lake, ignored the beautiful scenery and concentrated on stuffing himself with all kinds of food. She wanted to laugh: was it true that Chinese scholar officials down the ages were just a bunch of vulgar gluttons? Here she herself sat, stuffed to the gills with food and drink, apparently holding a dignified conversation, while she was secretly thinking that Xiaoming the driver must surely have seen her breasts just now when she was lying by the pool. No doubt they were seductively prominent, perhaps even with her nipples showing through the fabric. He could not have failed to see, could he?

Tianyi felt that the older she got, the more sexual she became. That young girl's purity, that aversion to the least smuttiness, had vanished. The more unobtainable sex was to her, the more her imagination ran riot. The problem was that before she married, a woman rarely had much insight into her own character. Take her, for instance, she had been convinced that she was someone who did not need anyone, was content to be proud and aloof from the rest of the world. She had imagined herself as one of those clever female scholars who featured in ancient, thread-bound books. But living with a man, even if it was a man she did not love, had opened her up. She had betrayed herself, and suddenly found herself interested in all the things she used to despise. She did her utmost to suppress these urges, but the more she suppressed them, the fiercer they grew. She sometimes had erotic dreams, which she dreaded, since all the books said they were extremely harmful to one's health.

When she was a newly-wed with a phobia of sex, Lian had thought of nothing else. But now she had become a sexually voracious woman, he could not do it anymore. After a few occasions on which he failed miserably, she was suddenly seized with a terrible panic. This was a problem that she simply could not solve on her own

To her dismay, she discovered that she was turning out like Tianyue, but perhaps even worse. The failure of her marriage and the onset of middle age had brought Tianyue a string of lovers to satisfy her sexual needs. But Tianyi was different, preferring to keep her distance from other people or rather, strictly speaking, from men. She was a woman who thought she could live forever in her dreams, now confronted by the very real challenge of her physical needs.

Times were certainly tough for her. The worst of it was that a young woman, Xi, turned up to add fuel to the flames of her desires. Xi brought her some porn videos, the first that Tianyi had ever seen in her life. The blood rushed to her face as she watched these naked men and women coupling shamelessly in every imaginable position. Xi just laughed: 'Tianyi, you don't know anything about anything!' The more Xi teased, the redder Tianyi became. To her relief, there was no one else with them, but Tianyi found it intolerable all the same. When they had finished watching, Xi said very seriously: 'Tianyi, you're just too innocent!'

Strictly speaking, Xi was one of Zheng's circle—she was his friend Tong's second wife. Tong had once had an animal virility but impotence struck after the painful break-up with his former wife. It taught him a lesson and when he looked for a new bride, he chose a virgin fifteen years younger than himself. No doubt the logic was that if he could get someone young enough, he could mould her and she would be subservient for the rest of her life.

Tong may have been politically astute but he knew nothing of female psychology. A girl like Xi, once the scales had fallen from her eyes, was as dangerous as a river in spate. When her grievances threatened to boil over, she came to Tianyi to get it all off her chest. 'Tong deceived me, Tianyi, he's nothing but a fraud!' she said after the videos were over. Then she reeled off a dozen offences without pausing for breath. The two chief ones were, one, he could not get it up, and, two, he did not want children. To enforce the second, he had forced Xi to have five abortions. Five!

Xi was so distressed by this point that she burst into tears and could not go on. Tianyi was at the point of shedding tears of sympathy when, to her surprise, she saw Xi start to undo her buttons. 'Look, Tianyi,' she was saying, 'Look, let me show you, I'm not even thirty years old and look at me!' Tianyi did not have time to avert her eyes before Xi had stripped to the waist. Xi was a tall girl, at nearly five foot nine, and to all appearances had a decent figure, but what Tianyi saw truly shocked her: Xi's large breasts hung slack and pendulous. Without a bra, they would have reached to her waist!

Tianyi had to turn away. However sympathetic she was, she could not bring herself to look at another's nakedness, especially such an ugly sight as this. But what followed astonished her even more. Xi carried on stripping off her clothes, saying as she did so: 'Tianyi, I've been thinking, why do we rely on men for everything? Didn't you see on the video, that women can give themselves orgasms? I've brought everything we need, will you be my partner? I've thought a lot about this, and you're the only one who'll do, even though you're older than me, you behave as you're young and innocent, and I feel at ease with you! Besides, I can see Lian's not a real man, so you must have the same problems as me!'

Tianyi was flabbergasted. At first, she simply froze, and even allowed Xi to remove her top for her. Xi was dazzled: Tianyi was wearing a rose-red, floral bra whose brilliant colour set off her alabaster white skin. Xi exclaimed joyfully at Tianyi's unimaginably deep cleavage: 'What a stunning body you have, Tianyi! It's so beautiful, I don't understand why you don't dress up more! You should wear tight-fitting tops and show a quarter of the breast, and you'd have men all over you!'

It was many years later, in a foreign country, when Tianyi heard that phrase 'show a quarter of the breast' again. She could not help secretly admiring Xi for having picked all this up on her own. But Tianyi was just too inhibited to go on, and so Xi, who dared to experiment where Tianyi did not, was left disillusioned and had to go and find herself another partner.

Tianyi still remembered how she turned away and went and

locked herself in the kitchen, refusing to open up to Xi who pounded on the door and cried bitterly. Xi kept it up for an hour or more, before finally flouncing off. Several months later, Xi came to see her again, her eyes shining with excitement, and told Tianyi she had found a lover. He was an artist in the Central School of Arts Woodblock Printing department. 'His name's Lang, and he's a real man!' Xi exclaimed, wide-eyed. 'We have sex on the floor, a dozen times a night! Oh, Tianyi, now I know how good it feels to be a woman!' As Tianyi listened, she felt envious, but also fearful, it seemed a little unfair on Tong, but before she could say so, Xi had further denunciations of her husband: 'Tong can't get it up more than once a month! He marks it on the calendar when we do! I can't bear a man like that, it doesn't matter how knowledgeable and capable he is! But now I've got this relationship with Lang, so I've got a husband and a lover, and what more could a woman want? What about you, Tianyi? It'll be more than ten years before Zheng gets out, shouldn't you find someone else?' Tianyi flushed scarlet and said nothing. She was actually thinking that at least Tong did the business once a month, whereas Lian had not even broached it for as much as half a year. Tianyi had far too much self-respect, she would have died rather than talk to Lian about it. She was utterly conflicted: intellectually open-minded, in her behaviour very conservative. In those days, she believed that the man should always make the first move. If she had initiated it, she would not have felt happy even if the man actually responded. As day after day passed in their busy lives, Lian never wanted intimacy. They had changed, it seemed, from being lovers to being friends, and from friends to comrades.

At least she still had the film company, and work to do for it. Wei Qiang talked to her about *Old City* and she got on the phone to the author. Wusheng was self-deprecating: 'Tianyi, is it really you? What an honour to hear from you! Six years ago, I had the privilege of reading your masterpiece, *The Tree of Knowledge* —that was such a good film—I read it through twice.' Tianyi hurriedly brushed the compliments aside: 'Oh, that's all in the past now! What I'm phoning about is your novel, *Old City*. I've heard a number of publishers are bidding hard for it, and my boss read the reports and asked me to contact you to ask if you would let us read the proofs?' Wusheng's voice instantly cooled: 'Ah, so it was your boss who asked you to contact me. Well, let me give *Golden Autumn* magazine a ring, they're previewing it. They can let you have a proof copy. But you may not like it when you've read it!'

Tianyi, however, was still brimming with enthusiasm for the project, or rather, to be truthful, for her boss Qiang. So she leapt on her bicycle and pedalled off to the *Golden Autumn* magazine offices where an old friend, Huilan, was the deputy editor. Huilan had been on the literary scene since the eighties, and was known for being blunt in her dealings with people. She was bit past her prime nowadays, but her fighting spirit was undimmed. When she met Tianyi, she gave her the low-down on *Old City* and how it was written. This was early in the nineties, and few authors had made it into film and TV. Talking to Tianyi about her company's interest in the book, Huilan was not slow to see an opportunity, and was canny enough not to commit herself to terms and conditions. The gist of it was that as soon as the film company had bought the rights, she wanted to be Planning Director. Tianyi thought a moment: 'I don't think that will work. As far as I know, we won't be doing any of that. The most we could swing is to get you made literary consultant.' 'Sure, that's fine,' said Huilan. 'At least I'll get something out of it.' And she gleefully got out a set of proofs and handed them to Tianyi.

That evening, Qiang called as usual and Tianyi gave him the good news: 'I've got a copy of *Old City.*' Qiang was delighted. Unluckily, Lian was in a foul mood that day. As deputy CEO, he felt he was really somebody now and, after going out to work all day, he was annoyed when he got home and Tianyi nagged him to do chores like give Niuniu a bath. In fact it drove him mad. Besides, the little boy was at a particularly mischievous stage and that added to his aggravation. So just as Qiang was settling down to his usual lengthy natter with Tianyi, he heard a roar at the other end of line: 'Get your clothes off!' Poor Qiang was so startled he nearly dropped the receiver.

Lian was of course directing the order to his son, who customarily dawdled over this duty for half an hour. But he was really getting at Tianyi. Why did he have to work all day and then come home and bath his son? While Tianyi, who didn't have to go to the office, could not even attend to her son's bath and spent all the time chatting endlessly on the phone. He was not going to stand for it a moment longer!

Little did he imagine that his shouted command had stirred sexual fantasies in Qiang. What would it be like, he wondered, to see Tianyi take her clothes off? What would she look like? He was certainly not unaware of her slender waist and full breasts, and when he was alone with her, he found her femininity thoroughly distracting.

A few days later, Wusheng arrived in Beijing. In high spirits, Qiang fixed up to go and meet him with Tianyi. He was banking on the fact that although Wusheng was now a celebrity author, he was an unsophisticated countryman at heart, and would be only too eager to accept an invitation from a film company. But when they arrived at the rather ordinary guesthouse where he was staying, he was taken aback to discover that Wusheng was in an uncooperative mood. Clutching his belly, he refused to get out of bed and complained: 'I've got terrible stomach ache, I'm not going anywhere!' Qiang had to grab hold of him: 'Hey, Wusheng, old man! The company bosses have invited you to a banquet! Don't mess us around like this!' Wusheng's reaction was to ignore Tianyi's presence and pull up his sweatshirt to reveal a sallow belly neatly covered in five big plasters: 'Just take a look at this! I'm not kidding you! I'm ill, I've got terrible belly ache!'

With the greatest difficulty, they managed to get Wusheng up and march him down to the Shunfeng Restaurant, famous throughout Beijing for its lavish dining. Here the deputy director of the film company, Mr Feng, splashed out on delicacies like shark's fin with papaya especially for Wusheng, but the author just sat there, pecking at his food, pale and morosely silent. Even when others spoke, he said nothing. It was Tianyi who finally succeeded in drawing him into the conversation: 'I've heard you're a master of the art of doing horoscopes, and your readings are very accurate,' she said. 'Why don't you do one for Mr Feng?' At that, Wusheng's thick lips parted and he turned to the director, speaking in a thick rural drawl: 'May I ask when you were born, sir?' The combination of the accent and his rather quaint way of expressing himself was comical, and Mr Feng suppressed a smile: 'I was born in 1944, the thirteenth day of the first month by the old calendar, between 5 and 7 in the evening.'

Wusheng picked up two chopsticks and made a lengthy show of turning them this way and that. Then he pronounced: 'It would not be appropriate for me to tell you now. I'll write you a letter informing you of my reading after I return home.' That certainly made the diners curious and there was a stream of questions. Tianyi hastily added her own time, day, month and year of birth. As she did so, she caught a slight smile at the corner of Qiang's lips, the sort of indulgent smile an older man might give a junior he had taken a fancy to, and she could not help blushing.

The dinner grew more uproarious, and no one mentioned *Old City* again. But just as the meal was ending, Wusheng suddenly said: 'You've been in such a hurry to get hold of the proofs, but I don't think you'll want it.' He was only too right.

Distressing times followed for Tianyi. Head office came down very hard on Qiang. When the company's executives read *Old City* they deemed it pornographic; Tangtang Film Productions would be mad to go for a work like that. It would be absolutely the wrong way to go! At the directors' meeting, Qiang was subject to heavy criticism. In turn, he dumped all the blame onto Tianyi. This was no surprise; almost any man in his position would have taken the same decision to save their jobs. In the Chinese media and cultural world a 'Duke of Windsor' who preferred a beautiful woman to his country would be a laughing stock!

Tianyi was completely isolated. For a long time, she did not know what was going on in head office meetings. All she knew was that Qiang had grown thinner, more taciturn and more guarded in his speech, all of which distressed her. She put out very discreet feelers but never got any real answers. She just had the impression that a gloomy Qiang was growing distant from her. She saw the situation deteriorate but could do nothing to redeem it. It felt like a knife turning in her gut.

She summoned up her courage and went to his office. Quietly, she asked him: 'Qiang, has there been a problem with *Old City*? If there has, then just dump the blame on me. Really, it doesn't matter a bit. I'm not planning to join the Party or become an official, so there's no way it can harm me.' For an instant, Qiang was genuinely moved. But the very next moment, he hardened his heart and waved her away.

Many years later, when Tianyi finally found out what had been going on, she smiled cynically. What had made her imagine that her love was returned?

At the time, the next thing to happen was that that she received a letter from Wusheng. It contained the horoscope he had done for her, telling her that if she took a trip to the South-West this springtime, romance might ensue. She threw the letter onto the table with a wry smile. However, some days later, she received an invitation from Yunnan TV to go to Xishuangbanna. By nature, Tianyi preferred to avoid confrontations by keeping out of the way. This invitation had come just at the right time. The one person she would miss was Qiang, but on the other hand, he might be in a better frame of mind by the time she got back.

Of course, there were strings attached. Yunnan TV wanted Tianyi to collaborate with a young local screen writer, Mo, on the script for a film about animal protection, and then get her company to invest in it. She and Mo went to a valley of wild elephants around sixty kilometres from Jinghong, the chief city of the Xishuangbanna area. It was very much off the beaten track. Tianyi was a well-travelled woman but the unusual scenery of this place truly amazed her. There was something uniquely chilling and mysterious about the atmosphere of the place. There had been no building at all here with the exception of some wooden shacks that did duty as guest houses. They were built up in the branches of lofty trees, and connected by rudimentary wooden steps and bridges. The tree canopy that hid the sky above and the rivulets that glittered beneath made this primitive valley look like something out of Dante's *Divina Commedia*. It was stunning and Tianyi was amazed that in their industrialized society, scenery as primeval as this still existed.

The screenwriter, Mo, was a local youth, and talked to Tianyi in a thick Yunnan dialect. They were eating their dinner outdoors that evening and Tianyi told him that this was the best and most special meal she had ever had in Yunnan. There were fragrant wild mushrooms and meat and greens, all mixed with rice. Exquisite.

The dusk seemed to last forever; the sun hung over the western horizon, a sharply outlined pale red globe, its lingering rays very soft while the colours reflected in the clouds glittered brilliantly. Tianyi and Mo walked down to the stream, to capture the last moments of the sunset. Dense layers of clouds were reflected in its waters, an array as gorgeous as one of Levitan's landscape paintings. The locals said that elephants relished salt, and on dark, windy nights when they came for water, they would eat up salt left to dry in the sun on its banks. Tianyi was captivated.

As night fell, they sat talking on the wooden veranda. There was no lighting so they each had a torch to guide them back to their sleeping quarters. Tianyi's room was built in the branches of an enormous, ancient tree. Inside, it was primitive but clean. There was a bed, a small table which held a lamp and a thermos, and a separate toilet. She put the padlock and the torch down on the table and her handbag by the pillow. Then she pulled back the blue-and-white batik curtains. From here she could just see the stream, glinting in the darkness.

It took her a long time to get to sleep, but very soon after, she was shaken awake from a dream that she was being chased by a black bear by a terrific trumpeting. She was instantly alert: it was a wild elephant! It must be! She jumped out of bed and pulled back the curtain. A gigantic elephant stood beside the stream. The beast was bigger than she could have imagined, and in the darkness, its sensitive ears gleamed like carved moonstone. As she watched, it was joined by another, then another. My god, there were four of them!

She turned on the torch and ran down the steps, shouting: 'Elephants! Come quick!' but by the time she had roused Mo and the driver, the elephants had melted away in the darkness. The two men calmed their shaken nerves by teasing Tianyi. She was just hallucinating, they insisted. There could not possibly have been any elephants. And Tianyi was never able to produce any proof. Perhaps she had dreamed it all.

Tianyi now took in young Mo for the first time: he was tall with the physique of a body-builder or, as the Yunnan TV station editors put it: 'a fine figure of a man'. Apparently he was also the son of a famous local painter. However, she found he made her uncomfortable. He had a lecherous look about him, and avoided her eyes.

Mo took her to visit the White Bird Garden, or rather, 'peacock garden' as Tianyi felt it should be called, because that was mostly what it contained. The birds were quite fearless. When a male displayed, you could walk quite close to one and have your photo taken next to it, with no fear that it might wander off or suddenly close its fan.

That day had a strange feeling about it, as though she had walked into the sort of fairy tale kingdom she used to long to enter as a child. You could communicate with all the birds and the beasts here. She even thought of having her picture taken with a peacock in her arms, but the young man looking after the garden would not let her. 'It'll peck you,' he warned.

She understood that. What these beautiful birds most prized was their freedom. They ambled around among the flowering bushes, uninterested in contact with any other creatures. She supposed all wild creatures were the same in that respect. In fact, surely all humans were too. In the west, when you were with strangers, you avoided physical contact like the plague. If you accidentally brushed against someone in the street, you both backed off immediately, saying 'Sorry'. That way, you maintained your freedom. When people came close, physically and emotionally, especially with those they loved, it was a trap, no matter how beautiful a trap.

One of the highlights here was when the peacocks were 'released into flight'. At ten o'clock in the morning, they gathered on a distant hillside, and were released into flight by their feeders. It was spectacular! One by one they took off in the distance and flew to the garden where they landed and the males displayed. One … two … three … Tianyi had never seen a dozen peacocks all displaying at once. It was splendid. The gorgeous, shimmering colours clustered together like so many rainbows, were indescribably beautiful. She was unable to take her eyes off them, did not dare even blink, as if she did, the whole scene might suddenly vanish. As she stared, she felt Mo leering at her, his eyes as usual half-closed, very close, and flickering.

She was astonished when Mo followed her back to Beijing. First he made a very long phone call to her. He told her that life was short and he needed some variety, otherwise he would have wasted his life. People who were truly in love, he said, did not need to marry, for instance the 1930s avant-garde lovers, Zhang Daofan and Jiang Biwei never did. Tianyi was familiar with that argument, having heard it once from her old university boyfriend Jianyu. There was nothing more beautiful than making love, Mo said, and asked her: 'Have you seen lovers making love on the grass, on river banks? Their bodies make the most beautiful shapes. When they're making love, that's when a man and a woman then are at their most beautiful, most vital.'

Mo certainly had a fine turn of phrase but what he said was hardly new, in fact, Tianyi found it appallingly clichéd. But clichéd or no, his words still stirred Tianyi's physical feelings. As Mo talked, there floated before her eyes scenes of green grass and seashores, and writhing naked people. Tianyi felt she was sinking ever deeper into a swamp of seduction.

Thinking back on it, it was Xi who started her on the slippery slope with those porn videos she brought over. Tianyi may have told her they were obscene, but those images set her body on fire. One evening she could not sleep, and the female porn stars came into her mind. How could they strip stark naked before the cameras and allow the male stars to violate them? Or maybe they did not feel it was violation but pleasure. As these thoughts went through her head, her hand crept downward. She was soaking wet. She made an effort to divert her energy to the *chakra* below her navel, but her hand was busy between her legs and it was no use. She brought herself off.

There had been so little real sexual joy in her life. The best she could manage was the brief thrill of fantasizing and masturbating, but that always left her feeling horribly ashamed, and feeling physically unwell. Her head swam and her loins ached. She wanted nothing more than to take herself off to another world, to get some peace and tranquillity. The three meals a day she shared with her husband and child were torture.

Chastity, loyalty, honesty … the words, so familiar from childhood, began to have a bleak ring to them. She felt like she was falling apart. At the same time, Mo's imminent arrival in Beijing filled her with a new spirit of initiative. It was very different from her encounter with Peng, when he had forced himself on her. Everything was taken care of. Her husband was off on business, his parents had Niuniu at weekends, and she had cleaned the house from top to bottom. And all this while waiting for a stranger to burst in on her.

But Tianyi still harboured a fear of sex. As young people, her generation had been sexually shackled, and it had destroyed them. Tianyi still had no real understanding of sex, only of her own needs. She tried to encourage herself to follow Xi's example. They were both women, and Xi wasn't afraid, was she? And she got pleasure from it too! Xi and the art student Lang had broken up in the end, and she and Tong were divorced, but her increase in sex, far from decreasing, grew. She was now living with a poet. They had been together for two years, but it seemed their ardour was undimmed.

So Tianyi was going to let herself feel some pleasure. She went through all her drawers until she found a sexy nightie, one she had bought a long time ago and had only worn once. It was made of purple silk, with a deep, revealing, V-neck. She was startled when she looked at herself in the mirror and quickly took it off again. When Mo arrived, she was just wearing ordinary clothes, without even her neck showing.

In the event, nothing happened in the way she had imagined. Still afraid, she insisted on turning the light off. She really had no idea that Mo, as a man, needed to be stimulated by seeing her to get turned on. Mo actually suspected that Tianyi had some physical blemish that she dare not let him see. He lost his erection and had some difficulty getting it back. Tianyi made a grab for the condoms. By now frantic, Mo begged her: 'Can't we do without?' 'No way!' Tianyi was adamant. 'I fall pregnant very easily.' Mo drooped again. After a lot of trying, he managed it in a more or less sort of way. *What a magnificent body, but it's good for nothing,* he thought to himself. Even his hick of a wife was a better bet. She might have been flabby, but at least she knew how to have a good time! He didn't know why he had gone to all this trouble. When the lights were out, all women were pretty much the same.

Watching Mo throw on his clothes and leave, Tianyi knew that yet another man had come and gone in her life. But this time, she had no regrets. His body had taught her to understand herself: she was not a woman who could separate lust from love, or go to bed with a man for whom she felt nothing, and she was deluding herself if she thought otherwise.

18

Qiang grew colder towards Tianyi. Finally one day he erupted when Tianyi got to work late, and lambasted her. Tianyi was mortified as she listened to his stinging remarks. From then on, they did not speak anymore even if they met. When Tianyi saw him from a distance, she lifted her chin and walked by as if he were not there. Qiang paid her back in her own coin, lifting his already lofty chin and turning on his heel. It was the gossip of the company—Qiang and Tianyi had had a bust-up. And everyone knew the reason: Tianyi had got hold of a book called *Old City* and Qiang had been severely criticized by his bosses for it, so severely that it could blight his career. According to colleagues in the Arts Department, what Tianyi had done was political entrapment!

Most of the staff in the Arts Department were women with some sort of acting background, and they loved to bitch. Tianyi remembered something her mother always used to say, that whores were heartless and actors immoral. The truism served her well now. The women quickly taught her, however, that certain other maxims were nonsense: return good for evil, persistent effort would be rewarded, no need to gild the lily, people will help you out in your hour of need. In this company, everyone was only out to make big bucks, and as fast as possible. Added to which, the place was full of flatterers and toadies, with a knife up their sleeves, a smile on their faces and a foot stuck out ready to trip you up. But she was treading on very thin ice, and she felt too intimidated to do anything about it. Whatever would be, would be. She was going unarmed into battle, so she might get shot at, but the wounds were unlikely to be fatal.

In the past, Tianyi had been under Wei Qiang's protection, and the ex-actresses had not dared do anything to her. But now they could see that she had been well and truly dumped and, as is the way of things, everyone was ready to hit a woman who was down. After all, she had been chucked out like an old cleaning rag, why shouldn't everyone scuff her underfoot? She had only written one big book, *The Tree of Knowledge* in the eighties, nothing more! She was just one among so many writers in that decade. And hadn't she just been an assistant in the Academy of Letters, a blue-stocking? What was she doing butting into the world of showbiz? She had no talent and no style in a world where both counted, and she was a bit of a ditherer, too. It was true she had put out some new stuff but she had not made any kind of a name for herself, and in the world of arts and entertainment, if you were a nobody, the safest thing was not to stick your head above the parapet.

Tianyi continued to hold her head high, but she also felt confused and distressed. She could not understand it. Qiang's entreaties that she should contact Wusheng for him still rang in her ears. She had taken on that responsibility unhesitatingly, for the sake of their friendship. Where had she gone wrong? Where?

But very soon, Tianyi was jolted from this particular crisis and plunged into a much deeper one. This time she was truly shaken to the core.

One day, a dismal drizzle was falling and the Beijing streets were unusually quiet. Tianyi, dressed casually in trousers and a top, slipped quickly into the military compound and to the door of the flat where Zheng's parents lived. Zheng's mother had phoned her. She found Mrs Ke with tears pouring down her face.

Even Zheng's father was weeping. Tianyi knew at once that it was serious.

With shaking hands, Zheng's mother gave her a piece of paper. Tianyi could see it was Zheng's handwriting but, for a long time, she could not bring herself to read it. She stared vacantly at his mother's hand, with its stubby, fleshy, carrot-like fingers. Can hands and fingers be inherited, she wondered vaguely? She seemed to see those fingers mixing the mayonnaise, clutching a pair of chopsticks with clumsy earnestness. The tears welled and her eyes misted over.

'Child, what's up! What is it? Read the letter!' Zheng's mother was shaking her with both hands. The elderly pair were alarmed at her Tianyi's deathly pallor and rigid expression.

Tianyi pulled herself together and peered at the scribbled writing. She had teased Zheng so often about his terrible handwriting but now all she wanted to do was to press those beloved words against her cheeks, into her heart. 'If prison conditions don't improve within two weeks, I'll take my own life in protest!'

She knew, as everyone who knew Zheng did, that he meant what he said. Just at the time when her head and her heart had been so full of Qiang, Zheng was enduring the hardships of prison. Number Two Prison was different from Qin Cheng Prison, he wrote. Here he only had four square metres of space, one-third of which was taken up with the latrine, which teemed with maggots in hot weather. The stink was terrible. He was tormented by flies, mosquitoes and fleas, and covered in lumps and bumps from their bites. The itching was unendurable, and he scratched and scratched, until he had wounds so deep that he could see the bone gleaming white underneath!

When she left Zheng's parents that day and got on the metro, she wept uncontrollably, beyond embarrassment and ignoring the shocked stares of her fellow passengers. She just wanted to know why. Why was the goddess of liberty so pitiless? People had not advanced a single step in a hundred years, and every step forward had to be paid for with someone's blood! The state was a meat grinder, one enormous meat-grinder that had destroyed the dreams of those whom the heavens loved. How many exceptional men and women had been minced to fragments in its jaws? Wasn't the law of nature survival of the fittest? But it was the best who were being destroyed by this process, the best! How many really excellent people had fallen in the last few years? Too many!

Many years later, when she mentioned Zheng's time in prison to his parents again, she found them indifferent. The old man chuckled: 'Wherever our boy goes, he's always lucky. Even those years he spent in prison, he really got treated well.' He talked as if it were all a lifetime ago. Distressed, Tianyi protested gently: 'He had a terrible time in Number Two Prison. He got a message out to me that he was going to kill himself in protest at the conditions.' But then she realized that this was quite the wrong thing to say. There was not the slightest reaction from anyone except for Zheng's mother. This woman who back then had wept and begged Tianyi to help, now said dismissively: 'That was only for a short time. Why rake it all up again now?' Tianyi's mouth dropped open and she looked from one person to another. Every one of them was busy stuffing their mouths with food. No one appeared in the slightest bit moved.

She was surprised at how very clear it all remained in her own memory. She had taken the letter that day to a friend, Fang, who ran the *Rule of Law* journal. He, in turn, took the risky step of informing someone very high up in the government via an internal memo. The official scribbled an instruction on it, the horrors that Zheng had endured at Number Two prison came to an end and he was transferred to the prison ward of a hospital on the outskirts of the city. She actually took Fang to meet Zheng's parents who were most grateful for his help. But memories fade, and the whole episode became for them something 'not worth raking up'. Tianyi found it chilling.

And so she came to realize that total amnesia had afflicted an entire people. The Chinese were so apathetic that they had simply decided not to pass judgment, to forget the disastrous decade of the Cultural Revolution. It had destroyed their lives, but they innocently imagined that this history would never be repeated. Yet it <u>was</u> repeated in 1989, on ground already soaked with blood, just because the perpetrators had escaped justice the first time round.

She was overwhelmed by her longing for Zheng, and wept until she had no more tears to cry.

19

One day, Xiao'ou reappeared in Tianyi's life. It was an unusually bright Beijing morning when someone knocked at the door. In those days, friends rarely phoned in advance, they just turned up. Tianyi opened the door, to see a tall figure silhouetted against the light. The sun's rays made the hairs of his head look almost transparent, and before she saw his face, she knew it was Xiao'ou. She was exhausted, not having slept well, and it showed in her puffy face. Worst still, she had not had time to wash her face and comb her hair. She looked a mess, and felt in no state to welcome an old friend, even one she had not seen for so long.

Xiao'ou did not seem to notice, though. He spoke excitedly about his recent doings, about the terrible night of 4th June, when by some lucky fluke he made his escape from the Square, and about the terrible scenes he had witnessed there.

'You're a friend of Zheng, aren't you?'

'Who told you?' she asked quietly.

'Fang.' Then, after a pause: 'A bunch of friends are going on an outing to Huairou County tomorrow. Do you want to come?'

'Who's going?'

'Fang, for starters. Everyone wants to know what's happened to Zheng, and do what they can to help.' That was how she found out that Zheng and Xiao'ou were friends. Small world!

The next day, she dressed carefully, putting on a blue-and-white batik skirt, tying her hair into a ponytail and applying a little makeup. Then she called goodbye to Lian and set off.

When they were in the minibus, she realized that this was a circle of people she had never met before. Such friendship groups had flourished after the Cultural Revolution ended, the more pretentious ones calling themselves 'Salons'. She always stuck by her friends—those she got to know through Zheng at the beginning of the eighties were like her family. But after June 1989, they had scattered, some going abroad, others taking refuge wherever they could. For Tianyi, a life swept bare of friends was no life at all so she was pleasantly surprised to be introduced to new ones today. You only had to exchange a couple of sentences in Beijing to get a general idea whether someone could become a friend. There was a sort of secret language that told you immediately.

Only one friend from the old days was on the bus, Zheng's ex-girlfriend, Xi. The famous boyfriend Tianyi had heard so much about, a rock singer, was there too. Rock stars were then as rare as the morning star in the sky and Tianyi was curious to talk to him, but he seemed to have nothing interesting to say. Xi, however, was as bubbly as ever, and full of endless questions, and the two women spent the trip catching up.

Fang was a respected figure within this circle of friends. After dinner, he called just a few of them, including Tianyi, to his room, to talk about Zheng. Everyone was talking about Zheng; all over China, he had become a hero. They were greedy for news, for any titbits of information about him: how was he getting on? What was he doing? Tianyi sensed their eagerness and found herself telling these people every detail of everything she knew, from beginning to end, because she was so anxious for him to get help.

Tianyi was the star of the show that evening. Everyone clustered around her. They seemed especially interested in Zheng's wife Yiyi's dramatic performance in court, and Tianyi thought again how in China there was no way of protecting ones secrets. Even those details she regarded as most private had somehow got out. For instance there were rumours that, since Zheng's imprisonment, Yiyi had been arrested for sleeping with foreigners, that Yiyi had stolen foreign aid funds to buy herself a silver fox coat ... But Tianyi had not the slightest interest in this sort of gossip, not only because it might affect Zheng adversely, but also because she found it all too boring. When she thought of Zheng shut away in lonely isolation in that dreadful prison, she felt thoroughly disillusioned at outsiders' prurient fascination with chewing over his private life. They were as bloodthirsty as the father who fed his son a blood-soaked bun in Lu Xun's story *Medicine*! Of course, they meant well, and Fang had been a huge help to Zheng, as she knew quite well. But even though it showed everyone was interested, it did nothing to raise her spirits.

She was secretly observing Xiao'ou. He was still extremely attractive but seemed in some way to have changed, become even more extrovert. When they used to swim in the reservoir, he seemed to make a point of strutting around in front of her in his swimming briefs, showing off his imposing physique and, especially, his luxuriant growth of chest hair. She had not enjoyed his behaviour. It reminded her uncomfortably of a Mister Universe. Her reaction was to cover up from head to toe, even if she did pour with sweat on a hot day, and to refuse to take off her long-sleeved shirt, thus successfully diverting the men's gaze to Xi's body instead.

But no ... it was not that Xiao'ou had changed. It was that she had simply not seen him clearly in the past. He was someone who liked to brag about how splendid he would be in a disaster. He might have made a Hermann Hesse, but Mahatma Gandhi or Martin Luther King was clearly beyond him, never mind Jesus Christ. It all made him the polar opposite of Zheng.

She felt now that it was even more difficult to divert their attention from herself than to attract it. It was an art apparently and she was no more than a beginner. For whatever reasons, the feelings she had once had for Xiao'ou, had evaporated. That was probably the only good thing that came out of this trip to Huairou County.

At work, Qiang was looking grimmer by the day. It never occurred to Tianyi that he was not an iron-man but a flesh and blood human being, in the prime of life, strong and vigorous, deprived of his wife and child (they had gone to live abroad), and in a position that gave him few opportunities for diversion. He had two choices: to grit his teeth and curb his desires or spend the midnight hours jerking off compulsively. Never in her wildest dreams did Tianyi imagine that she was the object of his masturbatory fantasies. So by day he scowled furiously at her, as if she had pried into some unspeakable secret of his private life.

Fortunately, Qiang had his decent side; he took pride in being a man of honour and principles, and putting his work responsibilities first. Looking very serious, he entrusted her with inviting three well-known avant-garde authors to the company, to sketch out the plot of a new film. At the same time, he got someone else to do the same with other authors, who wrote rather less highbrow stories.

Of course, Tianyi, who felt she had been wrong-footed over Wusheng, was over the moon. She had dreamed for years of 'author films', ever since seeing Alain Resnais's *Last Year in Marienbad*, in fact. She longed to get the chance to write the screenplay for a film like that, with its mixture of truth and fantasy. Her intelligence had not yet been tarnished by time, and those three avant-garde authors were not only good friends of hers, they were also very much on the same wavelength.

But creative ideas, as she was discover to her cost, looked quite different once they took practical shape. The authors settled on a thoroughly low-life theme, trafficking in women, for reasons she did not fully understand. As they planned the film, it was as if some sinister presence was manipulating them. Even the utterly matter-of-fact Qiang seemed strangely drawn in. One of the three, Xiang, got to his feet and held forth with gusto. This subject matter would certainly create a stir, he assured them. He was from Henan province, and he told them a whole series of extraordinary stories about Henan women who had been trafficked. His listeners were stupefied.

It was Carl Jung who made the great discovery of the 'collective unconscious'. On that midsummer evening in 1994, the planning meeting virtually sank into a 'collective unconscious'. Xiang's lively performance was totally absorbing. Tianyi did have a vague feeling that all was not right, but her objections were quickly overruled amid the general excitement. And in any case, Qiang was there. As he had complete responsibility for signing up the three authors on behalf of the film company, what was she worrying about?

So she relaxed and watched: Qiang, normally such a dapper figure, unbent so far as to take his shoes and socks off and sit cross-legged. His bare feet gave off a faint whiff and she looked away, secretly annoyed. It was really disrespectful, taking your shoes off in front of a woman! This detail brought her firmly back to the real world and she realized she had missed most of Xiang's speech.

Xiang's enthusiasm infected the two other authors, Song and Diao, and Song jumped to his feet and talked about a woman in Sanhe County, his old home, who had been trafficked to Inner Mongolia and sexually abused by the man for five whole years. Finally, she had succeeded in running away and made the long journey home. That got all the men in the meeting very worked up and they launched into a discussion of sexual abuse. It went right back even as far as the Vietnam War, said Diao, when the

American troops tortured female captives by piercing their breasts with bamboo spikes, whipping their private parts with belts and so on. There were detailed descriptions of this, he went on, in books such as *Letter from the South* and *South Vietnam Youth in Battle*.

From trafficked women to *South Vietnam Youth in Battle*, the discussion had gone wildly off topic, but Tianyi could not get a word in edgeways. She sneaked a glance at Qiang, who looked impassive but was clearly listening intently. She felt an obscure fury and would have loved to throw a temper tantrum. But she knew quite well that she was not at home and Qiang was not Lian. All she could do was excuse herself, go to the toilet and stand there at the window sighing at the stars.

Tianyi was surprised when she discovered that the three avant-garde authors had taken their fee and gone, just like that. As a result, she came under pressure from Qiang to complete the screenplay herself. She had never in her life written anything on this topic, one which moreover she found abhorrent. But this was the company where she worked and she had to get on with the job. No one had forced her to take up this position. She had to do her duty and she had to write well. And writing well in the context of this company meant that even the cook had to approve.

Actually, it all went unexpectedly smoothly and when she had written the synopsis and completed her first draft, she printed one copy for Qiang and one copy for his deputy, Zhi. Some weeks later, at the first discussion meeting, Zhi jumped in with a list of criticisms, thirteen of them, before Qiang could speak. The first criticism carried most weight, and it was this: it would be quite reprehensible for a highly reputable production company like theirs to make a film about the dark underbelly of society.

Instinctively, Tianyi looked at Qiang. Quite obviously, since this topic had met with Qiang's approval, Zhi's criticism meant one of two things. Either he was getting at Qiang, or the latter was too embarrassed to say anything and Zhi had to play the bad guy. Qiang still said nothing and sat there leafing through the photocopy of the screen play she had given him, as if he was deaf. She understood.

Zhi had started his career as a secretary, and was adept at divining the boss's intentions. He made it his business to get on well with his superiors, especially his immediate line manager. He was also at an age when he could hope for promotion, so there was no way he was going to jump out of line and offend Qiang. He must have got Qiang's approval before speaking out. He might even have discussed it with him.

Tianyi was devastated. Until now she had been ambivalent about Qiang, but from now on, she was finished with him! She did not even hate him anymore. Hate meant that she still had feelings for him, but now she just despised him. She felt suddenly liberated.

She stood up to speak, a mocking smile on her lips. She spoke to Zhi but her remarks were clearly intended for Qiang: 'I'm not as well as educated as you are, and I don't think I understand,' she began. 'As you well know, this theme was our manager's personal choice. The detailed synopsis got the nod from the company director, Mr Feng, himself. How come it's suddenly become "reprehensible to film the dark underbelly of society"? If that's what you're saying, where does that leave the director and Qiang?' Zhi was taken aback. The arts department staff had always been so amenable, he had not expected this pugnacious reaction. She had backed him into a corner! He looked uneasily at Qiang, and Tianyi, seeing the glance, was even more convinced that the two of them had been in cahoots with these thirteen criticisms. Qiang looked up, and swept Tianyi with his dignified gaze. 'All screenplays come out different from the synopsis. I'd strongly advise you to pay serious attention to this feedback,' he said. The old Tianyi would have flushed in consternation at this, which was no doubt what Qiang anticipated. Her haughty response must have surprised him: 'Excuse me! I am not in the habit of re-writing!' He was outraged. He was suddenly reminded of the *Old City* fiasco. This woman jinxed everything she touched. Resentments, old and new, rushed to the surface and he leapt to his feet, banging the table: 'That's enough from you, Yang Tianyi!'

There was shock at his enraged outburst. All the staff, from senior women to young girls, crowded around the doorway of Qiang's office, craning their necks to see what was going on. They heard the urbane Qiang bang the table again and shout: 'Let me make myself clear, Yang Tianyi! We make mass-market films these days, it's fast-food culture, for ordinary people to watch! So don't come to me with your highbrow ideas. No one's going to watch a film like the one you've written!' The staff were thrilled to hear Tianyi roundly condemned. *You asked for that, Tianyi! That's what you get for your smug hoity-toity attitudes! We've had enough of being treated like ignorant yokels by Madam Highbrow!*

But if they were hoping to hear Tianyi break down in tears, or even choke back a sob, they were disappointed. Tianyi startled them with her response. Quite calmly, she took back the two copies of the screenplay and, looking coldly at Qiang, said: 'You're a nasty little man and I despise you.' Then she turned on her heel and left.

A deathly stillness fell. The Arts Department staff were like an audience that needed time to absorb a highly significant play before bursting into applause. The trouble was that they did not know whom to applaud.

20

Tianyi went home from her confrontation with Qiang to be met by a long-faced Lian. He waved Niuniu's exercise book in her face and shouted: 'Just take a look at this! Look! Am I a single parent? I'm so busy and you pay absolutely no attention to Niuniu … Do you know what your precious son has been doing? He's been skipping school, that's what! Skipping school and going to internet cafes! He's spent the last forty-eight hours in one!'

Tianyi stared at Lian appalled. She could not think of anything to say. As Lian carried on shouting, she could not help thinking that she had come home from being yelled at at work to more yelling at home. Really! Chinese men! She found it rather funny, and started to laugh but that just made Lian angrier. 'Just what are you laughing at?' he demanded. 'Just tell me this: are you the slightest bit bothered about it?' Of course, the situation was serious, and it suddenly occurred to Tianyi to ask, if Niuniu had been in an internet café for two days on the trot, where had he got the money from? Lian did not appear to have thought of that: 'Well, I thought you'd given it to him!' Tianyi went through her bag, and discovered she was three hundred *yuan* short. She had never bothered to keep tabs on how much money she carried around in her bag, but as it happened, she had received some prize money just two days ago and knew she had not spent any of it.

Her heart sank like a stone. Her ten-year-old son was a thief! That was a terrible thing to call someone, but as she had always

XU XIAOBIN

been careless of her money, it was very possibly not the first time he had done it. And she had just let things slip and not discovered it.

Lian hauled his sleeping son out of bed, and dragged him by the ear into the hallway. Niuniu stood the way he always did before his father, feet together, head lowered, ready to receive his punishment. Lian was unmoved. He bellowed with rage at the boy, then began to pummel him with his fists. This was the umpteenth time Tianyi had seen Lian beat up his son and she felt too drained to react. Lian's temper had been getting worse and worse. When things went badly at work, a man could bring his bad temper back home to inflict on his family, but what could a woman do in the same situation? Tianyi felt like crying but found she had no tears. Something seemed to be blocking up her insides, something that would not come up, or go down. How much more would she have to put up with?

Niuniu finally admitted that he had stolen his mother's money, a bit at a time, more than 3,000 *yuan* in total. His visits to the neighbourhood internet cafes were not just occasional, he haunted them. But his mother had been the last to know. This was Tianyi's biggest crime in Lian's eyes. 'What kind of mother are you?' he accused her. 'Have you ever taken responsibility for your son? Or for the family?'

Having finished with Niuniu, Lian gave Tianyi a vicious tongue-lashing. When he was in a rage, he was terrifying. His eyes paled to yellowish-brown, and his mouth gaped as if he was going to devour them both. Tianyi looked at him and thought how capricious the human face was: when he and she were dating, his face had been soft and gentle, and now it had turned so ugly. The most dignified and cultured of men could turn into anything, once the mask slipped. It made her suspicious of the very nature

239

of marriage.

Tianyi did not know what to say in the face of Lian's accusations. She stared at him vacantly until finally he ran out of energy, went back to the bedroom and slammed the door hard. Then she heated some water, had a wash, and got under the covers in her little cubbyhole of a study. An odd smell emanated from the quilt, too much oestrogen, the smell of a woman who had not been with a man for a very long time. She and Lian had not had sex for two whole years. Just the thought made her groin suddenly burn. Flushed and restless, she got up and took two sleeping pills, then went back to bed again. She thought of the screenplay she had spent three months writing, shot down in an instant by her boss. She thought of the despicable features of the firing squad, of her impotent husband and her thieving son, and wondered what on earth the next decades would bring. Finally, the tears came. Once they started, the trickle became a torrent, and she could not stop. She felt that one of these days, she would simply keel over for good. The thought, strangely, did not frighten her. It almost brought her relief.

When Lian next went away on business, Niuniu's grandfather came to collect him, and Tianyi heaved a sigh of relief. She was relying on sleeping pills at night but they made her feel weird the next day, not just dizzy but depressed too. Utter dejection overcame her, until she almost felt life was not worth living.

She made herself cheer up, tried to be practical, tried to pull herself together but felt unable to get anything done. Listlessly, she got out her address book and went through the names one by one, trying to imagine what it would be like to talk to this or that person on the phone. But it all felt so futile. This was an age of futility, an age when everything produced was fake. When she thought of the defences she would have to put up to talk to any of them, she was filled with disgust. She was still true to herself, was a child of nature, and there was nothing 'civilized' values could do to change that. It was only when she got to their driver Xiaoming that she paused.

She had quietly begun to take note of this young man. He was a handsome youth with an air of mystery about him, taciturn and apt to simply disappear after ¬work, so that no one could find him. With her, however, he was different. Occasionally, when he was driving her and they were alone, he would open up and talk. One Mid-Autumn Festival, she and Lian had gone out to admire the harvest moon, but had had an argument. He had not hesitated to take her side and when she got her wish and was able to stand by the Beihai Lake to look at the moon, he suddenly made a comment: 'Mrs Yang, you appreciate beautiful things in a very deep way.' She had been startled. This was certainly a compliment, though not the sort of compliment you would expect from a driver. Her finger pressed his number.

He arrived less than a quarter of an hour later. 'Where would you like to go?' he asked with a smile. They drove around, with no particular destination in mind, until the sun was setting behind the mountains. 'Let me treat you to dinner,' she said. 'You choose the place.' He took her to Sun City Hotpot, a very popular place in the mid-nineties, but Tianyi could not summon up any interest in the food. On that early autumn evening, she was wearing a slim black wool skirt that showed off her figure nicely, although she was scarcely aware of it.

The diners served themselves to the ingredients, and she made Xiaoming sit where he was, while she went back and forth bringing tea and food to the table until Xiaoming began to be a little uneasy at such attentiveness from his boss. The pair ate slowly, and Xiaoming accompanied it with a drink or two. It was a very enjoyable evening. Tianyi felt completely relaxed. With Xiaoming, she did not need to put on a front of any kind. She had not felt so relaxed for a very long time.

There was another surprise to come. 'There's somewhere I'd like to take you,' Xiaoming said, when they had finished eating. When they were alone together, he always called her 'elder sister'. She agreed without a moment's thought. How mysterious, she felt, what fun.

It certainly was mysterious. A thick mist was descending. He drove north, a long, long way, for perhaps two hours, until they arrived at a hotel. When they went in, Tianyi realized that Xiaoming knew the hotel staff well—two hostesses greeted him warmly, took them to the bar in the foyer and served them tea. Xiaoming's mood was as upbeat as if he was back in his home town. After their first cup of tea, he became very talkative. He told her about his family: his father was deputy departmental head of some organization, his mother lectured in accounting at a university. He had skipped school a lot as a child and so did not get into university. He was married but he reckoned that had been a big mistake, he had slipped up just once and made a girl pregnant, and had had to make things right by marrying her.

'So what will you do?' Tianyi was genuinely concerned. She was surprised that he was talking about such a grave matter apparently so casually. As if it had nothing to do with him. 'There's nothing to be done,' Xiaoming smiled. 'Just get on with things, right? For the sake of the child.'

Tianyi said nothing. For the sake of the child, it was a phrase she had heard countless times, although she did not know whether the sentiment was uniquely Chinese or universal. Were human individuals really so acquiescent, so obedient to the diktats of fate? Why did Chinese men always put their mother and their child in first place, but treat their partners or lovers as if they were expendable? Did all Chinese men want to turn the women they loved into prostitutes, at their beck and call, without ever considering the woman's feelings? Suddenly she wanted to cry.

Xiaoming must have sensed a change in Tianyi, because he asked anxiously: 'What's up?' Tianyi made an effort to hide her distress. 'Nothing.'

He gave her a cautious glance and said in a low voice: 'I'll tell you something. You see, this place is my base.' 'Yes, I can see that,' she said vaguely. He dropped his voice even more. 'Please don't ever tell the boss. This is where my lover lives.'

She took a moment to react. 'What?'

He repeated it, then went on: 'I brought you here to meet her, but unfortunately she's gone home this evening.' Tianyi suddenly felt a wave of distress, which left her utterly drained.

Because of her fatigue, they started back late at night, driving slowly home through the fog. In all her forty years, she had never experienced fog this thick in Beijing. The car seemed to be floating in a cloud. Who knew where they were going? It was actually rather exciting.

Xiaoming was in good spirits. 'Are you afraid?' he asked her. 'No. Not at all,' she said. *What's to be afraid of,* she thought to herself. Better to die in this godforsaken place than to struggle along as she had been doing. She had a sudden vision: early dawn, the mist still lingering; a car crash, the vehicle smashed to pieces, the still-warm corpses of a man and a woman. Reports circulating that the pair had been carrying on an illicit affair. Then Lian's face, looking stunned. She found herself smiling a little.

The car nosed its lonely way through the mist. It was very, very late, two o'clock in the morning, when they finally arrived at her door. She had a sudden realization that this was not her home, it was a cage in which she was imprisoned. She had been delivered back to prison and she did not want to go in. He was puzzled at the dazed look on her face. Softly he leaned forward and planted a kiss in her cheek.

She was startled out of her dream. Instinctively, she knew she did not want to go back into that house, to that life that was like a living death, to that persistent smell of oestrogen. And her heart broke.

She suddenly flung her arms around him and burst into tears, clinging to him like a drowning person grips a lifebuoy. She was quite well aware that the lifebuoy would not save her because there were too many people drowning and the lifebuoy was destined to go to someone else, not to her. The tears scared him out of his wits. She wept and wept, a life-time of tears. He stammered some words, but she did not take them in.

Tianyi went into the house, her head spinning, too dazed to do anything. Then she gathered herself and sat down at the typewriter. It was 1994, and she did not have a computer yet, just a Sitong 2403 word-processor. She typed a title: *Drowning*. And so, that fog-laden night in the mid-nineties, Tianyi wrote the story of an ordinary Chinese woman. At the time, she just felt as if her heart was breaking. She had no idea that years later this story would get her into further trouble with the authorities.

Life did have its lighter moments, however. Tianyi took her material on trafficked women, called *Fenhe Bay Adventures*, to Tong. Tong, twice-married, twice-divorced, was now in charge of a TV production company. She got an answer a few days later. Tong had only two questions: 'What's this screen play about?' Trafficked women, said Tianyi. 'Who wrote it?' Me, she told him. 'In that case, I don't need to read it. Come and sign the contract tomorrow,' said Tong. It was as simple as that. Tianyi sold the screenplay, ten episodes, for 3,000 *yuan* per episode.

30,000 *yuan* was a huge sum for a media work in mainland China in the mid-nineties. When Tianyi actually had the money in her hands, and counted, she was half-aware of a smile on Tong's face. She suddenly felt that it was an immensely sunny smile. It warmed her to think of it for many years afterwards. It had emerged like the sun from behind clouds, and brightened the gloomy innermost recesses of her heart.

The year that followed was full of sunlight. In 1995, the Fourth World Conference on Women chose Beijing for its venue and instantly China's women, especially the intellectuals, came to life. A leading scholar brought out a collection of women's writing, and a piece by Tianyi was included. The concept of 'Women's writing' made its debut in the literary world and, more interesting still for Tianyi, she gained critical recognition as a representative of the genre. This was partly due to her old publication, *The Tree of Knowledge,* and even more because of *Drowning.*

Drowning caused an unimaginable commotion. It was as if this was the first time since the founding of New China, indeed since ancient times, that women's sexual needs, their deep inner suffering, and their ways of dealing with it, had been laid before the reader so clearly, so determinedly, so boldly, so painfully. Up until then, women's eternal diffidence ('Hiding half her face behind the *pipa*' in the words of the Bai Juyi poem) had caused people to misunderstand their sexual desires. It was as if Chinese women did not need sex, and were only passive partners, coerced into it by men. Chinese women's sexuality had always been an absolutely taboo topic. Only a fool would have tried to rip away the veil that covered it. And that fool was Yang Tianyi, and she was a fool through and through.

Not unexpectedly, retribution was swift. Although *Drowning* was chosen unanimously for a literary prize soon afterwards, it was subsequently dropped. The reason was an anonymous letter whose author did a thorough job of demolishing *Drowning*, and in the voice of sweet reason and moderation, too. The writer had even saved the authorities the trouble of reading the book, by meticulously going to the trouble of cutting and pasting sections of it into the letter, like a good, considerate Party comrade. The letter made its way right up to the Literary Censorship Bureau, where the cut and pasted excerpts stirred up a hornet's nest amongst its top brass.

Many years later, Tianyi found out to her amazement that the culprit had been Xi, Tong's second wife. She was divorced now, and a writer, having started first with flattering articles about her rock star boyfriend, Meng. With her passable English, she had then worked her way into the Foreign Languages Research Institute. Most recently, she had started writing novels.

Xi was generally a very mixed-up young woman, in and out of relationships like a yoyo. However, her relationship with Meng helped boost her career because he was convinced she had talent and encouraged her to write fiction. He was a bit of a connoisseur of good literature and well-connected too, being on back-slapping terms with all the most important people in the literary world. Meng's efforts were not wasted: Xi's success was a credit to him But as soon as he read Tianyi's *Drowning*, Meng began to have sleepless nights.

Meng had always felt that Xi was extremely talented, surely able to beat any of the newly fashionable women writers hands down. That is, until he gave *Drowning* a careful read and realized with alarm that this Yang Tianyi, whom he'd never heard of, posed a real threat to his lover. Of course, he could tell from her photograph that she was not a patch on Xi to look at, but in her style and depth of knowledge, she was far superior. There was scarcely anything in her writing that you could find fault with.

Over breakfast one day, Meng warned Xi: 'You better watch out for that Tianyi!' Xi was sceptical at first. After all, that silly woman hadn't written a word for years, why would she be a threat? But age and experience count for a lot and before long, Meng had convinced Xi that Tianyi was having a very bad effect on Meng's entire strategy for Xi. So Xi sat down in their bedroom and wrote that anonymous letter on Meng's instructions. Meng photocopied *Drowning* for her himself, tracked down all the bits that referred to the body, cut them out and pasted them into the letter.

Tianyi never in her wildest dreams suspected Xi. After all, the girl had always been so smilingly unstinting in her admiration. Around then, Tianyi was delighted to receive an invitation, together with another woman writer, to a literary get-together on 'Writing in the new age', to be held in a well-known hotel on the outskirts of Beijing. It was Xi who sent the invitation letter and called her to reassure her cheerfully that she did not need to prepare anything. They would just enjoy themselves.

Xi had appeared on the literary scene at a quiet time. Not to put too fine a point on it, she was not a very good writer yet; her writing was limited mainly to impassioned outbursts which expressed 'her reality'. Her language was full of the sort of malice endemic in an age of intellectual sterility. It just so happened that the Foreign Languages Institute was holding a get-together, and she took the opportunity to invite Tianyi and her fellow writer to go and 'enjoy themselves'.

And when evening came, Tianyi did enjoy herself. She may have been a good bit older than the others, but she was young at heart. She seized the mike and sang karaoke with gusto. In fact, she would have gone on all night if the karaoke hall had not shut its doors. But the instant she got home, the phone rang. It was the other woman writer, sounding gloomy: 'Tianyi, you're such a fool. Why are you letting yourself be Xi's doormat?' Tianyi was taken aback. Then the woman went on: 'Can't you see she's just using us as a prop for her literary career? She just wants someone to hold up her smelly feet for her! Didn't you see how she told us not to prepare anything, but she prepared very well and that certainly made her look good!' Tianyi could not believe her ears. This woman was just being bitchy, surely! She fobbed her off with a few words, then hung up. A few days later, Xi called: a well-reputed magazine from somewhere in China had asked for an article about her, and Xi would like Tianyi to write it. Tianyi did not raise any objections.

It was only when she came to write it that she began to worry: this was a really difficult article to write. They had just had a good time together. Good feelings could not be put into words. She was in a quandary.

As she racked her brains, she took a look at what one critic had written about Xi's writing. Normally, he did not pull his punches, but for some reason, he had treated Xi with kid gloves, in fact had heaped praise on her. As the months went by, she realized that all the critics, even the ones who savaged writers' work, behaved like pussycats where Xi was concerned. She certainly was a superb manipulator—she did not use money or sex, it was just that every time she opened her mouth, out came a barbed comment. And just one comment would do it, no matter how astute and savvy the intended victim was. Not a few seasoned authors, no matter how much of life they had seen and lived, fell right into the palm of Xi's little hand in this way. It all goes to show that sometimes it is someone quite mediocre who most easily makes people drop their guard.

Tianyi was a conscientious woman. In those days, there was no internet so she went to the library to look things up. She spent a whole three or four days there, even skipping meals, and finally found something to write for Xi's article. She mailed it to her. Xi was delighted with the article, and called simply to say: 'Tianyi, you're a darling!' To herself, she thought, but did not say: 'Tianyi, you're a fool!'

The literary world adores newcomers, and of course that included Xi. Once Tianyi's article was published, and some laudatory reviews, Xi ascended to the pinnacle of the pyramid that was the world of letters. But Xi, however brilliant, was comparatively new to all this and was forever calling on Tianyi to help her sort out this or that. Xi was child-like in her ability to enjoy herself and forget her worries. Once, Xi got very drunk at a meeting of the Writers' Association in some enterprise. On their way home, the boss of the corporation made a pass at her. Tianyi, sitting in the front passenger seat of the car, happened to turn around and was aghast: she could see quite clearly the man's hand kneading Xi's breast and Xi's hand had a firm grip on his prick. Tianyi instantly felt she wanted to stop playing this game.

Then a letter arrived from Tianyue in America. She needed her sister's help, she wrote, for an old college friend, Ke. Tianyue had met him again just before she left, he was now the CEO of a big company. And he was in trouble. Could she do a horoscope reading for him?

Ke turned up that very day in his Ford car, an impressively tall figure who greeted Lian enthusiastically and shook him by the hand. The pair began to talk of the old days, when they were in the Red Guards together, in the rebels' faction, all the people who ranked above and below them. Lian, of course, had ranked below Ke.

There were few top-class places to eat back then, but without further ado, Ke put Tianyi, Lian and Niuniu in his car and drove them off to the Hong Hong Gourmet Emporium, the most famous restaurant in town and virtually inaccessible to ordinary folk. He ordered platefuls of delicacies like braised shark's fin with rice and puffer fish. Tianyi was mortified when Niuniu demolished the lot, and then asked for more but Ke ordered another portion without hesitation. Tianyi secretly wondered whether she would have to pay the bill for her greedy son.

Ke did not beat about the bush: he needed Tianyi do a reading for him from the *I Ching*. Tianyi felt she was nowhere near good enough but the more she demurred, the more the other two told her to stop being modest. They had every confidence in her, they insisted. And so she agreed. She was always anxious not to let people down and put her best efforts into readings although she really was only a beginner. Nevertheless, the results sometimes astonished her. Take Ke for instance, she knew almost nothing about him but as soon as she cast the trigrams, everything became clear: Ke was currently facing a crisis and needed to get as far away as possible. When she told him, he fixed her with an intense stare, and was silent for a long time.

Soon after, Ke decided to quit and go to America. 'Do you want to come?' he asked Tianyi. He made it sound it sound as if they were popping off to somewhere in Beijing. She nodded. And a month later, she bought her air ticket. It was all extraordinarily simple. She thought of all the rushing around she had had to do a few years before, to get her passport. It dawned on her that everything had its time. No matter how hard you tried, if it was not the right time for something to happen, then it would not. And when the time was right, then things went through quite naturally.

Ke may have been a tall man but he had over-indulged and put on so much weight that his belly was as distended as a tin drum, on which he liked to sign his name. Ke was a great joker, so a dozen hours' flight time would not be so unbearable. Her sister was a lucky woman, Tianyi thought.

What really occupied her mind however was this: finally, she could see Zheng again! She had just heard from Peng that Zheng was through the worst of his ordeal—he had secretly been released and was in America.

21

Tianyi's first sight of America was Alhambra, Los Angeles County, and the first thing she noticed was the sky. It was the kind of azure that she remembered from her childhood, the sky of autumnal Beijing. An azure she had not seen for a very long time. This heart-warming sight immediately put Tianyi in a good mood. All thoughts of jetlag disappeared, and she felt she had shed years from her age.

However, what happened next was puzzling. Ke took her to visit his younger sister, but there was no sign of the sister and her husband (later she discovered he was actually just her boyfriend), even though they searched the whole house. All they found were some frozen leek dumplings, *jiaozi*, which Ke cooked for the two of them. When he saw Tianyi's expression, he said: 'It's just a stopgap. When they get home, we'll have a proper meal.'

But his sister, Mei, and her boyfriend were home very late. They had a little boy with them, Xiongxiong, Mei's child with her ex-husband. Tianyi was surprised at Mei's frosty welcome: Tianyi herself got a casual greeting while Mei ignored her brother completely. Even more astonishing, Ke, prone to swaggering and blustering in China, was as meek as a lamb here, bustling in and out of the kitchen as instructed and making dinner for the whole family.

When dinner was over, Tianyi presented the small gifts she had brought and Ke put a stash of American dollars into his little nephew's hand. This at least brought a smile to Mei's face. Ke had arranged for Tianyi to spend the night in a nearby guesthouse run by overseas Chinese. It was unimaginably shabby but she did not care. Nothing could dampen the excitement that bubbled within her. The next morning at nine o'clock, the phone rang—it was Ke inviting her for breakfast.

She was amazed that they were to eat an authentic Guangdong-style breakfast, and plenty of it, since Ke had ordered a lot as if to make up for the deficiencies of yesterday's dinner. They had a leisurely meal, talking as they ate, and gradually Tianyi came to understand Ke's problem. He had been drawn unwittingly into a property scam, he said, though Tianyi was sceptical that he was quite as squeaky clean as he was making out.

Ke gave her a few hundred American dollars so she could sign up for visits to Disneyland, Hollywood and San Diego. He told her these were all must-see places for anyone visiting the area, but he had been several times and did not want to go again. So Tianyi joined a tour group of local overseas Chinese and went off to enjoy herself—and enjoy herself she did. Everywhere there were dazzling colours and for someone like her who was so sensitive to colours, it was heaven! In front of a little wooden house in Disneyland was a mass of pink blossom, so perfect she thought the flowers must be fake. She touched the petals and was astonished to find they were real! She was delighted. It was a very long time since she had seen such gorgeous colours. How did the shrubs cope with air pollution, she wondered? Such brightness was in glaring contrast to anything back home.

There was a kind of simplicity in people's expressions too, a transparency. It was nothing like the look in people's eyes in China, a mixture of ignorance and cunning. Here their expressions reminded her of her childhood; that was when she had last seen such eyes, such expressions, or felt such an atmosphere in China.

Attracted by the deep blue waters of the ocean at San Diego, (and forgetting her US visa was single-entry), she boldly attached herself to a tour group going across the border into Mexico. Now she was in another country. She lingered over the displays of crudely-made but exotic souvenirs, caught up in her bargaining until imperceptibly the sun began to set over the mountains. Suddenly, she seemed to hear Ke's voice in her ear: 'Whatever you do, don't cross the border, or you'll be in big trouble. Your visa is single-entry.'

She was appalled. Clutching her bag of eclectic purchases, she looked hesitantly at the ill-marked border. There were only two Mexican guards standing there, and they looked half-asleep. There was nothing for it, she would just have to put a bold face on it. After all, she had done that plenty of times in her life. Nonchalantly, she strolled back over it. She was stopped by one of the Mexicans. She imagined the corpulent, dark-skinned guard suddenly turning fierce, and reaching out that dark-skinned, fleshy hand and, for an instant, she trembled all over. Then she realized that no one was paying the slightest attention to her and, concealed behind some much taller people, she simply slipped back past the border post. How casual these border crossings were, she thought to herself. She almost laughed as she remembered how difficult it had been for her to obtain her passport to leave China.

She stayed out until late at night. At the bus stop on her way back to the guesthouse, she saw some blacks talking and laughing under the dim street lamps. No longer afraid, she gave them a casual wave: 'Hi!' She got a 'Hi!' and genuine smiles, showing their gleaming white teeth, in return.

Everything she had been told since she was a child was a lie: the two-thirds of the world who lived out their lives in misery were not Americans, but her own countrypeople. The ideal country she had dreamed of since she was a child, was right here.

And soon Tianyue arrived from Salt Lake University, where she was studying to get a place on a Masters course. Tianyi had grown up worshipping her big sister. After her father, Tianyue was the one she was closest to. Now she scrutinized her, genuinely delighted to see her. Tianyue had never had children, and had a good figure. Her clothes fitted well, unlike Tianyi's. Tianyi had a fine bust but child-bearing had broadened her hips and given her a big bottom. Tianyi envied her sister her figure while Tianyue, naturally flat-chested, envied her little sister her breasts. Was there a woman in this world who was satisfied with the way she looked? Women's torment about their bodies went on until they died, just like that poor Brazilian model Luisel Ramos who, even though she was 1.75 metres tall, was determined to diet and diet until she was only 45 kilos. For a woman of her height, it would have been surprising if she had not died.

Tianyi noticed her sister's attitude towards Mei: despite forcing a smile, she avoided looking Mei in the eyes, and busied herself instead in getting out the presents she had brought. As she bent over to unzip her bag, Tianyi noticed that her permed hair had no shine to it all. It looked whiskery, and so brittle it might fall out if you touched it. Her sister's way of putting on a smile that was not a real smile reminded her of her father. Tianyue got all the presents out, and sat down, exhausted. Mei gave a grudging smile at the sight of a bottle of Chanel perfume. Much better than giving CDs, she said, and went into the kitchen. Startled, Tianyi looked at her retreating figure. Without the Chanel, would they have had any dinner, she wondered? Tianyi dutifully followed her into the kitchen. Mei, ladle in hand, said to her with a smile: 'You know about my brother and your sister, do you?' Tianyi was mystified.

Tianyue had just learned to drive and on their journey to Las Vegas, both Tianyi and Ke had to stay alert. Ke was in the front passenger seat, and responsible for looking out front and to the right, while Tianyi, in the back seat, looked out left and behind. All three were on edge. Tianyue told them to remind her when they saw the green Exit sign. That was the way off the expressway and you were in all sorts of trouble if you overshot it.

This was Tianyi's first experience of American freeways. In China in 1996, there were no roads of this sort, the sort that reminded her of the line from the famous Li Bai poem: *Like the Milky Way, fallen from the Ninth Heaven.* Looking at them, Tianyi understood for the first time why there were few traffic jams even though there were so many cars in America.

Nevada was a desert, from the middle of which there rose a monumental palace—the famous city of Las Vegas. To Tianyi's wonderstruck eyes, Las Vegas by night was like a jewel box, revealing an infinity of glittering gems everywhere she looked. There were fantastic light displays, and spectacular, gigantic fountains, four golden horse-heads spitting flames. No living creature could fail to be moved by these heart-stopping sights, let alone a woman like Tianyi, who still had something of the child in her,

Tianyi rushed around taking photographs with the Olympus Lian had brought her back from the US. It had been a good camera back then, and took good pictures. Besides, film processing in the US was of a much better standard than China. In the pictures taken of her, with her fashionable bob and loose-fitting red and blue-patterned jumper, she looked relaxed and pretty, far younger than her forty-odd years.

That trip was the first time she saw a striptease. It was not nearly as expensive as she had imagined, only thirty bucks a person, including drinks. In the dimly-lit room, she was amazed to see these unreal-looking beauties strip off the very last piece of clothing. The lighting made their private parts look unreal too, like patches of grey rubber. The men had clearly seen it all before and acted hard to please. Both men and women alike seemed quite unmoved by the experience. A big-breasted woman approached an overweight man in the row in front of her and gyrated her hips, until the man reached with some difficulty into his pocket, pulled out a hundred-dollar bill and tucked it into her G-string.

The casinos were something else again—quite dazzling. The slot machines with their brilliantly-coloured rows of fruit and numbers, the huge tables offering all kinds of games, roulette, vingt-et-un, dice. The slender young waitresses in their uniforms, going back and forth with trays laden with drinks, the pattering of coins cascading from the machines, the smells, a heady, decadent mixture of perfume, smoke and who knows what else.

Tianyi sat beside her sister, studying the way she pulled the lever of the slot machine, and then Ke bought a large pot of tokens for her. She enjoyed the tinkling they made as they dropped into the tray, and that sudden, wonderful feeling of winning the jackpot. The sisters did not dare gamble for high stakes, because they were playing with someone else's money. Even so, they had some success, winning two hundred bucks on the one-armed bandits alone.

When they had had enough, they moved to their hotel room, upstairs from the casino. The three of them shared a room, so did not undress. Tianyue had on the silk top she had worn often in Beijing, with small mauve flowers on it. They had one bed, with Tianyue in the middle, and Tianyi and Ke on either side. Ke cracked a few jokes then fell asleep as they were laughing, but Tianyue was restless. Tianyi dozed until the small hours when she was aware of Tianyue silently getting out of bed. It was a strange sort of night. The sounds of cascading coins from the casino downstairs were quite audible, but could not muffle Tianyue's footsteps as she quietly left the room. As if hypnotized, Tianyi collected her handbag and followed on her sister's heels.

Back in the casino, Tianyue showed her true mettle: she staked her entire thousand bucks and lost every cent. Tianyi felt herself drawn to follow her sister's lead: she fed the slot machine with her winnings, and the machine swallowed it all up.

Tianyi still remembered Tianyue's bewildered expression, but neither sister complained. Tianyi was reminded of the story of Ali Baba. They had both behaved just like the rich men in his cave. They were so self-righteous but they had no reason to laugh at other people. They were no better than anyone else. Humans were greedy and self-destructive by nature.

Salt Lake University, however, was in stark contrast to Las Vegas. This was Tianyue's home turf. The campus was carpeted in snow, through which poked exquisite flowers Tianyi did not know the names of. They somehow gave her the impression that she had been carried off to the realm of the Snow Queen. Her sister's rented house was much nicer than she had expected. It was built of sand-coloured brick, and stood in a row of others that looked like Lego houses, or rather cardboard cut-outs. For some reason, she had the impression that these houses were so flimsy that they could be dismantled just like that and then reassembled.

Silence. Tianyi felt as if she had been swallowed up by an unearthly quiet. At the start, she did not even dare raise her voice above a whisper. She was secretly rather fearful of Tianyue's landlady. She was quite a character, a jewellery-maker, or so Tianyi understood, and reeked of cheap perfume. She was old enough to have liver spots on her hands, but that did not stop her sporting at least six rings set with diamonds, gold, sapphires and emeralds. Tianyi was quite worried that the weight of them would deform her fingers. The woman wore thick blue eye-liner, and her eyelashes were long, curly and thickly mascara'd. But nothing could hide the fact that she was knocking on seventy. The overall effect was of some weird witch, with a glint in her eyes so sinister that Tianyi for a long time avoided meeting her gaze.

The landlady had been abandoned by her husband, Tianyue told her. She ran a one-woman business making jewellery and had a daughter. She apparently missed her daughter terribly but as soon as the two were together, they quarrelled. Mainly about money.

The woman gave Tianyi a hard, unfriendly look. Tianyi tried her very best to charm her, more for her sister's sake than her own. She paid the old witch so many compliments that she began to sound corny even to her own ears but, in any case, it appeared to have no effect at all.

Ke could afford to ignore all this, because he had money. He rented an apartment of his own as soon as he could, a generously-sized one with its own entrance, a spacious living room and an open-plan kitchen—the first time Tianyi had seen this kind of layout. She had grown up living in a cramped, Soviet-style terraced house allocated to them by her father's college, ugly but solidly-built, where the kitchen was too small to swing a cat.

The supermarkets in America astonished her. Growing up in Beijing, she had never seen anything like it. She watched as her sister and Ke piled all manner of things into their shopping trolley: pots and pans, vegetables and fruit, rice and other groceries appeared as if by magic. She was astonished to see that a large carton of concentrated fruit juice was reduced to 70 cents, because it was two days past its sell-by date.

It was so simple to make a new home. She bustled around in it, remembering how she had loved moving to a new home when she was little, because it brought her a whole new group of friends. But now they were in America. The neighbours were friendly but they kept their distance. She liked this feeling of distance, people ought not to be crammed cheek by jowl, it was cleaner this way.

And how clean Salt Lake University campus was! In Beijing, if you wore a pair of sandals outside for three days, they would be filthy but here they never got dirty. Even the piled-up snow looked spotless. Tianyi liked to go out in the early mornings for a leisurely stroll through the silvery landscape, wearing a bright red woollen cape that she had bought especially for this trip. As she walked along, someone might stick their head out of a passing car and call a friendly: 'Hi!' And, quite naturally, she would respond: 'Hi!' They might give a wink and a smile, and her own answering smile would come spilling out. These small gestures made her feel immediately at home. She could not understand why so many Chinese, including Lian, found America alienating. She felt as if she had been born here. How clean, innocent, friendly and unthreatening these winks were!

Tianyi was quite convinced that America was her ideal country. Her American dream lasted right up until she stepped on its soil for the second time, some years later, and found everything had changed. Nine Eleven destroyed this people, there were no more clean, innocent winks.

On this first visit, however, Tianyi fell in love with the place, its people, its scenery, everything about it. Every morning she got up early and went out for a walk in the snow, wearing her bright-red cape, enjoying the extraordinary blossoms, the fairytale-like houses, and those clean, innocent smiles.

Some of the shops opened very early but most at ten o'clock.

Any that had an OPEN sign, and a display of fresh flowers and souvenirs (often made by the native Americans), she would go in, saying in response to the sales assistant's friendly smile: 'I'm just looking.' Then she would subject the displays to a careful inspection, feeling quite safe and content. She made the occasional purchase, too. Everything was so ingeniously made, for instance a tiny house made out of wire, or a piece of light blue stone carved with the head of native American. Often, when she took them home, Ke teased her: 'You're just like Lian said, like a child!'

A Professor Jones had asked her to give a lecture at Salt Lake University, on the subject of women's writing and *Drowning*. The thought of her book reminded Tianyi that she was only here on a visit. The reality she had deliberately ignored came back with absolute clarity: far away in the East, in a very ordinary apartment building, she had a violent husband and a weakling of a son. That clarity turned in her guts like a knife.

All the overseas Chinese students, and students studying Chinese culture and language turned up. There was not an empty seat in the lecture theatre. From their expressions and their applause, she knew that they understood *Drowning*, and her. It was no doubt the first time they had had a Chinese author come to lecture them on Chinese literature here in this rural backwater. Most Americans imagined that Chinese were like the people in Zhang Yimou's films, the women tottering along on bound feet, the men smoking opium, or dressed in baggy trousers, herding their animals on the loess plateau. This ordinary-looking Chinese woman gave them a very different view of China. The world of Chinese intellectuals and scholars had been closed off to the rest of the world since the 1930s. The rulers of New China had been extremely hostile to the educated class, targeting them in one movement after another. By the modern era, there were no traces left of the moral principles of China's ancient scholars.

Tianyi often lay awake worrying about what kind of race the Chinese would turn into if things carried on like this. Over the centuries, most of those loyal officials brave enough to criticise their superiors to their faces had been punished with death while those who were lucky enough to escape that fate were subjected to one calamity after another. That just left sycophants prepared to work the system. A whole people had been bled dry of the quality of loyalty. Zheng was one of a kind and, by sheer good luck, had managed to survive, but only by risking his life and staring death in the face. She felt as if her heart was breaking.

From the day when she first trod on the soil of the United States of America, she had been searching for Zheng. All she knew was that he was on the East Coast, nothing more than that.

The evening of the lecture, Ke mysteriously pulled her to one side and said in a low voice: 'I've been thinking today of…of trying to get your sister on side. What do you reckon?' Tianyi almost laughed out loud: Ke's jokey way of putting things surely concealed a deep insecurity. She said offhandedly: 'Do you think it'll work?' Ke eyed her uncertainly. 'You know, my sister is pretty much immune to being "got on side",' she went on. Ke's thick eyebrows clumped together in a frown, and she softened: 'From what I know of my sister, she's someone who goes for spontaneity, so the less you plan it, the better the results will be.'

That evening turned into a seminar on Ke's problems. Tianyi had not realized just how serious they were. What Ke had told her was just the tip of the iceberg. Actually, he was in very deep trouble. He had started with a software company, and moved into property in the early nineties. His was probably the first real estate company on the mainland. He got himself certificated by a high-level local official who, in his words, was a 'hyena'. And not the only one. Ke had taken on a tower block, and when it was under construction, this official was just one in a whole pack of hyenas, all busily engaged in getting their rake-off from the wealthy investor who was funding the project.

Of course, the wealthy property investor was not above a bit of wheeling and dealing himself. He only knew Ke, never having met the officials who were on the take, so it was Ke he started to put the screws on. The odd thing was that, even before she knew the facts, Tianyi's *I Ching* reading had been that Ke needed to 'wade the great river' and start afresh. This prediction had earned Ke's undying admiration.

In any case, this investor had now brought a lawsuit against Ke's company. In Ke's view, the only way of clearing his name was to find the official concerned. Tianyi felt a flicker of doubt—she had never been quite convinced of Ke's probity. Not so Tianyue. Like so many women, she was completely blinded by love and insisted Ke was innocent. Ke spent that evening puzzling over the draft of a fax to send to his company in Beijing. He kept scratching words out and re-wording it, convinced it was full of mistakes. Tianyi could see that Tianyue could hardly keep her eyelids open and offered to draft the fax herself. Ke was sceptical that she had any talents in this direction but, by this stage, his options were running out. And that was how Tianyi did her bit to push her sister into bed with Ke. Once she had finished the fax, she got washed and went to bed herself.

The next morning, she was startled awake by Ke's shout of amazement. He had seen the fax lying on the table.'Ai-ya! I've met plenty of women in my life but I've never met one as clever as this! Tianyi, however did you think up such an amazing ruse?'

Tianyi looked in confusion at the happy couple and for a moment did not reply. Then she saw Tianyue's jealous look and realized that the fax she had written last night had been of considerable help to Ke. But Tianyue was far from grateful. She was extraordinarily pig-headed, and it was this determination in her which made up for her natural deficiencies. From then on, she spent every evening drafting and re-drafting for Ke, until finally Ke said: 'Good, that's enough.'

Tianyi was well and truly on her own now. But the news of her success at Salt Lake spread fast and she began to receive phone calls from other universities asking her to lecture. Since she had forgotten almost all the English she ever learned—it was so poor she could scarcely even manage to ask the way—could she travel on her own? She soon overcame her doubts; you hardly needed any English to move around freely in America. It was even easier, she felt, than moving around the country she had grown up in.

The first stop was Rocky Mountain University where she had been invited by a celebrated American sinologist. The professor had taken a Chinese name, Zheng Miaowu, and spoke excellent Chinese. Tianyi arrived, wearing a black woollen skirt under a dark blue-and-white batik cape that she had bought in Yunnan, and a Japanese necklace made from pieces of wood that tinkled pleasantly. The professor told her visiting lecturers came in three price tags; for instance, Wusheng, the author of *Old City*, did not get the highest fee when he came to talk. He told her she should take the highest fee she could, and so on. A great many people came to listen to Tianyi, far more than at Salt Lake, and Tianyi knew this was down to the prestige of her host. As before, she talked of women writers in China, taking pains to say nice things about her young friend Xi and her cohort of writers and equally carefully avoiding mentioning herself. She was to learn, many years later, that in this way she had sent her listeners off to the pinnacle of the pyramid that was the world of letters (Xi) while she found herself left far below. It is a truism, however, that people habitually find it convenient to forget the people who have boosted their careers, and so it was with Xi.

It was the Easter holidays. After the lecture was finished, half a dozen Chinese students offered to take her around. There was the university's 'golden couple', the boy apparently of Malay extraction, the girl with a slight limp. Tianyi immediately took to the girl who, she felt, looked positively angelic and put all the other students in the shade.

The pair took Tianyi around the Rocky Mountain University Museum and it was only because they were determined to see all four of the vast exhibition halls that they saw the most marvellous exhibit of all: in the very last room, one complete wall was hung with four long black dresses. They all gasped at the same moment. It seemed almost unimaginable that four black velvet dresses could have such an unsettling effect.

The dresses were pegged high up on the walls and their hems trailed right down to the smooth floor. Each one was so long that the pure black velvet lengths were like four eerily silent dark cascades. The effect in this great space was utterly mysterious and reduced them all to silence. What a pity they had no camera with them, the girl lamented. In fact, Tianyi had a camera but you were not allowed to use flash in the museum and she only managed one dim image.

They had a rice and omelette for dinner. It was Easter so you had to have something with eggs in. The omelette, golden yellow, was covered in a layer of tomato sauce. Tianyi found it delicious, and ate with a good appetite. She had had a very good appetite this trip, enjoying everything people cooked for her, the way a child does.

By way of a thank-you, Tianyi got out some presents and

presented her host with a cloisonné egg, appropriate for Easter she thought. It was skilfully engraved but the professor did not appear to appreciate it. She could not help remembering something rather astonishing that he had said that evening. 'Do you know who the best woman writer is in China?' he had asked. 'Lu Bei!' he had answered himself. Tianyi was startled, until she remembered that Lu Bei, who wrote low-grade political novels, was the professor's partner. Well, he was a human being too, wasn't he? It was not too surprising.

Tianyi did not get her pictures developed until she was back in China. The four dresses hung side-by-side in one photo, but the mysterious atmosphere, and its eerie power, were entirely gone, developed away in the processing.

22

Professor 'Zheng Miaowu' was a powerful figure at Rocky Mountain University and the news of the success of the lecture he had invited Tianyi to give quickly spread to the East Coast. Invitations from Pennsylvania and Maryland Universities followed in quick succession. In the blink of an eye, it seemed, she had become a travelling scholar. She travelled, she lectured, she earned a fee and that paid for the next leg of the journey. Most importantly, she was coming ever closer to the man she loved.

Finally one day she arrived in New York. As soon as she could, she took a boat trip and sailed under the huge hand of the Statue of Liberty. Looking up at the statue from below made her suddenly want to weep. She remembered reading a poem about it many years before: *Give me your tired, your poor, Your huddled masses yearning to breathe free, The wretched refuse of your teeming shore ... Send these, the homeless, tempest-lost to me.* The Statue, so familiar from photographs and painting, from her imagination and her dreams, finally appeared before her eyes. The oddest thing was that the fact that its colossal size in no way intimidated her the way Buddhas in the East did. Instead, it gave her a feeling of warmth and security.

Behind the State of Liberty lay New York, with its legendary sights: the Rainbow Room atop the Rockefeller Centre, Madison Square Gardens, Saint Patrick's Cathedral, Brooklyn Bridge and the Metropolitan Opera House, the splendour of Manhattan and the poverty of the Black areas, the yuppies, the rock singers and the punks, the gays and the migrants, people of every race and colour, the inherited rivalries, the dirty streets, the subways covered in graffiti, and the crime.

As far as Tianyi was concerned, the most important place was the Metropolitan Museum of Modern Arts. It was not only the paintings that she longed to see, it was also the place where she had arranged to meet Zheng.

When Zheng, an expat for five years now, appeared, she felt oddly calm. It was as if they had only parted yesterday. Of course, it dawned on her later, this was because their spirits had never parted, not for a single day.

Zheng was no longer the young man she remembered. He had arrived at middle age and, if you looked closely, there were signs of the struggle he had been through, that had worn him down and consumed him. It had left an indefinable mark on every pore of his body. Only his eyes were the same deep wells of goodness they had always been. Such great goodness, astonishingly still present after all his sufferings.

But Zheng clearly wanted to avoid saying a single word about that suffering, forestalling her with a barrage of words. She scarcely had a chance to get a word in edgeways. 'Do you know when the Metropolitan Museum of Art was built? It was actually started in 1866 … right, and now it's 1996, so it's 130 years old this year. A group of Americans got together in a restaurant in the Bois de Boulogne, Paris, to celebrate ninety years since the Declaration of Independence, and at the banquet, the lawyer John Jay proposed building a "national institution and gallery of art". This was to be America's first museum and the proposal won unanimous acceptance …'

Zheng's words came and went intermittently in Tianyi's ears, as other visitors pushed by with muttered Excuse me's. Instinctively, she took his hand and saw the corner of his mouth twitch. His hand was warm, but felt somehow petrified in hers. As she touched it, she wanted to cry.

At least she now had the opportunity to look at some of the paintings she most loved, and that helped to distract her. She suspected that Zheng had chosen this as a meeting place for that reason—she was unlikely to get too emotional and make a scene here. She caught sight of the painting by Henri Rousseau called *Le Repas du Lion* that had fascinated her since she was a young woman. Zheng helped her to push her way through and so that she could get a picture with the painting. She had first come across Rousseau at university at the beginning of the eighties. *World Art,* China's most prestigious arts journal, had devoted an entire issue to his work. For the Chinese art world, closed off for so many years, Rousseau's paintings were extraordinarily striking, and the artist had filled her dreams.

A forest of intense tropical colours, a white sun, just risen above the mountain, the tropical flowers and foliage, extraordinarily decorative, extraordinarily serene. A lion, half-hidden in the undergrowth, eating something. The whole painting was like a dreamscape, the branches and leaves so delicate they could have been cut out with scissors. She found it entrancing, too beautiful!

Afterwards, she learned about Rousseau's life. He had kept his distance from painting schools, acknowledging no one as his teacher, although he had gone to Africa and been influenced by African art. His works had an utterly primitivist feel to them and he was eventually recognized in France as the archetypal primitivist painter. His paintings were rich in a primitive lyricism, and had a beauty filled with harmony and a decorative quality, creating a world that was quite unearthly.

There were many painters she liked—Gustave Moreau, Odilon

Redon, Hieronymus Bosch, Reny Lohner, as well as Rousseau. Oddly, they shared one thing in common: they had not been famous in their lifetimes, only after their death.

Then came the Monet paintings. *Apple Trees in Bloom* reminded her of John Galsworthy's story *The Apple Tree*. This was just how she imagined the scenery he described. The lush beautiful abundance of apple blossom!

Everybody knew that the name 'impressionism' had come from Monet's painting *Impression, Sunrise*. Apparently, Monet's early teacher was Eugène Louis Boudin. Then he got to know Renoir, Whistler and others, as they left their painting studios and went out into the woods and meadows to paint from life. Monet greatly respected Gustave Courbet and Manet and was entranced by scientific experiments on light and colour. She recalled an anecdote from a book on Impressionism. One day, when he had not painted for a whole day, Courbet asked him why. He replied; 'I'm waiting for the sun.' *Apple Trees in Bloom* must surely have been painted after the sun came out. The sunshine filtering through the mottled clouds created a charming dappled effect on the apple blossom. The shadows thrown by the brightly-lit blossom contrasted beautifully with the green grass.

' "I am waiting for the sun." What a beautiful way to put it,' she murmured.

'What?' Zheng asked.

'I was saying thinking how beautifully Monet expressed it ... "I am waiting for the sun".'

She saw a shadow pass over his face. 'Actually,' he said, 'waiting is anguish, whether you're waiting for someone or for the sun.'

She looked hard at him. 'You must miss your family a lot.' He shot her a quick glance. She understood that look. He meant: *What nonsense!* But of course it was not nonsense. He was not made of iron, of course he missed his family.

And of course it was not only his family that he missed. He was someone who truly loved his native land. She was keenly aware that the minute he left that land, he was deracinated. He, who had been a luxuriant tree, had had his roots chopped away, and the only reason he had not died was that he had such vitality. The root runners still nourished him, but for how much longer?

'You can go and see another exhibition if you like, there's arms and armour, musical instruments, jewellery, not just drawings and paintings. I'm a bit tired, I'll wait downstairs in the café, look, go down the lift there by the fountain.'

She went on walking around until the museum closed. The café downstairs was huge, open-plan and filled with beautiful green plants. The fountain sometimes spurted as far as the little tables, and there were statues too, made of metal. He was sitting there, deep in thought. She sat down next to him, and ordered an apple juice. It was as if they simultaneously became aware of the sunset sky in the west. 'We aren't waiting for the sun, we're waiting for the sunset. And it's beautiful,' he said quietly.

They sat there, chatting. They talked of the rainy evening in Tiananmen Square in 1976 when they sang songs to commemorate the passing of Premier Zhou Enlai. They remembered eating peculiar-looking cream cakes at the Xinjiekou Street dairy products shop, and evening swims in the Miyun Reservoir ... it all felt like yesterday yet twenty years had passed just like that. They were old now, sitting in the Met Museum in New York. She found it hard to take in.

'You know what? Just yesterday, Song Meiling came on a visit here, at ninety-nine! She wanted to see the exhibits from the Taiwan National Palace Museum. I guess she saw this sunset too.'
She nodded. 'Red sky in the morning, shepherd's warning. Red

sky at night, shepherd's delight. Tomorrow should be nice.' He nodded, too. Then he looked her in the eyes for the first time that day.

'So you remember telling me I was the ultimate idealist?'

'Of course ... of course I do.'

'You're a good woman,' he said.

'And you're a good man.' Tears pricked her eyelids.

She was to take the last train to Boston late that evening. At the station, couples embraced and kissed goodbye. He and she kept their distance from each other, did not even look at each other, just exchanged a few meaningless words.

Suddenly, she said: 'I love American ice-cream.' He looked momentarily taken aback, then set off quickly down the escalator. Impassive, she watched him recede into the distance, a desolate figure. She felt a stab of anguish.

The train whistle had blown when Zheng finally returned, bearing a large tub of icecream, and quickly pushed it into her hand. In the instant that he turned away, she saw he was fighting back tears. She felt as if she was drowning, and her memories of the rest of the evening were blotted out.

23

It was 1996. Now that she was back in China, Tianyi found the contrast with America almost unbearable. The filthy puddles around the food market made her shoes dirty, and these were shoes that had walked the streets of America for three months and stayed clean. Lian just told her to get real. 'This is China,' he said.

But Tianyi's patience was wearing thin. Before, she just got on with things and kept herself to herself, but recently things had changed. The man she loved was unable to return home, her friends had scattered, the atmosphere was oppressive, and with her husband and her son, the two people she had to face every day. It was like her feelings were choking her. She could neither swallow them back, nor say how she really felt.

Her son had become a liar and a thief. She had to keep a close guard over her purse, although she was not happy about doing it. She searched her son's face and saw a gradual change. Of course, his skin had lost its flawless smoothness as he grew into a youth. But it was not that. She had noticed a new quality in him, a sort of viciousness. Yes, viciousness. It was not too strong a word to use. She kept an eye on him, and saw he was always with an older boy called Liang, a particularly vicious-looking young man.

One day she cracked her son's password on his computer. Her son had been surfing foreign porn sites! She clicked and clicked: photo after photo, one video after another. She was appalled. Oh my God! Do today's young people really look at this stuff? She thought back to the stifling rules they had had to live by in her youth. This is beyond belief. She felt completely powerless, like an ant whose life could be ground underfoot at any time by the relentless march of a new era. But she was too frightened to tell Lian.

Lian had become increasingly moody of late. His salary had increased tenfold since starting at the B. O. Holdings. His three hundred *yuan* salary had gone up to three thousand. But as far as Tianyi was concerned, it had actually dropped. Before, those three hundred had gone straight to her, but she never saw a cent of the three thousand.

Every evening Lian would come home and slump in front of the television until the programmes closed down and the screen filled with static. Then one day there was an explosion of rage. He went off, literally, like a rocket. It was around nine o'clock in the evening, and Tianyi had been reading. Suddenly she heard him bellow: 'Mother fucker!'

When she got to the other room, she saw that Lian's face was contorted with rage as he shouted abuse down the telephone. 'You fucking bastard, you still want to fucking control me? No way!' Tianyi felt her blood run cold. She marched up to Lian and tried to wrest the phone from him, but he pushed her away. She stood there gesturing furiously, but he completely ignored her. *Damn it,* Tianyi thought, *no more peace in this home.*

Lian was shouting at Qiankuan. He had been finding Qiankuan's stubbornness hard to take for quite some time, but he had held himself in check. As he had a tendency to go to extremes, this meant putting himself down until he was practically grovelling in the dust, and that just encouraged Qiankuan to trample on him, until one day he went too far and humiliated Lian in front of all the staff.

Lian had responsibility for finance, the part of the business that made Qiankuan most nervous. In fact, there were two things that worried him: first, that Lian often made stupid mistakes, and second, that Lian might fiddle the books. Lian had a lot of friends outside the company, and Qiankuan was afraid Wang might borrow money on the strength of the company's reputation. Qiankuan's worries were not unfounded: Lian had had this in mind for a while, but before he had time to do it, Qiankuan stepped in.

He hired a young man called Li Haibin, who had a masters in finance and practical experience too. Lian could see perfectly well what Qiankuan was up to, and it threw him into a panic. So he lost his temper with Haibin a few times, to see what would happen. Lu Qiankuan, however, had outsmarted him. Li Haibin ignored Lian as he let off steam, then chuckled and carried on as if nothing had happened. To add insult to injury, Qiankuan proceeded to interrogate Lian in front of Haibin and all of their colleagues about some entry in the accounts. Lian was mortified. He had bottled up his anger but now he was ready to exact revenge. He found a new job to move to.

As Tianyi listened to the phone call, she thought she had never heard her husband behave so childishly. For Lian, although he did not know it, that call would have lifelong, even life-threatening, consequences.

Lian threw himself enthusiastically into his new job—again he was deputy CEO. For the first few weeks, when everything seemed to have calmed down, Tianyi won herself a bit of peace and found a quiet moment to talk to her son. She gave him a stack of world classics she had bought for him to read, though he soon discarded them like so much junk. Everything nowadays is ersatz, she thought to herself, nothing real has any value. She could not let her son go on like this. What could possibly replace pornographic websites? She racked her brain until she was close to admitting defeat. Then she hit on a solution. During the summer holidays, she bought a martial arts classic, Louis Cha's *The Deer and the Cauldron,* and casually left it lying around at home. Once her son had picked it up, he could not put it down and took it with him everywhere, even to the toilet. She kept her delight to herself, afraid that a word from her might break the spell.

With her husband and son fully occupied, she opened a notebook and started to write what was probably going to be the most important book of her life—a story about destiny. As she wrote, Tianyi felt a suffering that was no longer psychological, but physical, stirring deep within her. Sometimes she was in so much pain she was unable to write. It was as if she was dying. Perhaps she really was terminally ill, in much the same way as the society she lived in was terminally ill. The two were connected. And nothing could cure this illness. The strange thing was that, as she wrote, memories long-dimmed by the passage of time resurfaced and were as vivid as if they had only happened yesterday.

Tianyi looked at some of her baby pictures. She had been a strikingly pretty baby. The future had seemed so full of possibilities then, as if that baby could have grown into a real beauty. But she had not. Tianyi felt that she was getting more average-looking the older she got. Before, when she was still single and felt the attractions of getting married, she was a lively young woman with a sparkle in her eyes. But now the vividness was gone, the vitality in her face was fading.

She studied the photographs carefully and made an unexpected discovery. After the age of five, something about the face of this angelic little girl had changed. She had lost a lot of weight, her big eyes were sunk deep in their sockets and her baby teeth had gone yellow. Of course, the trigger was the loss of her mother's love.

After her brother was born, her mother started to hate her. She did not know why, but she knew she was not mistaken: she sensed love and hate in other people acutely. Often she would sneak off to her room in the evenings and sit in the darkness crying, staring out at the red star on top of the Beijing Exhibition Hall, which in the late fifties was still known as the Soviet Exhibition Hall. As there were no taller buildings around it, the star was clearly visible from her home. She was ashamed to cry in front of people. Her feelings were complex and fragile, and she kept them carefully to herself. When she did show her feelings, she refused to let them out neatly and they exploded with a violence that belied the softness in her heart. Her longing for her mother's love consumed her, turned into a kind of hysteria. From childhood right through to adulthood, her heart had been filled with anguish. Deprived of love, that pretty, affectionate, lively child became ugly, introverted, and bad-tempered.

Now she realized, with some desperation, that her whole being, her life, her appearance, her everything, had been ruled by her emotions. When she was loved, she blossomed, she was beautiful. But without love, she withered. She had the same face, the same features, yet she looked like a different person. The only time she had ever really been beautiful again after babyhood was during her pregnancy. Now she was a sallow-faced old woman, with no spirit, just a bellyfull of resentment.

She sat for twelve hours a day, so engrossed in writing that she forgot to eat. When she did eat, she did not taste it. This was her way of escaping the world, of escaping herself.

One day, however, Tianyi's writing was interrupted. It was an ordinary evening, no different from any other. Tianyi had washed and got ready for bed as usual when there was a knock at the door. The two smartly-dressed men were polite. They got out a sheet of paper and presented it to Lian, who was visibly terrified. He shrunk into his chair, and tried to look ingratiating. Tianyi could tell the document spelled disaster. She caught a glimpse of it while pouring the tea, but all she could make out was a red seal: Xicheng District Procuratorate. And so Lian was taken away.

It took a while for Tianyi to pull herself together, but then she started making calls. She had an old-fashioned dial phone, and her fingers were swollen from turning the dial by the time she had found a way of getting him released. She reached Tong, or rather Tong's third wife Jiao, a celebrated lawyer, who asked a few preliminary questions in a cool, professional manner and passed her on to a friend of hers in the Xicheng District Procuratorate. Friends are friends, but money still had to change hands, and Tianyi paid over a substantial amount of the money she had earned through sweat, tears and her pen, although it distressed her to do so.

Lian was released forty-eight hours later. Without a word, he drew Tianyi into his arms. Tianyi quietly struggled free. It felt strange to be intimate with her husband after such a very long time. And his words sounded so insincere, they made her skin crawl: 'You know what they say, troubled times tests a relationship. And you came through for me!'

She felt acutely uncomfortable. This was the kind of thing he used to say when they were first married. But this was 1997, and thirteen years had passed. Thirteen years ... Tianyi felt she had done a very poor job of improving him.

What she found most unbearable was that Lian still refused to talk about what had really happened in the company. She felt deeply wounded, because it showed that he did not trust her. She had come through for him, as he put it, but he could discard her whenever he liked. Of course, she picked up a few clues when she overheard Lian shouting and swearing, it was something to do with his old company sponsoring someone, which led Qiankuan to accuse Lian of 'embezzling public money.' Even though it was the late nineties, the words still struck fear into Tianyi. How could they be used against her own husband? She tried not to hear the old cliché ringing in her years: No smoke without fire.

Back at home, Lian either slumped on the sofa at home, or took out his bad temper on his son. Tianyi found any excuse she could to get out of the house. Their home had become a powder keg ready to go off at any moment. One evening, as Tianyi huddled in her single bed under the chilly bedclothes, she wondered whether all marriages, all families, got to this point sooner or later. Perhaps everyone was unhappy, but some people put a brave face on it, while others were more upfront about their feelings. Her thoughts reminded her that a letter from Di had arrived the previous day, but she had not had time to read it. She ripped open the envelope. As usual, Di had written on thick, yellow paper lined in pale blue, and began her letter: Dear Tianyi. It was what came after that, though, that alarmed her.

Di said she had not written for so long because she had been on the verge of a breakdown. Of course, she and Du had broken up after a year of living together, Tianyi knew that because Di had written about it often enough. What was new was that Di had split up with her American, Brian Brown, and he wanted a divorce. There were many reasons, some of which she did not want to go into, but the main one was that he had wanted her to become a stay-at-home housewife. Di had put her heart and soul into her housekeeping but, to her astonishment, although she did everything perfectly capably, he and his mother never stopped criticizing her. Soon Brian was subjecting her to humiliating verbal abuse. He called her things like 'lazy' and 'dirty'. Di was frank. There was no way she was going to agree to a divorce, he would get more out of it than she would and she refused to walk away from the marriage with nothing. At the very least, she would drag her heels until she got American citizenship.

Tianyi put the letter down and stared into space. Two arms locked around her from behind. She knew it was Lian and shuddered. Physical intimacy with him disgusted her, and had done for quite some time. She forced a smile and tried desperately not to let her feelings show. Lian's eyes fell on the letter. 'A letter from Di?' he asked. She nodded. Lian picked it up. She was not happy, but managed to stop herself from snatching it off him. She could not keep something like this from him. Lian skimmed the letter and, sure enough, a sneer spread across his face.

'I knew it! I knew Di's marriage would never work. She thinks she's so great, but she's greedy and lazy. You know what, those sisters are jealous of you!'

'And what,' Tianyi replied coldly, 'do you think they're jealous of?'

'That you've got such a good husband!' Lian said. 'Don't all the neighbours say that I'm the model husband? Carrying the shopping for you every day. Where would you get another man like me?'

Tianyi gritted her teeth and said nothing. She could not rock the boat now. She had just been informed that she was to be sent on a writers' trip to the Czech Republic. In any case, she was coming round to the idea that she was the real problem, she was too negative. Instead of confronting problems head-on, she preferred to avoid them. She felt less and less inclined to talk. She had said goodbye to the chatty girl of her childhood and had turned into a sallow, silent old woman. She used to be in love with her mirror; now, feeling she was ageing more quickly by the day, she did all she could to avoid it. Classical poetry was full of couplets to describe a woman like herself. There was Lin, the heroine of *The Dream of the Red Chamber*: '*How can the lovely flowers stay intact, Or, once loosed, from their drifting fate draw back?*' Or the Tang dynasty lines: '*Pluck the blossom while it's there, Don't wait until the branch is bare.*' How right the ancient poets were! The problem was, who was going to pluck her? No good man would dare to. If he was bold enough to try, Tianyi would not let him. There was nothing left to her but to wither and fall.

Trips away were her only pleasure. They were a brief chance to escape. Tianyi had first become conscious of her desire to flee when she was a child. She and her mother were not getting on, and so she would imagine a tunnel that linked her to her past, a place of tranquility. She was imagining paradise, she realized afterwards. But she was no nearer to it now than she had been then.

Here at least was a chance of a respite: her trip to the Czech Republic. There would be three others going: two writers, a novelist, Zhao Ping, and an essayist, Wu Shanliang; the first was an old man, the second middle-aged. Then there was an older woman, a translator, Qiao Chun. Decent people, good writers. Tianyi was delighted to be going with them.

She had only ever known Prague through novels and songs, but now she was really here. Her first glimpse of the city was at night. The young man who came to pick them up from the airport, Tony, was the son of one of Prague's most famous sinologists. He had been given a Chinese name by his father, he told them: Lu Weida. Tianyi was wearing a plum-coloured velvet jacket, her short hair was neatly combed and topped with a few little curls. It was a feisty look, and her belted jacket showed off her figure. Today she was full of youthful energy. Tony gave her admiring glances.

Tianyi's heart gave a little flutter, too, when she first saw him. He was not exactly handsome, but there was an attractively saturnine look about him. He was tall and thin, rather how she imagined Kafka in his youth. (She told him this later in the trip, and to her surprise he was pleased: 'Yes, I played Kafka in my school play.') When they got to the hotel, she wheeled her suitcase towards her room. Then she glanced back and saw him still standing by the stairs, under the dim lighting, staring after her.

The trip passed off pleasantly. Tony's father, the sinologist, took them around and acted as interpreter. She did not take to the food, however. Once, the head of the Prague Writers' Association invited them out to dinner but the table was a desert, and the best thing on offer was a plate of fried potato cakes. The next day the Chinese delegation treated their hosts to dinner at a local Chinese restaurant. The table was filled with dishes to share, but to their amazement the head of the Association pulled a plate of fried meat in front of him and started shovelling it in. They stared at him in disbelief. He kept eating. Tianyi looked up from her plate and caught Shanliang's eye, and they traded half-smiles.

Tony was a fussy eater, full after a couple of mouthfuls, after which he would turn to his coffee, sipping at it endlessly. He looked down, seeming lost in thought, at least when he was not glancing sideways at Tianyi.

A Chinese student washing dishes at the restaurant was, in turn, staring at Tony. Then she boldly walked up to him and, taking a camera out of her pocket, said: 'Do you mind having a picture taken with me?'

Tony looked at her blankly, but in the meantime Tianyi had accepted the camera and took a few shots. Tony was serious, the girl all smiles.

Tony's father went by the Chinese name Lu Hua. When the elder Lu suggested they go and pay their respects at the grave of another famous sinologist, Dvorak, the Chinese delegation agreed with alacrity.

It was drizzling that day, and Prague was wrapped in a grey mist. The greyness made Tianyi think of *The Unbearable Lightness of Being* and *The Joke*, though this Prague was no longer the gentle Prague of Milan Kundera's novels. But, as Chun kept emphasising, the Czechs were gentle people. Indeed they are, Tianyi thought. The old sinologist and his son were very gentle. Two days before, when they were visiting the Czech National Library, Tianyi had spoken to a group of Czech students who were studying Chinese, Tony among them. Each in turn explained his or her Chinese name. Tianyi praised each one, hesitating only at Tony's. She told him it sounded rather ordinary. Tony became anxious, explaining that his father had given it to him, that it had a good meaning. Tianyi rushed to correct herself. Yes, of course, now that she thought about, it did sound like a good name. He gave a shy, gentle smile.

They stood at Dvorak's grave in the rain. They had brought flowers and a candle. To their surprise, Tony's elderly father was standing there, waiting for them. The head of their group hurried over to shake his hand. They had no idea how long he had been waiting in the rain.

Tianyi, not anticipating how cold it would be, was inadequately dressed and shivered. Tony removed his down jacket and draped it over her shoulders. Tianyi made a half-hearted attempt to refuse it, but he was insistent, saying in his stumbling Chinese: 'You … must wear it … because … you are a woman … I am a man … You are a guest, I am a host …' She accepted it and felt instantly warmer. Well, that was a good enough reason for wearing it, wasn't it? It made her look rather comical, and their group leader said she looked just like the Good Soldier Schweik.

They all posed for a photograph. Tony put the candle into the candleholder on the grave, and lit it. The small flame glittered like crystal in the rain, making the gravestone glitter in its turn. The gravestone in the rain was a warm, gentle memory, one she would never forget.

Many years later, Tony would come to Beijing. With him came the young Chinese woman who had been washing dishes in the restaurant in Prague, now his wife.

Autumn in Karlovy Vary was bathed in a majestic gold. A golden wind blew golden leaves onto golden rooftops. Under golden rays of sunshine, Tianyi walked past stalls lining the streets, full of glassware that glinted like melting snow on mountain peaks. She spotted a particularly fine and very cheap set of tall-stemmed glasses with gilded rims. Czech glass was famous, of course. But few people knew that the glass from Karlovy Vary was the finest.

The walls of an ancient fortress lined the shady side of the street. Here too were the springs, the most magical part of the town. Drinking from them required a special procedure, starting with the purchase of a ceramic pot. The market stalls around the springs were piled high with these pots, in all different styles. Unlike the clay in Chinese pots, this clay was warm to the touch, and had a mellow gleam like jade in the sunlight. Tianyi bought a pretty one, glazed a dark red, the colour of red bean paste, and decorated with a grey rose. It cost her almost nothing. According to the embassy's secretary, Gao, people used these pots to scoop up the water from the spring. She tried it and, although the water seemed a little saline, it was warm and tasted pleasant. At the springs, Tianyi saw something very odd: a Czech woman put a rose into the water, and before the eyes of the onlookers, it turned the colour of iron-sand. When she took it out, it was withered and had lost its fragrance, but acquired a strong mineral smell. So this was what Karlovy Vary was famous for! Little Gao told them that all the shops sold these chalky-gray, mineral-covered roses. The town was known for them.

After lunch they went shopping, and saw the roses everywhere. But for some reason, even after examining them more closely, Tianyi could not summon any interest in buying one. These once-beautiful flowers had metamorphosed into something else entirely. It was fun to watch them change colour, but then there was nothing special about them anymore. It seemed her companions felt the same way. The heap of roses, turned iron-grey, lay motionless looking like the slag left behind after iron smelting. Not a thing of beauty at all.

Tianyi sat very still by the hot spring and thought, so this is Karlovy Vary. This was the place where she had won her first-ever prize, for the film *The Tree of Knowledge*. That drew her to the town, as if they were old friends. The prize had aroused a flicker of hope in her, had awoken her ambitions. But that was all in the past. It would be foolish to hope for anything new to happen in her life now. No changes would be for the good. So many gorgeous fresh flowers in this life ended up as slag.

24

When the trip to the Czech Republic came to an end Tianyi returned to China. Strangely, she could not for the life of her remember what her husband looked like. She had forgotten him. It frightened her.

Cooking was now the fuse that triggered Lian's temper. He no longer wanted to be a model husband. Whenever he was at home he would lie flat out on the sofa watching the television. The house was like a powder keg, even the slightest spark could set it off. Tianyi had always been sensitive, and now she was a nervous wreck. To calm her nerves, she paid someone to come in and help out every day. The woman was from Anhui, and very capable, though a bit rough around the edges. It only took her two hours to do the laundry, cook and tidy up, but it took the pressure off Tianyi. These days she had to do her writing in secret. Lian did not say anything, but she was very tense all the same. Only once her husband and son had gone to sleep at night did she feel free to sit in front of her old Sitong 2403 word processor. She would stare at its small screen, tapping away at the keyboard, noticing how her fingers were looking rougher by the day, like a countrywoman's. Here, she could enter into another world, one of her own invention. She knew it was entirely illusory, but whatever it was, it was better than reality. At least in that imaginary world she could force herself to go on living.

Lian did not give her a cent; she was now the family's sole bread-winner. She knew she must not say anything, that Lian was waiting for her to say something. The barefooted don't fear the shod and Lian had nothing nowadays, so he had nothing to lose if they fought. But Tianyi did. Their building was full of Lian's colleagues, who could hear Lian's constant shouting. It was so ignominious.

Lian behaved like a man possessed. He kept coming up with one madcap idea after another. One day he came back with a gigantic fridge-freezer, then started buying the cheapest meat he could find from the morning market. The problem was, he kept forgetting about it, so it went bad and he had to throw it out. Every time, he would shout at Tianyi: 'What are you thinking of? Isn't this your home too? I buy all this food for you, why don't you defrost it and cook it once in a while?' Every time he had these outbursts, Tianyi would think of her brother, Tianke. Back then, her husband had been such an meek, easy-going character. Now he was as irascible as Tianke. How had that happened? Maybe he had been like that all along, and had just been hiding it.

He would cycle off to the market and buy up all sorts of rags and tatters, even stuffing them underneath their bed. Their home became such a mess that it really upset Tianyi. *One day ...* The thought reminded her of the time before her marriage. She used to think then too, *One day ...* Meaning: *One day I'll get away from the you all, and go to a happier place where I'll be free of worries and the world will belong to me.* Was Heaven the only place you could hope for happiness? The thought made her tremble. She had dreamed about it so many times as a child. Was death what it took for people to enter a world of contentment? She had made the decision, as a young woman, to leave her mother and brother, to find a world that belonged to her alone. But she was no longer young. If she left the people around her now, would she have the energy to create a world of her own? She doubted it, and that frightened her. Really frightened her. She had better hang on, make the best of things. Put up with the slings and arrows of outrageous fortune. She remembered Lin Biao's exhortation to the fighters going to Vietnam: 'Endure.' But what did 'endure' mean for her? Getting old and grey and sinking into dementia? She could not bear to think about it.

Her son was acting as cowed as she was. He was preparing his end-of-year exams but his grades were sliding rapidly, which was making Lian even more irascible. His temper needed an outlet, so he stood over his son every day as he did his homework. If he could not boss the show at work any more, at least he was master in his own house. He did not realise that to his son it was like having the devil breathing down his neck. How could he possibly concentrate on his maths homework?

She had to stick it out at home. She had another writers' tour coming up, this time to Taiwan. Everything at home troubled her. Her son was not going to get the necessary grades for upper middle school, and she knew why that was, but there was nothing she could do about it. She did not want to upset the apple-cart, because in some ways she still relied on Lian. If she left, he would be left in charge of their home and their son. But in the end, she could not keep the lid on her feelings.

Things came to a head the day before she left for Taiwan, when he gave her the new business cards he had printed for her. She inspected them. They were hideous. Was this really the man she had married, the man who, not ten years ago, had such good taste? The worst of it was, she told him so. The repercussions were awful. He threw the box of cards to the ground in a frenzy, scattering them everywhere, stamping on them, grinding them into the floor with his heel, shouting furiously: 'I was just trying to help! So I got it wrong again? Well, sorry, but this is the last time I'm waiting on you hand and foot!'

Her chest hurt as if it had been stamped on too. It was a dull sort of pain. She had to face up to things. She would wait until she got back, she thought, but one thing was certain, she could not sacrifice her life to this marriage.

Taiwan did not live up to her expectations at first. Taipei was no different from Beijing, though she at least she managed to pick up a nice set of coins with Chiang Kai-shek's face stamped on them. Kaohsiung was nicer. There the air was clean, the people honest and straightforward. Maybe because it reminded her of her uncle's family, the place gave Tianyi a warm feeling.

But even here she was disappointed. Her aunt had died and her uncle was living in an old people's home. Tianyi put the carefully chosen gifts in front of him, but he did not recognise her. She was overwhelmed by grief. She unwrapped the dried longans one by one and fed them to him. If only she could have chewed them for him too. The toothless old man gnawed and gnawed, dribbling as he did so. Tianyi sat by him, wiping his mouth and chin, until dusk, when the home was closed to visitors and her cousin, her uncle and aunt's only daughter, took her away from this dismal place.

Her cousin had grown to look just like her mother. Not exactly pretty but sweet-tempered, the kind of face rarely seen on the mainland. She was sweet-tempered in the way women used to be, a legacy from the Republican era. She had a lily-white complexion too, as if her skin had never seen the sun, a mark of her true Chinese heritage. Women on the mainland had had years of being toughened by labour. The times they lived through had left them soiled and weather-beaten, making them more masculine, stronger, and more resourceful than men. It was only when she saw her cousin that Tianyi realized that she herself had changed too. Surely all little girls wanted to grow up to be petted and protected by a man, but there was no chance of that for women from the mainland, even tenacious ones like Tianyi. They had a different destiny, and that was that.

Destiny! It was all destiny Tianyi had always despised the word, but now it forced itself on her, and she had to believe in it.

At least in Taiwan she could enjoy the beauty of Mount Ali. Mount Ali cleared Tianyi's mind. She could smell Mount Ali from far, far away. The fragrance of fresh greenery. Lush and wet. The endless swathes of green were so beautiful, it reminded her of a line from a Lu You poem: 'Towering green mountains, five thousand *ren* high.'

Tianyi and her companions walked through the trees on Mount Ali, taking pictures. It had been such a long, long time since they had seen such pure verdant greens, such lush, bright greens, greens without a smudge of mud or dirt. The cool fragrant air brushed their cheeks, making them tingle as if they having a facial. Greedily they breathed it in, letting it cleanse every organ of their body, making their bodies glow, reminding them that Mount Ali once had its own spirits. If you made a pilgrimage there, you had to light incense and bathe yourself until you were completely cleansed.

The most surprising thing about Mount Ali was its strangely-shaped trees. One species, in particular, grew almost horizontal, its long graceful branches reaching along the ground. On a twisting mountain path, it looked like the perfect modern sculpture, like those entwined tubes of metal you find everywhere in cities, though even the most imaginative of artists would have a hard time conceiving a tree this fantastic. They must be the creation of a higher being. When she had her photograph taken among the trees, she trod cautiously lest she disturb a wood sprite. Looking up, she saw layer upon layer of forest canopy. The towering trees and the undergrowth looked like something out of a Corot painting. She could imagine the spirits emerging to roam here after dark.

That evening, their host had organized a banquet in a restaurant on its slopes. They were all pleasantly tired and allowed themselves luxuriate in the heavy fragrance that emanated from the mountain. Their Taiwan host, an older man, was as warm and friendly as if they were all old friends. A young woman, a Ms Wang, told them about the customs of the indigenous people who lived on the mountain, and presented them with pretty, embroidered cases for their spectacles or mobile phones. Then there were the usual toasts and thank-you speeches from the visitors.

The conversation flowed. Only Tianyi was silent. The words of a song were running through her head:

Ali Mountain green
Ali Mountain so blue
Ali girls water-pretty
Ali boys mountain-strong …

The wooded surroundings and the enthusiasm of her companions made Tianyi's heart swell with emotion. She stood up and sang a song: 'Tomorrow Will Be Even Better.'

A Taiwanese poet grabbed hold of another microphone and sang along, and a local girl in an embroidered dress stood beside him and joined in. Tianyi had forgotten that it was a Taiwanese song. Everyone sang:

A gentle drumming wakes the sleeping soul

Slowly open your eyes
See if the busy world is still turning on its lonely way
Spring winds are unaware of love's glances
Setting young people's hearts alight
Let yesterday's tearstained cheeks
Dry in the wind of memories
Sing out your heart's passion
Reach out your hands and let me embrace your dreams
Let me possess your honest face
Let our smiles be filled with the pride of youth
Let us hope that tomorrow will be even better!

It was wonderful to be singing a song popular on both sides of the straits together with their Taiwanese friends. It was quite dark by now, and far above them, the stars were pinpricks of light. Had the forest sprites emerged to light those lanterns in the sky, for the benefit of these visitors who had come such a long way? Was this their way of welcoming them to Mount Ali, of joining in these joyous, intoxicated celebrations? On a night like this, you hardly needed wine. Just the fragrance of the forest could plunge you into a deep sleep.

Mount Ali by night was steeped in beauty. Tianyi, caught up in her own fantasies, imagined jumping on a flight and coming here any weekend she wanted, to this restaurant halfway up the mountain. It would be as easy as heading to a bar in Beijing's Sanlitun. They would brew tea from leaves freshly picked from the mountainside, and wile away the hours chatting. If it was a snowy winter's day, they would order drunken crabs with wild Mount Ali mushrooms, and talk of days long past.

One day, this might be possible. Tomorrow would be even better.
But tomorrow was not better at all. On the way home, she

stopped in Hong Kong to see her friend Di. Di had suffered a resounding defeat in her battle against Brian, her American husband, and, in a fit of depression, had headed for Hong Kong where she could at least get a long-term resident's permit. They sat in a bar on Wan Chai pier sipping cappuccinos. Both were well into middle-age by now, and time had left its mark on them, mentally and physically.

Di told Tianyi that her war with Brian had lasted ten years, though their marriage had lasted less than six months. Originally she had been determined to get an American green card but when, after ten years, they finally got to court, the court decided that she had no right to one. She should have guessed as much. Brian had worked for the American government, he was an American citizen, and she was just an interloper.

Di had aged in a way that Tianyi could not have imagined. She looked at her friend: 'You don't look like you've been suffering. You haven't changed a bit ...' Tianyi laughed bitterly, and sipped her coffee. 'I don't know. My life has never been what I wanted it to be ... I'm not living, I'm getting by. Does that make sense?'

'Of course. Total sense.' Di nodded. 'Everyone's getting by. But if you can get by, you're doing alright. Look at me, for the last ten years I haven't even been getting by ...' Dull tears ran down her face.

'Don't think that, you're doing well now, aren't you? You've got a Hong Kong resident's permit.'

'But now I'm asking myself, what's the point?' Di suddenly became animated. 'Ten years, ten of the best years of my life, all for a resident's permit. By the time I got a Hong Kong resident's permit, the island belonged to the mainland again. What was the point?'

'There never has been a point to any of it, you fighting for a resident's permit or me writing for a living. Absolutely no point at all. But we have to find a reason for living, right? We have to have something to do. Oh, by the way, I met Zheng in America.'

'Oh, did you? Has he changed? It must have been quite emotional to see him ... after all these years.'

'Not at all, I don't know why. I think we all live in our own imaginations, really. I can't tell anymore what's really happened and what I've imagined. Everything's so confused. She suddenly stopped talking. Far out on the horizon, where the sea met the sky, the sunset glow had caught her attention. It was utterly beautiful.

'We aren't waiting for the sun, we're waiting for the sunset,' a voice seemed to whisper in her ear.

Those were Zheng's words. Three years ago in the Metropolitan Museum of Art. They had been in the downstairs cafe, sipping their drinks and looking out at the sunset sky.

The sunset is lovely, but what if we wait and it doesn't come, there's only darkness?

'What were you saying?' asked Di, puzzled by Tianyi's distracted expression.

'Nothing ...'

'You may live in your imagination, but I don't. I've always lived in the real world.' Di blew a lock of hair from her mouth. She wore her hair short these days, and her face and neck were mottled with age spots. 'I've got a secret to tell you. For a while, I was very ill and almost died. Really. It wasn't scary. Death is only a window, once you open it and look out ...'

Tianyi looked at her, but said nothing.

'I've come face to face with death quite a few times now. When Brian and I had our worst fights, I wanted to open the window and jump. We lived on the twenty-fourth floor back then. It was really high, and once when I looked down a young girl in red looked back up at me. For some reason I thought it was you. For an instant, it took me back to the time when you used to wear that red skirt, and my sister and I used to wear the patterned ones. You'd just moved in, and the house was full of unpacked boxes. The place was empty, and the three of us used to play in there.'

'Xian ... I haven't seen her in ages ...'

'Mum says she's got herself a boyfriend and is about to get married.'

'She's brave! That's a big step.'

'Of course, don't you remember she was always the bravest of the three of us?'

Tianyi didn't reply. The sunset had faded. Before long, darkness would descend on the world again.

Back home in Beijing, she felt she was suffocating again. Her son was thinner, and seemed to want to keep her at arm's length. Lian was as miserable as ever and ignored her. She forced herself to put on a show of generosity, and brought out the Lacoste shirt and T-shirts she had bought for Lian. He turned away without so much as looking at them.

He came back with a piece of paper, which he threw at her. She glanced at it, eyes widening. *We are sorry to announce the death of People's Liberation Army General Staff Headquarters Comrade Vice-Minister Yang Huairen.*

'Uncle? Uncle's dead? When did that happen?'

'When? When you were off on your travels, that's when,' Lian said, with a sarcastic curl of the lips.

She looked at the date. The third day of her trip to Taiwan.

'What about Aunt Hui?'

'Your other uncle wrote saying your aunt wanted him to tell us the news. She absolutely doesn't want a visit, she's just letting the family know and then she wants nothing more to do with you.'

Lian sounded delighted at the news.

'No, I'm going to see her, right now.' She jumped to her feet. Go ahead and have your dinner. Don't wait for me.' Behind her, Lian asked sarcastically: 'Aren't you jumping the gun a bit? Are you sure it's the right thing to do? If she really doesn't want to see you, you'll just get egg on your face!'

She ignored him and went anyway. Her uncle and aunt's house held such happy childhood memories for her. Now, though, it was deserted. Just a couple of security guards, motionless in their sentry boxes. Not a breath of life in the place. Even the trees and flowers had disappeared.

In 1971, her uncle had been implicated in the fall from grace of Mao's one-time comrade-in-arms, Lin Biao. Demoted to chief of staff of Fuzhou Military Region far away in the south-east of the country, he returned to Beijing only when he retired. Tianyi visited them once. Aunt Hui had seemed much less spiky, even cracking jokes as she made chicken and mushroom stew. Her food was as good as ever. She had put on a lot of weight and was comfortably plump. When they had finished eating, she lay down and opened *Anna Karenina*. Then she spoke in a low voice: 'The old man's just like Karenin in this book, he's never given me an ounce of freedom in all our life together. He's crushed the life out of me. If it hadn't have been for him, I would have gone to university!' Tianyi looked at her, bewildered. Aunt Hui sounded like the bitter, sharp-tongued woman of the old days. She wondered if that would ever change.

Inside the compound, Tianyi found one of her uncle's aides-de-camp. He hesitated, then said: 'Tianyi, your aunt wouldn't want you to visit her, she's living with the minister, Mr Chai, now.' Tianyi was shocked. Never in her wildest dreams had she imagined her aunt, now in her sixties, as an Anna Karenina. Under her uncle's very eyes, his best friend and wartime comrade had become his woman's Vronsky. How dreadful. Her husband was scarcely dead before she was off, leaving behind only an empty, lonely house, desolate as a ruin. It made her own mother seem like a saint by comparison.

She thought of her uncle's final days. Had he known? There was little point in speculating about it now, but she hoped he had not. At least that way, he would be at peace, not buried with a broken heart that no one could mend. Tianyi remembered Lian's sarcasm. He said horrible things, but he told the truth. That was what happened nowadays. He was a shaman when it came to knowing what other people were up to. It was too bad he could not apply the same insight to himself.

The next evening Lian went out to dinner. Tianyi made a simple meal of noodles for herself and her son. He sidled up to her, leaned against her shoulder and said, 'Mum.' Then he buried his head in her chest. Tianyi put her arms around him and stroked his hair gently. Suddenly he raised his head and said something that made Tianyi tremble. 'Mum, I don't want to go on living.'

Tianyi was alarmed. She looked at her son's thin face, and felt as if a knife was being twisted in her gut. She waited for him to continue, but he said nothing more. When did her little boy become this withdrawn young man? 'Has your dad been giving you trouble?' He shook his head. She sensed his feelings bubbling like molten lava under the surface and knew that eventually they would erupt.

One evening—Tianyi would never forget it—Niuniu came back from school, called out his usual greeting, then went to his room. He closed the door. This was a mistake. Lian refused to let anyone in the house close the door. If they closed a door, he had the right to open it. It was proper to have the door open. In fact, he would kick it open if necessary. That day, he kicked the door open and discovered his son's secret. He had failed his physics exam, and was in the process of changing the grade on his report.

Lian grabbed him by the collar and hauled him out of the room. There was going to be a fight, for sure. Tianyi rushed to shield her son with her body. 'Lian, just say what you want to say, okay? He's a big boy now, if you keep hitting him, he'll end up hating you!' But Lian pushed Tianyi to one side, and she fell back onto the bed. The whites of Lian's eyes had turned a dreadful yellow and great gobs of spittle flew from his mouth as he yelled: 'I don't care if he ends up hating me! I don't care if anyone hates me! I'm not scared! If we don't get him under control, he'll be done for. Done for, get it? With grades like these, he'll be chucked out of school, and then what future has he got? He'll never be good for anything! He'll be nothing but scum!'

Lian said a lot of ugly things that day, she no longer remembered exactly what. The only thing she remembered was her son silently opening a drawer and taking out a knife.

The sight of blood galvanized her and she pounced, quicker than a female panther. She was in time, the blade had nicked the skin and drawn blood, but the wound was superficial. In that instant, she saved her son's life, and at the very same instant, abandoned fifteen years of marriage. 'I want a divorce. Now.'

The change in her voice surprised her. It sounded muffled, as if someone had covered her mouth. But it was loud, loud enough for the neighbours downstairs to hear.

Lian did not refuse. 'OK,' he said. 'We'll go now.'

Both looking angry and distressed, they got on the bicycle. Lian was in front, she sat behind, just like they had done fifteen years earlier when they were courting. The wheels turned, and they were back where they had started, with nothing.

This was not the sort of divorce registration office she had heard about, where the staff try desperately to save your failing marriage. A middle-aged man asked them a few perfunctory questions and made them an appointment to deal with the paperwork. They parted at Haidian Library. Lian went to buy books, and she took her son to her mother's.

Her mother was old, and finding walking a struggle. The sight of her hobbling around made Tianyi's heart ache. 'I'm getting a divorce,' she told her, as calmly as she had when she told her she was getting married fifteen years previously.

She thought she was being calm and resolute but the tears came anyway. Once she had started, she could not stop. Only the frosty look in the old woman's eyes helped her get a grip on her emotions.

'What are you crying for?' Her mother asked coldly. 'If you can't do without him, you know what to do.'

That was too much. She went into the kitchen and started hacking some vegetables into pieces, but could not help hearing the jibes. 'Listen to her! She wanted the divorce, so why's she crying?'

The thing that really scared her was that she felt no pain. She was numb. What had she ever done to deserve a mother like this?

Once she finished preparing the vegetables, she and Niuniu left. They would not stay for dinner, she decided, even though her mother tried to persuade her to stay, as she always did. Tianyi could at least wait until her brother, Tianke, came back, she wheedled. Tianyi could not look her mother in the eye, in case her resolve wavered. Instead, she decided to take her son out for a nice meal.

She chose an expensive Macau restaurant nearby, but after they sat down, her son looked disconsolate. Every time she suggested a dish, he said: 'I don't like that,' but refused to order for himself. The waitress stood for a long, long time, watching this strange pair failing to order their food.

Suddenly, to Tianyi's complete bemusement, Niuniu stood up and left. The waitress watched in disbelief. Tianyi was slow to react, but eventually she sprang to her feet and ran after him. Reason deserted her. When she caught up with him she slapped his face.

This was the first occasion she had ever hit her son. The first and only. Time froze.

He was a grown-up now. They stared at each other. She was a whole head shorter than him. All her anguish and resentment had turned to anger. His glasses had fallen to the ground, and passers-by were staring at them. Her son was desperate to appear macho, but his utter humiliation made him cry. Not even this softened her. She shouted, 'OK, go! Take yourself off wherever you want!'

She felt like she was going to collapse. She had no idea how she got home that day. The only thing she knew was that Lian was away on business. He was using the trip to delay the divorce proceedings, having had second thoughts.

She looked at herself in the mirror and wondered how she could have aged so much in only a few short days. But she felt no pity for herself, or indeed anyone else just now.

Suddenly she remembered the fortune-teller who had told her she would marry the man she met on the tenth of October, 1984. Why hadn't she said how long they would be married? Or when they would divorce?

She rested her head against the mirror, completely spent. Then a piece of paper caught her eye. She picked it up. It read, *'Wedding Anniversaries: Year One, Paper: First joined, the bond thin as paper; Year Two, Poplar: Drifting like the leaves of a poplar tree ...'* and so on. Her eyes scanned the page until *'Year Fifteen' caught her eye. 'Crystal: Lustrous, bright and dazzling.'* She stared at it blankly. 1984 to 1999, fifteen years. A lustrous, bright and dazzling crystal wedding! The name was lovely, but surely glass would have been a better name? So very breakable.

At half past ten, her son came home. His glasses were askew, he was holding his school bag slung over one shoulder, and he looked subdued. It was obvious he knew he had been in the wrong. She acted as if nothing had happened. 'Help yourself to the food in the wok,' she said quietly. 'Then have a wash and get ready for bed.'

He grunted in reply and went to eat. He ate and ate. She stood watching him, as she had done now for many years. She was used to it, liked watching her husband and son eat. They enjoyed her food. But to her, no matter how good it was, it tasted like candlewax.

She spread out the quilt on her son's bed and then got her marriage certificate out of the drawer. She needed it for the divorce. She needed to get all the documents ready, so that Lian had no excuse to back out. Once she made up her mind to do something, not even a team of oxen could pull her off course.

Before long, her son was asleep and snoring peacefully. She sat on the edge of the bed and looked at him, surprised that this little boy had grown up so quickly. A fuzz of whiskers was visible on his upper lip. He had his own fate, his own tomorrow, one that the people who had given him life were powerless to change. Not long ago he was kicking his little legs so hard she could hardly get his socks on. She still had those little pocket-sized blue socks in a drawer somewhere, but now they would only cover one of his toes. The tears started to flow.

It was two o'clock in the morning. In her room, she picked up the mirror again. There was nothing, just her tear-stained, puffy face. Then she caught sight of their wedding photo hanging on the wall behind her. The happiness they had shared then was long gone. Had it ever been real?

Happiness was this fragile. Fragile as crystal and glass, breaking when you touched it. No wonder they called it a crystal wedding.

She recalled what Di had said to her on the pier in Wan Chai. 'Ten years, ten of the best years of my life, all for a resident's permit. By the time I got a Hong Kong resident's permit the island belonged to the mainland again. What was the point?'

Xian had changed too, morphed into a frustrated spinster. When Tianyi saw her now, she always said she had too much on. Sometimes Tianyi was tempted to say, 'I know you're too busy to talk to me, but do stop throwing yourself at men.' Of course she did not say that.

The three girls had known each other since they were little. Found boyfriends, got married, divorced, one after the other. God had given them life and time to do things, but what on earth was it all for?

Why was she surprised? What were human beings when measured against infinity? They were so small, helpless, rudderless, fickle, anguished, stressed, depressed, deviant, useless, vacillating, acquiescent, self-betraying, self-negating, vile … She was all of these things herself. So was Di, and Xian, and Lian. Even Zheng, she thought.

She looked at her world-weary, battle-scarred reflection for a long while. Then, she felt a grim determination grow within her—she would endure, no matter what. As she sat thinking, the room seemed to grow brighter around her, to fill with a brightness like the lustre given off by a huge piece of uncut crystal.